Hubert Crackanthorpe

Wreckage: Seven Studies

Edinburgh Critical Editions of Nineteenth-Century Texts
Series Editor: Julian Wolfreys

Published titles
Richard Jefferies, After London; or Wild England
Edited by Mark Frost

Marie Corelli, A Romance of Two Worlds: A Novel
Edited by Andrew Radford

Sensation Drama, 1860–1880: An Anthology
Edited by Joanna Hofer-Robinson and Beth Palmer

Agriculture and the Land: Richard Jefferies' Essays and Letters
Edited by Rebecca Welshman

Maxwell Gray, The Silence of Dean Maitland
Edited by Julian Wolfreys

Jane Porter, Thaddeus of Warsaw: A Novel
Edited by Thomas McLean and Ruth Knezevich

Hubert Crackanthorpe, Wreckage: Seven Studies
Edited by David Malcolm

Forthcoming titles
William Barnes, Dialect Poems in The Dorset County Chronicle
Edited by Thomas Burton and Emma Mason

Geraldine Jewsbury, Critical Essays and Reviews (1849–1870)
Edited by Anne-Marie Beller

Hartley Coleridge, The Complete Poems
Edited by Nicola Healey

George Gissing, The Private Papers of Henry Ryecroft
Edited by Thomas Ue

Philip James Bailey, Festus: A Novel
Edited by Mischa Willett

William Morris on Socialism: Uncollected Essays
Edited by Florence Boos

Visit the Edinburgh Critical Editions of Nineteenth-Century Texts website at: edinburghuniversitypress.com/series/ecenct

Hubert Crackanthorpe

Wreckage: Seven Studies

Edited with an introduction by David Malcolm

Including additional writing by Hubert Crackanthorpe, Guy de Maupassant and Leila Macdonald

EDINBURGH
University Press

Edinburgh University Press is one of the leading university presses in the UK. We publish academic books and journals in our selected subject areas across the humanities and social sciences, combining cutting-edge scholarship with high editorial and production values to produce academic works of lasting importance. For more information visit our website: edinburghuniversitypress.com

Edinburgh University Press Ltd
The Tun – Holyrood Road, 12(2f) Jackson's Entry, Edinburgh EH8 8PJ

First published in hardback by Edinburgh University Press 2020

Typeset in 11/12.5 Baskerville and Times New Roman by
Servis Filmsetting Ltd, Stockport, Cheshire

A CIP record for this book is available from the British Library

ISBN 978 1 4744 4836 9 (hardback)
ISBN 978 1 4744 8466 4 (paperback)
ISBN 978 1 4744 4837 6 (webready PDF)
ISBN 978 1 4744 4838 3 (epub)

Contents

Introduction vii

Further Reading xl

A Hubert Crackanthorpe Chronology xliii

A Note on the Text xlv

Series Editor's Preface xlvi

Wreckage: Seven Studies
- Profiles 3
- A Conflict of Egoisms 25
- The Struggle for Life 47
- Dissolving View 50
- A Dead Woman 55
- When Greek Meets Greek 72
- Embers 94

Appendices
1: Realism in France and England: An Interview with M. Emile Zola 104
2: Reticence in Literature: Some Roundabout Remarks 111
3: 'The Haseltons' 121
4: 'The White Maize' 143
5: From *Vignettes: A Miniature Journal of Whim and Sentiment* 145
6: 'The Rendezvous' (*Le Rendez-vous*) by Guy de Maupassant 149
7: 'Jeanne-Marie' by Leila Macdonald 155

For Jennifer

Introduction: Hubert Crackanthorpe – Career and Reception

In Crackanthorpe's short life, his literary activities as such were restricted to the years 1892 to 1896. Between January and September 1892, Crackanthorpe was co-editor (with W. H. Wilkins) of *The Albemarle*, a political, social and literary journal, aimed at a literate, culturally aware, well-heeled and cosmopolitan readership. Besides essays on political affairs, social issues and artistic matters, *The Albemarle* published a substantial amount of poetry and several pieces of short fiction. Crackanthorpe himself contributed two short stories, 'He Wins Who Loses' (1.3, March 1892) and 'Dissolving Views' (2.2, August 1892). 'Dissolving Views' was republished by the author as 'Dissolving View' in *Wreckage*; 'He Wins Who Loses' has been republished only once, in an anthology in 1937 (Fisher 1994: 60). In his authoritative study of Crackanthorpe's life and work, David Crackanthorpe (the author's great-nephew) argues that between 1891 and 1892 Crackanthorpe was writing the fiction that would go into a later volume of short stories (David Crackanthorpe 1977: 46). Presumably he was also doing so in the year that he edited *The Albemarle*, and in the years up to his death.

In 1893, Crackanthorpe's first collection of short fiction, *Wreckage: Seven Studies*, was published by William Heinemann. It contains seven texts: 'Profiles', 'A Conflict of Egoisms', 'The Struggle for Life', 'Dissolving View', 'A Dead Woman', 'When Greek Meets Greek' and 'Embers'. A second volume of short stories, entitled *Sentimental Studies, and A Set of Village Tales*, appeared in 1895, again published by Heinemann. This volume is made up of two distinct collections. *Sentimental Studies* (the title means studies of sentiment, feeling and psychological state, rather than affected or mawkish ones) contains five stories: 'A Commonplace Chapter' (which is divided into two parts listed separately on the contents page), 'Battledore and Shuttlecock', 'In Cumberland', 'Modern Melodrama' and 'Yew-trees and Peacocks'. *A Set of Village Tales* is made up of six very short narratives: 'Lisa-la-folle', 'The White Maize', 'Saint-Pé', 'Etienne Mattou' (the longest at twelve pages), 'The Little Priest' and 'Gaston Lalanne's Child'.

In 1896, the year of his death, Crackanthorpe brought out a short volume entitled *Vignettes: A Miniature Journal of Whim and Sentiment.* This brief collection, published by John Lane/The Bodley Head, in sixty-three pages of text, consists of accounts of impressions, observations and reflections realised in a variety of locales in France, Spain, Italy and England. Crackanthorpe borrowed two passages from *Vignettes* for a later story, 'The Turn of the Wheel', published in his final volume of fiction. This collection appeared in 1897, after the author's death, as *Last Studies*, and was published by William Heinemann. It contains two long short stories and one relatively brief piece: 'Anthony Garstin's Courtship', 'Trevor Perkins: A Platonic Episode' (at thirty pages, this is the shortest text) and 'The Turn of the Wheel'. The volume also contains a poem by Stopford A. Brooke (a much better-known writer then than now) and 'An Appreciation' by Henry James.

That is Crackanthorpe's entire output of fiction. 'The Haseltons', published in volume 5 of *The Yellow Book* in April 1895, is effectively the second part of 'A Commonplace Chapter' from *Sentimental Studies*, barely differing from it. A few other pieces of work appear outside the collections – for example, 'Modern Melodrama' was first published in *The Yellow Book* (volume 1, April 1894), and 'Anthony Garstin's Courtship' first appeared in *The Savoy* in July 1896 – but these texts do not differ from those in the collections. Thus, the fictional *œuvre* (which is of most interest, I assume, to readers of this edition) consists of twenty-two short stories. Fisher (1994: 60) lists one other text as fiction: 'Bread and the Circus', published in *The Yellow Book* (volume 7, October 1895). To what degree this text is fiction or a piece of reportage (based on Crackanthorpe's four days of employment as a translator for Lord George Sanger's Circus in the summer of 1895 – David Crackanthorpe 1977: 104) is not clear, nor need it be. 'Bread and the Circus' is certainly a narrative piece, employing many fictional techniques, but that does not stop it being colourful travel writing. Even if we account this text fiction, Crackanthorpe's output is still slim.

Crackanthorpe's broader literary activities include several clearly non-fictional pieces. David Crackanthorpe (1977: 180) and Fisher (1994: 60) note two reviews concerning the theatre (one on Henry James's work for the stage), and an interview with the great and controversial French novelist Émile Zola, all published in *The Albemarle*. They also list an essay written for *The Yellow Book* (volume 2, July 1894) on developments in contemporary fiction. A brief piece on French fiction was published in 1897 after Crackanthorpe's death. In addition, a (quite awful) play that Crackanthorpe had written with Henry Harland came out in a private publication without a date (the British Museum stamp in its copy gives 1917 as the year of acquisition). The full bibliographical details of the above texts are listed in the Further Reading section of this book.

In 1897, in the *Academy*, Lionel Johnson wrote that Crackanthorpe's was 'a brief record of accomplishment, but all the finer, the firmer, the more successful for its very scantiness' (Johnson 1982: 12–13). One can only agree – on all counts.

Crackanthorpe's literary activities were made possible by family and individual wealth. David Crackanthorpe is in no doubt that Crackanthorpe's father financed the publication of *The Albemarle* (1977: 46, 57), although he provides no documentation for the assertion. Jad Adams writes that the publication of Crackanthorpe's first volume of short stories was partly financed by the author himself (to the tune of £47/10/–) (Adams 2009: 10), pointing out that this sort of self-publishing was common and not despised in the late nineteenth and early twentieth centuries. Shafquot Towheed (although his figures are not always reliable) indicates the same (2000: 53–4). Towheed also gives some publication data for Crackanthorpe's major volumes of fiction: *Wreckage* in two editions had a print run of 2,500 copies; *Sentimental Studies* came out in one edition of 1,500 copies (1,100 being sold); and *Last Studies* was published in an edition of 1,000 copies (with 700 sold) (Towheed 2000: 54). Towheed concludes that 'Crackanthorpe's fiction consistently failed to find success in the marketplace' (2000: 55). David Crackanthorpe disagrees with this assessment. Concerning *Wreckage*, he writes: 'The book sold well, his [Crackanthorpe's] publisher was enthusiastic, and much attention was drawn to his name' (1977: 76).

The critical response to Crackanthorpe's work is complex and discontinuous, but critical response there was and has been. It is clear that in the 1890s he was a writer who provoked a considerable degree of controversy. Contemporary responses to his work are mixed. There are certainly plenty of negative ones. An anonymous reviewer in the *Critic* of May 1894 comments on 'Modern Melodrama' that

> The gutter is celebrated in prose by Mr. Crackanthorpe, a young man who, when he writes of depravity, which he usually does, leaves nothing to the imagination. By the weak he is called 'strong', by the strong – but what do the strong reck of Mr. Crackanthorpe? (qtd. in Fisher 1994; 61)

Crackanthorpe's prose was certainly part of the realist fiction to which Arthur Waugh (who had reviewed *Wreckage* in 1894) objects in his essay 'Reticence in Literature' in volume 1 of *The Yellow Book*. It is mischief on the part of the journal's editors to place Crackanthorpe's 'Modern Melodrama' immediately after Waugh's essay, and Crackanthorpe was allowed a reply to the essay in the following volume in July 1894. In *The New Review* (May 1893), H. D. Traill writes, of 'A Struggle for Life' from *Wreckage*, that

> its repulsive subject' is 'depicted in equal fullness of detail, and . . . even more graphically descriptive power, by reporters dealing with the lowest class of unfortunates at the time of the Whitechapel murders. (qtd. in Greenslade 2013: 166)

Some of the most hostile criticism came after Crackanthorpe's death. Writing in the *Critic* in early 1897, Jeannette Gilder remarks,

> I am not at all surprised by the tragic death of Mr. Hubert Crackanthorpe. No young man, or old one for that matter, could write such morbid, loathsome stories as he wrote and still have a sane mind. . . . A man must have a diseased mind who finds pleasure in writing of diseased morals. (qtd. in David Crackanthorpe 1977: 145)

Fisher notes a moderate and ambivalent attitude in the work of early reviewers such as William Archer in the *Westminster Gazette* (March 1893) (1994: 61). However, there are many positive responses to Crackanthorpe's work (the first edition of *Sentimental Studies* contains two pages of admiring reviews from the contemporary press), although several of the writers that offer such positive responses can be judged far from disinterested in their plaudits. They were part of the *avant-garde* as much as Crackanthorpe was. Fundamentally positive comments on Crackanthorpe's work turn up in articles in *The Yellow Book* by 'The Yellow Dwarf'. In volume 7 (October 1895), the pseudonymous critic writes in praise of the stories in *Sentimental Studies*, noting 'the actuality of his subjects, the clearness of his psychological insight, the intensity of his realization, the convincingness of his presentation, and the sincerity and dignity of his manner'. Such advocacy is modified by strictures that Crackanthorpe's work is too explicit and too detailed, too much marked by 'moral earnestness', and striving 'too hard, a little too visibly for the *mot juste*' (1895: 141). An article by 'The Yellow Dwarf' in April 1896 (volume 9), celebrating the second year of the existence of *The Yellow Book* and lauding the first volume in 1894, contains the exclamation 'and then the Literature!', and counts Crackanthorpe among the stars of that volume: James,

Max Beerbohm, Edmund Gosse, George Moore, John Davidson, Ella D'Arcy and others. '*Wasn't* it a jolly company!' writes the jocose reviewer (1896a: 19–20). Crackanthorpe is seen as an important innovative writer too in volume 10 (July 1896), to be mentioned alongside D'Arcy, Henry Harland, Beerbohm and James (1896b: 16–17).

Crackanthorpe's work certainly had admirers. Thus, Lionel Johnson in 1897 writes appreciatively of the stories in *Wreckage* 'with their helpless misery and grim irony'. In 'The Struggle for Life', he notes that 'The telling of the misery becomes a thing of desperate beauty, and in its intensity goes nearer to the heart of the whole dark matter than many a moving sermon' (1982: 13, 14–15). Summing up Crackanthorpe's work, Johnson insists that 'his writing had in it *soul*, an [sic] high distinction of temperament, which, with his technical power and pains, makes us feel certain of how much was lost to literature in the loss of him' (1982: 18). Grant Richards reports that William Heinemann, the publisher of *Wreckage*, was delighted with the collection. 'That was the sort of book he was then proud to publish. Crackanthorpe was, he said, to do great, great things' (qtd. in David Crackanthorpe 1977: 63). David Crackanthorpe also notes that Crackanthorpe himself saw several reviews as very positive (1977: 63). In a tribute to Crackanthorpe, published in the *Star* in January 1897, Richard Le Gallienne unambiguously lauds the author, his adventurous work and his great potential (qtd. in David Crackanthorpe 1977: 145).

In his 1897 essay, Johnson is certain that Crackanthorpe's 'accomplished work, whatever be its shortcomings, flaws, will not fall into the obscurity of neglect' (1982: 18). In this belief, Johnson was wrong. After the 1890s, Crackanthorpe's work was largely forgotten and never made it into the canon of late nineteenth-century literature. But neglect is relative, and there has been a recurrent interest in his writing in the more than 120 years since his death. Stories are included in specialised anthologies of the period: for example, Derek Stanford's *Writing of the 'Nineties: From Wilde to Beerbohm* (1971) and Ian Fletcher's *British Poetry and Prose, 1870–1905* (1987). Holbrook Jackson places the 'youthful, accomplished realist' in the company of famous exemplars and agents of 'a renaissance of art and ideas' in literature in the 1890s (Jackson [1913] 1950: 222, 33, 46). In 1942, in *The English Novel in Transition*, William C. Frierson writes of Crackanthorpe's fiction, noting 'the precision and concentration of Crackanthorpe's phrasing' (54). In an earlier text, published in French in 1925, on the influence of French naturalism on English novelists between 1885 and 1920, Frierson devotes some fifteen pages to Crackanthorpe, and three to an analysis of 'A Commonplace Chapter' alone. He concludes that, but for his early death, Crackanthorpe 'serait probablement devenu un des maîtres du roman anglais' (would probably have become one of the masters of the English novel) (1925: 120–35). In 1969, William Peden edited and introduced a facsimile edition of Crackanthorpe's *Collected Stories (1893–1897)*, published in a scholarly imprint in the USA. In 1977, Peden writes of Crackanthorpe's work in the Foreword to David Crackanthorpe's study of his great-uncle's life and *œuvre*. His judgement is that 'Of the lesser-known fiction writers of the nineties . . . the most talented, the most important and the most undervalued is Hubert Crackanthorpe' (1977: ix). In 1978, Peden discusses Crackanthorpe's work in *Studies in Short Fiction*. He sees him as a 'Forgotten Pioneer' (1978: ix). Fisher's entry in volume 135 of the *Dictionary of Literary Biography* runs to fifteen pages, and the critic judges that 'Creative quality in Crackanthorpe's stories . . . is unusually high' and that 'his writings warrant detailed attention' (1994: 61), attention that he duly gives them in his essay. In 1990, Michel Haurie notes Crackanthorpe's precocity, potential and interestingly controversial status (1).

Crackanthorpe has, indeed, recently achieved some of the critical attention I believe he deserves. In her excellent study of British short fiction, Barbara Korte writes of his interest in the theme of 'the problematic marriage and failed relationships between the sexes generally' (2003: 110–11). In another fine book on the short story, Adrian Hunter sees him as an important figure in the circle of writers connected with *The Yellow Book* and with the influence of Henry James's work. Hunter finds his stories germane to 1890s debates relating to psychologically oriented fiction, to innovative abandonment of traditional story materials and to gender issues (2007: 34–7). In studies co-edited or written by me, I have attempted to redress the relative neglect into which Crackanthorpe's work has fallen since his death (see: Malcolm and Malcolm 2008: 11–13; Malcolm 2012a: 101–2, 191–3; Malcolm 2012b: 98–9). Even more recently, William Greenslade focuses his essay on 'Naturalism and Decadence' on 'The Case of Hubert Crackanthorpe', in which he discusses Crackanthorpe's complex and shifting response to contemporary debates on fiction dealing with the abjectly sordid aspects of social life, and his deployment of a sophisticated narrational technique (2013: 163–80). It is not all obscurity, although nearly so.

The life

The relation between an author's work and his/her life is never simple and direct. The accuracy of many authors' biographical and autobiographical narratives is questionable. However, it is worth looking at Crackanthorpe's life for two reasons. First, it was and has been seen as a life representative of some cultural trends in the late nineteenth century. Holbrook Jackson saw it as such, and although he gets Crackanthorpe's age wrong, places him within the roll-call of the early dead of the 1890s: Oscar Wilde, Aubrey Beardsley, Ernest Dowson and Lionel Johnson ([1913] 1950: 130). Such a view of Crackanthorpe's life as somehow typical of a time and a place is echoed by Jerome Hamilton Buckley in *The Victorian Temper* ([1952] 1966: 236–7). Second, some details concerning Crackanthorpe's wealth and his family's support for his literary endeavours may surprise modern readers, so used to artistic narratives of obstacles overcome with heroic persistence. There was suffering aplenty in his short life, but it was not from material want or a result of philistine opposition to an artistic career on the part of his family. The best accounts of Crackanthorpe's life are those given by David Crackanthorpe (1977), Fisher (1994) and Adams (2009). David Crackanthorpe's is by far the fullest; Adams has an axe to grind in his. What follows is based on those three texts. But all narratives of Crackanthorpe's life have intriguing gaps in them, and there is a surprising lack of documentation at points. The circumstances of his death are particularly opaque.

Crackanthorpe was born in London on 12 May 1870. His father, Montague Crackanthorpe (1832–1913), was an eminent lawyer and writer on social and political issues, including birth control and eugenics. His mother, Blanche Crackanthorpe (*née* Holt) (1847–1928), had strong literary interests and wrote extensively on women's issues. In the 1890s, she held a literary salon at the family's London home in Rutland Gate, Kensington, close to Hyde Park. It was attended by major contemporary writers – George Meredith, Thomas Hardy and Henry James – but also by rising younger writers, such as John Galsworthy. The Crackanthorpes were very well off. They became even more so when, in 1888, Montague Crackanthorpe inherited the Newbiggin estate in the historic county of Westmorland (now Cumbria) in the north of England, several thousand acres of farms, woodland and moors. Indeed, the family changed its name from Cookson to Crackanthorpe as part of the provisions of the inheritance. They were wealthy, intellectual, liberal and Liberal. Montague Crackanthorpe twice stood unsuccessfully as a Liberal Party candidate in elections. They were progressive in their artistic views. For example, Hubert Crackanthorpe and his parents were members of the Independent Theatre Society in London in the 1890s, an institution set up to obviate late Victorian theatre censorship.

Hubert Crackanthorpe's education was partially typical for a male of his class and time. He attended Eton from 1883 to 1888. However, he did not go to university. The years between 1888 and 1892 are scantily documented and have drawn some lurid speculations (David Crackanthorpe 1977: 29–30). He certainly went to France in 1889, living in Orthez near the Pyrenees, where he not only improved his French, but made the acquaintance of the notable French poet Francis Jammes (1868–1938), who records his liking for and gratitude to Crackanthorpe, 'ce gentleman au regard byronien' (this gentleman with the Byronic gaze). (In 1893, Crackanthorpe used his connections in the French literary world to bring Jammes's verse to the attention of Stéphane Mallarmé and André Gide. One can only be impressed that he had such connections.) After his return from France, Crackanthorpe spent time in advanced literary circles in London, particularly that of Selwyn Image, whose Fitzroy Group gathered young innovative writers like Lionel Johnson, Ernest Dowson and Richard Le Gallienne, and overlapped to an extent with the now more famous Rhymers' Club.

In January 1892, the first number of *The Albemarle* appeared. The journal, of which Crackanthorpe was co-editor, ran for nine months until September 1892. Priced sixpence, it contained a mixture of social, political, artistic and literary essays, with some quite eminent and largely Liberal and progressive contributors, including Sir Charles Dilke, Ben Tillett, Elizabeth Hollister, David Lloyd George, R. B. Haldane and G. B. Shaw. Artists who contributed work included J. McNeill Whistler and Walter Sickert. The journal published literary work by R. B. Cunninghame Graham, Lionel Johnson, Ernest Dowson and Crackanthorpe himself. The cosmopolitan and advanced tastes of projected readers are obvious: contributions on French literature, including Crackanthorpe's interview with Zola (in volume 1, number 2), and on Impressionism and modern art. The educated and well-heeled nature of the readership is also marked by the extensive use of foreign languages (especially French), the range of sophisticated topics, and the advertisements for luxury goods and services that accompany articles (*inter alia*, fine art insurance, artistic furniture, sixty-guinea wedding cakes, the Richmond Bed Rest and Lounger, silver-mounted silk umbrellas, solid gold opera glasses and electro-plated 'entré' [sic] dishes). David Crackanthorpe is certain that Montague Crackanthorpe paid the bills to establish and keep the journal running (1977: 46, 57). There is no suggestion that his family disapproved of his literary career. *The Albemarle* ceased publication in September 1892. David Crackanthorpe judges that the editorship of the journal was part of a consciously undertaken apprenticeship in literary activity by Crackanthorpe, one that had served its purpose by late 1892 (1977: 57).

In February 1893, after a brief acquaintance, Crackanthorpe and Leila Macdonald were married at St Paul's Church in Knightsbridge. Macdonald's father had been an eminent lawyer with intellectual concerns beyond the law. After her parents' deaths (both were dead by 1876), Macdonald, who was born on 7 February 1871, was brought up by her grandfather, Sir William Grove, a wealthy judge with scientific pursuits and a home on Harley Street. Like Crackanthorpe, Macdonald had no money worries. Also like Crackanthorpe, Macdonald had literary interests and ambitions. After the wedding, the couple went to France, to Orthez, where Crackanthorpe had spent time in the late 1880s. They associated with Jammes when they were there. Jammes did not care for Macdonald, describing her as 'une sorte d'amazone à l'œil dur' (a sort of hard-eyed Amazon) (Adams 2009: 11). While in Orthez, Macdonald suffered a serious accident to her eyes, which entailed extensive treatment, both then and in later years. The couple returned to England by late 1893, living in London (finally, in a wing of a house on Cheyne Walk in Chelsea, which they commissioned Roger Fry to decorate), travelling abroad, and involving themselves in advanced literary circles in the capital. Crackanthorpe published his short stories; Macdonald contributed four pieces to *The Yellow Book*, the most substantial of which is the short story 'Jeanne-Marie', published in volume 3, in October 1894 (reproduced in the appendices to this edition).

Accounts of Macdonald's and Crackanthorpe's marriage suggest that it was a complex one. Macdonald had a miscarriage in early 1896 and blamed Crackanthorpe for it. Later, Macdonald claimed that she had contracted syphilis from her husband. In the spring of 1896, Macdonald left London for Italy. Crackanthorpe entered into a relationship with Mary Elizabeth Welch (known as Sissie), wife of the actor James Welch and sister of Richard Le Gallienne. According to Crackanthorpe's younger brother Dayrell (a biased source), at Viareggio in Tuscany, Macdonald became involved with a Frenchman called d'Artaux. Her grandfather died in mid-1896, making her even wealthier, and independently so.

The events of late 1896 unrolled thus. Sissie Welch and

Crackanthorpe travelled together to Paris in August 1896. Macdonald and d'Artaux arrived in September. They established a *ménage à quatre* at 18 avenue Kléber, which lasted for some two months. Macdonald sent for her lawyer, who arrived on 4 November. She and d'Artaux left the avenue Kléber. Macdonald informed Crackanthorpe that she meant to divorce him. Crackanthorpe sent Sissie back to London and appealed to his parents for help. His mother came to Paris. On the evening of 5 November, Blanche Crackanthorpe, Crackanthorpe, and Macdonald's lawyer Hills met at the Hôtel de France on the quai Voltaire by the Seine. Hills informed the Crackanthorpes that Macdonald intended to sue Crackanthorpe for divorce on the grounds of adultery and legal cruelty, the latter meaning that she was accusing her husband of knowingly infecting her with venereal disease. After this meeting, Crackanthorpe left the hotel with Hills. He was never seen alive again. On 24 December 1896, a body was discovered by the pont de l'Alma, several bridges downstream from the quai Voltaire. The body was in an advanced state of decay, but on Christmas Day 1896, Crackanthorpe's younger brothers, Dayrell and Oliver, identified the corpse as their brother's on the basis of a signet ring, cufflinks and other personal items found in the dead man's pockets. The body was placed in a sealed coffin and returned to London. Suicide? Murder? An accident – for the waters in the Seine were unusually high that November? It all reads like a melodrama or the exposition of a detective story, but played out for real.

Adams adds another dimension to the narrative. He argues that after Crackanthorpe's death, there was a concerted and successful attempt on the part of the Crackanthorpe family to put an end to lurid speculation about their eldest son's disappearance and death. This is certainly true. They also, he goes on, set out to persecute Macdonald, deprive her of an inheritance from her husband, and reduce her to obscurity. The evidence for the last is slim but Macdonald did fall into obscurity. A single volume of her verse was published in 1904. Adams claims that she died in Paris in 1944. Sissie Welch returned to her husband. They divorced in 1906 and Welch died in 1907.

The *fin de siècle*

Crackanthorpe's mysterious and early death, the sensational circumstances surrounding it (which were known to and embellished by many commentators), and the sense of a potential unrealised made (and make) that life, death and work particularly resonant in and of the late nineteenth and early twentieth centuries. That was certainly how contemporaries saw the matter, both those hostile to him and the kind of life and literature he represented, and those who thought the opposite. Jackson writes of Crackanthorpe's typicality:

> Nothing is more remarkable in looking back at the Nineties than to note how Death has gathered to himself so many of the period's most characteristic and most interesting figures. All of these men 'lived their own lives'. . . . Most of them died young, several were scarcely more than youths; some died of diseases which might have been checked or prevented in more careful lives; some were condemned to death at an early age by miserable maladies, and some were so burdened by the malady of the soul's unrest that they voluntarily crossed the borderland of life. It would seem as if these restless and tragic figures thirsted so much for life, and for the life of the hour, that they put the cup to their lips and drained it in one deep draught. ([1913] 1950): 129–30)

So much was lost with his death, some argued. 'I venture to believe', writes Le Gallienne in his obituary to his friend, 'that posterity will deem the youth who could write *Wreckage* at the age of twenty-two something like the Chatterton of the English novel' (Le Gallienne 1897: 1). 'So much promise, and so little time for adequate performance!' exclaims the anonymous commentator in *The Speaker* on 24 December 1897 (qtd. in David Crackanthorpe 1977: 157). But 'He was the most pronounced type of decadent,' proclaims Jeannette Gilder in *The Critic* in the same year (qtd. in David Crackanthorpe 1977: 145), which combines a sense of typicality with disdain.

The term *la fin de siècle* (the end of the century) is as questionable as it is current. It is understood to refer to a variety of cultural phenomena in a variety of European countries from the 1870s through to the first years of the Great War (thus not literally only the end of the century). Perhaps Gilles Philippe's witty formulation of *l'entre-deux-siècles* (the inter-century period) (Philippe 2016: 23) might be more appropriate. However, the notion and the term were available for use and satire by 1891. In Chapter 15 of *The Picture of Dorian Gray*, after a dense array of inversions of conventional wisdom, the following dialogue ensues among Lady Narborough, Lord Henry Wooton and Dorian Gray.

> '*Fin de siècle*', murmured Lord Henry.
> '*Fin du globe*', answered his hostess.
> 'I wish it were *fin du globe*', said Dorian with a sigh. 'Life is a great disappointment.' (Wilde [1891] 1968: 198)

The dialogue captures newness, disappointment and self-indulgence in equal measure.

There is a widespread consensus as to the instabilities and shocks in culture and society of the late nineteenth and early twentieth centuries. One needs to be cautious with such general commonplaces, all the more so because if the argument is correct, one would like to know what period has been without instability and shock. None the less, the consensus concerning cultural and social transformations in Britain between roughly 1870 to 1914 is persuasive. On a political level, the period was marked by imperial aggrandisement and checks in South Africa and in Ireland. Socialism, organised labour, increasing male enfranchisement, a strong awareness of the massive economic disparities among British people, and mass education challenged an existing *status quo*, as did Irish nationalism, and feminist argument and political organisation. 'New Women' seriously destabilised a strongly patriarchal order. Economically, British industry and commerce were increasingly challenged by those of Germany and the USA. Technologically, developments were as shocking as those of fifty years earlier. By 1914, much modern technology was firmly in place: telephones, wireless technology, the cinema, the motor car, the aeroplane, although, as Bernard Bergonzi remarks, quite what all that had to do with literature is not always entirely clear (Bergonzi 1980: xv). In intellectual life, Darwinian ideas, notions of decadence and publishing for a mass market are seen as eroding mid-Victorian certainties (although whether there were such certainties is open to question). Even if all the above is true, it must be remembered that how one saw all this inconstancy and innovation depended on who one was and where: for a young woman of advanced views and for an Irish nationalist, such impermanences were liberating; for an unreconstituted, patriarchal, English middle-class male, they were threatening.

The newness of the times was echoed in newness in literature. As Crackanthorpe himself noted: 'Books are published, stories are printed, in old-established reviews, which would never have been tolerated a few years ago' (Crackanthorpe 1894b: 262). His essay 'Reticence in Literature' (reprinted in the appendices to this edition) is a lucid review of tendencies in literature and other arts, and the responses provoked by them, from admiration to a sense of a decadent horror that life was heading towards a cultural and social apocalypse. Crackanthorpe wrote the essay in response to Arthur Waugh's essay of the same title, published in the previous number of *The Yellow Book* (1, April 1894). In it, Waugh argues for a literature that is honest, but still in touch with 'the normal taste of the hale and cultured man of its age' (Waugh 1894: 208). He bemoans a tendency away from both emotional and topical reticence.

> The two developments of realism of which we have been speaking seem to me to typify the two excesses into which frankness is inclined to fall; on the one hand, the excess prompted by effeminacy – that is to say, by the want of restraints which starts from enervated sensation; and on the other, the excess which results from a certain brutal virility, which proceeds from coarse familiarity with indulgence. The one whispers, the other shouts; the one is the language of the courtesan, the other of the bargee. What we miss in both alike is that true frankness which springs from the artistic and moral temperament; the episodes are no part of a whole in unity with itself; the impression they leave upon the reader is not the impression of Hogarth's pictures; in one form they employ all their art to render vice attractive, in the other, with absolutely no art at all, they merely reproduce, with the fidelity of the kodak, scenes and situations the existence of which we all acknowledge, while taste prefers to forget them. (Waugh 1894: 217)

Modern scholars concur with the outlines of the dispute, which goes well beyond Waugh and Crackanthorpe, and the pages of *The Yellow Book.* Korte points out how ethereal aesthetes and muck-raking realists alike challenged literary and social norms (Korte 2003: 108–9), and Hunter discusses how the psychological-realist writing that modern readers take for granted was seen as innovative and contentious, indicating a feminisation of literature in its movement away from traditional story materials and their organisation (Hunter 2007: 34–5). Crackanthorpe addresses this issue directly when he quotes Edmund Gosse's verdict that

> we cannot return, in serious novels, to the inanities and impossibilities of the old well-made plot, to the children changed at nurse, to the madonna-heroine and the god-like hero, to the impossible virtues and melodramatic vices. In future, even those who sneer at realism and misrepresent it most wilfully, will be obliged to put their productions more in accordance with veritable experience. (Crackanthorpe 1894b: 268)

Another way in which British literature renewed itself in the last decades of the nineteenth century was in the revaluation of the short story that took place then. (For a fuller discussion of this subject, see Malcolm 2012b: 91–102.) Whatever the complexities of the situation before 1880, it is true that, for much of the nineteenth century, the prestige of the long novel was great and that major writers did not devote much time or thought to the shorter form. The situation changed radically in Britain in the 1880s. Literary economics played a large role. Many new journals were set up to cater to an increasingly literate urban population (*Tit-Bits* and *The Strand Magazine*, for example). Such magazines were prepared to pay substantial sums of money for new short fiction. Bohemian journals, like *The Savoy* (which, just before his death, Crackanthorpe offered to edit) and *The Yellow Book*, looked for topically and technically adventurous short fiction for a more *avant-garde* bourgeois readership. In addition, the three-decker novel had clearly become an ossified kind of fiction, offering writers little scope and opportunities for novelty. The day of shorter forms had come. Novels, in general terms, became more concise, and as H. G. Wells wrote later in 1911, 'short stories broke out everywhere' (qtd. in Hanson 1985: 34). Indeed, according to Henry James (writing in 1898), short fiction became 'an object of almost extravagant dissertation' in the 1880s (qtd. in Shaw 1983: 3). An impressive roll-call of British and Irish authors tried their hands at the short story in the last two decades of the nineteenth century and the first decade of the twentieth: Robert Louis Stevenson, Rudyard Kipling, Joseph Conrad, Henry James, George Gissing, George Moore, H. G. Wells, M. R. James, Arthur Conan Doyle, Ernest Dowson, Crackanthorpe, Ella D'Arcy, George Egerton and Oscar Wilde. Many made money out of their short stories: for example, Conan Doyle's fees for his Sherlock Holmes stories were very high indeed.

The short story was certainly a form of status in the contemporary literary world. It was also a matter for conscious reflection. James, for instance, thought hard about the short story, arguing that it was not a boiled-down novel, but that its shortness was a crucial element in its make-up, one that opened a range of possibilities and made a range of demands that were unique to the form (Hunter 2007: 7–8). Frederick Wedmore, Henry Harland, Bret Harte and Brander Matthews – like James, Americans – developed Poe's earlier ideas about the short story in the 1890s (Korte 2003: 93–4). Their observations were published and read in Britain.

That James, Wedmore, Harland, Harte and Matthews played a substantial role in the British literary scene of the *fin de siècle* indicates that foreign influences were important in the development of British short and longer fiction from the 1880s through to the Great War.

Writers from outside Britain and Ireland deeply influenced British and Irish short-story writing and novel writing in this period, both in person and through textual inspiration. Americans play a great role in this, but with regard to Crackanthorpe and many others, it is French examples that are particularly germane. (For further discussion of this issue, see Malcolm 2012b: 91–102.)

'We get a realistic fiction abroad, and we begin to copy it at home,' Waugh writes in 1894 (216). He means, principally, French fiction. Widespread interest in Britain in the work of late nineteenth-century French novelists and short-story writers – the Goncourt brothers, Émile Zola, Guy de Maupassant – is well documented. French fiction was a contentious issue; for some, these writers were admirable models; for others, they were anathema. Crackanthorpe was consistently identified as an English Maupassant and an English Zola, both in approval and in contempt (Frierson 1942: 52; David Crackanthorpe 1997: 75). David Crackanthorpe notes that Crackanthorpe's collection of books has been preserved and contains mostly nineteenth-century French texts. These volumes are heavily marked, indicating Crackanthorpe's interest in them. The authors whom David Crackanthorpe particularly mentions are Paul Bourget, Henri-Frédéric Amiel, and the Goncourts. Passages marked include those related to 'literary theory and criticism', narrative technique, and pessimism, melancholy and death (David Crackanthorpe 1977: 43–5). It is striking that David Crackanthorpe does not record editions of Maupassant's or Zola's fiction among Crackanthorpe's books (72).

In a recent study, Gilles Philippe discusses what he calls 'le moment français' (the French moment) in English literature, which he dates from 1880 to 1930 (2016: 6).[1] He identifies this as a period (which includes Crackanthorpe's career) in which there was a widespread belief among English and French writers that French fiction was superior to English fiction, and that the British could and should learn from their French colleagues. For example, Philippe quotes Robert Louis Stevenson, in 1885, touching on technical concerns that echo those of Gustave Flaubert (35), and Henry James, in 1899, unambiguously declaring a debt to French prose of the last fifty years (7). According to these and other sources cited by Philippe, it is above all in the area of style that innovative British writers and men and women of letters felt the need to catch up with and model themselves on the French

1. I am grateful to Professor Marc Porée of the École Normale Supérieure in Paris for drawing my attention to Philippe's study.

(7–8). The French influence on English writing in the late nineteenth and early twentieth centuries seems unambiguous.

In his rich and ground-breaking work, however, Philippe questions this assumption. He dislikes, in any case, the term 'influence', preferring 'référence' (19, 243), for he argues that English writers are not so much influenced by French models, as they discovered French examples to back up English questions and solutions (17–18). He further questions whether the reference between English and French writing is actually one of style (63). Writers, he argues, borrowed certain concerns and ideas, but they did not borrow, in any substantial measure, features of French literary prose (syntax, for example) (17–18), for how could you in reality write in English as in French (84–5)? Indeed, Philippe's text becomes what he calls 'l'histoire d'une illusion' (the history of an illusion) (25, 221). There is no such thing *sensu stricto* as French style in English. (I would argue, in fact, that such a thing would be grotesque. Joseph Conrad's much-bruited Gallicisms are minor deviations from the usual repertoire of English syntactic possibilities; indeed, lexical issues in his writing can often be seen to be echoes of Polish phrases, and, in any case, even they do not seem entirely alien in English.)

But this is not to deny borrowings and references: for example, an increasing interest in impersonality in narration (39–40), an enhanced employment of the device of free indirect speech (18, 89–90), and a presentation of character psychology as fragmentary (87–8). These have French models – the prose of Flaubert, Zola, Maupassant – underlying or underpinning them. In the analysis of Crackanthorpe's short fiction that follows in this introduction, I point out where and how his prose illustrates these points of French *référence*. However – and I move beyond Philippe's study here – one can also see a *francité* (Frenchness) in English writers' increasing obsession with style (which they do not define very clearly), but which becomes a motif in much self-reflection about writing in the late nineteenth and early twentieth centuries. I doubt if Dickens or George Eliot was any less concerned with writing well than Stevenson and James; they simply saw no need to rattle on about it. Another substantial borrowing (relevant to a study of Crackanthorpe's work) is in subject matter – an interest in the sordid, a sexual explicitness – and this comes, at least partly, from France. In 1890, William Barry is in no doubt in an essay in the *Quarterly Review*. Recent literature's interest in sites of social and pathological degeneration, 'the shambles, the surgeons' hall of "demonstration", the house of shame, the prison, the pawnshop and the reeking tavern' – these are a debt to Zola (qtd. in Greenslade 2013: 167). The work of Crackanthorpe was continually identified with that of Maupassant and Zola (Peden 1977: ix–x; Fisher 1994: 61; Hunter 2007: 34), but commentators have also pointed to the ways in which James and Hardy, too, are models for the young writer (Peden 1977: ix–x; Fisher 1994: 61).

Wreckage: Seven Studies (1893)

The title of the volume immediately makes claims on the reader's attention. 'Wreckage' suggests much: disaster, the waste that is left after disaster, a cheerless perspective on life, and a general view of things (after all, wreckage must run through all seven stories; it is no isolated phenomenon). Further, the texts in the collection are not immediately presented as stories, but as 'studies'. Are they artistic studies (fragmentary, unfinished, tentative) or scientific studies (objective, testing, probing) – or both?

The studies themselves are preceded by an epigraph in (untranslated) French:

> Que le roman ait cette religion que le siècle passé appelait de ce large et vaste nom: 'Humanité'; – il lui suffit de cette conscience: son droit est là.
> (May the novel have that religion which the previous century called by the broad and vast name 'Humanity'; – this conscience is enough for it: its right is there.)

The quotation comes from the Preface to the first edition of Edmond and Jules Goncourt's novel *Germinie Lacerteux* (1865), a very controversial and highly regarded text, considered as a major attempt to refresh literature by opening up the lower depths of society and human behaviour to literature, a text full of lurid and pathological material that it seeks to claim for tragedy and readers' attention. The brief quotation is part of the final paragraph of the Preface, in which the authors acknowledge that their novel will be calumnied. However, they argue that, since the novel has become a major form, a means of 'enquête sociale' (social investigation), and by 'recherche psychologique' (psychological research) has become 'L'Histoire morale contemporaine' (contemporary moral History) and has assumed the duties of science, it can demand freedoms and privileges. The quotation used by Crackanthorpe in his paratext is preceded by the following:

> Et qu'il cherche L'Art et la Vérité; qu'il montre des misères bonnes à ne pas laisser oublier aux heureux de Paris; qu'il fasse

> voir aux gens du monde ce que les dames de charité ont le courage de voir . . .: la souffrance humaine, présente et toute vive, qui apprend la charité.
> (And may it [the novel] seek Art and Truth; may it show miseries that it would be good not to let the happy people of Paris forget; may it make the people of the world see what the ladies of charity have the courage to see . . .: human suffering, present and completely alive, which teaches charity.) (Goncourt [1865] 2017)

The Goncourts' programmatic Preface sets out Crackanthorpe's aims in *Wreckage*: to set forth miseries that the prosperous and happy world would do well to remember, to show suffering that will lead to charity, to do so through quasi-scientific and psychologically oriented studies, and to claim the sordid and the forgotten as legitimate subjects for literature. Crackanthorpe is not alone in advancing such aims; for example, these are George Moore's in *Esther Waters* (1894) and Thomas Hardy's in *Tess of the d'Urbervilles* (1891) and *Jude the Obscure* (1895). Crackanthorpe simultaneously locates *Wreckage* within a set of concerns drawn from French literature, and squarely within what is modish in contemporary British writing.

The texts in *Wreckage* show a considerable degree both of range and of coherence. They go beyond the lower social depths implied in the quotation from the Goncourts, but they do treat of psychological states of a complex and also at times disturbing kind. The story materials are sordid and shocking enough. In 'Profiles', Maurice (a gentleman lieutenant in the Army) and Lilly (somewhat lower down the social scale) are keeping company with a view to marriage. Maurice's family is likely to be hostile. Baited by her embittered aunt, with whom she lives, Lilly assaults her and flees to London. She and Maurice live together there for a few days, after which Maurice must return to his regiment in Guildford. Lilly is immediately and willingly seduced by the saturnine Safford, who rapidly abandons her. Lilly tells Maurice, leaves him, and seeks her lover and then replacements for him, finally descending into low-class prostitution. In 'A Conflict of Egoisms', Oswald Newall, a novelist, and Letty Moore, a journalist, enter into an ill-considered marriage. Oswald is incapable of meeting Letty's passion or expectations; they start to live separate lives. In vengeance, Letty destroys a manuscript her husband is working on. Although Oswald hears her praying to get him back, he sets off to commit suicide in the Thames, dying, however, just before he does so. 'A Struggle for Life', the briefest and most commented on of the stories in *Wreckage*, truly plumbs social depths. The anonymous but intradiegetic narrator enters a vile riverside bar in London. He observes one particular client in the company of a prostitute. The man's young wife (or partner) enters the bar, asks him to come home and begs for money for their children. He refuses, the prostitute laughs and the girl leaves the bar, followed by the curious narrator. She walks by the river and at the text's end sells herself for two shillings and sixpence for an hour to a prowling stranger. Part of the social milieu is completely different in 'Dissolving View'. Vivian Marston is very wealthy and about to make a socially very advantageous match. Some ten months previously, he has had an affair with Kit, a semi-literate chorus girl, one she has ended by running off with a French violinist. Marston receives a much-forwarded and delayed letter from Kit. She is dying and her child is his. Vivian sets off to find her, although he wishes for her death. In a mean district of London, Vivian finds that she and her child have died. Relieved, he returns to his world of beauty, wealth, and insulation from the world's hardships.

'A Dead Woman' moves beyond the capital to the north of England. This story, the second longest in the collection, tells of Rushout, the landlord of a public house, who gradually works out that his dead wife Jane has had a long-term adulterous relationship with a local farmer called Hays, whom he knows very well. Parts of the action involve Hays's attempt to obtain the white mare that Jane Rushout used to take her to meet with him. Other parts involve Rushout's towering rage towards Hays and his attempt to do him violence. In the end, the two men are reconciled and, drinking whisky together, calmly discuss the dead woman and her affair. 'When Greek Meets Greek', the longest story in the volume, is a tale of the fast world of high-stakes gambling. Simon Avery is a skilful, successful and high-class card sharp. His companion is Pearl, a French girl whom he has saved from a drunken and violent father. Ralston, an ex-Indian Army officer with a dubious past, is devoted to Pearl. He borrows money from her to gamble with (he is an obsessive gambler). He and Avery gamble at a London club. Ralston cheats and is discovered; Avery cheats and is not. Ralston is a broken and disgraced man. Avery brings home a lot of money. He and Pearl look forward to a good future together. In the final story, 'Embers', Frank Gorridge is a poor but respectable clerk and copyist. In the past, he has been married to a woman who has left him and who now inhabits a base world of drink and prostitution. By chance, she comes across her ex-husband, disrupts his life, extorts money from him, and leads him to the edge of financial and emotional ruin. However, finally, the ex-wife, Mags, is moved to compassion for Gorridge and disappears from his life.

The story materials all involve failed male–female relations at every level of society – from the wealthy ('Dissolving View' and 'When Greek Meets Greek') to the poverty-stricken (either humble and respectable, as in 'Embers', or utterly debased, as in 'The Struggle for Life'). Emotional disturbance is apparent everywhere and is analysed in detail. Adultery and betrayal are rife (in 'Profiles', for example). Dishonesty is recurrent (for example, Simon Avery in 'When Greek Meets Greek' is a crooked gambler, Jane Rushout and Hays are secret adulterers in 'A Dead Woman', and Mag in 'Embers' is utterly mendacious). The world is a dismal place. It is also melodramatic. The stories in *Wreckage* certainly involve story materials that have long been the stuff of melodrama: the women who turn to prostitution in the great city; card-sharping in the bright lights of a fancy London gambling den; a rural affair that is uncovered; the rich socialite who exploits a show girl. The reader who takes *Wreckage* seriously – as I do – must acknowledge the highly coloured story materials that the collection employs. After all, though, nineteenth-century fiction (and later fiction) has never had any compunction in employing the melodramatic to serious ends. We would have to stop reading Charlotte Brontë or Kate Chopin if we let such things bother us too much.

The story materials may be sensational, but in terms of narrative (that is, their chronological and logical organisation) they are accessible and far from innovative. All the stories possess a very familiar linear narrative organisation, and, in 1893, it would be surprising – despite George Eliot's supple chronology in *Daniel Deronda* (1876) – if they had anything else. 'Profiles', 'A Conflict of Egoisms', 'The Struggle for Life', 'A Dead Woman' and 'Embers' are without extensive analepses or prolepses. Logical and chronological order is adhered to, with the ellipses that are the stuff of all narratives. 'Dissolving View' and 'When Greek Meets Greek' do involve analepses, however: when Marston recalls his relationship with Kit, and when there are several pages that fill in details of Pearl's and Simon's (and Ralston's) lives before that night in London when the narrative begins. The latter is the only extensive retrospect in the collection. Most of the stories come to some kind of narrative conclusion: the final vanishing of Lilly in 'Profiles', Oswald's death in 'A Conflict of Egoisms', the reconciliation of Rushout and Hays in 'A Dead Woman', Mags's final departure in 'Embers'. 'Dissolving Views' and 'The Struggle for Life' are less conclusive. In the former, Marston's reputation has been saved and his responsibility for Kit and her child is over, but the future is not entirely clear. A sequence of important action has terminated in the latter story, but one has a sense that the young woman's future is open at the end of 'The Struggle for Life'. A great deal from the narrative (a useless and abusive partner, poverty, the lure of prostitution and of suicide) has still not been dealt with.

The ordering of texts (a kind of over-narrative) in the collection is of interest and shows planning and symmetry. The first and last stories ('Profiles' and 'Embers') both end in a woman's departure into dire misery. 'The Struggle for Life', as well as 'Dissolving View', involves sexual exploitation of poor women, seen from slightly different perspectives. 'A Dead Woman' and 'When Greek Meets Greek' both end with reconciliation between two characters. Overall, there is a movement from utter hopelessness in the first four stories to a guarded hope (not for Mags, of course, in 'Embers') in the last three.

If narrative is traditional in the texts of *Wreckage*, narration is much less so and shows markedly innovative features. It is in this respect that Crackanthorpe shows his reference to the latest French models. On one level, little could be more traditional than the narrator's configuration in the stories in *Wreckage*. Six of the seven stories employ a third-person omniscient narrator, one who, at times, albeit in a very limited fashion, is prepared to comment on the action depicted. 'The Struggle for Life' is, strictly speaking, a first-person narration, and it is important to note that it is one. However, the narrator is restricted to the role of an observer of events and plays no part in them. In Gérard Genette's terms, he is both homodiegetic and heterodiegetic (Genette [1972] 2007: 260). Thus, even when the narrator is present in the story material, as 'I', he is external to the events that he recounts.

Such externality is central to the figure of the narrator in most of the texts in the collection. In 'Profiles', the reader is initially offered physical descriptions of Maurice and Lilly, and later of Safford. In the opening pages of 'A Conflict of Egoisms', the narrator provides succinct presentations and analysis of the principal characters and of their lives up to their first encounters. 'The Struggle for Life' takes the form of a piece of reportage of London low-life, a quasi-journalistic one. 'A Dead Woman' records events and conversations. 'When Greek Meets Greek' opens with a depiction of Ralston and provides details about his past and present; the narrator offers the events of Pearl's and Simon's first meeting in Nice and its subsequent developments over some three years. 'Embers', too, is marked by close but external observation.

> Outside, a drizzling rain. The gas lamps shone a dim, filthy yellow, streaking the slimy pavement with their reflections. There was no sky, only a murky atmosphere overhead. And

> save for a woman creeping along, the street was deserted. Her slatternly clothes hung loosely about her skirt trailed in the mud. She was quite wet, for she had no umbrella.

Even the highly focalised 'Dissolving View' ends with a sober piece of narratorial observation: 'A month afterwards, Gwynnie and he were married. It was a smart wedding. There was a fashionable crowd, and the couple started to spend their honeymoon in Italy.'

Such externality on the part of the narrator to the narrated events is further demonstrated by the extensive use of dialogue in most of the stories. Such passages indicate a withdrawal of the narrator; texts become quasi-dramatic. Thus, Lilly's unhappiness and desire for change emerge clearly in the dialogue with Maurice in Section VII of 'Profiles'. The crisis of her abandonment by Safford in Section XII is rendered primarily through dialogue. The same is true of the climax of her rejection of Maurice's overtures in Section XVI. Dialogue plays an important role in 'Embers' too: Letty's and Oswald's ill-advised decision to marry and the emergence of a serious rift between them are enacted through dialogue rather than narrational recounting. 'A Dead Woman' is full of passages of dialogue in which the narrator is in the background, conversations primarily between Rushout and Hays, but not only them. Section III of 'When Greek Meets Greek' largely consists of passages of dialogue between Pearl and Ralston, and Pearl and Avery. The conclusion of 'Embers' is a piece of dialogue between Frank and Mags.

Despite such externality, however, one of the most striking and most innovative features of the narration of the stories in *Wreckage* is the extensive use of free indirect speech or thought, whereby selected characters' thoughts and feelings are given via indirect speech, unmarked by 'he/she said', and in words that closely render the flow of reflections and emotions within the character. The reader steps close to the character, but that character does not become a narrator him- or herself (Abbott 2008: 77–8). This device is one that is often seen as being a French-influenced introduction in the later nineteenth century (Philippe 2016: 89–90, 224–5), although examples of it can readily be found in Jane Austen's novels. Crackanthorpe uses free indirect style in most of the stories in *Wreckage*. Thus, in 'Dissolving View', which, in terms of narration, possesses fewer of the recurrent technical devices of the other stories (there is little externality and limited use of dialogue), the story is entirely rendered through Vivian Marston's consciousness. For example, as he travels in a cab towards his former mistress's last known address, his thoughts are presented thus:

> And his thoughts writhed under the increasing pain – then, a quick twinge of hunger, reminding him that he had had no breakfast. Back came the object of his journey. He was going to see Kit. It was as if he and she had never had anything in common, as if he only knew of her by hearsay – but somehow, she and her child had spoilt everything for him. And he understood how he hated going, how he shrunk from bringing her back into his life. But for the irresistible force inside him, urging him forward, he would have turned homeward again. Gwynnie, how could he marry her after this ? Strange that he felt no anger against Kit, for having come between them, only he wondered vaguely if it would be easy to get rid of her. But perhaps she was dead – oh! to know for certain that it was so; and the sense of relief, which he knew to be a delusion, was so keen that it hurt him. But the child? – the child – that would live on. They always did. Gloomily, incoherently, he brooded over what was to be done with it.

Over half the lines of this excerpt (those underlined) must be taken to be Vivian's thoughts, or his words to himself, but are rendered as unmarked indirect speech. 'When Greek Meets Greek' moves among the consciousness of the three major characters. Thus, in the gambling club, Ralston's point of view is given directly and rawly, when he begins to cheat (II).

> Then Alvary turned up his cards –seven! – and immediately a loathsome terror swept through Duncan. Some one must have seen him – he would be exposed – and he fell to wondering whether they would let him get his hat, or whether they would hound him bareheaded into the street. He dared not look up. He felt the gaze of the whole room upon him. But at last he mustered courage. Strange! no one seemed to be paying any attention to him. Alvary, surely he? but no – and look! the croupier unmoved was pushing a gilt piece towards him. Then he was not discovered. He was free! ha! ha! and a wild spasm of joy swept through him. When it was gone his head swam, and tossing off a brandy and soda, let three deals pass, while he struggled to calm himself.

Again, at least half the lines in this quotation consists of a close rendition of Ralston's thoughts. Another example from the same text is apparent when Pearl is waiting for Simon's return (III).

> Her father! what had become of him? Dead – a round, green, nameless grave, or perhaps still alive, sitting in a dingy café, with the yellow-green drink before him. Simon! oh, why did he not come?
>
> Duncan! Was he winning to-night. Those notes! How angry Simon had been when he had snapped his fingers. What was he doing? Perhaps at this moment, now at this very moment, he was taking their money. Oh! why did he not come?
>
> Ah! Stop! What was that? A noise – a knocking – muffled, as if something soft against the door. Ah! there it was again. What could it be? Simon! *It* had come then. She rushed into the hall and struggled to unfasten the door.
>
> Outside the figure of a man. Not Simon – he was too tall. No hat, wet through, his clothes were clinging to his body.

Here the text closely follows Pearl's thoughts and emotions, but without the character's direct address to the reader.

All the stories in *Wreckage* illustrate Crackanthorpe's use of the device of free indirect style. Thus, narration in *Wreckage* is marked by externality, extensive use of dialogue and extensive use of free indirect style. These three techniques are far from incompatible, as they all involve a narrational withdrawal, even when the narrator renders a character's consciousness closely but indirectly. Indeed, the final striking feature of the configuration of the narrator in *Wreckage* is a refusal to pass moral judgement on characters and actions. The reader is meant to see Vivian Marston as exploitative and irresponsible, but the narrator nowhere draws that verdict. Lilly's self-destruction and her destruction by Safford do not produce commentary from the narrator. The pity and the shame are implicit. Such neutrality is, above all, apparent in 'The Struggle for Life'. The vileness of the lower depths and its mores is clear, but the narrator nowhere passes explicit judgement on the characters and their actions.

The narrators' language is also worth commenting on in *Wreckage*. Above all, it is a demotic and informal language. This is the case in passages of dialogue. Here are two examples from quite different social milieux. The first is from the relatively genteel world of 'Profiles':

> 'Why, Lilly, doesn't it interest you?'
>
> 'I don't think I could ever go back,' she answered slowly.
>
> 'But we can't live any here else, unless I exchange, and that would take time.'

A pause, during which she was nervously tearing strips off the edge of the newspaper.

'How long will you be away?' she asked at length.

'Let's see, to-day's Wednesday. If I go tomorrow morning, I ought to be back by Friday night or Saturday morning. But what on earth will you do with yourself?'

'I don't know, but I can't go back there. You don't know how impossible it is.'

'But after we are married?'

'Perhaps it will be different then,' she answered musingly. (VII)

A second useful example is drawn from 'A Dead Woman', in which Crackanthorpe notably renders northern English with some skill and, I believe, accuracy:

'Mornin', I thought ye were off to the auction mart.'

'Nay, I thought better on't. There's scarce a bit doin' jest now.'

'Ye'll take a drop to warm ye. It's raw.'

'Nay. I've come for a bit o' business.'

'Ye're welcome, business or no business. Step inside.'

He led the way into the room where they had sat the night before.

'Well,' said Rushout, when he had settled down in his chair.

'I've come to buy t'mare.'

'Not the white one?'

'Ay, that's her.'

Rushout reflected: 'What, in the name of goodness, d'ye want with her?'

'I want her,' answered the farmer doggedly.

'But what for?' testily retorted the other.

'Maybe I've taken a fancy to her.'

Rushout's face broadened to a smile.

'Are ye lookin' for a bit of blood to spank ye to church?' (II)

Such informality of language is reflected in what is strictly narrator's discourse throughout the collection. Paragraphs are frequently very short (the texts are full of examples), and narrators show a predilection for sentence fragments. For example, 'The Struggle for Life' begins thus:

It was a chilly October night in a notorious 'den' beyond the water – since closed by the police.

> Half a dozen gross gas-jets lit up the long, low room; making a procession of queer-shaped shadows dance restlessly about the walls: here and there, dotted about, crudely coloured chromos of the Queen, the Prince of Wales, and one or two half-naked prize-fighters.

This is the beginning of 'Embers':

> The room was small, but the twilight shadows made it appear larger. An iron bedstead; two tables, one covered with papers, the other with a white cloth; a chair by the door, and on it a mud-splashed pair of trousers and a dirty shirt, with a pair of old slippers, trodden down at the heels, underneath; a black, shiny armchair, its horsehair stuffing protruding in places; a deal chest of drawers – this was all the furniture. No kind of ornament, bare walls, not a spot of colour to relieve the cheerlessness.
>
> Yet presently, as one looked, two or three details betrayed something of the individuality of the occupant.

Lexis is not entirely informal (although syntax usually is). In the above passages, 'notorious', 'making a procession' and 'restlessly' ('The Struggle for Life'), and 'protruding', 'to relieve the cheerlessness' and 'betrayed the individuality of the occupant' ('Embers'), are more formal and sophisticated than the rest of the vocabulary, but only to a limited degree. Crackanthorpe's language in *Wreckage* is not entirely informal, but it is predominantly and strikingly so, and, in this respect, much more like parts of Hardy's later fiction than James's work. In language, too, as in narrational technique, Crackanthorpe is – like many other late nineteenth-century British writers – moving fiction away from the relative formalities of earlier prose (especially in narrational discourse) towards something much more demotic and accessible. Stevenson, Ella D'Arcy, Wells, Arthur Conan Doyle and Wilde, among others, can be seen to be doing the same.

Settings and characters illustrate the range and consistency of *Wreckage*. Each story has a different social coloration, and several stories vary internally. 'Profiles' moves largely within a relatively respectable and well-off milieu: Maurice comes from a wealthy family; Lilly is just at the respectable end of the social spectrum; Safford may be a cad, but he is a wealthy one. However, at the end, Lilly descends into a sordid world of low-class prostitution. The story also shifts from the rural idyll of the opening section to the excitements and dangers of the great city. 'A Conflict of Egoisms' is wholly set in London, among hard-working but far from wealthy characters concerned with fiction-writing and journalism, in unglamorous but respectable lodgings. 'The Struggle for Life' takes a plunge into the lower depths of lumpen London, with settings, characters, dialogue and events to match. 'Dissolving View' rises considerably up the social scale. Marston is wealthy and socially successful; his life is one of luxury, hunting, shooting and a splendid marriage. In the course of the text, however, the protagonist travels into a quite different locale: the mean streets of dingy restaurants, foreigners and seedy lodgings. The city is central to Crackanthorpe's created world in *Wreckage*, and the city is typical of many *fin-de-siècle* depictions: a place of threat, confusion, misery and unhappy ends. Lilly's progress after Safford has abandoned her represents this well.

> And then the seething turmoil of the great city, ruthless in its never-flagging lust, caught up the frailty of her helpless beauty, and playing with it, marred it, mutilated it. Like a flower, frost-bitten in the hour of its budding, she dropped and withered. (XIV)

'A Dead Woman', however, is set outside London in north-west England, its characters a publican, a farmer and servants, its principal setting a public house. 'When Greek Meets Greek' is cosmopolitan in its settings: a respectable enough house in Maida Vale, a high-stakes gambling club, Nice, and casinos in Paris and fashionable continental resorts. Characters correspond; Ralston is ex-Indian Army with a dark past; Pearl is a French foundling; Avery is a sleek, sophisticated, secretive master of cards, moving between English and French with ease. But 'Embers' descends again into a metropolitan world of bare respectability, shabby poverty and drunken shiftlessness. Clearly, Crackanthorpe is aiming at a generality in his pictures of human life. Wreckage, as an existential and emotional state, is part of a wide range of social situations and marks a spectrum of human life from low to high and in between.

The distinct worlds of *Wreckage* make one consistent world in several respects. The principal focus of Crackanthorpe's writing in these stories, and, indeed, in all of his texts throughout the *œuvre*, is intimate male–female relationships, whether by way of marriage or unauthorised liaison. Thus, Lilly's relationships with Maurice and Safford are at the centre of 'Profiles', as is Oswald's and Letty's marriage in 'A Conflict of Egoisms', the girl's and the mason's connection (and hers with her customer and, perhaps, future customers) in 'The Struggle for Life', Vivian's and Kit's affair in 'Dissolving View',

Jane Rushout's past relationship with her husband and her lover in 'A Dead Woman', Pearl's and Simon's liaison in 'When Greek Meets Greek', and Frank's and Mags's marriage and its aftermath in 'Embers'. All these relationships are complex and most of them work out unhappily for one or both of those involved. Lilly betrays Maurice, and Safford rejects her. Oswald and Letty prove incompatible. The mason rejects, humiliates and abuses the young woman with whom he lives and has had a child. Prostitution – both in the figure of the prostitute in the bar, and in the young woman's bargain with her customer on the street – is sordid. Kit has run off with a French fiddle player; Vivian has scarcely felt her departure, and his relief that she and her child have died is palpable. Jane Rushout has consistently betrayed her husband with Hays. Frank's marriage with Mags leads to desertion and mercenary exploitation. Only Pearl and her gambler husband have a stable and loving relationship, and even she distrusts him at times.

It is notable that in the relationships in the stories, female figures are frequently, if intermittently, active. Lilly walks out on Maurice and decides herself to drift into self-destruction. Letty becomes so enraged with Oswald that she destroys the manuscript of his book (in their world, a major act of aggression). Kit, too, runs off from her relationship with Marston. Jane Rushout has pursued her own desire with her lover, and Mags, for all that she behaves in a dreadful fashion, chooses to extract support from her estranged husband. However, the girl in 'The Struggle for Life' is, above all, a passive figure abused by men, and Pearl is utterly dependent on Avery, her saviour and patron, in 'When Greek Meets Greek'. In fact, it is striking that, in several stories, female characters end up dead (and, thus, particularly passive): Lilly, Kit and Jane Rushout (who is dead from the beginning of the story). Some kind of balance and reconciliation is, occasionally, possible, although only between Pearl and Avery in 'When Greek Meets Greek', and between the two male figures in 'A Dead Woman'. The sexual explicitness of male–female relationships is also marked. Lilly clearly has sex with Maurice and Safford. Sexual relations are at the fore in 'The Struggle for Life', 'Dissolving View' and 'A Dead Woman'. Pearl and Avery live together for a year before marriage.

The complex and shifting nature of gender roles and perceptions is a further focus of the stories in *Wreckage*. There is an interplay of activity and passivity among male and female figures. Some male characters are strikingly passive: Maurice in 'Profiles' (set off against the decisive, if wicked, Safford), Oswald in 'A Conflict of Egoisms' (his passivity is part of what irritates Letty) and Frank in 'Embers'.

Even the hugely wealthy and socially successful Vivian in 'Dissolving View' is pitched into action only by Kit's letter. Rushout and Hays are both passive figures, left alone by the woman they both love. Ralston, in 'When Greek Meets Greek', if not exactly passive, is a pathetic failure throughout, sponging money from Pearl to lose in futile gambling. As I have suggested above, some female figures show a kind of agency, if only a destructive and self-destructive kind. Indeed, the only decisively active male figure is Avery in 'When Greek Meets Greek', and he is a card-sharp. Thus, traditional gender roles (male activity, female passivity) are at least queried in *Wreckage*. Further, these stories do scrutinise the themes of male power over women. Abuse of male power is not class-specific: Safford, Marston and the mason in 'The Struggle for Life' all use women for their sexual ends, and the women pay.

A final, albeit minor, focus in these stories relates to the figure of the artist. In 'A Conflict of Egoisms', Oswald is a well-known, if not wealthy, writer, who meets and generates disaster through an ill-considered marriage. In 'Embers', Frank is a copyist, a writer figure of sorts. In 'When Greek Meets Greek', Avery is an artist (and a hard-working one) among crooked gamblers. The figure of the writer is paradoxically prominent in 'The Struggle for Life'. He enters the 'notorious "den"', presumably looking for material. He watches the sordid scene that plays out there and then, 'curious to see the end of it', follows the girl out into the street. He passes close by her and watches her as she weighs up suicide and prostitution, noting her tears in the moonlight. He sits as the 'slinking' customer takes her off for sex. There is no intervention, no excess of pity, only observation and the assembly of material for a short story.

Remaining fiction

Crackanthorpe's fictional *œuvre* consists of three other texts: *Sentimental Studies, and A Set of Village Tales* (1895), *Vignettes* (1896) and *Last Studies* (1897). It should be noted that the last text was published posthumously, and one wonders to what degree it was, in fact, organised by Blanche Crackanthorpe, who wrote the dedication to the volume. The title is clearly not Crackanthorpe's own, and we do not know whether the ordering of the three texts it contains was authorial. The volume is meant as a homage to Crackanthorpe (the inclusion of Brooke's poem and James's 'Appreciation' show this), and is not strictly a collection put together by the author. However, much in the text is consistent with Crackanthorpe's other work.

Indeed, the remainder of Crackanthorpe's output shows that the author was using a very similar technique and working over very similar concerns to those in *Wreckage*. This coherence is scarcely surprising, given that we are dealing with what must be the work of four years at most by a relatively young author.

Sentimental Studies contains five or six texts, depending on whether one takes the two parts of 'A Commonplace Chapter' as separate, or the same long short story divided in two. I will treat the parts here as belonging to one fiction. 'Modern Melodrama' had been published already in *The Yellow Book* in April 1894, and 'In Cumberland' had been published as 'A Study in Sentimentality' in the same journal in October 1894. The texts in *Sentimental Studies* echo much that is in *Wreckage*. Narrative is linear, although there is an inclination to open endings, which is less prominent in *Wreckage*. 'Modern Melodrama' and 'In Cumberland' are both less conclusive than the other texts, especially the former. In terms of technique, narration is marked by a widespread use of dialogue and free indirect style. Strong character focalisation is current in all stories, very clearly in 'Battledore and Shuttlecock' and in 'A Commonplace Chapter' in the presentation of Ronald Thorneycroft's and Ella Haselton's consciousness. Much of 'In Cumberland' plays out in Alec Burkett's mind and feelings.

Settings are as varied as in *Wreckage*: largely metropolitan in 'A Commonplace Chapter' and 'Battledore and Shuttlecock', rural in 'In Cumberland' and 'Yew Trees and Peacocks'. The variety of social milieux is also marked: from the *demi-monde* to respectability in 'A Commonplace Chapter' and 'Battledore and Shuttlecock'; the world of a kept woman and her sponsor in 'Modern Melodrama'; provincial life among the respectable and the poor in 'In Cumberland'; and a country-house setting in 'Yew Trees and Peacocks'. Central characters are all complex in their psychologies and their relationships. 'Sentimental Studies' means, in this volume, examinations of far from simple feelings and emotional lives. 'In Cumberland' is a particularly detailed scrutiny of obsession on the part of the central male character; 'Modern Melodrama' is centred on Daisy's sense that she is going to die soon. The sexual explicitness in character presentation is marked in several stories: Haselton has mistresses in 'A Commonplace Chapter'; there is no doubt how Midge and Daisy make their living in 'Modern Melodrama' and 'Battledore and Shuttlecock'. As in *Wreckage*, passivity marks many characters: Ella in 'A Commonplace Chapter', Ronald and Helen in 'Battledore and Shuttlecock', Alec Burkett in 'In Cumberland', Daisy in 'Modern Melodrama', and even Hallam in 'Yew Trees and Peacocks'. Inevitably, given the collection's focus on male–female relationships, there is a scrutiny of gender roles: men are exploiters of women, as in 'A Commonplace Chapter' (although this exploitation is complexly shaded in 'Modern Melodrama'), but many male figures, as I indicate above, are remarkably passive and malleable.

A Set of Village Tales is part of the *Sentimental Studies* collection, but shows Crackanthorpe's fiction moving in a different direction. It is in these stories that he comes very close to some of Maupassant's fiction of lower-class life. Always cosmopolitan in scope (think of 'When Greek Meets Greek'), Crackanthorpe's fiction here consists of six narratives set in the south-western French countryside, involving, primarily, characters who are small farmers or village dwellers. Narration is complex. The narrator is present in all the stories, as an English outsider who becomes privy to the experiences of those who surround him (and who bears some resemblance to Crackanthorpe himself in his good French and taste for fine horses). But in two stories, 'Lisa-la-Folle' and 'The Little Priest', the narrator reports others' stories. None of the stories in the collection is short of event, although sometimes these events are seemingly trivial: mould on the maize, the death of a dog, the teasing of a naïve priest. But these events are important for the characters involved, often having substantial material and emotional consequences, and the stories explore the characters' psychological responses to them. 'Etienne Mattou' shows Crackanthorpe's interest in the criminal and the melodramatic (compare 'When Greek Meets Greek'): Etienne Mattou arranges what looks like his own murder in order to cash in on his life insurance, but his wife Jeanne frustrates him and leaves it all to the Church. 'Gaston Lalanne's Child' demonstrates the author's recurrent focus on the complexities of adultery.

Vignettes, too, shows Crackanthorpe extending his range. Several of these texts had been published previously in 1895, in *The Speaker* and *The Saturday Review*. These are observations and impressions of various places in various countries, and more than a few comments on those places, dated over the course of a little more than a year. The epigraph – 'The pursuit of experience is the refuge of the unimaginative' – is of some interest. It is an adaptation of Wilde's dictum that 'Consistency is the last refuge of the unimaginative' (in 'The Relation of Dress to Art', *The Pall Mall Gazette*, 28 February 1885). To quote Wilde, even in a modified form, in 1896 was surely to make some kind of gesture towards subversive behaviour. In addition, the epigraph must be a piece of self-irony, given that *Vignettes* is full of experiences and of impressions gained from experience.

The thirty-seven separate texts in *Vignettes* move between the rural and the city: for example, from a description of trees, leaves, blue flax and purple orchises in Béarn in south-western France (9) to Paris, 'all white and a-glitter under a cold, sparkling sky' (28). The narrator (we can assume it is Crackanthorpe speaking in his own voice and person) presents some harsh views of the city. Paris is marked by 'parochial modernity coquetting with cosmopolitanism' (28), and London by 'portentous provinciality' (52). Naples is colourful but sordid (40–1). However, country landscapes are not purely lovely. Against 'the rank, luscious green of the Rhône valley', Jeanne-Marie Latou tells of her nephew in the French Army in North Africa, of the pleasures of a humble excursion to Marseille, of the legacy of the Revolution (1–5). But urban squalor abounds. A description of 'dingy-brick houses' in London also contains an image of a shabby male figure, the red flesh of his feet visible through the cracks in his boots (56–7). The impressions of London are often menacing and dismal (see the passage 'In the Strand', printed in the appendices to this edition). Descriptions of sunsets and night-time recur throughout many of the texts, giving the whole collection a constant air of ending and decline. The collection concludes with a dream rêverie and its perfect cloudscape, self-ironisingly entitled 'Enfantillage' (Childishness). *Vignettes* is an odd text, to some extent a genre (fragmentary impressions and *obiter dicta*) with which modern English-language readers are not completely familiar. It demonstrates, above all, the range of Crackanthorpe's interests (nature, the city, the sordid, the beautiful, the shabbily human, the power of the imagination), and his attempts to find striking and perhaps (for a writer) useful locales and to get them down in words. He certainly recycled two of them, a 'Rêverie' on the times, and a description of the traffic on the Strand in London, in the last story in *Last Studies* (see the last two extracts from *Vignettes* printed in the appendices).

Last Studies contains three stories. One of them, 'Anthony Garstin's Courtship', had appeared in *The Savoy* in July 1896. Although Crackanthorpe cannot have had a hand in the ordering of the texts in the collection, they form a coherent whole. They also clearly relate closely in technique and subject matter to the earlier fiction. The first story, 'Anthony Garstin's Courtship', is set in the rural north-west of England, among respectable, hard-working but not wealthy people, in a world reminiscent of that of 'A Dead Woman' and 'In Cumberland'. It is a harsh, rural tale of a man's stubborn pursuit of the woman he is obsessed with, and his final winning of her, despite her vagaries, her reluctance and his mother's deep antagonism to the match. However, what the future holds for Garstin and Rosa Blencarn, ill matched as they are, is not clear. The presence of a considerable number of passages of dialogue, a great deal of it in dialect, gives the piece a sense of authenticity, reminiscent of Hardy's work and anticipatory of D. H. Lawrence's. The sexual openness and the psychological complexity of the piece echo much of Crackanthorpe's earlier work.

'Trevor Perkins: A Platonic Episode' shifts to an urban world, that of a shabby shop assistant with intellectual interests and of the waitress in London with whom he has a relationship. Perkins himself is a figure who is echoed in E. M. Forster's Leonard Bast in *Howards End* (1910). Perkins, whose consciousness is frequently rendered through free indirect style, is, as so often in Crackanthorpe's work, a passive figure, malleable by circumstance, who determines to have a non-sexual relationship with the waitress Emily Hammond, only to succumb move by move to the circumstances of an evening tryst in Hyde Park. The reader can only think that the relationship means the end of his high-flown intellectual ambitions.

'The Turn of the Wheel', which concludes the volume, is a long short story of wealth, success, power and betrayal, set in fashionable and wealthy London society. The central male character, Lingard, a hugely successful businessman and politician, has been betraying his wife Bessie for years, keeping his secret from his admiring daughter Hilda but not from his wife. The short story charts Hilda's discovery of her father's corruption, of her despised mother's strength and suffering, and of her own desires in relation to her suitors, for she is a very desirable match. Like all the stories in *Last Studies*, the ending is ambiguous and, to a degree, open. Does Hilda choose Walsh because she loves him, or because he will be undemanding and open to manipulation?

Conclusion

It is undeniable that Crackanthorpe's output is slim but it is substantial. His technical competence and interest in innovation, the range of his fictions, his ability to render characters' complexities in depth, his sexual frankness, his fascination with the disturbing city (and his ability to render rural themes and persons with skill and tact), and his interest in the intricate interplay of gender roles – all these make his work a considerable achievement. His early death can be seen only as a loss to English literature. His relative exclusion from accounts of English prose fiction is regrettable. This edition of *Wreckage* (with its appendices and apparatus) is an attempt to rectify the situation.

Further Reading

Abbott, H. Porter (2008), *The Cambridge Introduction to Narrative*, 2nd edn, Cambridge: Cambridge University Press.

Adams, Jad (2009), 'The Drowning of Hubert Crackanthorpe and the Persecution of Leila Macdonald', *English Literature in Transition, 1880–1920* 52.1, pp. 6–34.

Bergonzi, Bernard, ed. (1980), *Poetry 1870 to 1914*, London: Longman.

Buckley, Jerome Hamilton [1952] (1966), *The Victorian Temper: A Study in Literary Culture*, Abingdon: Frank Cass.

Crackanthorpe, David (1977), *Hubert Crackanthorpe and English Realism in the 1890s*, Columbia and London: University of Missouri Press.

Crackanthorpe, Hubert (1892a), 'He Wins Who Loses', *The Albemarle* 1.3 (March), pp. 104–11.

— (1892b), 'Dissolving Views', *The Albemarle* 2.2 (August), pp. 80–3.

— (1893), *Wreckage: Seven Studies*, London: William Heinemann.

— (1894a), 'Mr. Henry James as a Playwright', *The Albemarle* (January), pp. 34–5.

— (1894b), 'Realism in France and England: An Interview with M. Émile Zola', *The Albemarle* (February), pp. 39–43.

— (1894c), 'Modern Melodrama', *The Yellow Book: An Illustrated Quarterly* 1 (April), pp. 223–32.

— (1894d), 'Reticence in Literature', *The Yellow Book: An Illustrated Quarterly* 2 (July), pp. 259–74.

— (1895a), *Sentimental Studies, and A Set of Village Tales*, London: William Heinemann.

— (1895b), 'The Haseltons', *The Yellow Book: An Illustrated Quarterly* 5 (April), pp. 132–70.

— (1895c), 'Bread and the Circus', *The Yellow Book: An Illustrated Quarterly* 7 (October), pp. 235–60.

— (1896), *Vignettes: A Miniature Journal of Whim and Sentiment*, London and New York: John Lane/The Bodley Head.

— (1897a), *Last Studies*, London: William Heinemann.

— (1897b), 'Notes for a Paper on Barrès and Bourget', *Tomorrow* 3 (February), pp. 83–92.

— and Henry Harland (1917?), *The Light Sovereign: A Farcical Comedy in Three Acts*, London: Lady Henry Harland, n.d.

Fisher, Benjamin Franklin (1994), 'Hubert Crackanthorpe', in William

B. Thesing, ed., *British Short-Fiction Writers, 1880–1914: The Realist Tradition, Dictionary of Literary Biography*, Detroit, Washington, D. C., and London: Brucoli Lark Layman/Gale Research, vol. 135, pp. 60–74.

Fletcher, Ian, ed. (1987), *British Poetry and Prose: 1870–1905*, Oxford and New York: Oxford University Press.

Frierson, William C. (1925), *L'Influence du naturalisme français sur les romanciers anglais de 1885 à 1900*, Paris: Marcel Giard.

—(1942), *The English Novel in Transition 1885–1940*, Norman: University of Oklahoma Press.

Genette, Gérard [1972] (2007), *Discours du récit*, Paris: Éditions du Seuil.

Goncourt, Edmond and Jules Goncourt [1865] (2017), *Germinie Lacerteux*, Paris: Flammarion.

Greenslade, William (2013), 'Naturalism and Decadence: The Case of Hubert Crackanthorpe', in Jason David Hall and Alex Murray, eds, *Decadent Poetries: Literature and Form at the British* Fin de Siècle, Basingstoke: Palgrave Macmillan, pp. 163–80.

Hanson, Clare (1985), *Short Stories and Short Fictions, 1880–1980*, London and Basingstoke: Macmillan.

Haurie, Michel (1990), 'Le Révélateur de Francis Jammes', *Hommage à Hubert Crackanthorpe, Association Francis Jammes, Bulletin No 14* (December), pp. 1–3.

Hunter, Adrian (2007), *The Cambridge Introduction to the Short Story in English*, Cambridge: Cambridge University Press.

Jackson, Holbrook [1913] (1950), *The Eighteen Nineties: A Review of Art and Ideas at the Close of the Nineteenth Century*, Harmondsworth: Penguin.

Johnson, Lionel [1897] (1982), 'Hubert Crackanthorpe', *Poetry and Fiction: Reflections on Three Nineteenth Century Authors*, Edinburgh: The Tragara Press, pp. 12–18.

Korte, Barbara (2003), *The Short Story in Britain*, Tübingen and Basel: A. Francke.

Le Gallienne, Richard (1897), 'Hubert Crackanthorpe: In Memoriam', *The Star* (2 January), p. 1.

Macdonald, Leila (1894), 'Jeanne-Marie', *The Yellow Book: An Illustrated Quarterly* (October), pp. 215–40

Malcolm, Cheryl and David Malcolm, eds (2008), *A Companion to the British and Irish Short Story*, Oxford and Malden, MA: Wiley–Blackwell.

Malcolm, David (2012a), *The British and Irish Short Story Handbook*, Oxford and Malden, MA: Wiley–Blackwell.

—(2012b), 'Foreign Transfers: Or, What Happened to the British Short Story in the *Fin-de-Siècle*', in Sabine Coelsch-Foisner, Manfred Markus and Herbert Schendl, eds, *Transfer in English Studies*, Austrian Studies in English 100, pp. 91–102.

Peden, William, ed. (1969), *Collected Stories of Hubert Crackanthorpe (1893–1897) together with An Appreciation by Henry James: Facsimile Reproductions with an Introduction by William Peden*, Gainesville, FL: Scholars' Facsimiles and Reprints, 1969.

—(1977), 'Foreword', in David Crackanthorpe, *Hubert Crackanthorpe and English Realism in the 1890s*, Columbia and London: University of Missouri Press.

—(1978), 'Hubert Crackanthorpe: Forgotten Pioneer', *Studies in Short Fiction* 7.4, pp. 539–48.

Philippe, Gilles (2016), *French Style: L'Accent français de la prose anglaise*, Paris: Les Impressions Nouvelles.

Shaw, Valerie (1983), *The Short Story: A Critical Introduction*, London and New York: Longman.

Stanford, Derek, ed. (1971), *Writing of the 'Nineties: From Wilde to Beerbohm*, London: Dent.

Towheed, Shafquot (2000), 'Reading the Life and Art of Hubert Crackanthorpe', *English Literature in Transition, 1880–1920* 43.1, pp. 51–65.

Waugh, Arthur (1894), 'Reticence in Literature', *The Yellow Book: An Illustrated Quarterly* (April), pp. 201–22.

Wilde, Oscar [1891] (1968), *The Picture of Dorian Gray*, Harmondsworth: Penguin.

'The Yellow Dwarf' (1895), 'Books: A Letter to the Editor', *The Yellow Book: An Illustrated Quarterly* 7 (October), pp. 125–48.

—(1896a), 'A Birthday Letter', *The Yellow Book: An Illustrated Quarterly* (April), pp. 11–28.

—(1896b), 'Dogs, Cats, Books, and the Average Man', *The Yellow Book: An Illustrated Quarterly* (July), pp. 11–23.

A Hubert Crackanthorpe Chronology

1870	Hubert Crackanthorpe is born, on 12 May, in London. The family name at this time is Cookson.
1883–8	Crackanthorpe attends Eton.
1888	Crackanthorpe's father changes the family name from Cookson as a requirement for inheriting his cousin's estate, Newbiggin, in the north of England.
1889	Crackanthorpe spends several months in south-west France. He makes the acquaintance of French poet Francis Jammes (1868–1938).
1889–92	Crackanthorpe is assumed to be in London in these years, moving in *avant-garde* artistic circles, including that centred on Selwyn Image. The lack of information concerning this three-year period gives rise to outrageous rumours.
1892	Crackanthorpe co-edits *The Albemarle*, a political and cultural monthly. It runs for nine numbers from January to September. The second number publishes Crackanthorpe's interview with Émile Zola.
1892	Crackanthorpe makes the acquaintance of Leila Macdonald.
1893	Crackanthorpe and Macdonald are married on 14 February. The couple travel to France, where they stay for a longer period. They also probably visit other European countries. They return to London at the end of 1893.
1893	*Wreckage: Seven Studies*, a collection of short stories, is published by William Heinemann in March.
1894	Crackanthorpe publishes a short story ('Modern Melodrama') and an essay ('Reticence in Literature') in *The Yellow Book.* Macdonald publishes a short story ('Jeanne-Marie') in *The Yellow Book.* In spring and summer, the Crackanthorpes travel in Italy and France.
1895	Macdonald publishes verse in *The Yellow Book.* Crackanthorpe's second collection of short stories, *Sentimental Studies, and A Set of Village Tales*, is published by Heinemann in July. The Crackanthorpes travel in France and elsewhere in Europe. In the summer, Crackanthorpe spends four days travelling with a circus.

1896 Macdonald publishes verse in *The Savoy*. She suffers a miscarriage in the early part of the year. She departs for Italy alone. In August, Crackanthorpe and Mary Elizabeth (Sissie) Welch travel together to Paris. *Vignettes: A Miniature Journal of Whim and Sentiment* is published by John Lane in October. On 4 November, Macdonald informs Crackanthorpe that she plans to divorce him. On 5 November, in the evening, Crackanthorpe is last seen near the Seine. On 25 December, Crackanthorpe's brothers identify a corpse, recently recovered from the Seine and in an advanced state of decay, as the author's.

1897 *Last Studies* is published by Heinemann.

A Note on the Text

The following text follows the first edition of *Wreckage*, published by William Heinemann in 1893. The second edition of *Wreckage*, again published by Heinemann, differs only in insignificant ways from the first. There are no other editions from Crackanthorpe's lifetime. Original spellings and punctuation have been followed; differences between Crackanthorpe's and modern British usage are, in any case, minor. Notes have been added where I have thought it necessary, especially in connection with Crackanthorpe's extensive use of French vocabulary, which would, however, have been well within the competence of most of his original readers.

Series Editor's Preface

The nineteenth century saw an unprecedented, prodigious production of literary texts. Many of these, often best-sellers or offering vital commentaries on cultural, political and philosophical issues of the period engendering debate, did not survive in print long into the twentieth century, regardless of putative quality, however measured. Edinburgh Critical Editions of Nineteenth-Century Texts seeks to bring back to the reading public and the scholarly eye works of undeniable importance during the time of their first publication and reception, which have, often unjustly, disappeared from print and readers' consciousness. Covering fiction, long and short, non-fiction prose and essays, and poetry, with comprehensive critical introductions and carefully chosen supporting appendices, germane to the text and the context of the volume, Edinburgh Critical Editions of Nineteenth-Century Texts provides definitive, annotated scholarly reprints.

WRECKAGE: SEVEN STUDIES

BY HUBERT CRACKANTHORPE

PROFILES

I

It was one of the first warm afternoons of the year; the vigorous rays of the sun lent the young leaves, whose delicate green suffused the wood, an exquisite transparency.

All was still; the rushes clustered immobile on the banks of the little stream; no breath of wind ruffled its surface.

Alone a water-rat splashed, and gently rippling the water, swam across.

On the bank a girl was sitting, her white cotton dress rucked about her knees, displaying a small pair of muddy boots, which dangled close to the water's surface. Her body was thrust forward in a cramped position, as with both hands she held a long, clumsy-looking fishing-rod. She was watching intently the movements of a fat, red float, which bobbed excitedly up and down.

She was bareheaded, and her crisp, auburn hair was riotously tumbling about her ears and neck.

Quite pale was her skin, but pale, transparent, soft; exquisite was the modelling of her fresh, firm lips.

There were great possibilities of beauty in the face; but now an all-absorbing look filled it, the forehead puckered over the eyebrows, the lips set tight together.

A little way off, on the grass, a young man, in a grey flannel suit, was lying on his back, his face shaded by her big-brimmed straw hat, inside the ribbon of which were tucked some bunches of primroses; one hand thrust in the armhole of his waistcoat, the other thrown back over his head – the limp abandon of his pose betrayed that he was asleep.

Down darted the fat, red float. Awkwardly the girl tugged at the rod; the line tightened, swaying about from side to side.

'Maurice!' she called; then louder, as he did not wake.

Maurice started, pushed the hat from off his eyes, murmuring sleepily –

'Hullo! what's up?'

'Make haste, do! I can't hold the rod any more.'

He jumped up, took it, and in a minute or two the fish was floundering on the grass, its sleek, silver sides gleaming in the sunlight.

'Why, Lilly, it's quite a big one,' he exclaimed.

Tall, with fine, broad shoulders, and a small, well-shaped head, evidently not a quite young man; but a trick of raising his eyebrows with an air of boyish surprise, made him appear some years younger.

'He pulled like anything. I should have had to let go the rod in another minute. My arms ache all over,' she added, ruefully.

'That rod's too heavy for you. I'll have to get another, if we're coming fishing again.'

'Oh, yes! Of course we are. I love it.'

Quite beautiful she looked, her face lit up in a delicate flush of excitement.

'Put on another worm, quick. There's sure to be some more, aren't there?'

Maurice pulled out his watch.

'Nearly four o'clock,' he said, shaking his head. 'I've got a guard at half-past five. We must pack up.'

At once her face clouded, the eyes half-closed, the mouth drooped, the chin pouted.

A pettish exclamation was on her lips, but, catching sight of an amused twinkle in Maurice's eyes, she checked herself, and her face cleared.

Together they unscrewed the rod, and when they had put the joints into their canvas case, they started off through the wood, along the narrow path that led to the village.

Maurice, with the rod under his arm, and a long cigar in the corner of his mouth, Lilly bareheaded, her hair more unruly than ever, carrying her hat and her parasol in her hand.

II

They were engaged to be married, Lilly and Maurice. It had been so for nearly three months.

Lilly lived with her Aunt Lisbet in a semidetached villa on the outskirts of Guildford, where Maurice's regiment was quartered.

She had never known her mother; when she ransacked the dim memories of her childhood, there was nobody further back than Aunt Lisbet. Her father she scarcely remembered at all, for he had died when she was quite a little girl. He had been a bookmaker, and a coloured photograph of him – a burly, red-faced man, in a white top hat, and a long, grey dust-coat with a scarlet flower in the button-hole – hung over the fireplace in Aunt Lisbet's bedroom. Underneath the photograph was written, James Maguire – 'Big Jock.'

During his lifetime 'Big Jock's' good luck had been almost proverbial, so that he was reputed to be worth a 'tidy pile.' But at his death, when all his debts had been paid, scarcely a hundred pounds remained. What had become of it all no one knew, and Aunt Lisbet had never forgiven her brother for this mystery. The disappearance of the money itself exasperated her; but the thought that for years he had been secretly making away with large sums without a word to her, his sister, who had kept house for him since his wife's death, and who had been a second mother to his child, made her especially furious.

This bitter feeling against her brother, instead of subsiding as time went on, only rankled the more in her mind; and now, except in terms of abuse, she never mentioned his name.

She was a thin, sharp-boned, little woman, with red lids to her greenish-coloured eyes, a long, aquiline nose and a pointed chin. When she spoke to Lilly of her father, there came into her voice a curious, rasping intonation.

Aunt Lisbet drank; chiefly brandy, and her drunkenness took the form of fits of ungovernable passion.

These outbursts were almost always directed against Lilly; not that Aunt Lisbet had any particular personal animosity towards her niece, but because Lilly was the handiest object on which to vent her feelings.

She would begin by recalling some evil trait in Jock's character. Lilly had no really tender affection for her father's memory, the little she knew of him was far from creditable. But this disparagement of him by Aunt Lisbet somehow made her blood boil, and at times the scenes between them were very violent.

And though, except for these occasions, they seldom quarrelled, Lilly loathed Aunt Lisbet with an instinctive, imperious loathing.

And this afternoon, as she drove home in the dog-cart by Maurice's side, her hatred for her aunt seemed fiercer than it had ever been before.

III

The horse's hoofs rang clear on the hard, white road, as they sped swiftly along, Lilly leaning against Maurice's shoulder, plunged in a brown study.

Presently she said, meditatively: 'What is the earliest date on which your father can arrive?'

'Well, he won't leave Bombay for another fortnight, then he'll not hurry himself on the journey, so it will be at least a month before he reaches England. It's a beastly long time, isn't it?'

'Oh, Maurice! What's the good of waiting? He will never consent, let's get married at once.'

Recklessly he dropped the reins and taking her face in his gloved hands, held it up to his. Their lips met, and putting both his arms round her, he strained her to him. The kiss was a long one; at last she gave a little moan; he let her go.

'You don't know the old gentleman, you see,' he continued. 'My infernal busybodies of relations have been writing all sorts of tales about you – at least, not about you, but about your aunt and your father, and about – well, a lot of damned rot. But directly he's seen you, I shall be able to make it all right with him. Of course, if you really wish it, we could get married next week, but I think it would be more prudent to wait. The very fact that I had not waited till his return might put his back up, and he might cut off my allowance on the spot.'

'Of course, Maurice, we'll wait. It was selfish of me to think of it. But – but – .'

'Well?'

'I do hate Aunt Lisbet so.'

'I know; but it's not so very long now.'

They were entering the town.

'Shall I drive you to the door?'

'No, drop me at St. Luke's. I'll walk home from there.'

He pulled up and she got down.

'Be at Mrs. Newton's in good time to-morrow afternoon,' he called out, as, smartly flicking the horse, he rattled away down the street.

IV

The solitary candle flickering on the dressing-table made the shadows of the coming night creep back into the corners of the room, as Lilly, with swollen eyelids, and red patches on her cheeks, looked out through the window-pane.

All was still. The earth slept.

The moon poured her white light on the meadows opposite; a few fleecy clouds lazily chased one another across the sky. In the distance a dog barked, then all was again still.

Lilly threw herself on the bed, burying her face in the pillow.

And presently the cool linen began to soothe her burning forehead.

It had passed, the wild impulse to throw herself out of the window that people might know to what Aunt Lisbet had driven her. Now the resolve never to see her again ousted all else from her mind. Absolute, irrevocable was this resolve: any departure from it was as a physical impossibility. Only she must wait till morning, and she turned to a cooler spot on the pillow.

And as she did so, a vivid vision of the scene in the kitchen below started before her eyes. Aunt Lisbet leaning against the dresser, her hair slipping down on one side, and in her voice a hissing sound.

It was the first time that she had said things about Maurice; that was what had made it worse than it had ever been before.

A blind desire to silence her, to stamp the life out of her, swept over Lilly. Seizing the parasol which lay on the kitchen-table, with all her strength she hit Aunt Lisbet across the side of the head.

And over the thought of that blow she lingered, recalling it again and again, repeating it in her mind with a strange, exquisite pleasure. For into it she had put the hatred of years.

Aunt Lisbet uttered a low, plaintive moan – the curious moan of sudden pain – and fell, dragging with her on to the floor a pile of plates.

The crash sent every nerve in Lilly's body tingling, piercing her through and through; in a fit of hysterical sobbing she sank into an armchair.

Slowly Aunt Lisbet rose to her feet, and muttering incoherently under her breath, staggered out of the room.

Round and round all these incidents Lilly's thoughts revolved, dwelling on them, brooding over them, unable to escape from them.

And each time that she thought of the hissing sound in Aunt Lisbet's voice, the blind, murderous feeling swept over her, and each time that the thud of Aunt Lisbet's head on the floor sounded in her ears, the tears welled up in her eyes.

V

The Charing Cross platform was alive with people, some hurrying hither and thither, others standing together in groups or sauntering up and down.

The fierce panting of an engine echoed through the building, and a cloud of dense smoke rose to melt away under the curved roof.

It was nearly a quarter to one, for when Lilly had awoken in her little bedroom at Aunt Lisbet's, weary and unrefreshed through having slept in her clothes, the morning was already half gone. Downstairs and out of the house she had crept, meeting only the servant-girl, who told her with a smirk that her aunt was still sleeping.

Her first impulse had been to go straight to the 'Barracks' to ask Maurice to take her away and marry her at once. It seemed the only alternative, for never again would she set foot in Aunt Lisbet's house.

But, as she hurried through the town, there came upon her, like a spasm of physical pain, a feeling of irresolution. She remembered what Maurice had said yesterday – 'It's not for so very long.' She foresaw that he would advise her to go back and put up with it for a few weeks more, and that she would have to argue with him about it. The courage to face such a prospect was wanting.

No, there was only one thing, take the train for London, telegraph to Maurice to meet her there. Then he *must* understand how impossible it was for her to go back.

And this she had done.

Three hours and three quarters to wait till the next train from Guildford, even if Maurice got the telegram in time. He might not be at the barracks when it arrived. At four, of course, he would go to Mrs. Newton's, as they had arranged yesterday. But would he go back home beforehand? And if not, would his servant send on the telegram, or keep it till his return? These and many other possibilities whirled through Lilly's brain as anxiously she paced the platform.

* * * * *

Four hours had passed. The porters lined the platform edge as rapidly the train drew up. The doors flung open; out swarmed the crowd.

But Maurice was nowhere to be seen. Eagerly Lilly looked for him, up and down; once she fancied that she saw him talking to a porter at the other end of the train.

Desperately she pushed through the crowd, only to find herself face to face with a stranger.

There was not another train till five, and then not another till half-past seven.

With a numb feeling of hopelessness she wandered out into the Strand.

It had just stopped raining. Noisily the omnibuses splashed past, while the hansoms,* one after another, crawled along the edge of the pavement.

Some hungry-looking boys were yelling the contents of an evening paper, two flower-girls and an old man selling bootlaces, stood in the gutter. Along the pavement, brown, and a-glimmer with the wet, poured a continual stream of men and women.

No one took any notice of Lilly, they only jostled roughly past her. And somehow the sight of all these strange faces and the movement of this seething turmoil made her feel sick and faint.

For the first time she realised her absolute loneliness.

* Hansom cabs. A hansom is a two-wheeled cab for two persons. The driver is mounted outside at the rear and the horse's reins pass over the roof.

* * * * *

The five-o'clock train and the seven-o'clock train had both come in, but still no signs of Maurice.

The last train was due at twenty minutes past nine.

Lilly sat staring lifelessly before her. She had scarcely eaten anything all day; exhausted, she was suffering much, but so great was her nervous tension, that she did not know that it was hunger.

What she would do if Maurice did not come she never considered. All her energy was occupied in counting the minutes till the train was due.

At last! That must be it! She had not the strength to move, but intently watched the passengers as they poured out through the barrier.

Yes! Maurice! – hastening towards her, yet somehow not looking as she had expected him to look.

VI

Maurice, rising abruptly from the breakfasttable, and throwing open the window, looked down on to the crowded street, for their rooms in the hotel faced the Strand.*

Delicate, grey–blue streaks of smoke curled restlessly upwards; in streamed the morning sunlight, bathing Lilly in its full flood.

A newspaper lay before her on the sofa; but she was observing Maurice with stealthy glances from under her dark eyelashes. Solemnly the clock ticked, while, with obvious constraint, he hummed discontentedly to himself.

An instant ago their voices were raised in angry dispute – not the first, though they had been but three days together. And Maurice, as he gazed out on to the sea of roof-tops, recalled the trivial incident from which their quarrel had sprung. The thought formed a central spot of pain amid the monotony of his gloom.

For the twentieth time he was aimlessly brooding on the change that had come over her.

Never for a moment had he treated her dislike for Aunt Lisbet seriously, though he had sympathised with it, vaguely, distantly. Lilly was to blame for this he thought: beyond occasional references, she had told him nothing, and, in his blind contentedness, he had never troubled to question her. Besides, instinctively, even in thought he had shrunk from that side of her life. It jarred upon him.

* A major London thoroughfare, running out of Trafalgar Square.

They had spent the night after his arrival together; it had seemed the more natural thing. Maurice only had hesitated for an instant with an indefinable shrinking. And when in the morning Lilly suddenly sat up in bed, and began the explanation of her flight, he listened impatiently to what seemed a series of clumsy and unnecessary exaggerations. He had imagined, with a subtle tickling of vanity, that somehow she had been driven to it out of love for him, and he felt an annoyance, vague but real, at learning that it was not so.

But in a minute or two this had passed; in bewilderment he lay watching her.

Tremulously, with a look of passionate fierceness, her face was working as if some strange light were playing on it.

She had done. He knew that every word was true.

And afterwards, if, at odd moments, the improbability of it all flashed upon him, the recollection of that look would at once drive all doubt from his mind.

No longer could he love her lazily as before. The half-girl, half-child, simple and heedless, with occasional moods of confiding, dreamy gravity, and fits of charming pettishness, the easy dispelling of which he had enjoyed, was gone.

The events of the past few days had broken down the barrier, behind which the strong passions of her nature had laid dormant, and now, let loose for the first time, they mastered her; she was their slave.

Capricious and irritable, with outbursts of nervous exasperation, followed by hot tears of remorse and a desperate sensuality that disturbed and almost frightened him.

And strangest of all, when he had proposed yesterday that they should be married at the end of the week, with an evasive reply she had at once started another topic.

As he turned to throw away his cigarette, he saw that she was by his side. How silently she had crossed the room! Putting both hands on his shoulders, she murmured:

'Maurice, dear Maurice, kiss me; don't be angry with me.'

VII

'We must go back to Guildford, to-morrow,' he said, after a pause. 'I can't get any more leave, and there are all kinds of arrangements to be made down there – fresh quarters, servants, and heaps of things. You can stay at Mrs. Newton's till everything is ready,' he went on hurriedly, 'it will only take a few days and then we will come back here and get married. I will keep on the room, so that there will be no difficulty about a licence.'

'I don't want to go back. I hate the place,' she muttered sullenly.

'But, Lilly dear, do be reasonable. There's nothing else to be done.'

'You can go alone, I shall stay here till you come back.'

Angrily he was on the point of replying, but the words died away on his lips. Expostulation, he saw, would be worse than useless.

He went on to tell her about a red-tiled house just outside the town, on which he had had his eye for months, but catching sight of her face, he stopped short, and burst out despairingly:

'Why, Lilly, doesn't it interest you?'

'I don't think I could ever go back,' she answered slowly.

'But we can't live anywhere else, unless I exchange, and that would take time.'

A pause, during which she was nervously tearing strips off the edge of the newspaper.

'How long will you be away?' she asked at length.

'Let's see, to-day's Wednesday. If I go tomorrow morning, I ought to be back by Friday night or Saturday morning. But what on earth will you do with yourself?'

'I don't know, but I can't go back there. You don't know how impossible it is.'

'But after we are married?'

'Perhaps it will be different then,' she answered musingly.

He drew her to the sofa, and putting both arms round her, began with infinite tenderness:

'Lilly, darling, what is it? Tell me. Is it that you don't care for me as you did? What is it? Tell me, little woman. Oh! I can't bear the thought of leaving you here all alone by yourself.'

'Maurice, I don't know what it is. Only I feel very miserable. Everything seems in such a tangle. I feel as if something strange were going to happen to me. I want to think about lots of things. That's why I want to be alone, quite alone.'

VIII

Eight o'clock had just struck; a continuous hum resounded through the restaurant, a Babel of voices and a clatter of knives and forks.

'I do love the crowd, the bustle, and all that,' exclaimed Lilly, excitedly.

Then,

'Oh! Maurice, who's that? I'm sure he knows you; look!'

Against the pillar in the centre of the room a powerfully built, dark-faced man was leaning. His face, in contrast to the whiteness of his shirt-front, seemed copper-coloured, and there was a singular massiveness about it; bushy eyebrows, heavy, black moustache and vermilion lips.

Dominating the whole room, he stood leisurely casting his eyes over the crowd of diners.

'That man by the pillar?' answered Maurice. 'Yes, I know him a little. His name is Adrian Safford. Some more soup?' And he went on with his dinner.

Safford's eyes were on them now, travelling from one to the other with a deliberateness that was almost insolent.

Lilly's eyelids dropped; she hurriedly crumbled a piece of bread.

But the temptation was irresistible; nervously she glanced up. Quite close now, his back towards her, both hands in his pockets, and a crush hat tucked under one arm.

'Maurice, he can't find a seat.'

'Can't find a seat – who can't?'

'That big man – Mr. Safford. Tell him that there's room next you.'

In the glass opposite she could see the reflection of his face. As she spoke he made a sudden, half-arrested movement of his head. He had overheard.

Maurice touched him on the shoulder. And, as shaking hands they exchanged greetings, Lilly noticed the prickliness of his eyebrows, and the strong muscles on each side of the bull-like throat.

And Maurice introduced him to her; under the stare from his lustrous black eyes she flushed hotly.

He was speaking, his voice sounded slow, drawling almost.

But she scarcely heard what he was saying, she was watching his hands, as they smoothed the cloth in front of him – white and fat, tipped with pink finger-nails, carefully trimmed to a point.

IX

All the morning and during luncheon Maurice had been gloomily taciturn; this had induced in Lilly a strained, nervous gaiety.

The moment of parting drew near and the tension became more and more painful.

Yet it did not snap till they were slowly pacing the platform before the departure of the train. Then, of a sudden, he turned his face, contorted as in acute physical pain, and with a dryness in his voice, passionately implored her to return.

But he did not touch her. Strange that she was observing him, curiously, for the first time conscious of distinct antipathy towards him. He looked – yes, ridiculous, as if ashamed of having betrayed his emotion. The sight of this emotion sent a spasm of irritation through her. Next she felt an almost uncontrollable inclination to laugh.

But he did not press her any longer, for he dimly saw how it was. The porters began to slam the doors; in silence he entered the train.

After it had gone she sauntered about the streets, staring at the people, reading the posters on the hoardings, gazing into the shop windows, now and then buying with the money he had given her little objects that took her fancy.

At last, hot and dusty, she found herself back at the hotel. Tired out, she stretched herself on the sofa, and, closing her eyes, let thoughts float aimlessly across her brain.

There passed visions of a woman with yellow hair indolently reclining against the cushions of a victoria*; of the red-bearded policeman who had told her the way to the hotel; of the stare of a thin man in frock coat pinched at the waist; of the goldspotted veil, and of the brooch set in imitation pearls, which she had carried home with her.

Then the bronzed countenance of Safford, his bright, red lips, and fat, white hands appeared as he leant against the central pillar of the restaurant.

And now Maurice was there too. Side by side they disputed for her. Maurice troubled, with tears in his eyes; Safford still, massive as a statue.

'Which loves her best?' cried the crowd.

'I do,' answered his slow tones. He encircled her cheeks with his hands, which were soft and warm, and his bright, red lips kissed her softly on the eyes.

X

Abruptly, without effort, her eyes opened. And immediately their gaze fell upon Safford. For an instant, the impression of her dream remained vivid; to see him there seemed natural. But before the returning sense of reality, it faded quickly; bewilderment sweeping in, arrested all thought.

Astride of a chair, the broad expanse of his back blocking the light, he sat, looking out of the window, apparently absorbed in the street below. This unconcernedness alarmed her.

* A light, four-wheeled carriage, with a collapsible hood and seats for two passengers.

How did he come there?

A minute or two slipped by, then he shifted his chair, as if to rise. Her eyes shut hastily, involuntarily; she pretended to be asleep. He came to her, so close that his breath played on her cheek, but in spite of the loud throbbing of her heart, she never stirred. He moved away: his heavy tread sounded about the room. Then silence.

Had he gone? No, she would have heard the click of the door-handle. The darkness, the suspense became intolerable, yet it was a full minute before she could summon courage to reopen her eyes.

Her gaze met his.

'I say, if I couldn't sham better than that, I wouldn't try at all,' and his broad teeth gleamed.

Somehow his voice calmed her. His self-possession communicated itself to her, giving her confidence.

'I wasn't shamming.'

'I could see it.'

'How?'

'Your eyes were trembling.'

She smiled, almost frankly.

'Weren't you surprised to see me?'

'Yes, no – I mean yes.'

'Where's Radford?'

'Maurice? He's gone.'

'Gone? Where?'

'To Guildford.'

'And you're here all alone?'

She nodded.

A moment's pause – he thoughtfully jingling some money in his trouser-pocket; she, wondering that he looked so much darker than he had done in evening dress.

'When is he coming back?'

'I'm not sure, either to-morrow night or Saturday morning.'

Another pause.

'What did you do last night – after I went away?'

'We went to the theatre.'

'Did you like it?'

'Yes, awfully.'

'You're fond of the theatre?'

'I've only been twice – in London at least.'

'Would you like to go again to-night?'

'I couldn't.'

'Why not?'

'Maurice – I promised him.'

'What a pity! You'd have liked it.'

'Yes, I should.'

'Look here, it will be all right; he won't mind, he knows me well enough.' And again the broad teeth gleamed.

'I don't know – perhaps – .'

But as she spoke, his soft, warm hands encircled her face, his bright, red lips kissed her on the eyes, just as in her dream.

The blood rushed to her face, in hot gasps her breath came and went, everything but Safford swam in a mist and was gone; impulsively she lifted her burning face to his and murmured:

'Tell me that you love me. Then I'll come.'

XI

Adrian Safford's chambers were sombre; even on this summer morning shadows lurked in the corners of the lofty spacious room. There was no window; the light struggled in as best it could, through a ground glass skylight. On the walls, maroon-coloured hangings; from the fireplace to the ceiling reached a huge overmantel of black, carved oak. The rich scent of a burning pastille struck a note of sensuous mystery. It was all curiously characteristic of the man.

Amid the dark tints, a single patch of colour – the white tablecloth on which an exquisitely fresh breakfast was laid. Safford had just seated himself before it, a scowl deepening the bronze of his face. Yet he ate in a vigorous, businesslike way. His appetite was always splendidly regular.

The girl asleep in the next room was the cause of his scowl.

Something about the crispness of her hair; something about the modelling of her chin; something in the questioning look that darted out from the liquidness of her big eyes; something – he knew not what – had haunted him, ever since their first meeting. A spark of caprice fanned into fitful flame by the offensiveness of Radford's ill-concealed pride of possession.

And so the day before yesterday he had gone to the hotel. To find her alone was more than he had hoped for, but directly he saw her lying asleep on the sofa, he knew instinctively that she was his. Women were so easy.

The rest had been the old story, only this time more commonplace than ever – a dinner at the Café Royal,* a box at the Empire, and back

* A fashionable London restaurant.

to his chambers afterwards. And yet she was different from the others; she remained; he kept her for her mutinous freshness.

He had asked nothing about her relations with Radford. He had made a rule never to question them about themselves; the tedious monotony of their stories bored him immensely.

It was she who, in her wilfulness, had blurted it all out. He saw it coming and did his best to stop her. But it was not to be. And when he heard that she and Radford were to have been married in a day or two, his feeling was one of pure disgust – not disgust at her treachery, but disgust at the blunder he had committed – blunder ahead of which he foresaw a whole series of unpleasant complications.

And in that instant he tired of her – her passion, from being a thing to be toyed with complacently, suddenly filled him with active dislike. The very searching gaze which had amused him before now seemed merely stupid. With the exasperation of a trapped animal, he realised that she was one of the clinging sort, whose dismissal was generally difficult, always disagreeable.

'Damn,' he muttered, savagely biting the end of a cigar.

XII

Safford, his huge frame stretched on two chairs, from time to time carefully inserted the cigar between his teeth. He smoked thoughtfully, deliberately, yet the cigar had nearly burnt to an end before Lilly ran in, with the fresh morning bloom upon her.

'Why, how late! Ten o'clock,' she cried. 'And you've eaten nearly all the breakfast. For shame! I believe that's why you got up without waking me.'

'There's some left under the cover. Ring for more if it's cold,' he answered, without removing the cigar from his mouth.

But she, in her radiant unconsciousness, did not notice his gloom.

'Do come and cut this bread for me,' she called out presently, 'it hurts my fingers, it's so awfully hard.' He did as she asked; then flicking the ash from his cigar, stood looking down at her as she ate.

'Sugar, please. I say, what shall we do to-day? It's so splendid out. I can't stop inside. Besides, it's so stuffy in here.' Safford shifted his feet uneasily. 'I tell you what – I know. We'll go down to Kingston and go on the river. It's awfully jolly down there. I went once last summer.'

'With Radford, I suppose?'

'Why, I believe you're jealous of him – yes, you are, else you wouldn't look so solemn. Come, aren't you?'

No answer.

She rose, and both hands toying with the lapels of his coat, said hurriedly:

'But I don't care for him – not a bit. He seems like a stranger now. It seems months since I saw him. I love you – oh! I can never tell you how I love you. I want to be with you always – you know I do. Come kiss, kiss me again like the first time.' Her voice, though rapid, had great earnestness in it.

With an impatient movement he repulsed her.

'You must go back this morning,' he said, more brutally than he had intended, but his exasperation had got the better of him. 'When I sent for your things yesterday, they said he would return this morning.'

She stepped back, as if he had struck her; the light went out of her face; her eyes blinked quickly as she tried to grasp his meaning, her under-lip began to twitch.

'You're joking! Oh! Don't! Say it's a joke! You don't know how it hurts!'

'No, I'm quite serious. Now be sensible and listen. I should never have brought you here if I'd known about you and him. You must go back – at once.'

'You really mean it?'

'Yes, I mean it.'

'Then you don't love me any more,' she burst out. 'I don't believe you ever did. It was only just to amuse yourself that you brought me here. You made me love you, and now that you've had enough of me you want to send me back to him. You – '

Unheeding, he went on slowly: 'Besides, I'm going away.'

'It's a lie! You only want to get rid of me.'

'Do as I tell you, and don't make a fuss.' There was an imperiousness in his voice that cowed her. The passionate fierceness left her. 'And if you are careful,' he went on, 'it will be all right; not a soul knows where you've been. Very likely he won't find out that you've been away. And even if he does, he's quite fool enough' – and with a grim smile at the words that were rising to his lips, he checked himself.

But she did not hear what he was saying. Like some nightmare procession, the incidents in her life since her departure from Guildford were passing before her.

'I sha'n't tell any lies. I shall tell him straight out,' she said half to herself.

Impatiently he shrugged his shoulders.

'And then, when I've told him, I may come back, mayn't I?'

'Come back? Here?'

'Yes, when it's all over with him. I mean when he's gone away again.'

'It's quite impossible. Just understand that.'

'But what am I to do, then?' It was the cry of concentrated despair.

'You've got to do what I've told you. It will be all right. I know what I'm talking about. If you don't choose to – well, then, it's your lookout. You can't come back here, that's certain. I'm going away.'

She was not looking at him; her big eyes, wideopen, were staring vacantly at something beyond.

'Where are you going?' she said faintly, after a pause.

'Never mind. Nowhere where you can come.'

'Oh! for God's sake, don't send me away.' The vacant expression had given way to the feverish pleading of her childish passion. 'You will kill me if you do. Can't you see how I love you. There seems to be nothing else in the world for me but you. Perhaps you think that I shall be in the way. But I promise you that I will do whatever you tell me; I will be no trouble; I will not speak to you if you do not want me to – I will do anything.' And down streamed the tears.

'Poor little devil,' he muttered under his breath.

He drew her towards him and her frail body shook convulsively on his chest.

'Lilly, dear, you must go, you really must. It's for your own good. There are lots of reasons why you must, that you don't understand – you will soon forget all about this. Now come, kiss me, and say you will go quietly.'

Her sobbing had ceased. His slow tones had mastered her.

She looked up through her tears and nodded. 'I will go,' she said through her teeth, 'because I can't help doing what you tell me. But I shall come back.'

So absorbing was his sense of relief that he did not hear her last words.

'Make haste and get your hat. I'll see you into a hansom. I'll get your things packed and sent after you at once, And remember all that I told you. You've only got to play your cards well, and it will be all right.'

So fearful was he lest she should repent her submission, that the unnatural calm which had come over her passed unnoticed.

XIII

'Lieutenant Radford has just come back; he was asking for you just now ma'am,' said a waiter as she mounted the staircase.

Pushing past him, she laid her hand on the door of the room. As she did so, it opened suddenly from within, and a man, whom she recognised as the manager of the hotel, held it open for her to pass.

Maurice was seated at the table, writing. 'Lilly,' he cried as she entered. 'Thank God!'

Wildly he poured kisses on her hair and face. She submitted passively, quite white, her teeth set, in her eyes a stony stare.

The first rush of emotion passed, he let her go.

'But where have you been?'

She made no answer, only a dangerous light – a light that boded mischief – suddenly animated her face. He was so different from him whom she had just left. And, as she recalled Safford's massive frame and bronzed countenance, she found herself looking at Maurice, critically, as at some stranger, each detail of whose person was acutely repulsive. But for him Safford would never have sent her away. She hated him for it.

'Lilly, they tell me that you've been away since Thursday. What have you been doing?'

She had expected anger; but there was none in his voice, only a tone of tender entreaty that made her wince. An irresistible, evil desire to wound him came to her.

'I've been with Adrian.'

'Adrian? Who? Safford?'

'Good God!' and as the truth dawned on him, with a gradual, ugly contraction, his face turned a greyish colour.

Sinking into a chair, he buried his head in his hands.

Some minutes passed, but he did not stir. The silence soon became intolerable to Lilly; fiercely she fidgeted with her glove, pulling at a button, trying to wrench it off.

At last she could bear it no longer. She spoke, and as she did so, the sound of her own voice startled her.

'Have you anything more to say to me?'

He looked up, tears were in his eyes. 'What do you mean?'

'I'm going if you haven't anything more to say.'

'Going? Where?'

'Back. I only came to tell you.'

In supreme unconsciousness of his suffering, she spoke quite naturally, as if the matter was of no consequence.

His lips moved, but he uttered no words, only a choking, gurgling sound.

Again dropping his head in his hands, he sobbed audibly.

The sobs rose, and fell regularly, harshly. It was the first time that she had seen a man cry. And an element of contempt entered into her bitterness.

Then for one short moment she pitied him. Vaguely, as one pities an animal in pain.

She stepped forward, as if to say something, but almost immediately the impulse died away. She went quickly out through the door, closing it softly behind her.

And Maurice, blinded by his grief, did not know that she was gone.

XIV

Lilly was now alone. Maurice and she had parted – probably for ever. And Safford had disappeared. They had told her at his chambers that he was gone. At first she believed that they were lying, and obstinately waited for him during long hours. But it was in vain. Then she searched for him in the streets, wandering hither and thither in the hope of meeting him. But amid the crowd there were no signs of his massive frame.

So for several days. And then the seething turmoil of the great city, ruthless in its never-flagging lust, caught up the frailty of her helpless beauty, and playing with it, marred it, mutilated it. Like a flower, frost-bitten in the hour of its budding, she drooped and withered.

Against the inevitable she made no continuous resistance. How could she? Only for a while; with the feeble struggles of a drowning creature she clung to the memory of her great love for Safford, and to every little thing that reminded her of it.

First, it was a dark-faced foreigner about Safford's build and height. He was kind to her – at least he treated her with no selfish brutality – and listened indulgently when she opened her heart to him. As he listened she would feverishly strive to delude herself into believing that he was the lover she had lost. But even this consolation of self-deception was denied her.

After a while, she somehow lost sight of him, and then it was any one who by some detail of his person recalled Safford to her – a drawling voice heard one night in a restaurant; two prickly eyebrows caught sight of one night under a lamp-post in Piccadilly; a red and black necktie like the one he wore the afternoon that he had come to the hotel.

Fierce, fitful loves, prompted by curious twistings of caprice, born to die within an hour or two.

She grew careless of her dress and of her person, and at last callous to all around her. She sunk into the irretrievable morass of impersonal prostitution. She ceased to live; mechanically she trudged on across the swamp-level of existence.

One evening, before starting out, as she dragged through the ceremony of her toilet, wearily staring in her glass, there flashed across her murky brain a resemblance between her own wasted, discoloured face, and the hard angularity of Aunt Lisbet's features.

After that the recollections of her girlhood – Aunt Lisbet, Maurice and even Safford faded into the twilight of the past. With no common speed, the end was drawing near.

XV

Pain beyond a certain degree of intensity ceases to be pain. Thus it was with Maurice. In a state of mental numbness he went back to Guildford. His mind, stunned as it was, could only feebly revolve about these words of Lilly's: 'I'm going back to him. I only came to tell you.' All else was blurred; this alone, and the vision of her white, set face, and stony stare stood out distinct and sharp.

It was many days before consciousness began to return, before his thoughts, emerging from their torpor, started to explore the extent of his pain.

But when the awakening came, with a morbid craving for self-inflicted torture, he lingered over every detail; starting from the very beginning, he lived once again through the events of the last three months.

Now and then, the memory of some happy day they had spent together would come back so vividly as to drive away the dull pain, but it was only for an instant. With a quiver like that caused by the turning of a knife in an old wound, he heard the words ringing once more in his ears: 'I'm going back to him. I only came to tell you.'

And yet, realising the grim hideousness of it, he felt no resentment against her.

Of a sudden, an infinite pity for her filled him. From that moment all was changed. His love for her, which had lived on in spite of it all, and the new-born pity, each nourishing the other, lessened the sense of his pain, lifting him above it.

For the first time the mechanism of her nature was laid bare before him. He saw many things that he had never heeded before, passing them over as of no significance, things that now, with curious intuition, he understood.

And the exaltation of his love and of his pity rose.

The tragedy was no longer his, but hers. It was not his life that was spoilt, but hers. Pitilessly he upbraided himself – to have left her in the hands of a brute like Safford (the very thought of the man's swarthy skin made his blood boil) – Lilly – his Lilly – who was to have been his wife. How had he ever done it ? How contemptible, what a weak creature he was! Poor little child!

And the exaltation of his love and his pity rose yet higher.

Yes, he must save her. It was not too late. All the fine elements in his nature forced their way to the front in support of this resolve.

This resolve was the outcome of no blind impulse; he knew to the full the extent of the sacrifice he was about to make. His eyes were opened; he had counted the cost, but he never wavered.

On the contrary, the very sense of her unfitness to be his wife only strengthened his determination to do what was right.

XVI

A small servant-girl, slatternly in her dress, led the way up some narrow stairs, and Maurice stumbled once or twice, catching his feet in the torn stair-carpet, which was colourless with dirt.

'This is the room,' she said, and he followed her in.

The first thing that struck him was its shameless disorder – on the table, in the centre, a great litter of old newspapers; some tattered, yellow-backed novels; a half-finished cup of tea, stale and greasy; the remains of a cake, with crumbs scattered on the floor; a packet of cigarettes, two almost empty glasses. There were only three chairs, and on each some article of clothing had been thrown, a bonnet, a petticoat, or a pair of stockings. On the mantelpiece lay a bunch of withered roses, and opposite the mantelpiece stretched a curtain which evidently divided off the bedroom.

Presently a voice – her voice, just the same as in the old days – called out from behind the curtain.

'Who's there?'

'It's some one to see you,' answered the servantgirl.

'All right. I'll be out in a minute.'

A sound of splashing water; and the strained humming of a music-hall song.

'I say, who are you?' she called out.

He did not answer.

'Speak up, don't be shy. You're Dick? Ned Chalmers, then? Eh? Well, I give it up. Just wait till I've brushed my hair a bit, and I'll come and see for myself.'

At each fresh word revealing the extent of her downfall, he winced.

But his resolve was as strong as ever.

The curtain moved. In a gaudy, pink dressing gown, stained and torn, she stood before him. Lilly, and yet not Lilly – like, but different with a difference that chilled him.

At the sight of him, her whole body stiffened in astonishment.

'Maurice!' she gasped.

Face to face they stood, looking into each other's eyes. 'Lilly,' he heard himself saying at last, 'come away.' He could find no other words, so imperious was the desire to remove her immediately out of these loathsome surroundings.

'Come away,' he repeated, 'away from all this.'

'Yes, it is rather messy,' she assented, looking round the room with a forced smile. 'But I'll get the girl to tidy up a bit. Sit down, chuck those things on to the floor. How it took me aback seeing you all of a sudden like that! Fancy your finding me out. I never expected to see you again. I thought you had forgotten all about me.' (She spoke hurriedly to conceal her agitation.) 'Just look at this table, did you ever see such a beastly mess ? The people here never think of cleaning out the room.'

'Lilly,' he heard himself saying again, 'you must come away with me at once. You shall make a fresh start with me. I will marry you, and together we will forget all this awful time.'

'You're quite serious?' she asked slowly. 'You want to marry me now – after all that has happened?'

'Yes,' he answered steadily, yet with the absolute futility of it quite clear before him.

'Well, you're more curious than I thought you were,' was all her reply.

'What have you been doing all this time?' she added presently.

'I've been back at Guildford. But you must come away from here first. I can't talk things over with you in this horrible place.'

'All right, I'll come if you like. But it's no good.'

'What do you mean?'

'I mean about your marrying me. I could never marry a man I didn't care for.'

He took a full minute to grasp her meaning. The possibility of this had never crossed his mind.

'But you can't go on like this.' He was so staggered that words failed him. 'Do you know what the life you're leading means ? Don't you see how it must all end?'

'Oh! I know all that as well as you do. You don't suppose I find it so extra pleasant, do you?' she burst out bitterly. 'But they say it won't last long; that's one comfort. I'm done for, and the sooner it's over the better.'

Her voice was hard and reckless.

'For Heaven's sake don't talk like that.'

'Look here,' she interrupted almost fiercely. 'It's no good your going on about it. I could never marry a man I didn't love. And I don't love you. I thought I did once. But it was all different then.'

'Is there any one else then?'

'Any one else,' and there was a savageness in her voice as she caught up his words. 'They're just a lot of beasts, the whole lot of them. And if you go on talking about it you'll make me just mad – yes, they're all beasts – I hate them – every one of them, and the sooner it's all over the better. Have a cigarette, there's some on the table. For God's sake do something, say something; don't stand staring at me like that – you've seen me often enough. I'm a precious fright, I know. But how's a girl to keep her looks in this hell of a life?'

'But it's not too late to mend it all.'

'Oh! Don't go on saying that over and over again. Just get the idea out of your head, once and for all. That's my last word.'

And he saw that she meant it. Somehow an immense relief that it was not to be came to him and struggled with his pity for her.

'At least give up this life. Here's some money. Go away somewhere, where you can make a fresh start.'

She took the sovereigns from his hand, quickly, with an angry movement as if to fling them on the floor. But, instead, she poured them into a china box on the mantelpiece.

'I'll see about it,' she answered.

But he saw the deceit written on her face, and he could bear the strain no longer. An irresistible longing to escape from the stifling atmosphere of the room, to be once more in the street, swept over him.

And as he groped his way down the dirty staircase he felt physically sick.

XVII

The next day Maurice went back to her lodgings.

She was gone, leaving no address behind. He set to work to trace her, and found her at last, late one rainy night, in the Charing Cross Road, but she passed by without recognising him.

And when he entreated her, she was sullenly obdurate.

In despair he went back to his regiment.

For some time more she was seen at intervals in a little public-house at the back of Regent Street. Then she disappeared. What had become of her, no one knew and no one cared.

Maurice alone remembered her, but he never saw her again.

A CONFLICT OF EGOISMS

I

The sun must have gone down some time ago, for the room was darkening rapidly. Still Oswald Nowell went on writing, covering page after page with a bold, irregular scrawl. Since breakfast he had been there, and large sheets of paper littered the table and the floor around it. In front of him, by the inkstand, was a plate filled with half-burnt cigarettes.

Of a sudden he became aware that the light was very bad; so he laid down his pen, rose and paced up and down impatiently, his canvas shirt unbuttoned at the throat, his coat discoloured, and worn quite threadbare at the elbows, his thin, grey hair dishevelled as after a sleepless night; his eyes with the dull look of brain exhaustion in them.

For some moments he stood blinking thoughtfully down at the sheets on the floor, and passed his fingers roughly across his forehead, and once more sat down at the writing-table; with the reckless pluck of a blood-horse, struggling on for a few minutes longer. But in vain. He was dead beat. This was how he always worked – a brief spell of magnificent effort following weeks of listless idleness.

For twelve years he had been writing. In all, he had published five novels and a volume of short stories. The work was singularly unequal, now so dreamy and vague as to be almost unintelligible, now grand with largeness of handling and a power of vision that lifted it at once into the front rank. He had learnt nothing from modern methods, neither French nor English; he belonged to no clique, he had no followers, he stood quite alone. He knew nothing of the disputes that were raging in the world of letters around him: when they told him that a popular critic had set him up as a chief of the idealist school, to do battle with an aggressive and prosperous band of young realists, he puckered his eyebrows and smiled a faint, expressionless smile. For in reality, he had grown accustomed to his own ignorance of what was going on around him, and, when people talked to him of such things, he never expected to understand. And so, day by day, his indifference grew more and more impregnable. His books achieved a *succes d'éstime** readily enough, but the figures of their sale were quite mediocre: the last one, however, probably

* This should be '*succès d'estime*'. The French phrase means critical as opposed to popular or commercial success.

owing to his having been labelled chief of a school, had run through several editions.

All by himself, in a quiet corner of Chelsea,* he lived, at the top of a pile of flats overlooking the river. And each year the love of solitude had grown stronger within him, so that now he regularly spent the greater part of the day alone. Not that he had not a considerable circle of acquaintances; but very few of them had he admitted into his life ungrudgingly. This was not from misanthropy, sound or morbid, but rather the accumulated result of years of voluntary isolation. People sometimes surmised that he must have had some great love trouble in his youth from which he had never recovered. But it was not so. In the interminable day-dreams, which had filled so many hours of his life, no woman's image had ever long occupied a place. It was the sex, abstract and generalised, that appealed to him; for he lived as it were too far off to distinguish particular members. In like manner, his whole view of human nature was a generalised, abstract view: he saw no detail, only the broad lights and shades. And, since he started with no preconceived ideas or prejudices concerning the people with whom he came in contact, he accepted them as he found them, absolutely; and this, coupled with the effects of his solitary habits, gave him a supreme tolerance – the tolerance of indifference. This indifference lent a background of strength to his artistic personality. It was for this reason perhaps, and also because no one knew much about him, that every one spoke of him with respect.

Just now his power of work was exhausted: stretching himself on a sofa and shutting his eyes, he loosened the tension which was causing his brain to ache. His thoughts, as if astonished at their sudden liberation, for a minute or two flitted about aimlessly; then sank to rest as he fell into a dull slumber.

II

Below, in a tiny sitting-room, daintily but inexpensively furnished, a woman, broad-shouldered and large-limbed, was stirring a cup of tea, with the unconstraint of habitual solitude. She sat facing the light, which exposed the faint wrinkle marks about the eyes and mouth and made her seem several years older than she probably was; and these, coupled with the absence of colour in her cheeks, gave to the whole face a worn look, as if the effort of living had for her been no slight one.

* At that time modestly respectable district of west London. The protagonists are later married on the King's Road, which must be nearby.

And so indeed it was.

Eight of the best years of her life had slipped away in a hard-fought, all-absorbing struggle for independence. At last, a year and a half ago, it had come, and ever since, the emotional side of her nature, hitherto cramped and undeveloped, had been expanding with a passionateness that was almost painful.

Her childhood and her girlhood till she was nineteen, had been spent with her father, who was sub-editor of a halfpenny evening daily – a joyless, homeless existence, moving from boarding-house to boarding-house. Then one dirty November evening brought the first turning-point in her life. An omnibus knocked down her father as he was crossing the Strand, and the wheels passed over his chest. Death was quite instantaneous. Letty gave way to no explosion of grief, only she uttered a little gasp of horror at the sight of the distorted, dead face.

She had never cared for her father, the outbreaks of whose almost uncontrollable temper were the only dark incidents that relieved the dreariness of her colourless memories; and she had never learnt to pretend what she did not feel.

Old Stephen Moore, thriftless and dissolute all his life, left behind him nothing but a month's unpaid salary.

A couple of days after the funeral, she appeared at the office, and doggedly demanded to be given something to do. The manager peered suspiciously through his glasses at this gawky, overgrown girl and put one or two questions to her. Her apparent friendlessness and her determined spirit touched him; he promised to see what could be done.

The next day, and every day for the following six years, she spent in and out of the narrow, grimy building in Fleet Street,* doing all manner of odd jobs, carrying messages, copying and answering letters, after awhile working up paragraphs and even writing leaderettes. Into whatever she was set to do, she threw her whole soul, always bright-faced and quick of intelligence, always eager to learn. And three or four times her salary was raised.

Then the sub-editorship of a ladies' weekly was offered her. She accepted it eagerly, for, though it meant but a little more money, there seemed good prospect of promotion. Here, as before, she was indefatigable. Two years later the editor died; the post was at once given to her.

The new sense of authority and of responsibility was a source of great pleasure to her; she liked to recall the old Fleet Street days, when she was at every one's beck and call, to remind herself that no one had helped her, that her exertions alone had done it all. This thought

* At that time the centre of London newspaper and periodical publishing.

repeated itself constantly, never failing to send through her a warm thrill of self-satisfaction. Hitherto she had had no desire, no interest outside her work; in complete unconsciousness of self, in complete ignorance of her own emotional possibilities, she had lived on, day after day.

Little by little, she began to realise herself in her relation to the corner of the world in which she mixed; insensibly to compare herself with others; dimly to perceive that life had perhaps many things in store for her, that were not included in the daily routine of work. And this process of awakening, once begun, proceeded with a curious rapidity.

Formerly she had always spent the couple of hours between her dinner and bed-time typewriting or doing other light work, making or mending her own clothes.

Now the necessity for this was gone, and at first she found the filling of the daily gap by no means easy, for she had never learnt how to be idle. She could, of course, have found plenty of work for herself in connection with the paper, but when she thought of it, she became aware that somehow the idea was distasteful. In reality, an undefinable but growing longing for something – what she knew not – was unsettling her.

One evening the dinginess of her lodgings struck her, and from that moment she took a violent dislike to them. A week later she moved into the rooms she now occupied, half-way up the pile of flats overlooking the river.

The choosing of the furniture gave her a fortnight of excitement, for she set about it, as she set about everything, with an intense seriousness.

Next followed a period of restless arranging and rearranging; directly the dinner was cleared away, hammering in nails and wrenching them out again, pushing chairs and tables from one corner of the room to another, the whole accompanied by protracted consultations with the newly engaged servant-girl.

Sometimes on her way back from the office, it would occur to her that the looking-glass ought to be hung higher or lower, or that the table-cloth on the square table would look better on the round one; hastening home, and without waiting to take off her hat and gloves, she would at once try the effect of the alteration.

And, when everything was done, the clean, new chintzes, the stiff, white muslin curtains, the Japanese fans, and the hundred and one other bright-coloured knick-knacks on the walls, all, instead of delighting her, as she had expected, made her feel awkward and ill at ease. Her well-worn, work-a-day clothes seemed out of place in this new interior, which made their deficiencies appear all the more glaring. In her daily work she had of necessity acquired a considerable knowledge of the fashions, but to use that knowledge for the adornment of herself had never occurred to her before.

The new elegancies in her dress led her to self-admiration, and to the delicious discovery of her own beauty. It came one afternoon, through a glimpse caught of the reflection of her own profile in a shop window. She stopped, turned and passed before it five or six times, examining herself anxiously. Then, as she walked on homewards, she found herself eagerly comparing her own appearance, which remained clearly visualised, with that of the passers-by.

About this time, too, she became infected with a passion for reading – chiefly inferior, sentimental novels. A considerable number of these were sent each week to the office for review. One afternoon, when things were slack, she happened to open one of these volumes that was lying on her table. Before long her attention was absorbed, and, in the evening, she carried the book home with her. All through her dinner, and on till nearly twelve o'clock, she pored over it, till the three volumes were finished.

The habit, once set going, rapidly ate its way into her life, so that, soon, she never sat down to a meal without a novel before her. And directly one book was finished, she would start on another; hence she remembered scarcely anything of what they contained, but their incidents, piled up and jumbled together in her mind, inflamed her imagination and brought on inexplicable fits of dissatisfaction and depression. Her thoughts took to dwelling on man's love; vaguely she marvelled that it had always been divorced from her life, that no one had ever whispered softly to her, 'Letty, darling, I love you.'

But surely one day, now that she was well dressed and smart – yes, it seemed that it must be, when she thought of the others, dull and ugly, who were married. And the care with which she dressed herself each morning was for the sake of this unknown new-comer, for whom she was waiting with vague expectation.

This evening however, as she sat over her half-finished cup of tea, her expression – sensitive reflection of all that was passing in her mind – started to fluctuate from radiancy to perplexity, from perplexity to despair.

III

'I beg your pardon,' he said, 'but may I offer you half of my umbrella? It's not quite so bad now.'

The shower had been a fierce one covering the roadway with a thick crop of rain spikes, filling the gutters with rushing rivulets of muddy water; now, through a rift in the ink-coloured clouds, the sunlight was filtering feebly, and the swirl of the downpour had subsided to a gentle patter.

Under a doorway they stood, side by side. Having no umbrella, she had fled there for shelter, when the shower had overtaken her on her way home from the office. And as soon as she had recovered her breath, she saw that he was there too, leaning against the wall, staring absently before him, puffing at a short pipe, his hat pulled over his eyes, his clothes hanging loosely about his large frame. She knew him well by sight from having passed him often on the stairs of the flat; but they had never exchanged a word.

When she had first learnt who he was, she had bought his books, and had set about reading them, not as she usually read, but attentively, almost religiously, because the fact that she was constantly meeting him, and that he lived overhead, gave her an almost personal interest in them. And hence, though there was much in them that she did not understand, they remained distinct in her memory,

She encouraged her servant to repeat to her all sort of gossip about the inmates of the flats, and in this way she learnt much concerning him. And all that she so learnt, coupled with his picturesque appearance, only set her imagination working the more. So that, insensibly, she slipped into the habit of thinking a great deal about him.

As he spoke, she flushed under her veil, and endeavoured by an anxious scrutiny of the sky to disguise her nervousness.

'Thank you,' she answered. 'Thank you very much; but I think it would be better to wait a few minutes longer. It looks, over there, as if it were going to quite stop.'

Two or three minutes passed. She was waiting for him to speak; but he said nothing. She was growing angry with herself for not having gone with him at once: the silence oppressed her. A dozen different ways of breaking it passed through her mind, but she rejected them all as soon as they occurred to her. Why did he not say something? She glanced at him – back in the listless attitude, gazing vacantly across the street; the sight of this unconsciousness considerably relieved her embarrassment.

Presently he seemed to become aware that she was looking at him; rousing himself, he took the pipe from his mouth and said:

'I think you should be getting home; you ought not to stand here in your wet clothes.' He spoke easily, with a quiet familiarity, as if he had known her for a long time.

They started out together: quite slowly, for in order to keep herself out of the rain, she was obliged to accommodate herself to his pace. And as they strolled along through the drizzle, he clumsily pecked at her hat from time to time with the points of his umbrella. She longed to ask him to walk quicker, or to let her hold the umbrella; but she dared not, on account of his self-possession. He was talking leisurely, questioning her about herself, about her life, with a directness that would have been presumptuous but for the half-disguised indifference of his tone. Then gradually the uncomfortable edge of the strangeness wore off and his calm communicated itself to her.

She was not listening attentively to what he was saying; she was thinking about him as the author of his books, vaguely wondering that he did not talk as she had expected him to talk.

There was a pause; he had done speaking and she had nothing to answer.

Suddenly, almost with surprise, she found herself saying:

'I've read your books.' And immediately she felt a sense of relief flowing through her, as if the weight of some heavy thing had been all at once removed.

He started and answered with a change of tone:

'Which ones?'

'All of them.'

For the first time he seemed embarrassed, uncertain what to say. Surprised at his silence, she looked, and saw that his lips were moving hesitatingly; but he said nothing. Then a crash, just behind her – a heavy dray-horse fell, and lay helplessly floundering on the slimy pavement. They turned and stood watching its vain efforts to rise.

'What a shame not to put down some sand!' she exclaimed.

But he answered:

'Did you like the last – "Kismet"?'

Smiling a little at the irrelevancy of his question, she answered him at first with trite, meaningless phrases; but as she tried to explain how it had affected her, she found herself talking as she had never talked before, as it were inventing ideas that sounded astonishingly clever and well expressed. And, one after another, they rose to her lips.

She was unconsciously charmed by this new pleasure of listening to her own talk; oblivious of all else, she walked on by his side, till the sight of the familiar, red-brick doorway abruptly brought back the sense of reality.

'Good-bye,' she said hurriedly. 'Thank you so much. I hope,' – she wanted to apologise for her outburst of garrulity – she wanted to express a hope that he would come to see her – to tea some afternoon; but somehow she did neither, and without finishing her sentence, mounted the stairs. He waited till she was gone; then filling his pipe again, lit it, and went out slowly, his large figure growing more and more indistinct as it receded down the brown pavement.

The rain was over: the countless little streams that trickled down the roadway gleamed yellow in the sunlight.

IV

On the morrow, as Letty, hastening homewards, approached the spot in the Strand where she had met him yesterday, she became aware of a thrill of expectation; for she was half counting on seeing him leaning against the doorway, his hat pulled over his eyes, his short pipe in the corner of his mouth. She even stopped and looked about her. But the crowd flowed thick on the pavement; there was no sign of him. And, since he was not there, just as she had imagined he would be, her expectation died away, her thoughts drifting to other things.

And so till she was home; then, by the entrance to the flats, she caught sight of him – how she liked the loose way his coat hung from his shoulders!

'Won't you come up and have some tea?' she said nervously.

'Thank you,' he answered, and they mounted the stairs together.

She had been scheming the evening before, as she lay awake in bed, how she should get him to come to tea with her; she had imagined him sitting in her armchair, consulting her about his books, or admiring her yellow silk curtains and the plush hangings behind the door. But with their entry into the room, a constraint seemed to come over both of them. Without even glancing around him, he sat down and drank his tea, awkwardly, obviously not accustomed to holding his cup in his hand. And when he spoke – and he said but little – it was with a slight stammer that she had not noticed before. She, too, was ill at ease: it had been easy enough to talk to him in the street, now she could think of nothing to say. And more and more keenly she resented her disappointment, growing quite indignant with him because it was all so different from what she had expected. So that, when at last he rose to go, it was almost a relief, and her petulance was scarcely concealed.

And he, noticing her change of manner, gave her a look half-puzzled, halfpained.

* * * * *

During the week that followed, she met him almost every day on her way home: each time it was in the same, absent, almost casual manner that he accosted her. But she knew that he came out expressly to meet her. All day, as she went about her work in her little room at the office, she would look forward to the walk home by his side; in the evening she would sit, as it were, living every incident of it over again. Beyond his books they had found no common interest, so they talked of little else; but this alone seemed to her full of possibilities, indefinable but endless.

One evening she was sorting a bundle of letters she had brought home from the office, when her servant opened the door and he walked in.

'I can't get on with that chapter; I want to talk to you,' he said abruptly.

She saw the yellow look on his face; she noticed, too, that his shirt was unbuttoned at the throat, and that there were inkstains on his fingers; it was as if he had risen from his writing-table and had come straight down to her.

'I can't get on with it at all,' he repeated, half to himself.

There was something in this appeal which, outside her own personal feeling for him, went straight to her heart, and put her quite at her ease.

He began to talk, walking up and down the room, and, in a minute or two, she perceived that he had forgotten all about her. For he was not talking to her, but to himself, thinking aloud; now blurting out headless, tailless phrases, now breaking into long, rhythmical sentences which he recapitulated and corrected as he went along. She was listening, a little impatiently, waiting till he should stop, anxious to turn the conversation. But when at last there was a pause, it seemed impossible for her to break the silence with any other topic, so impregnated did the very air of the room seem with his words.

'And after that, what happens?' she asked, not really wanting to know, but only to hear him speak again.

He gave her a sudden glance, as if surprised that she should have overheard him; then, picking up the thread of his thought, continued as before.

Presently he stopped abruptly, just in front of her.

'Good-night.'

She held out her hand: he took it in both of his.

'Good night,' he repeated absently, 'things are much clearer now.'

'Then I have really helped you?' Her eyes fell on her hand which he still held, and she flushed a little, drawing it away. But he never noticed her movement: he was staring straight in front of him.

'Yes, things are much clearer. I think I'll go up and put them on paper. I'm afraid I've disturbed you,' he added, glancing at the papers on the table. 'It was good of you to listen to me for so long.' And with his hand on the door he continued: 'It is all well marked out in my mind now.'

She stood listening to his footsteps, as they died away up the staircase. Then glancing down at her right hand, as it hung by her side, she flushed again, more deeply this time, and moved almost impatiently to the chair by the table. She took up the paper again, but it was only for a minute or two. The loneliness of the little room struck her: the knick-knacks that brightened it irritated her, and this for the first time. Her head sunk on her hands.

'I have really helped you?'

'Yes, things are much clearer now.'

The question, the answer, and the faint smile which had accompanied it were repeating themselves in her mind over and over again.

* * * * *

How long she had been there she did not know, for she was thinking of him, sitting at his writingtable upstairs, putting it all on paper as he had said he would do. What was his room like, she wondered, for she had never seen it. Of a sudden – a step – his step – coming down the stairs. Instinctively she felt that he was coming back to her; so she rose and opened the door. Without a word he walked in, she following him. So continuously had she been thinking of him that the strangeness of his proceeding never struck her: it seemed quite natural that he should return.

'Well?' she said inquiringly, as he did not speak.

'I've done it, it's all come splendidly. Thank you, thank you.'

A pause.

'But I came down again because I want to ask you something, Miss Moore.' He spoke with the slight stammer that she had noticed once already, and he called her by her name, which sounded strange, as if he had never done so before.

'Well? what is it?'

'Would you care to be my wife?' He said it quite easily.

'Yes,' she answered, quite easily also, not realising the situation, but knowing by instinct that there was no other answer possible.

'I haven't much, only a few hundreds a year, about four or five I think. I don't suppose I spend half of it myself. There will be enough for both of us.'

At the sound of this bald statement of the practical side of the matter, she winced; but almost immediately, with a woman's quick intuition, she saw that the words had not come naturally, that he had only said them in a blundering endeavour to rise to the situation.

'I don't see many people,' he went on in the same, clumsy way, 'but I think it would help me having you – with the work, I mean. Would you really care to live with me?'

'Yes.' The word came back through her set teeth with a little hissing sound. Her joy struggled with the disappointment she could not help feeling at the way he had said it, and the struggle hurt her considerably.

He crossed the room and stood quite close to her.

'May I kiss you?'

In answer she held up her face; the light of the lamp fell on it, and there was no colour in it. As he bent down, with a sudden movement she clasped both arms round his neck and dragging his face down to hers, said:

'You will love me, won't you?'

'Yes, of course.'

There was a silence painful to each of them. At last with an evident effort he broke it.

'Good night once more.'

But she had caught his hand and was holding it tightly, looking anxiously into his face.

'Please,' she whispered.

'I – I don't understand.'

The blood rushed to her face.

'Please,' she repeated under her breath.

He understood; and when he had kissed her, he went slowly out. On the landing he stumbled heavily over the mat, for the gas on the stairs had been turned off.

V

Mechanically, in a state of unnatural passivity, drifting on as if impelled by some invisible outside force, she lived through the next few days. Some great thing was about to happen to her, but somehow she shrank from questioning herself concerning it. Outwardly there was little change in her daily life. She went down to the office as usual, for to throw up her situation at a moment's notice was impossible; besides, she clung to the old life instinctively; partly because, at the thought that soon it would all be gone, a feeling of dismay, almost of terror, would creep over her; partly because its daily routine enabled her to ignore her own suppressed excitement.

She saw him a good deal oftener now, for every evening be would come down and sit with her. He no longer talked to her about his work since that strange night, now far receded into the past, when he had asked her to marry him; all his fever for it seemed to have passed away. And so, for the first time, their conversation drifted to other things, to the insignificant incidents of their daily existence. Then came the first half-realisation of her ignorance of him, which bewildered her.

For he was quite different now – so different that at times on looking back over the old days she could scarcely believe that he was the same man. The abrupt self-absorption had given way to a simple kindliness, with a trustful look in his eyes, which sent all her love for him leaping up within her. He had no variation of mood, his easy familiarity, at once gentle and respectful, was always the same.

And, as for Letty, her feeling for him, sprung at first out of her own overwrought sentimental imagination, soon began to grow each day in strength and richness. Into this newborn love for him her whole being fused itself in impetuous rebellion against the life of solitude which had cramped it for so long. With a rapidity, that at first sight seemed startling, she absorbed every detail concerning him, till the whole perspective of her life veered round, everything being subordinated to its relation to him. And all these new things accumulated themselves within her, till their accumulation was painful to endure. For through his easy kindliness of manner she soon divined his supreme unconsciousness of all that the marriage meant to her, and thus her yearning to bring herself at once quite close to him became anguish; looming in front of her, as it were, she began to dimly perceive the barrier of his own personality, a barrier which was the outcome of years of accumulated habit, and which had grown so natural to him that he ignored its very existence. Yet, following a common paradox of human nature, the further she felt herself from him, the more she loved him.

As the days went by her listlessness concerning practical details became almost wilful, so that he was driven to making most of the arrangements for the marriage, foreign though it all was to his nature. Of course there was to be no ceremony; everything was to be as simple as possible. One morning they were to walk together to the Registrar's office in the King's Road – that was all; and there was no need to hunt for fresh lodgings, for Oswald's flat contained two empty rooms. When he suggested this as he sat with her one evening, she assented without a word of comment. Next, the matter of the moving up of her furniture arose.

'I should think it could all be done in a day,' he murmured, looking vaguely round the room.

'Yes, while we're away.' He looked up, puzzled.

'Away? ' he repeated after her.

'Yes, we're going away, aren't we – for – for – the honeymoon,' and her voice quavered a little.

'Of course – of course,' he answered hurriedly, 'but where?' There was a despairing accent in his voice, so dismayed was he at this new, unforeseen difficulty.

The comic side to it never struck her, only she continued, staring vacantly before her:

'I should like to go where we could walk together under tall pine trees, where the bracken grows high and thick, where there are mossy banks to rest oneself upon, and a little inn by the roadside with a gabled roof.'

'But I don't know where it is,' he said blankly.

'Nor do I,' she answered. 'I must have read about it in some book.'

So they never left London; but on the marriage day, he took her down to Greenwich* by steamer instead. And to her that was all the honeymoon.

VI

The crowd, black and restless, swarmed aimlessly round the flaring kiosque, whence rose and fell the sensuous cadence of a Strauss waltz; behind, amid the trees, winked yellow and sea-green lights, lending an air at once weird and fascinating; while beyond, the buildings of the Exhibition† lifted their fire-rimmed roofs.

Oswald and Letty were sitting a little apart from the rest. Since they had come there, the band had played, and ceased, and played and ceased again several times; but, as yet, neither of them had spoken. At last, however, Letty began, realising as she spoke, the length of their silence.

'Look at the people. How silent and sad, all of them! Why is it? Why is every one so sad to-night?'

But not a muscle of his face stirred; he had not heard her.

* A short trip downriver. Letty does not get much of a honeymoon.

† It is possible that this is the Crystal Palace, the great glass building, home to the Great Exhibition of 1851, moved from Hyde Park to south London shortly afterwards.

'Tell me, why is it? Why is every one so sad to-night?' she continued, a shrill note of exasperation in her voice.

Still his lips did not move, and she began moodily to dig up the gravel with the point of her umbrella.

After a pause, with perverse determination to make him speak, she broke out again:

'I wonder if any of them are as unhappy as I am.'

This time at her words he started; he did not know to what she was referring, but the tone of her voice made the anger rise within him. He resented this unhappiness of hers which he saw she was trying to force under his notice. And now he remembered how soon after their marriage it had begun – reproachful generalities, fits of inexplicable irritability, of exacting affection, or of studied coldness. They had been married several weeks; how many he scarcely knew, only the old life seemed to have receded far, far into the past.

Since the night when he had asked her to marry him he had done no work. There was nothing strange in this, for in between the outbreaks of work-fever, he had always been accustomed to spend weeks without once putting pen to paper – unbroken weeks of eventless peace, as it seemed to him to-night. But now she was always there, with her air of suppressed discontent, from which he shrank, never meeting it openly, pretending to ignore it. To arrive at an explanation of it he never attempted. The necessary effort, and a vague dread of consequences were more than sufficient to deter him.

It had been a strange thing this marriage of his – a thing so sudden, so impulsive, that, as he thought, he marvelled at it. This woman by his side, her full-lipped mouth quivering with an expression that he disliked – all at once, she seemed no longer near him; but, from a distance, as it were, he was looking at her as one looks upon a stranger – a stranger who had come into his life and who was changing it all for him.

Back his thoughts drifted to his unfinished book, and the craving for work returned, coming as a great relief. To-morrow morning he would start again. There were passages, especially in the last chapter, that sadly needed revision. Yes, to-night he would begin. And, all at once, a whole multitude of ideas, leaping up, chased one another across his brain. Expressionless his eyes stared out across the crowd, while a wonderful intuition seemed for a moment to lay bare the whole secret of his life. But it was for a moment only, gloriously it all flitted past and was gone.

He rose.

'Shall we go home?' Letty asked. There was a note of penitent tenderness in her voice.

'Yes, I want to look over a manuscript. I'm going to begin work again to-morrow morning. Come, this is the shortest way. We can get a cab at the entrance.'

'Oh! my Oswald,' she exclaimed, 'I *am* glad. You will talk it all over with me, just as you used to do before, in the old days, won't you? That will be splendid. And I will help you – ever so much. Listen, I've thought of something. Do you remember how once you said to me that ideas came to you in talking, but that when you tried to write them down, they all slipped away? Well, you shall talk to me, I will write it all down. I can write quite quickly enough, I'm sure. I used to take down articles like that years ago at the office, when they were in a hurry. That will help you, won't it?'

They had left the gardens and were walking rapidly down the main hall, she, her face lit up to excited radiancy, he, preoccupied, frowning a little.

VII

The next morning, when she awoke, he was already dressed and gone. Should she slip on a dressing-gown and go to him? Not just yet – presently; for she shrank from· the reality that awaited her. So she lay on in bed, and closing her eyes, half asleep and half awake, dreamed that they were together on a desert island and that he was loving her in a new, wonderful way. After awhile she awoke more completely, and she grew restlessly curious to find out what he was doing.

Breakfast was ready in the little dining-room, but only a single place was laid.

'Mr. Nowell's writing in his room, ma'am, and he said he shouldn't want no breakfast, and that he mustn't be disturbed,' explained the servant.

She sat down; but beyond a cup of tea and half a slice of dry toast, she could eat nothing.

A mental pain, dull at first, growing in intensity as she brooded over it, was settling down upon her. This was the first time that she had breakfasted alone since their marriage: so he did not want her – yet last night, when she had proposed that she should help him – no, it struck her now that he had made no movement of assent. And she had somehow taken for granted that he would like it. How happy the thought of it had made her. For a long while as he slept heavily by her side, she had lain awake thinking of it in a state of excited happiness. 'He mustn't be disturbed' – that was his message. All at once, tumultuously, her wounded pride rose within her. He did not want her – she, who had loved him – ah! how she had loved him. There was nothing she would not have done for him; and he scorned it all – who was he to treat her in this way? She had thrown herself away on him – he did not care for her, not a bit; a dozen small signs of his indifference occurred to her. Why had he married her, then? Oh! why had he made her love him, since he did not care for her? And in bitter, reckless desire for self-inflicted pain, she strove to conjure up all the silly day-dreams she had had about him.

Then, of a sudden, her mood changed. Her love for him, pent up and unsatisfied, cried out in anguish, 'Oswald, Oswald,' and big teardrops rolled down her cheeks. 'Come to me, my Oswald, you are the whole world to me.' Yes, she would go to him and tell him all; she would break down this barrier that lay between them. But not now. He was at work. She must not disturb him. He would not like it. Perhaps he would answer her crossly. And, with a rush, her pride broke forth again, fiercer this time. Thus, while the hands of the clock slipped round, they wrangled together, her wounded pride and her wounded love.

* * * * *

'Mr. Nowell says you needn't wait lunch for him, ma'am; I've just taken him some coffee and bread-and-butter, and he says he won't want anything more till tea-time.'

* * * * *

Tea-time – so he meant to stop work at tea-time – nearly four hours to wait. A quarter of an hour of it she killed, trying to eat some luncheon. After this she fetched her bonnet and went out, wandering disconsolately down the Embankment.* Unconsciously she took the way along which she had walked so often with him. And her thoughts were very bitter.

* * * * *

With Oswald hour after hour was slipping by – only the scratching of the pen, and the tick-tick of the clock. How good it was, he felt, as two or three times he leant back, stretching his arms, back to the regular grind after the nerve-exasperating idleness of the past weeks! Then he would turn to again.

As for Letty, her image never once crossed his mind. Outside the work in which, with the exhilaration of new-found freedom, he was revelling, he had forgotten everything; all things were alike.

* By the River Thames.

When he had finished, he strolled downstairs and out into the street, never looking to see what she was doing. The summer evening was clear and cool, the roadway glowed like a track of beaten gold, and his brain, lazily drinking it all in, sank into a delicious torpor.

* * * * *

About five o'clock he came in. Letty was already drinking her tea; she had not waited for him. She gave him no word of greeting; only a look expressive, as a woman alone can give.

But he noticed nothing; he did not even remember that he had not spoken to her before that day.

'It's been splendid,' he broke out. 'Splendid. I feel a different man.'

'Your tea is getting cold,' she answered in icy exasperation.

'I've written that last chapter from beginning to end, and nearly finished another one,' he went on, taking up the cup, 'there's a real rhythm about the last three pages.'

'The muffin is down by the fire.'

'Look here,' putting down his tea untasted, 'I'll just fetch them and read them.'

In a minute he was back again, the manuscript in his hand.

He walked up and down, trying the sound of the sentences sometimes over and over again before passing on to the next, or appealing to her as to the justness of a word, or continuing without waiting for her verdict.

The scene in her own old little room underneath, the evening that he had asked her to marry him, came back to Letty. She felt that she could bear it no longer, but, with a last effort, clenching her teeth, she restrained herself.

When he had finished he turned to her:

'Well?'

But there was no answer from the white, set face.

'Come, say something,' he went on almost roughly.

Slowly her head began to droop, the lips pressed tighter and tighter together, till they were quite bloodless. Suddenly, burying her face in her hands, she burst into a passionate fit of sobbing.

'What on earth's the matter with you?' he exclaimed, making no attempt to conceal his annoyance.

'Can't you see?' she burst out. 'Are you as heartless as that ?'

'Heartless! What do you mean? Whatever do you want?'

'Oh! nothing,' she answered in a hard voice, and there the conversation ended; a few minutes afterwards he went back to his study.

VIII

After this, in grim serenity, a whole month passed, while the breach between them steadily widened. On Letty's part all signs of the smouldering fire within her disappeared beneath a permanent attitude of chilly apathy. By a mutual, tacit understanding neither spoke to the other, beyond attempting now and then some forced commonplace remark, when the tension of silence became especially intolerable. But even this pretence of intercourse was rare, for, except during the evening meal, they were never together. And, as often as not, Letty would sit with an open book before her plate, taking refuge in the old habit of reading, which she had dropped since her marriage.

All this while, the fever of creation was consuming Oswald more rapidly than it had ever done before. In a sort of blind recklessness, fostered, at first, to a considerable extent, by an instinctive striving to forget the strain of the daily life with Letty, he would shut himself up in his study every morning, and struggle on till evening, with scarcely any food, till his eyes throbbed and it seemed that endless regiments of heavy soldiers were tramping across his brain. When he had done, he would lie in his armchair, a helpless prey to fits of depression, inexplicable as it seemed to him, but which were in reality the reaction that inevitably followed the long hours of cerebral excitement. The effort required to seat himself each morning at his writing table grew greater and greater, and the progress achieved was each day less and less. His brain under the continual, accumulated strain, became impotent with exhaustion, and he would sit for hours, feebly grappling with a single sentence.

Letty never appeared to observe that anything was the matter with him; she made no comment when his appetite grew smaller and smaller. Only once, as he furtively glanced across the table at her, he perceived that she was scrutinising him with a strange, searching look that he did not understand.

And, with the acute sensitiveness of an overstrained nervous system, he grew to hate this halfhour face to face with her over the evening meal; in her presence he felt painfully uneasy, as if there were hanging over his head a storm, which, at any moment, might break and overwhelm him. So that every time she began to speak to him, he was conscious of a spasm of alarm; and all through the day, the dread of meeting her was present in his mind.

One evening – he had been working later than usual – when the servant came in to tell him that dinner was ready, and that Letty had already begun, he felt that he could bear it no longer. He waited till the girl was gone back to the kitchen; then crept stealthily along the passage, took down his hat from the peg behind the door, and hurried out down the stairs, into the street.

From the river came a fresh breeze. Before he had walked a dozen yards, his brain began to reel, and a black mist floated before his eyes. He clutched at a railing to steady himself, and crawled on to an eating-house round the corner.

The place was sordid-looking and far from cleanly, and a hot smell of cooking pervaded it. Oswald found his way to one of the narrow tables covered with greasy and yellow oilcloth and sat down. Presently a young man, in his shirt-sleeves, fetched him from the counter at the far end a steaming plateful of hot food. Oswald began to eat feebly, glancing up at the door between each mouthful. Letty! if she should come and find him out here; and he fancied she was standing before him, beckoning to him to follow her. His fork slipped from his hand. He was asleep over his food.

He awoke with a start; some one was shaking him roughly by the shoulders. It was the young man in his shirt-sleeves who had waited upon him. The room was empty, and all the lights but one had been extinguished. With a shiver, Oswald rose and went home, slinking up the stairs of the flats. All was dark; Letty had gone to bed. For the first time since their marriage, he unlocked the door of the room where he had always slept in the old days. And, fetching some blankets from a cupboard, he arranged them, as best he could, on the narrow bedstead.

So that now they were separated day and night.

The next day Letty expressed no surprise at his behaviour, and that evening and each following evening, he went out to the eating-house round the corner, sitting there stupidly over his food, till the young man in his shirt-sleeves turned out the lights.

And as time went on the thought of death began to haunt him till it became a constant obsession. In the daytime, fascinated by it, he would lay down his pen and sit brooding on it; at night, he would lie tossing feverishly from side to side, with the blackness that was awaiting ever before him. And with the sickly light of the early morning, there met him the early relief of having dragged on one day nearer the end.

IX

'Don't go out this evening. I ask you to stay in to dinner. I have a particular reason.'

She was standing in the doorway of his study, on her face a look of infinite pleading, strangely out of harmony with the stiffness of her phrases.

All day he had been writing, squandering in a sort of fierce delight the last desperate rally of his brain, and now that he felt his strength to be running low, goading himself on with pitiless obstinacy.

After she had spoken, there was silence, for he could not immediately transfer his thoughts to what she had said. When at last he did so, it was in savage irritation that he answered:

'I can't – I don't know – I'm busy.'

* * * * *

An hour and a half later the servant came in to tell him that his wife was waiting dinner for him. The phase of irritability was gone. With weary docility he collected the scattered sheets of paper and followed her into the dining-room, the manuscript in his hand.

He was unaware whether the expression with which she greeted him was angry or pained, for he never looked at her. Without a word he walked straight to his place and sat down. Putting the manuscript on his plate, he began mechanically to turn over the pages. In a few minutes he ceased, and leant back wearily in his chair.

* * * * *

A long while, a short while, he knew not which, and consciousness began to return. A white table before him – a half finished pudding. He was alone; she had gone. The manuscript! – surely he had had it in front of him. Where is it? – gone! He looked up, and the first thing that met his glance was Letty, her face half turned away from him, evidently unaware that he was awake, on her lap the manuscript. Presently the crackling sound of crumbling paper, next, the harsh noise of tearing; she was tearing it, slowly, deliberately. Then, again and again; it was with a sort of frenzied fierceness that she was tearing now, and the fragments were fluttering on to the floor. She stood upright, and quickly, without heeding him, went past.

It was dead; she had killed it – this was the end. He picked up some of the fragments, handling them gently, tenderly almost. A wild look came into his face: he followed her out of the room.

* * * * *

Softly he pushed the door open, and stood, in hesitation, on the threshold. From below, through the open window, came the rattle of wheels and an instant after the distant wail of a steam-tug. The room was almost dark, only the dim night-light from outside. Yet he was quite familiar with its arrangement, and this somehow astonished him a little. Almost simultaneously two thoughts occurred to him. That it was a long time since he had been inside the room, and that he had slept there with her many nights. Where was she? Suddenly, quite close to him, so close that he shuddered, the sound of heavy breathing. It was she. He could see her huddled form, shapeless in the dark, crouching by the bedside. The rumble of wheels died away, the noise of her breathing grew in intensity till it filled the whole room.

Holding his breath in dread lest she should discover him, he peered through the obscurity at her. By degrees he perceived that she was kneeling with her head buried between her two arms, which were stretched out straight on the bed in front of her. Then, a queer, muffled sound, breaking in upon the stillness – she was speaking, and his fingers closed on the door handle.

'Oh God! Merciful God! Listen to me; hear me. Almighty God! They say that Thou helpest people who are in trouble. Surely it cannot be much to Thee just to help me. Dear God! (here she began to sob) I cannot bear it any longer, indeed I cannot. Bring him back to me, God, just for a moment. I wanted him. Oh, how I wanted him! And I will give up my whole life to Thee. I swear it, my whole life shall be Thine. I have been wicked, very wicked in the past. Give me this one thing, and I will do whatever Thou wishest. Almighty, merciful God, say that Thou wilt help me!'

For a while her sobs choked her utterance. Oswald's fingers pressed tighter and tighter on the door-handle. She broke out again:

'Oswald, my Oswald, come back to me. Oswald, Oswald, my husband, speak to me – oh! speak to me, just one little word. What have I done that you will not speak to me? What is it that has taken you from me? Oh! I want you, I want your love. Oswald, my Oswald, I cannot live without it. Come back to me, come back to me. I cannot bear it any longer. It is killing me. Oh! it is killing me. If only it could be.'

X

He stood in the middle of the suspension bridge, peering down through the iron-work at the river.

A long fall through the air – the water black, cold and slimy, the rush down his throat, the fight for breath, to sink down, down at once, and the yearning for the peace of death swept through him.

Could he crawl through the iron-work? No, it was too small. And some one might see him. He must clamber over, quickly. As he looked round him to see if he were observed, his eyes fell on a heap of flints a few yards off; where the road was under repair. He went up to it, and stooping down, began, with the feeble slowness of an old man, to fill his pockets with the stones. Then he went back to the bridge edge, and gripping the stanchions, prepared to swing himself on to the top of them. As he did so, a blackness filled his eyes; a dull thud; his body dropped back on to the roadway – dead.

THE STRUGGLE FOR LIFE

It was a chilly October night in a notorious 'den' beyond the water – since closed by the police.

Half a dozen gross gas-jets lit up the long, low room, making a procession of queer-shaped shadows dance restlessly about the walls: here and there, dotted about, crudely coloured chromos* of the Queen, the Prince of Wales, and one or two half-naked prize-fighters.

It was a Saturday night, so the place was quite full – bargemen with grimy furrows across their bronzed faces; plenty of typical river casuals sucking stumpy clay-pipes; in a corner a group of pasty-faced youths quarrelling over their greasy cards; and scattered about the room some riverside prostitutes, their cheap finery all bedraggled with mud. A veritable Babel rose from these dregs of a population – hoarse laughter, snatches of songs and oaths.

It was hot, a foul, unhealthy heat; the very walls were sweating, and a bluish haze was filling the room up to the blackened ceiling.

I was vainly looking about me for a seat, when a mason, whose corduroys were still white with lime, pulled my arm and motioned me to a place next him, at the same time lifting the woman who was occupying it on to his knees.

Then he began again to beat the table, with an empty pewter-pot, to the refrain of a popular song. At intervals he would stop, grin across at me, and hug his companion.

She, too, was young: perhaps she had been striking-looking once; at least her eyes were still fine, but the lips were shapeless, the voice was hoarse and overpitched, and the complexion was muddy-coloured. I was watching this typical couple, when suddenly I heard a plaintive voice behind me.

A girl stood there, death-white, with dark rings round her eyes. The corners of her bloodless lips were quivering, as though she were in great pain.

'Jack,' murmured the plaintive voice, 'ain't yer comin' back?'

The mason looked across at her with drunken solemnity, shrugged his shoulders, and put his arms round the woman on his knees.

In one flash the eyes of the two women met; of a sudden the whole expression of the young girl's face changed. Like wild beasts, they glared at each other: the one, with all the exasperated fury of

* Chromolithograph. An often crude image produced by the use of printing blocks in various colours.

interrupted appetite; the other, with the instinctive desperate hatred of a mother defending her young.

She clutched at a pewter-pot as if to fling it in her rival's face, but the impulse passed away, and letting it fall listlessly, she turned again to the mason and said in the same, plaintive voice:

'Jack, come along, do.'

''Ee knows when 'ee's well off, my dear,' said the prostitute, pursing up her heavy lips and offering them to her companion.

'At least give us some money,' went on the other, 'the kids ain't touched a bit since morning, and I've nothing.'

The mason, by this time exasperated, burst out, bringing his fist down on the table:

'Go to hell!'

'But baby'll die, if she don't get something,' persisted the girl.

A hoarse laugh from the prostitute was all the reply. This little scene was beginning to attract the attention of the occupants of the surrounding tables – the gambling group in the corner threw down their cards at the prospect of a fight; two women opposite began to jeer.

Whiter than ever, the girl stood there, braving them all; then dropping her head, she ran out of the room like a hunted animal. I had already left my seat and was watching the scene from the doorway. When the girl passed out, I followed her, curious to see the end of it.

She hurried along, through the ill-lit streets till she came to the river.

It was a starless night, but the full moon had just risen from behind the thin, headless necks of a cluster of chimneys which stood out black against the lurid glow reflected by the lights of the city; across the river lay a ragged pathway of quivering, silver light.

There was an uncanny stillness about the spot. The water flowed sluggishly, stealthily by; not a sign of life on board the black hulks* moored to the banks, only from the distance came the feverish rumble of the great city.

A cab was crawling up, its yellow lamps gleaming like the round eyes of some great night beetle; nearer, at the street corner, a policeman and a woman stood talking. The girl, crossing the road, made straight for the river; and the policeman turned to follow her. She stopped when she came to the edge, for she saw the policeman was close behind her; leaning against the parapet, she stared down at the water, her head between her hands.

I passed close by her. The moonlight made her pinched face seem

* Cargo ships.

whiter than ever, the tears were dripping on to the pavement. I sat down on a bench a few yards off and waited.

Presently, the small, black figure of a man came slinking along under the wall. When he saw the girl leaning over the parapet, he stopped and went slowly up to her.

He passed behind her, turned, and passed again. She had not stirred. He was now standing by her side, examining her from head to foot, cynically, as a horse-dealer examines a horse. Presently he put his hand on her arm and spoke to her.

I could not hear what they were saying; but I saw the girl shake her head several times, while the other seemed to be speaking very fast.

After a while, they moved away together, and as they passed in front of the bench where I was sitting, I heard her saying in a broken voice:

'Half a crown* then, and I can go home in an hour.'

* Two shillings and sixpence. There were eight half-crowns in a pound. This is not a very large sum.

DISSOLVING VIEW*

In a low, roomy armchair, puffing gently at a longstemmed pipe, Vivian Marston was listening to the wail of the wind as it swept fitfully down the street, complacently pitying the wretches who, cut by its blast, were shivering outside, this bleak November evening. Slowly his eyes travelled round the luxuriously furnished room, every detail of which reminded him of his own cosiness, and he became conscious of a vague glow of internal satisfaction. Resting his feet on the fender-bar, he began to think of himself.

Leisurely he recapitulated all that conduced to his self-satisfaction. His silky hair, which one woman had liked to stroke; his large grey eyes, 'expressive,' another had called them; his money, it pleased him to remember that he was rich, richer even than most rich people; next, how his new hunter, thanks to the excellent line he had taken, had shown the whole field the way on Saturday, and how, last week, he had crumpled up pheasant after pheasant in a tearing wind, when the others couldn't touch them; last, of Gwynnie, the biggest triumph of all, Gwynnie, his Gwynnie, whom he was going to marry in the spring. And before him defiled, in a grotesque procession, all the men who wanted to marry her; each one, as he passed, looking up in jealous admiration.

From Gwynnie, his thoughts wandered to the others to whom he had made love before her. And a gentle, sentimental melancholy, which was delicious, stole over him. The images of most of them were blurred, half-effaced by time; one alone remained clear-cut. Many weeks it was since he had thought of her, for there was nothing in his life now to remind him of her. She was only a little chorus-girl, yellow-eyed and freckled, with a cracked voice that grated on the ear. He wondered, looking back over it all, what had been the link between them. Perhaps her splendid masses of hair, dark chestnut shot with gold; perhaps her quaint, clinging winsomeness. Towards the end she had grown capricious and fretful, and he had tired considerably of her; but that he did not remember. Only he heard once again the small imperfect voice raised in anger, as they stood together the last evening in the narrow, theatre corridor, with the single gas jet flaring behind. The next day she was gone, with a Frenchman who played third fiddle in the orchestra, so they said. And Vivian, the first moment of pique over, forgot her.

* A term used for a type of magic lantern show in which images dissolve into each other and there appears to be movement.

With curious ease she dropped out of his life. At the end of a week the gap she had left was scarce perceptible. All that happened ten months ago.

He unlocked a drawer in the writing-table, and took from it a packet of letters – ten or perhaps a dozen in all, and three of them much longer than the rest. These last she had written in the autumn, when he was away in the Mediterranean yachting. One after the other he read them, and, as he did so, a curious uncomfortable feeling crept over him. The vision of the thick, rich hair, encircling the yellow eyes, and little freckled face, seemed to change, charged with new meaning. Between the lines he began to read all that the mis-spelt scrawlings on these cheap, shiny half-sheets of note-paper had meant for her. He remembered how their illegibility had used to amuse him, and he was puzzled that he had not understood them then as he did now. There was one, worse written than the others, full of reproaches, that she had not seen him for three days. After that he read no more, but impatiently threw the packet into the blazing grate.

He lit another pipe, and for some little time more sat on exasperated, trying to force his thoughts into another channel.

* * * * *

96 PAXTON STREET, W.C.
Sunday.

'DEAR VIV,

'i am very ill the Dr says i shall get better but it is not true. i have got a little boy he was born last tusday you are his farther so you will see to him when i am ded will you not dear Viv. Louis is gone to Parris he was mad because of the child. Viv dear for the sake of old times com and see me gest once it is not a grand place were i am but I do long to see your dear face again. Plese Viv forgiv me for going of with Louis but i thought you did not care for me anny more and it made me mad i am sending this to the old adress i hope you will get it alright.

'Your loving
'KIT.'

Motionless, he was staring at the sheet of paper in his hand. He could not think; stunned, his brain refused to function. Thus a whole minute passed. At last, mechanically, he picked up the envelope which was lying on the breakfast-table. He turned it over, absently at first, but, with returning consciousness, he noticed that there were two addresses on it; it must have been forwarded from his old lodgings, and, looking closer, he saw that one of the postmarks was nearly a month old. Once more he read the letter through, then again, and then a third time. Gradually a dizzy faintness and a sickening feeling in his stomach came over him. The air seemed close and stifling, but he had not the strength to cross the room to open the window. He sat down feebly by the fire, and, as he did so, he became aware that his hands were clammy with perspiration.

A moment or two and it passed. His thoughts were liberated; he was able to think again.

Kit was dying; by this time perhaps dead. Kit dead – stiff and cold between white sheets, lying flat all but her feet, which upright, projected at the foot of the bed, her face expressionless, the freckles yellower than ever against the deathpale skin. And the child? He felt a thrill of exasperation against the useless, unwanted child. But it was his child – then it was he who -

Suddenly the door opened. He started, every nerve in his body tingling. It was the servant bringing in his breakfast. The man set down the shining covers and steaming coffee-urn, while Vivian, half-dazed, watched him curiously, for there seemed something strangely unreal about his unconcernedness.

At last he moved towards the door.

'Get me a cab,' said Vivian, huskily. Then perceiving the astonished look on the man's face, he added hurriedly:

'I have to go out – at once – important business.'

* * * * *

As the hansom rolled along, Vivian's thoughts rushed back over the past. Incident after incident crowded up in his memory, and this hideous sequel to his love for Kit gave to each a new, ugly significance. It was the culmination towards which all the rest pointed. The cab shot past an omnibus lumbering city-ward, and he found himself marvelling at the difference between the people seated inside it and him. Surely they had never had things like this in their lives. And his thoughts writhed under the increasing pain – then, a quick twinge of hunger, reminding him that he had had no breakfast. Back came the object of his journey. He was going to see Kit. It was as if he and she had never had anything in common, as if he only knew of her by hearsay – but somehow, she and her child had spoilt everything for him. And he understood how he hated going, how he shrunk from bringing her back into his life. But for the irresistible force inside him, urging him forward, he would have turned homeward again. Gwynnie, how could he marry her after this? Strange that he felt no anger against Kit, for having come between them, only he wondered vaguely if it would be easy to get rid of her. But perhaps she was dead – oh! to know for certain that it was so; and the sense of relief, which he knew to be a delusion, was so keen that it hurt him. But the child? – the child – that would live on. They always did. Gloomily, incoherently, he brooded over what was to be done with it.

The cab turned into a side street, scattering some squalid children from off the narrow, asphalted road. There was an untidiness about the neighbourhood, an untidiness that was almost indecent, the untidiness of a bed that has been slept in. Here and there, in the doorways, lounged slatternly women in dirty, colourless petticoats. As the cab passed they looked up, and under their gaze, Vivian winced. All the repulsive features of the neighbourhood stared him brutally in the face. Surely it must be close now? Here? The hansom pulled up before a dingy Italian restaurant: the driver was asking the way of some men smoking cigarettes before the door. They were foreigners, and answered him, all speaking at once, with gestures. A spasm of impotent rage passed over Vivian: he could almost have struck them. The cab moved slowly along: then stopped again at the end of the street. Vivian got out.

He knocked, and, before the narrow seedylooking door, stood waiting. His excitement made his teeth chatter as with cold. This annoyed him, and, in the struggle to divert his thoughts, he forced himself to take stock of the house. There was nothing peculiar about it; its sordidness was neither greater nor less than that of those next to it or opposite to it. Only across the ground-floor window there stretched a card bearing the words 'Apartments.'

Kit was inside this house: perhaps in the very room into which he could almost see from the doorstep. He imagined himself arguing with her, persuading her, reminding her of the old days, giving her money – a large sum of money, the loss of which he would not feel – enough to make her and the child comfortable for life – doing anything and everything to get her to go away at once, to some spot where he would never even hear of her again. Surely she would agree to that. It would be for her own benefit, quite as much as for his. Yes, after all, he would be doing the handsome thing by her, and for an instant, he deluded himself into a glimmer of self-satisfaction.

The sound of a voice, breaking the train of his thoughts – in the area below a grimy woman, her sleeves rolled back over her red arms.

'Well, what d'yer want?' she asked, defiantly.

'I want to see Miss Gilston.'

'Thur ain't no Miss Gilston livin' 'ere,' she called back fiercely, evidently angry at having been disturbed for nothing. She prepared to re-enter the house.

'But,' Vivian went on, 'didn't she – about a month ago.'

'No, I tell yer, I ain't 'ad no Miss Gilston 'ere. Thur was a Mrs. Marston' – at the sound of his own name shouted up through the area railings, Vivian's hands clenched, and instinctively he glanced up the street to see if any one was within ear-shot – 'a few weeks back, but she was took ill with a baby, and she died, poor soul.'

Mrs. Marston – his name – she had taken it then – and his head began to swim a little – but she was dead – dead – gone – dead!

'What's become of the child?' he heard himself asking. The sound of his own voice startled him, for he did not recognise it.

'The baby died along with 'er,' shouted the woman. 'She didn't leave a blessed sixpence behind 'er. Two week and a arf rent she owed me, besides 'er food, all sorts of delictasses I used to git for 'er.' Then with a change of tone, perhaps desirous of a gossip, perhaps struck by Vivian's prosperous appearance, 'Jest wait a minute. I'll come up and tell yer all about it.'

He was leaning against the area railings, scarcely hearing what she was saying, conscious only of the immense relief that was creeping over him. The child dead too. Both of them gone for ever. He became aware that the high-pitched voice had ceased; the woman had left the area. And he looked feebly around for her, the monotonous squalor of the close-packed, brown-brick houses hurt him more than before – oh! to get out of it, away from it, quickly, at once. Kit – it was as if she had never existed. It was like an episode in another man's life.

With a sudden, imperious impulse, he left the doorstep and walked rapidly away down the street.

Twenty minutes later he was seated before his breakfast-table, eating voraciously; for the morning excursion had given him a splendid appetite.

* * * * *

A month afterwards, Gwynnie and he were married. It was a smart wedding. There was a fashionable crowd, and the couple started to spend their honeymoon in Italy.

A DEAD WOMAN

I

'Mary, two bitters and a small Scotch to the Commercial Room, and a large Irish for Mr. Hays here.'

'Yes, Mr. Rushout,' answered the girl, measuring out the spirit and swinging down the silver-knobbed handles.

Then she whisked herself out of the room, and the two men were alone. Neither spoke, but their silence evidently resulted from no constraint; it was quite natural that each should be all content with his own thoughts.

There was no mistaking the dejection of Rushout, the landlord. His corpulent and unwieldy frame lay inert; the features of his smooth, congested face hung limp in gloomy abstraction.

Opposite him, stiffly upright on the edge of his chair, sat Jonathan Hays, bony and gaunt in his rough frieze coat, corduroy leggings and iron-bound boots, while his bushy, red hair and untrimmed beard added not a little to the uncouthness of his appearance.

One end of the room gave on to the entrance of the inn, through a window, across which stretched the broad, brown shelf that did duty for the bar. On either side of this opening were ranged row upon row of glasses, of all shapes and sizes, and all along the edges of the shelves were suspended glistening pewter mugs. Sporting prints, a rackfull of walkingsticks and hunting crops, a large coloured almanack, some pictures of fattened sheep and cattle, illustrating the results of using certain artificial foods, adorned the rest of the room. In the grate glowed a lavish fire, before which a cat lay curled.

'Are ye takin' nothin' yeself?' asked Jonathan, as he filled up his glass from the water-bottle. 'Have a drop o' port: it'll cheer ye, maybe.'

Rushout made a faint sign of dissent.

'Ye're for a smoke then,' persisted the other, producing a battered tin box, half full of tobacco.

'Nay, I've lost all inclination for't.'

The farmer pulled out a blackened pipe and filled it with slow precision. He had all but finished when there burst down the passage a strident guffaw of laughter.

'That'll be Mike, I'll swear.'

'Ay,' Rushout replied listlessly.

'How's t' house doing, Richard?' asked Jonathan.

'Middlin.'*

The other drank and sucked his moustache appreciatively,

'Jonathan,' Rushout began.

'Well?'

'It'll be a twelvemonth to-day.'

'Ay, sure, that it be,' and he started all at once to puff vigorously at his pipe. 'Ay, jest a twelvemonth. Lord, how time flies! It don't seem as it was last back end, do it? Ye'll best be soon looking about ye, Richard. T' house can never prosper while there be no missus, and jest a look at that broomstick woman ye've got now is sufficient to drive even Mike over the way. I tell ye man, ye'll have to bestir yeself,' he continued, raising his voice as he saw that his words had produced no effect on the other's apathy, 'the custom'll go to pieces, right off, mark my words.'

And, with an air of profound conviction, he repeated, 'Mark my words, Richard.'

'Jonathan,' said Rushout presently, 'I'm partin' with the white mare.'

'What? – not -'

'Ay, *her* mare. She be jest spoilin' herself in stable and I can't abide drivin' her myself.' 'Who's for buyin' her?'

'Dr. Wilkinson. He was in this mornin' about her.'

'What're ye askin'?'

'Forty-five.'

Once more they both relapsed into silence. It was again Rushout who spoke first.

'Jonathan, it's a twelvemonth to-day. I'm goin' to drink to her soul.' He drained the wineglass to the dregs and set it down again with almost reverent precaution. The other stared at him in stolid astonishment; then mutely raised his glass to his lips and did likewise. The glances of the two men met, and parted again hastily. It was as if the one had detected the other in some secret deed. The publican obstinately examined the fire; the farmer toyed with his glass, rinsing the spirit round and round.

'Did ye part with them ewes?' asked Rushout. He was obviously struggling to appear unconcerned; but the huskiness of his utterances belied the effort.

'Every one of them. 'Twas a good job too; they were always a troublesome lot.'

'Jonathan, do ye believe in ghosts?' A shout of laughter from down the passage followed immediately on the question which was delivered in impressive solemnity.

* In the north of England, this means something like 'so-so'.

The farmer took time before answering: the matter was too serious to be settled off-hand.

'I don't know but what I should, if I se'ed one,' he said at last.

'It'll be near eleven likely?'

'It wants half an hour.'

'I believe she'll come to-night.'

Jonathan started violently; his clay pipe fell to the floor, smashing into a dozen pieces.

'Ye're a fool, Richard,' he exclaimed, stooping forward and ruefully picking up the fragments.

'Ye never knew her when that likeness was taken,' Rushout continued, pointing to a photograph surrounded by a deep black border, which hung on the wall. 'I had it done jest after we were married. It's simply magnificent. That was when we kept the "King's Head" at Dewston. She *was* a beauty in them days. Why the whole place was jest wild about her. And we'd ha' been married thirteen years come Martinmas.* God! it do take the life out of a man!' he concluded. His speech had grown thick, and the gurgle of a stifled sob sounded through the room.

Jonathan was engaged in fitting together the fragments of his broken pipe. Gradually his fingers stiffened, his eyebrows contracted, a sullen look swept over his face. He never raised his eyes but kept them fixed on his fingers. Next he blurted out, pushing back his chair roughly:

'I'll ha' to be gettin' home.'

'Good night, old man,' answered the other feebly, without moving.

Jonathan went out. In the passage he stumbled over his dog who lay across the doorway; with a vicious kick he sent him yelping into the street The night was clear and frosty, and his footfall over the cobbles, as he strode away, broke with strange brutality the silence of the sleeping village.

II

The village shops were drowsily divesting themselves of their shutters, and the two or three loafers hanging about the parapet of the bridge over the river, their hands thrust deep in their trouser pockets, were stolidly watching the rickety one-horsed omnibus as it rattled past on its way to meet the early train, when Jonathan, his collie at his heels, swung round the corner.

* The feast of St Martin (11 November), an important date in the traditional rural calendar, when servants were hired and animals slaughtered to be salted for winter food.

One of the men on the bridge jerked a 'marnin'' at him as he strode by; then he had passed, and through the swing door of the 'Bear,' disappeared.

Inside, the discordant note of a woman's angry voice met his ear. 'It was that "broomstick woman" giving it to the girl,' he guessed. And so it was.

The flow of her wrath ceased when she caught sight of him; screwing up her ill-conditioned countenance into a caricature of a smile:

'Good morning, Mr. Hays; grand mornin' this,' and turning to the girl cried: 'Now what're ye standin' gapin' there for? Get along and see after that breakfast for the coffee-room.'

'Ye do let her have it,' remarked Jonathan dryly.

'Let her have it,' she retorted, 'let her have it. I should like to know who wouldn't let her have it, lazy, good-for-nothin' hussy. Her goin's on 'ud try the patience of a saint, and as for her impudence, why – '

'Is t' master in?' interrupted Jonathan.

'In! In! Gracious! In! where d'ye think he'd be? In, indeed! Why it 'ud be a wonder if he's out o' bed yet. And for all the trouble he gives himself he might jest as well stay there. Jest settin' and mopin', the whole blessed day. Senseless, downright senseless, I call it. Ye'd think his wife had been a sort of female paragon, to see the way he behaves himself. *She* wasn't such a lot to mourn over, by all accounts. No better than she should be,* and there he sets, moonin' and soakin'† like a great baby.'

'Stop that jabberin',' shouted Jonathan, banging his stick down flat on the bar. 'Ye know nought agin' her.'

'Oh! I know nothin', don't I? Oh! very well, I know nothin'. No, of course I don't. How should I? Only let folks as pretends to have nothin' on their conscience and can't keep a civil tongue in their heads – let 'em look out, I say. I'll teach 'em to march in here with their airs and graces.'

But of a sudden the rest died away on her lips, and snatching up a tray, she bounced down the passage into the kitchen. Jonathan faced about seeking the reason for her precipitate departure: behind him stood Rushout.

The landlord's vitality had perceptibly bettered since last night, for he sent an angry glance in the direction of the kitchen-door.

'Mornin', I thought ye were off to the auction mart.'

'Nay, I thought better on't. There's scarce a bit doin' jest now.'

* Here this means guilty of improper behaviour.

† Drinking.

'Ye'll take a drop to warm ye. It's raw.'

'Nay. I've come for a bit o' business.'

'Ye're welcome, business or no business. Step inside.'

He led the way into the room where they had sat the night before.

'Well,' said Rushout, when he had settled down in his chair.

'I've come to buy t' mare.'

'Not the white one?'

'Ay, that's her.'

Rushout reflected: 'What, in the name of goodness, d'ye want with her?'

'I want her,' answered the farmer doggedly.

'But what for?' testily retorted the other.

'Maybe I've taken a fancy to her.'

Rushout's face broadened to a smile.

'Are ye lookin' for a bit of blood to spank* ye to church?'

'Never ye mind, Richard. It's none o' your business why I'm wantin' her,' replied Jonathan, nettled.

'Well, it don't make much odds, anyway, because ye can't have her.'

'She's not gone yet ?'

'Nay, she's not gone, but she's promised. I told Dr. Wilkinson he should have her. Ye know that.'

'He's givin' ye forty-five?

Rushout nodded.

'I'll give ye fifty!'

'I tell ye man, it's no good. The affair's concluded. Dr. Wilkinson's to have her. Why if I'd advertised her, I'd have got half that price again, and many a time over, easy. She's jest about the bonniest mare, for her size, I ever saw. And I'm determined Dr. Wilkinson shall have her, and cheap too; for (lowering his voice) there's not another doctor in the neighbourhood as would have done what he did for Jane.'

'Settle yer own figure then, I'll give it ye. I'll make it a hundred,' persisted Jonathan.

'Are ye crazy?'

'I tell ye I want her.'

'And I tell ye, ye can't have her.'

'When's she goin'?'

'To-morrow mornin'.'

'I'll come back this afternoon. Maybe ye'll have changed yer mind.'

And, with that, he marched out into the street.

* Move or travel quickly, briskly.

III

But neither that afternoon nor that evening did Jonathan return to the 'Bear.' For about sundown, while he was re-penning some sheep in a bare field all strewn with half-gnawed turnips, he heard the stride of the white mare pounding down the road towards him. Ay, t'was she: many a time had he waited before, listening for her action along the road. Behind, in his mustard-coloured ulster,* sat Dr. Wilkinson. On perceiving Jonathan, he reined up and called out over the hedge:

'How are the sheep doing, Hays?'

But the question fell unheeded on Jonathan's ears. He was surveying the mare – her legs, straight, slender, sinewy; her lithe and gracefully rounded body; her undersized head erect, neck arched, and ears cocked, while at regular intervals she shot out bars of breath from her quivering nostrils.

'Isn't she a beauty?' said the doctor, following Jonathan's gaze. 'By Jove, she does take some driving, too. She hasn't been between the shafts these ten days. By the way she rushes at her work, you'd think she hadn't stretched her legs since poor Jane Rushout's death.'

Jonathan did not answer, so the doctor continued:

'Ah! there wasn't a prettier whip this side of the county than poor Jane Rushout. It was a sad thing! And Richard's getting in a very bad way. I wish something could be done for him. He's got no spirit left – just as cut up as if it all happened yesterday. When I sent my man just now to fetch the mare, he was as overcome as if he were parting with an only child. It *was* a pity they never had any children.'

The mare, who had been fidgeting with her bit, now began to paw the ground. The doctor, poking the rug under his legs with the whip-stock, lifted the reins preparatory to starting again.

'Hold hard, doctor,' broke in Jonathan. He pushed fiercely through the hedge and laid one hand on the mare's neck, pressing his cheek against her nose and speaking softly and soothingly to her. This for a few seconds, till she tossed up her head, and he was forced to let her go.

'Good day, doctor.'

'Good day to you, Hays.'

Jonathan watched the retreating gig till it was gone round the corner; then, roughly brushing the back of his hand across his eyes, climbed back into the field. The sheep lifted their heads a moment and fell to nibbling the turnips again. Folding his arms across the top of a hurdle, he rested his chin on them, gazing straight out before him. His ruddy

* A long overcoat.

beard glowed as the light from the setting sun caught it, and the look of suppressed suffering on his face lent a curious refinement to its ruggedness. And the fantastic tracery of a couple of gnarled oaks stood out against the glare of some burning city on the horizon.

IV

After this an obstinate combination of calamities made a busy time for Jonathan – an outbreak of sickness among his sheep, coupled with the unexpected departure of his shepherd, and the destruction of fence after fence by a sudden rising of the river; and as his energy, dogged, desperate almost at times, overcame one difficulty, a fresh one would discover itself.

Two miles away, in the village, the procession of eventless days defiled in sluggish regularity. Rushout rose from his bed in the morning only to lie torpid for hours before the fire in the little room behind the bar, now staring into the glowing coals, now sunk in stupid slumber.

At all hours the shrill voice of the 'broomstick woman,' as Jonathan had nicknamed her, grated on his ears, till he agreed with himself that she must go. Yet he took no step, procrastinating, first for one reason, then for another. Every hour saw his indifference to the mechanism of the little world around him take deeper root.

One morning, however, he was conscious that the wrangling voices in the kitchen waxed higher than usual, and presently Mary, the maid, stood before him, her cheeks aflame, and her voice tremulous with emotion. 'She couldn't stop to be treated like dirt. She desired to give warning* – she had put up with it long enough.' And when Rushout, remonstrating, endeavoured to soothe her, the girl, bursting into sobs, poured an elaborate, though spasmodic, category of the abuse, tyranny and insults to which she had been subjected. 'It'd never ha' been so if the poor missus were here.' And, at these words, Rushout felt all his apathy lift, like a curtain of fog, and the momentary recovery of his old self, stirred him strangely.

'There, there, lass; ye needna' fash yerself so,'† he said. 'I'll not part with ye. Faith! I'd sooner give her the sack this forenoon right off, than lose ye.'

And at the end of three or four such speeches, the girl, pacified, returned to the kitchen.

* Notice of quitting her employment.

† You needn't trouble yourself so.

She had not been gone a moment before the wrangle of voices recommenced, as fierce, nay fiercer, than before. Then the door burst open violently, and the other woman, her soured face grotesque with passion, stalked into the room.

'I jest want to ask ye, Mr. Rushout, if ye told that girl just now that ye intended me to go sooner than her?'

'Ye're quite correct.' He spoke with quiet determination that was not without dignity.

For nearly a minute she was unable to articulate a word.

'Then ye mean to signify that I'm to clear out to suit that chit of a gal.'

'If ye can't give over frettin' agin her from mornin' till night,' he answered. 'She's a downright good girl, that she is; she's been with me these three years and a half, and I've had scarce a fault to find with her, and my wife had never a word agin her.'

'Oh! that's it, is it? It's for that that ye're wanting to turn me off – me that's slaved my soul out to keep the custom in the house, while ye lie soakin' over the fire. Yer wife never had a word to say agin' her – nothin' to say agin' her (mimicking Rushout's intonation). Where's the wonder? I'm not surprised. Of course she hadn't – she was too busy gallivanting about the country.'

Rushout struggled to his feet, and advanced threateningly towards her.

'By God! ye dare to say another word agin' her. Ye jade, why ye aren't fit to scrape the dirt off her gig-wheels.'

'Ay, ye great, louting coward ye – ye'd be for strikin' me, wouldn't ye? But jest lay so much as yer little finger on me, and I'll have the law agin' ye. Who be ye to call me names? Jade, indeed! D'ye mean to insinuate that I'm not what I should be?'

'Nay, it'd be powerful curious if ye'd ever had the chance.' The adroitness of his retort pleased Rushout, restoring his self-possession.

The woman craned her neck, as if to break into a torrent of abuse; but her impulse changed. With deliberate and concentrated venom she began:

'Ye poor deluded fool, Richard Rushout! Ye little think how that doll-faced minx hocussed ye the minute yer back was turned. Ye little reckon the proper laughin'-stock she made of ye.'

'Shut that sewer of a mouth,' thundered Rushout. His wrath had trebled in intensity with its return flow, and the hue of his face darkened to an apoplectic purple.

But the woman was not to be silenced.

'I'll teach ye to throw mud at honest respectable women,' she cried back, 'a giddy, wanton thing she was, I tell ye. Did ye fancy she'd be satisfied with the boozing good-for-nothing that ye are.'

'It's a blasted lie!'

'A lie, is it? Ye can spare me your filthy language, Richard Rushout. Ask Jonathan Hays if it's a lie. Ask Jonathan Hays if he never had his arms round her. Ask Jonathan Hays if he never – '

A spasm of atrocious suffering convulsed Rushout's face – the poison was doing its work. Snatching at both her wrists, he wrenched her on to her knees.

'Ye'll not stop me – nay, not if ye beat my head in,' she hissed, 'I'll teach ye to throw mud at me. Ask Jonathan Hays, I tell ye. Ask him where she used to drive that high stepping horse of hers, when ye sat soakin' yeself with a roomful of sots. Ask Jonathan Hays, I – '

'Ye she-devil' shouted Richard, with a guttural cry of anguish, as he flung her into the passage.

Then dizzy and dazed, he dropped into a chair.

V

Rushout never saw the woman again, though her voice resounded outside several times. He sent her out her wages and her railway fare back to Newcastle, whence she came, by Mary, with a message that the omnibus would call to convey her luggage to the station. After which he ate his lunch, cold beef, beer and cheese, which was all quite tasteless. And early in the afternoon he heard her depart. The rumble of the omnibus died away in the distance bringing him real relief, for as long as her presence in the house continued to irritate the activity of his rage against her, he felt himself unable to settle down and grapple, face to face, with the new anguish of his doubt. And this he longed to do.

But now that all was still again, he unhooked the photograph from the wall and stood looking into the eyes, long and earnestly. They told him nothing. The guileless candour of their gaze seemed to exhale first tenderness, then mockery. Which was the truth? He set the photograph down on the table, and, going back to his chair, started to ransack the incidents of the past. 'Where did she go when she went out driving?' the woman had said. 'The white mare.' And the first time that they had sat together behind her, the day after he had bought her, came back to him – a crisp, frosty morning, with the sunlight sparkling coldly on the whitened hedges. Next, another time, the week of the Agricultural Show; after lunch they had set off along the North Road to a farm where he had some business, she holding the reins, he smoking by her side. When they arrived, she had declined to come in, declaring that the mare was too hot to stand, and he, with a glow of pride at her workmanlike solicitude for the animal, why, he himself had asked her to take a message up to Jonathan's about some heifers he was entering for the President's prize. Perhaps – God! – and in his mind's eye he saw the two, locked in each other's arms. He watched the whole scene as it was played before him; she, giving herself with all the gestures and caresses with which he was familiar, till its vividness became almost unbearable. He lifted up the photograph once more. But underneath the faint smile lurked a wealth of smothered corruption; on the half-parted lips he detected the imprint of Jonathan's kisses. Hemmed in, as it were, on every side, he appealed as a last resource to the memories of all their common life; but these, obstinately blurred and confused, came not to the rescue, and his belief in her, losing foothold irrevocably, tumbled headlong into the abyss. Then by sheer intensity his desire to establish the certitude of her faithlessness was fulfilled. Fragments of conversations, chance meetings and exclamations, all were pregnant with damnatory clues. Even meaningless remarks he interpreted as fresh proofs of her guilt.

And if Jonathan, why not with others? With Mike, who was in and out of the house all day – with this and that acquaintance. On, on, the Satanic extravagance of his imagination whirled, till at the zenith of his agony, he was conscious that he loathed her virulently. This discovery made him uneasy, and by some quick, unaccountable process his mind wandered off to the advisability of giving a trial to a new blend of whisky, a prospectus of which had reached him that morning. For the moment, all else, receding into the background, was forgotten; outside this fresh track of thought his mind was a blank. The spirit was cheaper, certainly; but that would be balanced by heavier carriage, unless indeed, he ordered a large quantity. But he was not certain concerning the flavour. As he debated the matter with himself, the idea occurred to consult Jonathan. Immediately the full strength of his pain was upon him once more. And once more the whole round of self-torturing doubt recommenced, each time with a fresh crop of detail, new pretexts for suffering. That night in his longing for forgetfulness he went to bed drunk. And he had been sober for years.

VI

He made no effort to acquire fresh proofs. The seed of suspicion sprouted in his mind with the luxuriant growth of a noxious weed; and at the same time his devotion to his dead wife reasserted itself in all the earnestness of its profundity, so that he would turn without transition from the contemplation of her faithlessness to tender recollections of her personality. There was no lifting of the gloom of existence without her; day and night he longed for her; could she have returned he would have shared her with Jonathan willingly. In the sluggish meanderings of his mind he often faced such a contingency, and the consideration of it was in nowise painful. Jonathan – he had never settled with himself what attitude he should adopt when next they met; indeed, whether he felt any vindictiveness against him or not, he did not know. It was that he simply never considered him in the present, apart from his connection in the past with her who still was everything to him, connection of which now his certitude was quite absolute.

After a while it began to seem many days since he had seen him, and he fell to expecting that he would be in, day after day. That it was because Dr. Wilkinson had got the white mare, he guessed, and he resented no longer the other's anxiety to possess her, though the reason for it was now quite clear. And the thought that the doctor had got her, ceased to give him satisfaction; for he understood how carefully Jonathan would have treated her. He was sorry he had spoken so sharply to him about it.

In the mornings when he woke, then the depression lay heaviest, the fatigue at the joyless prospect of the day in front of him. He cared not a jot that the custom of the house was dwindling daily, that every corner revealed some sign of dirt and slovenliness. Everything outside his own bodily wants was growing indifferent to him. And the expectation of seeing Jonathan was the solitary daily event that remained.

One Sunday evening, about six o'clock, there began to fall, slowly, silently, big flakes of snow, so that by the time the congregation trooped out of the square-towered church the white carpet lay soft and thick on the ground. Rushout elbowed his way through the group, loitering in the porch, and buttoning up his coat, hurried down the street, as briskly as his ungainly gait permitted. As he pushed through the swing door of the 'Bear' the first sound that struck his ear was Jonathan's voice:

'Ye can cart the load Tuesday forenoon,' he was saying.

'Right, Mr. Hays, that'll suit,' answered another voice.

Rushout walked straight into the commercial room, whence the sound came. As he entered the third man greeted him with the cordiality due to the landlord, but Jonathan remained silent. Rushout stood irresolute: the sight of his beard and pale face caused him an unexpected agitation. It brought back the past with, as it were, a change of perspective, that filled him with excitement. He discovered that there was something about Jonathan's physiognomy offensive, violently, imperiously. Yet it was not all at once that he realised this impression, so overwhelming was its unexpectedness.

Presently the third man bid them good-night, and the door banged behind him.

Almost immediately Jonathan, awkward-looking in his ill-fitting Sunday suit and stiff, black hat, prepared to depart also.

'A wintry evening,' he mumbled.

'Nay, ye cannot go,' said Richard in a voice at once low and full of determination. And he blocked the doorway. 'Sit ye down again.'

The farmer obeyed. He turned his hat round and round on his lap: a twinge shot across his face and was gone. It was evident that he had guessed what was coming.

Then he waited, stolidly resigned. Rushout was still too agitated to determine where to begin. At last, when for a moment his astonishment got the better of his anger, he broke the silence with:

'How did she come to be fond of ye?'

Jonathan shifted his feet in noisy uneasiness.

'It commenced with the Foresters' picnic, three years ago.'

'Where did ye used to see her?'

'At Coney Standish's old cottage, along the North Road.'

The blow was a heavy one; but Rushout never winced. All outward signs of his agitation had vanished.

'Ye might have let me have the mare,' Jonathan went on, powerless to keep back the bitter thought that lay uppermost in his mind.

'How often did ye use to meet her?' asked Rushout, entirely ignoring the other's remark.

Jonathan paused to consider.

'On Mondays and Fridays, mostly.'

A sudden thought struck Rushout.

'Did she go there that time I was away at my father's funeral?'

Jonathan nodded.

For a long time they remained silent, as if oblivious of each other's presence. Of a sudden Rushout looked up; from around his eyes all the blood had retreated, leaving broad, white rings, and making a deep-toned patch of red on either cheek. He seemed to have come to some great resolution, for the whole expression of his face was different.

'Jonathan Hays,' he said solemnly, 'there'll not be room for both of us.'

The farmer did not answer. And there was nothing in his face to reveal whether he had heard. This time the silence was longer than ever, then Rushout continued:

'I'll be at Helton cross-roads at ten.'

Jonathan slowly uncrossed his legs, and walked to the door. And, as he crossed the threshold, he blurted out:

'Ye'll find me there.'

VII

After the darkness of night had descended, savage gusts of wind started to sweep across the country, mysterious-looking, clad in tatters of ghostly white. And the myriad snow-flakes, which had ceased awhile previously, appeared again, fleeing before the wind; the big trees moved their limbs as if racked with pain; the little trees writhed, taking queer, fantastic shapes.

Inside the 'Bear,' each time that the wind passed in its frenzied passage down the village street, the windows rattled, and the smoke burst into the room from under the mantelpiece in dense puffs, as if it shrank from facing the storm outside. Rushout raised the tumbler to his lips, unsteadily, knocking the edge of the glass against his chin.

The hands of the slow-ticking clock pointed to close upon ten. Presently he must set off to meet Jonathan at the cross-roads. He was quite hazy as to what would happen there; but he had a vague notion that something was to be settled between them – and, indeed, he cared but little. Jonathan had wronged him, and the consciousness of injury begat a spirit of quarrelsomeness within him amounting to pugnacity, fitfully violent.

The rush of the wind gave way to a crooning wail of distress: the window shook furiously in its casement. Too stupefied to heed the storm, he added some more spirit to his glass.

It was half-past ten before he had put on his great-coat and crammed his hat all awry on to his head. He stepped into the street and immediately the blinding force of the wind and driven snow struck him: he tottered, and only kept on his legs by clutching at the wall. Catching at his breath he paused. His senses were sufficiently dulled to render him indifferent to the cutting cold of the blast and the icy wet of the snow: besides, the strain of maintaining a foothold demanded all his attention.

By the parapet of the bridge he halted, hopelessly struggling to rally his faculties. The strangeness of the storm completed his bewilderment. Behind him, out of the blackness, trooped the multitude of snowflakes: in front of him, back into the blackness, they disappeared. Where was he? Had he crossed the bridge? Then he knew that the night air had made him drunk. It was a vague sense of unfulfilled purpose that roused him again – he must avenge the memory of Jane. And he started forward once more. He crossed the bridge and even mounted the ascent on the other side, though the journey took him a long time.

Now the cold was beginning to penetrate him. The cross-roads were scarcely a hundred yards distant; but he was completely ignorant of his whereabouts. Then his foot tripped against something, and he floundered headlong in the snow.

* * * * *

'I jest catchéd seet o' him, leein' all o' a heap by t' road-side: ef I had'na stoppéd he'd ha bin leein' there yet,'* said the carter.

'Lift him on to the sofa – here,' called the ostler.†

'Get your arms under him – now then.'

'He be na featherweight,' the carter remarked, as they deposited the body.

'However did he come there?' asked the maid.

The three figures stood grouped together. The carter's lantern was on the table: there was no other light.

'Light one of them candles; let's have a look at him,' said the ostler.

The maid did so.

But the draught blew the flame to a tiny spark. 'Shut the door – the outside door. Hark to the wind.'

'There's a nasty place on his forehead,' said the carter.

'Ye'd best run for the doctor,' suggested the maid.

The ostler went out.

'He be jest stupefied-like,' remarked the carter. 'I reckon I'll loose him at t' throat.'

Five minutes later Dr. Wilkinson was in the room, directing the two men how to carry him upstairs to bed. And when that was done, the carter went on his way.

VIII

All traces of the snow were gone; the sun glinted warm on the house-tops opposite; inside, a red hot fire was piled up in the little room behind the bar, and before it, extended in his accustomed armchair, lay Rushout. His half-grown beard transformed his whole physiognomy, veiling the coarseness of it here, adding vitality to it

* 'I just caught sight of him, lying in a heap by the roadside: if I hadn't stopped, he would be lying there still.'

† Stableman.

there. Since his illness the ruddiness of his face had paled considerably. After the fever-tossed delirium had come the gentle lassitude of convalescence.

Mary was bustling about the room, retailing divers scraps of village gossip which had accumulated during the past fortnight.

'And Mr. Hays, too,' she was saying, 'he's been in most every day to ask how ye was doin'. I bid him come upstairs many a time; but he was frightened to disturb ye. He'll be around this afternoon sure; I told him ye were for coming downstairs.'

Unreal, shadowy as a dream, the past – the storm, the white snow, the slippery road, the story about Jonathan and Jane – came back to Rushout. Jonathan and Jane – his thoughts lingered over them – not angrily, not bitterly, not sadly. His bodily weakness rendered his emotions indolent, and this indolence precluded any feeling but that of passive good-will. Only he wondered lazily concerning it all.

Then he heard the triple slam of the swing door outside, and Jonathan was before him.

'There, Mr. Hays,' cried the girl, 'ye see he's come downstairs after all.'

'Jonathan, I'm downright glad to see ye,' Rushout found himself saying, and just for an instant it seemed a little odd that he should speak so.

The farmer gripped him by the hand with unfeigned cordiality; as their eyes met his red beard and pale face looked at once strange and familiar.

'I scarce should ha' known ye, Richard, the beard makes ye look different.' And he seated himself opposite, adding:

'Mary, jest a drop of Scotch – the same that I had yesterday.'

'What's your opinion of the spirit?' asked Rushout.

'It's just to my taste. Ye'll be feelin' feeble-like?'

'Ay, I do a bit.'

'It was a close touch of it ye had.'

'I reckon it was.'

'By God! it was a wild night.'

Richard shot across an inquisitive glance, but he did not speak. And simultaneously there appeared to both of them a vision of the dead woman – to Jonathan clear-cut and living, to Richard halfeffaced by time. And each remembered that she had belonged to the other, and, at that moment, they felt instinctively drawn together: each was conscious of a craving to talk about her, to hear the other mention her name. All this was keener with Jonathan, hence it was he who began:

'Richard, she *was* a grand woman.'

'That she was – sich splendid hair.'

'Nay, but t'was her eyes that were the finest.'

'Black – jet-black.'

'Did you ever take notice of the lashes?'

'And a dresser – more style than any lady. And the cleverest understander of horseflesh!'

Here they paused.

'Richard,' Jonathan began again at last in an altered tone, 'the white mare's gone lame.' 'Lame!' Rushout sat of a sudden upright as he repeated the word after him. 'Lame!'

'It's a nasty strain on t' hind fetlock. The doctor says she's been kickin' in the stable.'

'Stuff and nonsense,' Rushout retorted angrily. 'Kickin' in the stable – she's as quiet as a sheep. He's been drivin' of her too hard, that's what it is. A hammerin' of her over the stones. He isn't fit to sit behind her.'

'I'm goin' to put her out to grass.'

'Ye goin' to! But the doctor? Isn't he for usin' of her?'

'He's parted with her. He reckoned she would na stand his work.'

'And it's ye that have bought her.'

Jonathan assented. Rushout reflected, then:

'Jonathan, I'm powerful glad. I've always regretted ye didn't have her first. I reckon Jane would ha' sooner that ye had her, if she was to go.'

'And to mind that on her death-bed she bade ye be tender with the animal. I'd ha' given most anything for her to ha' kept sound,' returned Jonathan reproachfully.

'Ay, I know ye would,' answered Rushout repentantly.

Yet a moment later he began again:

'D'ye mind how wild she was the day I was for lettin' young Will Dykes drive the mare?'

'That I do.'

'Were ye sweet on her then?' he put the question in hesitating timidity.

''Twas the first occasion I had a kiss from her,' answered Jonathan, defiantly.

'When was that ?'

'Whilst ye were fetchin' the new skin rug.'

* * * * *

'What made ye fix on that old house of Coney Standish's?'

'I canna rightly say. There was a great amount o' reasons – it's a long tale. Yet I don't know but what I've any objection to relating it to ye. I reckon it'd be best out.'

'Ay, ye're right. Ye know I bear ye no malice. Hold on though till the girl fetches me a drop more of this barley-drink. It's grand coolin' stuff when ye're feverish.

WHEN GREEK MEETS GREEK*

I

'Why don't you say at once that you hate me? Of course you do. What have you to do with a poor, broken-down devil like me?' and the concentrated exasperation of his sneer was ugly.

He stood planted on the hearth-rug, his face flushed, and a swollen vein standing out across his forehead. He had finished speaking, and there was silence in the room now; yet the figure of the girl opposite remained motionless. Seated in the far corner of the room, she was but an indistinct mass of shadow, for the feeble light of the shaded lamp did not reach her.

There was no freshness on the man's face – the battered skin, wrinkling at every corner, was stretched as loosely as an old man's, and hung in folds under the chin; the hair, scanty on the temples, was here and there strongly streaked with grey; but the moustache, with its slender waxed points, was coal black, and the frame, despite the stoop in the shoulders, had all the spontaneous elasticity of youth. Fifty or thirty? Which was nearer the mark?

Duncan Ralston had lived a long time in India. Those in England who had known him before he had gone out as a young subaltern, freshly commissioned, talked vaguely of his brilliant bravery in the Afghan War, though no one could say exactly the manner in which he had distinguished himself. Then, about three years ago, selling out under apparently disadvantageous conditions, he had come home for the first time. When he appeared in London, some said that the climate had aged him strangely; but others, who knew him better, hinted that hard living had done as much as unhealthy heat. Now and then there were ugly rumours of a scandal with the wife of a Government officer up at Simla†; but since no one spoke with certainty on the subject, they never attained any definite form.

After a minute or two, the girl came and stood by his side before

* The title refers to a well-known saying, usually something like 'When Greek meets Greek, then there comes a tug o' war.' It has come to mean that a serious conflict is inevitable when two like persons meet. The title is particularly relevant to the story since, from the sixteenth through to the nineteenth century, a meaning of the word Greek was a card-sharp and a cheat (see: Eric Partridge's *The Penguin Dictionary of Historical Slang* (1972)). This meaning is also given in *The New Shorter Oxford English Dictionary* (1993).

† Simla, or Shimla, was the summer capital of British India from the 1860s. It is situated in the lower ranges of the Himalayas.

the fire, stretching out one foot towards the grate. The flickering light which played about her face revealed that the violence of his words had not affected her self-possession; there was only a tired, weary look, as if she had played the same scene many times before, and it palled upon her.

Her hair was drawn into a single coil on the top of her head, and her black evening dress revealed her warm-tinted throat and breast and her delicately modelled arms: she wore no ornament of any kind, and this enhanced the purity of her charm. Though she stood almost as high as he did, she was little more than a child.

The contrast between the two was a violent one, the man, with infinite possibilities of one kind in the past, the girl with infinite possibilities of another kind in the future.

And to Duncan the sight of her seemed to bring the bankruptcy of his own life very near at hand. Gradually the hardness went out of his face, all his anger fading as it had come, quickly. A glance of almost abject self-abasement and he laid one hand on her bare shoulder, while with the other he lifted her fingers to his lips, slowly, almost reverently.

'I'm sorry, Pearl,' and he kissed her fingers again; 'I couldn't help it.'

But on her part there was no movement in response to his, passive with the same dreary look she let her arm fall limp to her side again; and he, all occupied with his own emotion, noticed nothing.

Duncan Ralston was a ruined man. Eighteen months ago he had fancied himself within a few days of the crash; yet, week after week, month after month, he had managed to stave off the disaster, till he accepted his difficulties as a natural part of his life, and, a victim to the almost incredible blindness of self-deception, imagined that, sooner or later, by some means or other, he would emerge from them all. Perhaps, but for his passion for Pearl, despair would have taken the place of this reckless hopefulness; perhaps it was her presence alone that encouraged him to go on living. Yet it was only occasionally that he resented, as he had done just now, that she made no pretence of returning his love, and it was very rarely that the whole extent of his degradation betrayed itself in her presence. The scattered remnants of a craving for religion or its equivalent, which years of loose living had not been able to eradicate, had centred themselves in his worship of her, so that there were moments when he could have knelt down before her, and prayed to her as a child prays to God. Once, nay twice, when he was absolutely penniless, she had given him money to go on gambling with, and on each occasion her money had brought him remarkable runs of luck. Hence there grew up in his mind a superstition that when the worst came, she would be there to save him, and this superstition was a source of considerable comfort to him in his worst moments of dread.

In the beginning, when his passion for her was purely selfish, he had determined to become her lover, cost what it might; but as, with each fresh batch of losses, he sank deeper and deeper into the mire, the reality of this resolve dwindled, and now the idea, had it been put before him, would have seemed little short of sacrilege. The fierceness with which the passion for gambling – become of late an almost nightly struggle for existence – had fastened upon him, had chastened his love for Pearl, making of it a haven wherein all the better part of his nature took refuge; and he had enough moral sense left to recognise his own enslavement.

'Pearl,' he said in a low voice, 'can you let me have another hundred? I must have it,' he went on, speaking more rapidly. 'I haven't five pounds left, and I must play to-night. Your husband's banking, and it's my last chance.'

'Simon's banking?' she murmured after him. She spoke with a foreign accent that made the words very musical. 'Simon's banking,' and a change came over her face, whether of anger, or of dread, or of pain, it would be difficult to say.

She crossed the room, and unlocking a drawer, handed him some notes.

He took them, counted them, and gave her in return a long look of hungry gratitude.

Pearl went back to her old position before the fire, gazing vacantly into the flames.

'I shall come to-morrow,' said Duncan briskly, moving towards the door.

'Yes, come to-morrow,' she answered absently.

The door shut. She was alone. And, as the twilight creeps over the earth, steadily, stealthily, a feeling of loneliness crept over Pearl. Everything grew greyer and greyer, blacker and blacker. She was ignorant of the reason for her gloom, and indeed it would have been vain for her to attempt to arrive at its subtle and complex causes. There was, too, at the back of it all, a sense of uneasiness, the dread of some nameless disaster. 'Simon's banking to-night,' she repeated to herself, and at once the dread doubled in intensity. Then the reaction. How often had she not felt like this before, and there had been nothing? Besides, after all, what did she know? perhaps it was all right. Yes, it must be all right. But, as if by command, a crowd of incidents leapt up in her memory to remind her of the truth of her suspicion. To speak to him about it never occurred to her; to implore him to give up playing was more than she would have dared. Once or twice indeed she had thought of it, but almost immediately, appalled at her own audacity, she had rejected the idea. For how could they live? He could not work, that was out of the question. Besides had he not saved her? Did she not owe everything to him? And for the fiftieth time the conflict between right and wrong distracted her, till from sheer weariness she gave it up, as she had done many times before. Already eight o'clock, why was he not yet back?

* * * * *

Three years, and several months of the fourth year had come and gone, since that early morning when Simon Alvary, on his way home, after a heavy night at the *Cercle du Mont d Or*,* Nice, was attracted down a narrow side street by a sound of muffled moaning. The figure of a man was stooping over a black mass lying in the roadway. It was a girl crouching all huddled in a heap on the cobbles, her elbows raised across her face to protect her eyes. The man was hitting at her with a piece of rope. As Simon came up, he paused before swinging the rope above his head and bringing it down heavily on the girl's neck. In an instant Simon's gloved fist was in his mouth, the fellow reeled and dropped with an incoherent oath. The girl lay on a moment; but presently, surprised that the blows had ceased, she cautiously lowered her arms. Next she crawled up to the groaning body of her assailant, and when she saw the blood trickling from his mouth, she whispered hoarsely to Simon:

'*Merci, monsieur. Il allait me tuer si vous n'étiez pas venu. Merci*,'† then turned over in a faint face downwards.

Simon ran for a cab, took her home in it to his lodgings, sent for a nurse from the hospital, and the best doctor in the town, gave her his own bed, and slept that night on a sofa in the dining-room. It was three weeks before she was able to get up again, and during that time he did everything that could be done for her, waiting on her himself, as anxiously and as tenderly as if she were his own child. Two nights even when her fever was running dangerously high, he was absent from the card room of the *Cercle*, though the luck was with him, and he had been winning largely.

He made cautious inquiries and discovered that the man from whom he had rescued her was her father, an *ancien professeur de lycée*,‡ whom absinthe was fast driving into the gutter. This and the fact that he led

* A casino.

† 'Thank you, sir. He was going to kill me if you hadn't come. Thank you' (French).

‡ A former secondary school (high-school) teacher.

his daughter a dog's life was all that Simon could learn, for the man was not a native of the town, and the day after the encounter he disappeared – either afraid that he would be arrested for ill-treating his daughter, or anxious to take the opportunity of ridding himself of her.

Meanwhile Simon was exercising the faculty for secretiveness, which in him amounted almost to genius, inducing the doctor, the nurse and the *concierge*, all, by different means, to keep their tongues from wagging, so that the incident was kept absolutely quiet. And since for certain reasons it was necessary, that his life, when he was not at the *Cercle* or locked up by himself as was his wont for a certain number of hours each day, should be as retired as possible, afternoon upon afternoon he would relieve the nurse by her bedside, smooth her pillows, mix her medicines, shift her poultices, and often, when she grew stronger, read aloud to her in his hard, English voice, chapters from a dog's-eared copy of the *Le Capitaine Fracasse*,* which he found lying in the room.

At first this playing the nurse amused him, varying as it did the forced monotony of his life; after a while, as the fascination for her blanched, childlike face and of the big, brown-ringed eyes, wide open in wondering gratitude, grew, he came to regard her as belonging to him absolutely. This sense of proprietorship was especially pleasant – he liked to think of that straight, clean blow – he had never delivered a better – by which she had come into his possession; and of her hundred and one charming little ways of showing her gratitude, not one jarred upon him. From the moment when she had first realised what he had done for her, she had started to worship him, with a sort of wondering superstition, telling herself that he had been sent by Providence to save her. This idea when she told it to him charmed him and strengthened the bond between them. The first morning that she was well enough to leave the house, it occurred to him that he should like to keep her, so with the promptitude of action that was habitual with him, he took her back with him to London. It was not till a full year later that he had consented, with a smile of good-humoured indulgence, to go through the marriage ceremony with her. For months before this they had been living as man and wife, and any ratification had seemed to him quite superfluous.

This was the story of their marriage – a strange enough binding together by chance of two individualities.

Pearl – for so Simon always called her, though her real name was Marie – was now nineteen, ripening every day from a quaint, winsome

* A popular French historical novel (1863) by Théophile Gautier.

child into a finely built, beautiful woman. The cowed look had gone from her face – or rather it had developed into an air of delicious gravity, the mysterious thoughtfulness of one for whom the task of living had some hidden meaning.

The many months of their life in common had dulled but little the vividness of her gratitude to Simon. She had felt that the least she could do in return for what he had done for her was to give herself up to him, body and soul, studying all his tastes and habits that she might the more easily merge in them all her own desires and aspirations. And this she had accomplished with no ordinary single-mindedness, till her submission was so complete that he was never aware of it. Yet, in spite of it all, there was not that close sympathy between them which would have made of this sense of duty a source of joy.

Simon was kind to her – more than kind to her – just as he had always been. Ah! that was it, it was the perpetual monotony of his kindness that at times maddened her, stirring up within her a fierce desire to break out into bitter reproaches against him. She was conscious of a distantness in his indulgence towards her, that he was constantly 'thinking apart' from her, as if he were never quite off his guard in her presence. It was not of a sudden that this impression had flashed upon her, it had grown up, built bit by bit from the observation of subtle changes of manner, look, tone. And yet, strong as the temptation to pour out her heart to him was, an indefinable dread had up till now prevented her from yielding to it.

Once she had imagined that it was the memory, of some other woman over which he was brooding; but something – what she had forgotten – banished this idea from her mind.

Then appeared the suspicion, which at certain moments crystallised itself into a certainty – it was the card-playing. Wherever they went, London, Paris, or the various fashionable resorts on the Continent – and they were constantly moving from one place to another – Simon played. Even this she did not learn all at once; for when he started out late at night, he never volunteered where he was going. At first in the full flush of her gratitude she had given but little thought to this, the idea that he was playing for large sums never entered her head. But once, when he came back in the middle of the night, she watched him, as she lay in bed, take from the pocket of his ulster a leather bag, and lock it away in a drawer of the writing-table. And as he carried it across the room she heard the muffled chink of money. When the morning came, and he was still sleeping heavily, she slipped out of bed and, unlocking the drawer, loosened the string round the mouth of the bag. Inside lay gold and silver, and a bundle of papers – notes? – yes, notes.

The sight of all this money – thousands of francs, as it seemed to her – scared her. Hastily she tied up the bag again and, locking the drawer, crept back into bed.

After this, though she had never dared say a word to him about it, she began to spy upon him. She had always taken for granted that he possessed *rentes** – the word to her meant something at once vague and reassuring. How much she had never stopped to calculate; but that it must be a good deal she felt sure, for they always lived at the best hotels, and he gave her more money than she knew how to spend.

Now, frequent spyings on the writing-table drawer made her understand that all the money he gave her came from the card-playing, and that he had nothing but what he brought home at nights.

At the beginning of the third year after their marriage they went back to London, to the set of rooms in a little hotel near King's Cross, where he had first taken her. This was a great change from the lavish living to which he had accustomed her on the Continent; but meekly she accepted as final his curt explanation – they must reduce their expenditure.

For a whole fortnight he never once went out at night-time; but after eleven o'clock, when she had gone to her bed-room, he would remain by himself in the sitting-room till past midnight.

Now, since the solitude of her life caused every trivial incident to assume the proportions of an important event, this change in his habits inflamed her curiosity to fever heat. Seated on the bed, or standing in the doorway of the bed-room she would wait listening. Presently a scraping as of the gentle turning of a key. Then for a long while, sometimes an hour, sometimes two hours – nothing – only the movements of the other inmates of the house as they retired for the night. At last the scraping sound again and his tread in the passage.

One night she had worked herself up into such a state of nervous excitement concerning this mystery that she stole out in her stockinged feet to listen at his door. All was still. What could he be doing? She put her eye to the key-hole. Yes, there! he was sitting at the table. There was no one else in the room. He was muttering to himself then. What was he doing with his hands? Cards? Yes, cards! He was lifting them from a heap in the middle of the table, and was scattering them over the table. For a long while she remained watching breathlessly, till the draught against her eye became very painful: stealthily she slunk back again.

From that moment the great suspicion lived with her, at times

* An income from investments, stocks.

attaining the definite proportions of a certainty, at times fading to the indistinctness of a blurred shadow.

Not long after this the little hotel saw them no more. They had moved to a house in Maida Vale.* And here, excepting a month spent in Paris towards the end of the last year, they had been ever since. In reality her life remained as retired as before, though outwardly it was much less so. There came to the house a certain number of men – yet with not one of them did she feel she had anything in common. It was certainly not their low standard of taste before which she recoiled, for many of the chance acquaintances with whom she had been thrown on the Continent could boast of but little refinement, but rather as if a portion of her husband's secretiveness had communicated itself to her, teaching her to retreat more and more within herself. To Duncan Ralston alone was she at all accessible; but even with him it was little more than a passive tolerance of his presence, partly on account of his dog-like devotion to her, partly because the pathos of his wrecked life touched her sentimentality.

And so he was with her constantly. And Simon, reticent as usual, made no comment: only when he remembered the soundness of her fidelity, he smiled inwardly, and the smile was entirely pleasant.

Women friends she had none. Barely half a dozen acquaintances – the wife of an actor in whose house (next door) she had met all the others – mostly mere names.

* * * * *

'Well, Pearl, how are you?'

A rotund figure, insignificant in height, but sturdily built, curly, black hair, no moustache or beard, a healthy pink and white complexion, the eyes small and metallic, the mouth thin-lipped, the chin full and heavy. But for his voice, a hard, mechanical voice, with no modulation of tone, the last word sounding the same level note as the first, he would have seemed a mere boy. And when he spoke every feature of his face remained impassive, as if he had no consciousness of what he was saying. Thus the first impression that Simon Alvary conveyed was one of well-fed, crass stupidity, But to Pearl he was the all-important centre of her tiny world; and the hardness of his voice – of course she had never heeded it, for it had always been the same.

As he came in she ran towards him, saying impulsively.

'Oh! I thought you were never coming.'

'Poor little Pearl!' and he patted her on the cheek. 'Has it been very

* A district in west London.

dull all the afternoon? Well, little woman, you shall have a treat this evening, and we'll go to the theatre.'

'*Chéri*,' she answered, nestling her head on his shoulder.

Presently he moved away from her, arranging his white tie, which she had crumpled, in the mirror.

'By the way,' he said (his back was still turned towards her), 'just give me back those notes I gave you yesterday. I shall want them to-night. You shall have them again in the morning.'

'Give you them back!' she repeated.

He said nothing, only went on straightening his tie.

'I – I haven't got them.'

'Haven't got them? Haven't got them? What have you done with them?' His voice was a tone louder, and every syllable sounded with ruthless distinctness.

'Where are they?' he repeated, facing her.

'I – I gave them away – to Ralston,' she faltered.

His face was unmoved, but he snapped his fingers once or twice, and this movement, which she knew, made her still more frightened.

'What did he want them for?' he went on.

'For to-night – he said it was his last chance – I am so sorry – forgive me – *je ne savais pas*.'*

'*Sotte*,'† was all his reply. She burst into tears.

'*Je ne savais pas*,' she cried.

'It's no good making a fuss. But this is the last time.'

'*Je te jure*,'‡ she interrupted.

'All right. Now let's come to dinner. Stop! How often have you done this before?'

'Twice. Once a long time ago, and once after we came back from Paris.' She answered him eagerly, hoping by the fulness of her confession to atone for her fault.

'How much?'

'Twenty the first time, and fifty the second.'

'Was that the fifty I gave you on your birthday?'

'Yes.'

He laughed a short, contemptuous laugh, and then they went in to dinner.

* 'I didn't know' (French).
† 'Silly girl' (French).
‡ 'I swear to you' (French).

II

It was half-past twelve before Simon entered the card-room of the Athenian Club. Still and silent stood the shapeless mass of figures which crowded the far end of it. So still, so silent, that the ticking of the clock was distinctly audible. Then, suddenly, the brutal outburst of a fierce gabbling of voices; incoherent and indescribable, and the crowd started to sway to and fro, feverishly.

Simon handed his overcoat and crush hat to an attendant, leisurely bit the end from a cigar, and sauntered up to the table; that quick glance of his scanning the crowd, it flashed across his face and was gone. But so high ran the game that no one heeded his arrival. It was indeed a full night – not only was every seat round the oval table occupied, but on both sides they stood huddled together, two or three deep, some grey-headed, some bald; some stout and horsey-looking; some boyish, beardless and flashily dressed; some with dark skins, coarse lips and hooked noses; some insignificant like the people one meets every day in the street, a few in evening dress, several with their hats on; most smoking cigars or cigarettes; each and all craning over the table and the disorder of counters, white, gilt, and silvered, which lay strewn up and down it.

Simon stepped on to the dais which skirted the room, and stood there, a little apart, stolid and expressionless, revealing nothing of the quickening glow that was stealing over him – the deliciously exhilarating glow of fine expectation, coupled with a sense of entire satisfaction with himself.

'Gentlemen, please make your stakes.'

(The chink of counters, accompanied by a shower of the disjointed remarks which form the gambler's ritual.)

'*Rien ne va plus*,'* called a voice.

'Cards?'

'Cards?'

'Six,' and a fresh outburst of hubbub drowned the voice of the banker.

Simon was not a constant visitor at the Athenian – the scene of his operations was usually laid elsewhere – most of the faces were unknown to him; yet he was at once conscious from the demeanour of the crowd that something unusual was taking place. But the gap in the wall of bodies surrounding the table was now closed, and, from where he was, he could see nothing of what was going on.

* This French sentence means that no more bets may be laid.

'Hulloa; good evening.' It was Duncan. Simon nodded shortly, and after a pause:

'The bank's low.'

'A devil of a run,' the other answered excitedly. 'The German started at three hundred and was broke in half an hour. This chap took one at five hundred and he's only been on about ten minutes.'

At that moment the voice of the croupier was heard.

'Gentlemen, there are only twenty-three pounds in the bank.'

A sullen murmur of grumbling, a reckless laugh or two, not a few astonished oaths, an expansion of the crowd, and a noise of the shifting of chairs as the punters rose from their seats. The buzz of conversation swelled till it filled the room, there was a popping of corks, and waiters, armed with glasses, glided in and out of the various groups. The croupier was sweeping away the mess of cards by his side; gazing at him absently, bald and flabbyfaced, sat the banker. Presently, however, he swept the little pile of counters before him into the palm of his hand, rose and was lost in the crowd. It was the merchant Stendermann.

The buzz of conversation flagged and rose, flagged and rose again. The croupier had cleared the table, and now was idly examining a crack in his rake.

So the minutes slipped by. But the chairs remained untenanted. No one would risk another bank. A few anxious-looking punters, excited by their gains, were wandering restlessly about, others were moving towards the door, a group was forming round a couple of *écarté** players, who had just seated themselves at the other end of the room.

Simon was biding his time; he loved to toy with the temper of the crowd. At last he stepped forward and, without a word, seated himself in the banker's chair. Instantly there was a rush for seats at the table; those who were on the point of going divested themselves of their overcoats; the two *écarté* players were left almost alone.

'A thousand,' he said, throwing a bundle of notes on the table. The croupier ran his fingers through them with the precision of a bank clerk, and the light from the chandelier glinted on the counters which he poured on the table in return.

Then he began dexterously to churn together the six packs of cards.† Simon, calling for a match, relit his cigar, disguising with admirable skill his keen scrutiny of the punters. On his right sat Duncan, the swollen vein standing out across his forehead as it always did when he was excited – meddling fool! – he at least should go to bed that night

* A card game for two players.

† The game is a form of baccarat.

with empty pockets; next to him, a hollowcheeked, filmy-eyed fellow, whose straggling black beard he remembered having seen before in other gaming rooms; beyond, three young ' bloods'* in evening dress, all chattering in noisy excitement over their winnings off the last two banks. (Simon's eye lingered almost lovingly on this little group, and he observed that two more of the same party stood behind.) Of the punters seated on the other side of the table, three at least, by the quiet determination of their demeanour, were players of calibre, and, next the croupier, a seedy-looking individual, whose fingers were tremulously sorting his small pile of counters – a broken-down specimen, tottering on the brink, without one of which at least no gaming-room is complete. Ah! there in the crowd behind, the fat Stendermann (he had come back then) – a noble loser he, for, during Simon's last visit to Paris, had the merchant not written him out a cheque for seventeen hundred without a murmur after an hour's piquet!†

A few minutes later the game was in full swing. Simon had not yet begun to work; as yet he was only playing. For fine as was the pleasure of controlling chance, he was epicure‡ enough to render it quite exquisite by a period of preliminary deliberation. Playing was to him what the *hors d'œuvre* is to the glutton – and what are the joys of the gambler compared with the joys of the Greek? Besides, in spite of, or rather on account of, the previous runs against the bank, all were staking in small sums, except the three young 'bloods' in the corner, and Stendermann, who threw down a heap of ten-pound counters before each deal. Nothing makes the veteran gambler so cautious as heavy winnings.

As yet there were no signs of a run. The hesitation of the cards, declaring first in favour of the punters, then in favour of the bank, had been up till now almost complete, as if, conscious that the struggle had not begun in real earnest, they feared to commit themselves to one side or the other. It was nearly five weeks since Simon had had the chance of a serious game at the Athenian – one of the few clubs open to him where the banker was allowed to handle the cards. Hence the ridiculous proportion of the stakes to the amount of his bank irritated him, or rather provoked that almost imperceptible ruffling which was all he ever allowed himself to indulge in. He determined to raise them by a method all his own, which, though dangerous, was rarely unsuccessful. Waiting till the cards were almost exhausted, he called for three fresh

* Late nineteenth-century slang for a fast and fashionable young gentleman.
† A card game for two players.
‡ A person who cultivates a refined taste.

packs. Directly they were placed on the table, he exchanged them, all but the last dozen or so, for a 'poultice' which he carried concealed in his waistcoat pocket. In this 'poultice' every figure-card, every eight, every nine, and a quantity of combinations making up these two numbers were delicately cogged, so that by passing his fingers along the edges of the pack, he could at once detect their whereabouts. Next, he proceeded to 'slip' in favour of the punters five 'naturals,'* three to one side and two to the other. The manœuvre cost him over a hundred pounds, but it accomplished his object. At the beginning of the tenth deal there was more money on the table than there had ever been before, and henceforward with each deal the stakes rose higher and higher. The blood of the players was warmed. He could now begin to work. Yet for a while he continued to dally with the game; that was the weak spot in his strength. How he loved to refine upon the thrill that the consciousness of his power sent through him. So, if he still led the punters on, first to the right, next to the left, it was only to render the joy of plundering them in the following deal all the more acute. The preliminary operation of deposing the 'poultice' successfully accomplished – and in truth, for him, this was no difficult feat – all was secure; for the indentations on the cogged cards were so delicate as to be invisible to the naked eye, and imperceptible to any but his exquisite touch. So absolute was his control over the cards, that any moment he could have dealt fifteen 'naturals,' or fifteen baccarat hands running, had he been so minded. His whole being was concentrated on the game, and he made no attempt to disguise it. The assumption of carelessness, or of nervousness, of high spirits, of loquacity, of bluster, or of extreme civility – the hackneyed devices of the modern Greek – he scorned them all. For tonight at least, he was on a higher plane; he could afford to dispense with them; no salad-shuffle, no churning together of the cards, however conscientious, could impair his omnipotence.

Meanwhile Duncan, whirled along by the savage tide of the vice, won and lost, lost and won again in blind senselessness, only alive to the fluctuation of the pile of counters before him. Off the first two banks he had taken eighty pounds, and his madness wrought in his mind out of this sum the annihilation of all his difficulties. Tradesmen's debts, overdue promissory notes, miscellaneous debts of honour, all vanished, lost to sight amid the magnificent vista of possibilities now stretching before him.

Before now, in a single night, men had won fortunes – fortunes, ay, fortunes large enough to enrich them for life. And he? Why not he? The

* In gambling, a natural is a combination or score that immediately wins a game.

luck was with him. And did not Pearl's money always bring him luck? The sight of the masses of counters strewn up and down the table fed the fierceness of his lust, intoxicating him, causing him to plunge more and more desperately. He was losing now, but a couple of 'naturals,' at the rate at which he was staking would right him again; then in real earnest he would start to break the bank. Alvary – little sleek-faced devil! – he had always hated him – he would break him yet, down to his last farthing. And when he had broken his bank to-night, he would dog him from gaming-room to gaming-room till he had stripped the very clothes from off his back. He sent a glance of hatred at the stolid, round face. Pearl, when he was rich, he would take her from him, and Alvary, he would kick him into the gutter. And, when all these things were done, he would never touch a card again. He would settle down to enjoy life. Ha! there were two winning cards, and as the croupier pushed half a dozen counters towards him, the glow of self-sufficiency that accompanied the vision of a new life of unbroken enjoyment was as vivid as if it had been real. Yet he was losing again. Two 'baccarat' hands shattered his castles in the air. His eyes ran rapidly over the counters – thirteen gilt ones, £130; eleven silvered ones, £55; about a dozen white ones. Barely two hundred. Damn these cursed cards! Why he had only won twenty pounds on this bank.

Six and a figure card.

'Seven,' sounded Alvary's clear voice.

While the croupier swept away five of his gilt pieces, Duncan gave vent to a smothered exclamation of fury, and the vein across his forehead swelled as if it would burst. He was a bad loser.

The next deal saw five more disappear. He swore a foul oath between his teeth.

'*Il faut savoir perdre, mon ami,*'* said Simon, his teeth gleaming.

The blear-eyed owner of the straggling beard laughed nervously; but Duncan heard nothing.

The following hand was a winning one, but the next two, four and five against Alvary's seven and six, brought him back to where he was before. And for a while he plunged on, neither winning nor losing. Once he possessed at least half a dozen gilt counters, then a run of four losing hands in succession, and they were gone every one. A couple of five pound counters and a small heap of white ones were all that remained. With the caution of despair, he refrained from staking them all, pushing only the silvered ones over the line. Knave – six – thank God!

* 'You have to know how to lose, my friend' (French).

'Stand,' he gasped.

'Seven,' called Alvary.

And the last of the silvered pieces went to swell the mass in front of the banker. Unconscious of all around him, as if stunned by a heavy blow, he forgot to stake. In the agony of his despair, he was trying to recollect whether, when he had left her, Pearl was wearing the coral necklace he had given her. Then gradually his thoughts came back to the game, and mechanically he pushed forward three white counters. They followed the others, and he sank to staking in sovereigns. One by one they were swept away, and, as they disappeared, the lust of his greed waxed imperious within him, at the sight of the enormous mass heaped within a few feet of him in front of Alvary. Once more he staked again, and, as he lifted his cards, the players, the table, everything seemed blurred and distant. Nine! God! and he only had a sovereign on. Swiftly, like a wild beast from its lair, sprung up the impulse – passionate, ungovernable – the *poussette.** There was no time to lose, now, at once. Instantly all his self-possession returned. Coolly he looked round the table, and dropped four counters by the side of the ones he had already staked.

Then Alvary turned up his cards –seven! – and immediately a loathsome terror swept through Duncan. Some one must have seen him – he would be exposed – and he fell to wondering whether they would let him get his hat, or whether they would hound him bareheaded into the street. He dared not look up. He felt the gaze of the whole room upon him. But at last he mustered courage. Strange! no one seemed to be paying any attention to him. Alvary, surely he? but no – and look! the croupier unmoved was pushing a gilt piece towards him. Then he was not discovered. He was free! ha! ha! and a wild spasm of joy swept through him. When it was gone his head swam, and tossing off a brandy and soda, let three deals pass, while he struggled to calm himself.

He was better now. Good God! what an escape. Never again as long as he lived. It fell to him to hold the cards. Eight! – 'natural.' In an instant he had pushed a second gilt counter over the line. This time a cold sweat came out over his body, and his mouth grew suddenly quite dry. He made a supreme effort to conceal his agitation by beckoning the waiter to bring him another brandy and soda. Twenty pounds he had won. He had three shining gilt pieces.

After this he was wild to win. In the recklessness of his intoxication

* Derived from the French word for push, this denotes a way of cheating in which one increases one's stake surreptitiously after the conclusion of laying stakes.

he had lost all self-control. It was with a clumsiness that was quite pathetic that he was cheating.

He noticed nothing. Alvary whispered to the croupier, the croupier to a man standing behind him; there was a hushing of the hubbub; the game suddenly flagged. But still he noticed nothing. He was staking three gilt counters on each deal now, increasing them to five if the cards were favourable. All fear of detection had vanished. He only knew that he was winning. It was as if some strange force within him were driving him on – as if he were performing some task, imposed upon him by some unknown authority. Half the room was watching him. But he was aware of nothing.

Yet for a while no onc made any comment. Each shrank from being the first to speak. At last a nervous laugh burst from one of the young bloods in the corner.

'I say, this is a bit too thick!'

The spell was broken. The storm burst.

'Good God!'

'Who is he?'

'What?'

'He must have been at it all night.'

'I know him. Ralston – army man.'

'No – retired.'

'Kick him out.'

'Yes, out with the skunk.'

'The window!' yelled the young 'bloods,' leaping to their feet.

Then above the uproar, quelling it with its harsh imperious note, rang Alvary's voice:

'Gentlemen, gentlemen!'

By degrees there was silence. He was the banker. He had a right to be heard. They waited for him to speak.

'Let the poor devil go,' was all he said.

'No, no.'

'Out with him.'

'Open that window,' yelled a sallow-faced youth.

But from the other side of the room arose a murmur of dissent. Some of the older men made themselves heard.

'No violence.'

'Shut the window.'

'Don't shout.'

And again every one began to speak at once, till the uproar grew quite incoherent. The sallowfaced youth was disputing violently with a man who was trying to shut the window.

'Now's your chance,' said Alvary to Duncan. 'Out you get.'

But the wretched man sat limp, helpless, amid the storm that was raging around him.

'Come, man.' And Alvary, gripping him by the shoulder, shook him. 'They'll chuck you if you don't run for it!'

'Here get him out of the way or those fellows over there will kill him, if they once get at him,' called the fat Stendermann.

Duncan rose and two attendants, at a sign from Alvary, half pushed, half dragged him out of the room.

When those who were for summary measures learnt that he was gone – so great was the uproar that it was fully a minute before they did so – they shouted the louder.

'Who let the blackguard go?' howled the sallow-faced youth.

'I did, young man,' thundered back Stendermann, shouldering his way through the crowd. The threatening attitude of the merchant's bulky frame had its effects on the other. Changing his tone considerably, he stammered:

'Why did you let him go?'

'Because we're not going to have an infernal shindy* because some of you fellows can't play without getting drunk,' interrupted Alvary. The contrast between the heat of his words and the coolness of his demeanour was very striking. The crowd was impressed, for, as he finished speaking, a chorus of approval went round the room.

'Drunk? What the -? Who are you?' burst out the other.

'Look here, stop it,' thundered the merchant, seizing him roughly by the arm, while two or three bystanders instantly put themselves menacingly between Alvary and his antagonist.

'There's been enough for one night,' remarked one.

'Yes, the young idiot. What does he want?'

'Something to settle the drink inside him,' facetiously answered a third.

Alvary stood, his face absolutely unmoved, waiting while the croupier counted his bank.

'Come, let's get out of it,' said some one.

And there was a general move towards the door.

III

Pearl had not gone to bed. Outside the rain pattered against the window-pane; inside the fire was dying, slowly but surely. She wrapped

* A brawl, a quarrel.

the shawl closer about her shoulders; the book that lay on her lap glided on to the ground. And the rain beat against the window-pane a little louder than before.

After Simon had brought her back from the theatre, and, going out again into the night, had left her to herself, the old sinking sense of uneasiness had come upon her. Vain were all her attempts to beat it back. 'It is only because I am unwell,' she kept on insisting to herself. But against the advance of the growing dread she was helpless. Waiting, waiting, waiting, listening for the sound of his key in the door, she sat on.

Her father! what had become of him? Dead – a round, green, nameless grave, or perhaps still alive, sitting in a dingy café, with the yellow–green drink before him. Simon! oh, why did he not come?

Duncan! Was he winning to-night. Those notes! How angry Simon had been when he had snapped his fingers. What was he doing? Perhaps at this moment, now at this very moment, he was taking their money. Oh! why did he not come?

Ah! Stop! What was that? A noise – a knocking – muffled, as if something soft against the door. Ah! there it was again. What could it be? Simon! *It* had come then. She rushed into the hall and struggled to unfasten the door.

Outside the figure of a man. Not Simon – he was too tall. No hat, wet through, his clothes were clinging to his body.

'Who are you? What do you want?' she gasped, hoarse with terror.

'It's me.'

'Ralston. Oh! *comme vous m'avez fait peur! Que faîtes-vous là? Qu'est-il arrive?** Speak, for God's sake! Come in out of the wet.'

She seized his dripping sleeve and pulled him inside the door.

'Here, in here; there's a light here,' as he stumbled in the dark.

She still held him by the sleeve. He dropped heavily into a chair. His matted hair clung close to his forehead: the water dripped from his fingertips on to the carpet.

'Simon – where is he? *Dîtes, je vous supplie!*'† Where is he? What has happened?'

He sent her back a dull stare: he had not understood.

'Speak! for the love of God, speak!' she cried. 'Where is he?'

'He's – he's at the club,' he answered, grasping her meaning with a visible effort.

* 'Oh! how you frightened me! What are you doing there? What has happened?' (French).

† 'Speak, I beg you!' (French).

'There's no danger. Nothing's happened to him?'

'Nothing's happened,' he repeated mechanically. 'No, I suppose nothing's happened to him.'

'But why are you so wet? Where's your hat? and your coat? See! your trousers are covered with mud.'

'Are they?' he asked listlessly.

For an instant neither of them spoke. She, lost in wonder at his woeful appearance; he, stupidly examining the mud on his boots.

'Pearl, I'm done for at last!'

'Done for. How much have you lost? Are they all gone?'

'Lost! worse than lost. They all went. I had only five left, white ones. I tried to win, but – the cards were awful, I was mad – *poussette*. I couldn't help it; it was stronger than myself. At first I won, five times I think. Then they saw. I had to go out – into the street – pouring rain,' and he shivered as he spoke the last words.

She tried to stir the dying fire to a flame.

'Come near,' she said. ' It's not a grand fire. You must take off those wet things. You'll catch cold.'

'No,' he answered, 'leave it.'

'And Simon? What did he do?'

'Simon? He won a great pile. I don't know how much.'

'But when you were discovered?'

'He told me to go out. He and a big, fat man. Don't know his name. German, I think.'

'But you mustn't sit in those wet things. You will kill yourself.'

'I'm going home.'

'Let me get you a coat.'

'No, good-bye.'

'Why good bye? *Au revoir, n'est-ce pas?*'*

'It's good-bye.'

'What are you going to do? You're not going to – '

'No, I've thought of that; I'm going away abroad. I shall start to-morrow. Good-bye.'

'*Adieu.*'†

An instant later, he came back and said, 'Give me a couple of shillings to get home with.'

She handed him her purse.

'Have you got any brandy open?'

She pointed to a decanter and glasses by the door. He drank a wine-

* 'It's just au revoir, isn't it?' (French).

† A more permanent form of farewell than 'au revoir'.

glassful, greedily, as if it were water, then went out again, quickly, without looking behind him.

An instant later the ball door slammed, shaking the whole house.

And Pearl, burying her face in her hands, burst into tears.

In the distance a rattle of wheels, louder and louder – before the house it stopped. She ran to the window and, pushing aside the blind, peeped out. Through the murky atmosphere she perceived that it was a hansom cab. Bang! Bang! the doors flew open. A man stepped out on to the footboard, and stood there, paying the driver. Simon! at last. Now he was opening the door! Now he was in the hall! She did not go to meet him.

There he was! To her surprise, he was unchanged. There was nothing unusual about him – his hair was unruffled, and his shirt-front was spotless and uncrumpled.

'Hulloa, little woman, not gone to bed!' The hard, toneless voice was the same as ever.

She made no answer.

'Has my little Pearl been sitting up all alone for me? But she mustn't do such silly things. Why it's nearly three o'clock.' He put his arms on her shoulders, drawing her towards him.

A slight shudder ran through her; she wrenched herself away.

'*Ne me touche pas.*'*

He stepped back, surveying her critically, puzzling for the reason of her anger.

'What's up?' he asked, not interrogatively, but rather to gain time.

Still she made no answer.

'Come,' he said, taking both her hands in his and softening the hardness of his voice. 'Come, you may as well tell me.'

'*Je sais tout.*'†

'Ah!' The exclamation was deep-drawn, but the slightly theatrical form of her reply had not escaped him. 'That fellow has been here,' he added rapidly.

She nodded, and something in that nod betrayed to him her weakness. There would be no battle, after all, he saw.

Instinctively, he divined what to do. Picking up the novel that lay on the floor, and holding it to the lamp, he turned over its pages. Presently his eye travelled to the mud on the carpet. His eyes blinked briskly, as he sought the interpretation of this sign; as its meaning came there was an almost invisible twitching of his nostrils.

* 'Don't touch me' (French).

† 'I know everything' (French).

He turned and faced her. Their eyes met. He had calculated the strength of his influence. She made one step towards him, and threw both arms round his neck.

'*Simon, je suis si malheureuse!*'* she sobbed.

'There, there,' he said soothingly, stroking her on the back. 'Don't take it so to heart. Don't cry. There, *ma petite* Pearl. Why, you'll make your eyes all red. Now sit down here on my knee and tell me all about it.'

He dropped into an armchair and drew her on to his lap.

'*Je t'aime*,'† she murmured, burying her face in his shoulder.

He sat quite still, waiting, till she should grow calmer. At last she lifted her head. He wiped away her tears and kissed her on both eyes. Then with parted lips, he looked her full in the face. She smiled.

But immediately her face clouded again; the vision of Ralston's bedraggled figure had come back; but it had lost much of its vividness.

'Now tell me all about it,' said Simon. 'What did he want?'

'Nothing; he was wet through, and he had no hat – he said good-bye. He said he was going abroad. *Que deviendra-t-il? Dis!*'‡

'He'll find something to do. They always do.'

'*Mais c'est affreux!*'§

'Well, but if people will do these things.'

'*Mais toi. C'est la même chose, n'est-ce-pas?*'¶

'What do you mean?'

'*Oh! Je l'ai soupçonné depuis – oh! Il y a bien des mois – dis, je t'en supplie. C'est vrai, n'est-ce pas? J'aimerais mieux savoir. Est-ce la même chose?*'**

'You're hurting me – sit a little higher, more to one side. That's it. No, by Jove! it's not quite the same thing – not by a long chalk,' and he laughed mirthlessly.

'*Mais tu gagnes toujours!*'††

'And where would the little Pearl be if I didn't?'

This indirect reminder of all she owed him touched her; she drew a little closer to him.

'*Mais si tu gagnes toujours.*'‡‡

* 'Simon, I'm so unhappy' (French).

† 'I love you' (French).

‡ 'What will become of him? Say!' (French).

§ 'But it's terrible!' (French)

¶ 'But you. It's the same thing, isn't it?' (French)

** 'Oh! I've suspected for – oh! months now – tell me, I beg you. It's true, isn't it? I'd prefer to know. Is it the same thing?' (French).

†† 'But you always win!' (French).

‡‡ 'But if you always win' (French).

'Yes, I always take good care of that.'

'*Le danger. Ce doît être terrible!*'

'No.'

'*Mais lui.*'

'That's different. He lost his head.'

'*Il n'y a pas de danger, alors.*'

'No, not for me.'

'*Mais si tu étais découvert?*'*

'I never shall.' At the absolute decision in his voice, her face brightened. The movement was not lost upon him.

'Now, little woman, are you reassured?'

She did not answer, yet he could see the conflict within her was practically at an end.

'*Combien as-tu gagné ce soir?*'†

'Six hundred and thirty-four.'

'Pounds?'

'Of course.'

She caught her breath in astonishment.

'*Mon Dieu!*' she exclaimed.‡

Then she looked up at him, and there was admiration in her eyes.

'You won't hide things from me now. Promise, when you are away, you will tell me what has happened – everything. Won't you? You can trust me. I swear you can trust me.'

'Yes, *ma petite* Pearl. In the future you shall know everything. You shall be the banker and keep all the money for me. Would you like that?'

'*Oui.*' The word shot out quickly between her teeth.

'Six hundred and thirty-four pounds!' she repeated, half to herself. 'How much is that in francs?'

'Nearly sixteen thousand.'

'And my Pearl isn't angry any more?

'*Je t'aime*,' she murmured in reply.

Their lips met.

* Pearl's four utterances (in French) mean respectively: 'The danger. It must be terrible!'; 'But him'; 'So then there's no danger?'; and "But if you were discovered?'

† 'How much did you win this evening?' (French).

‡ 'My God!' (French). Pearl's surprise and admiration are warranted. This is a large sum of money in 1892.

EMBERS

The room was small, but the twilight shadows made it appear larger. An iron bedstead; two tables, one covered with papers, the other with a white cloth; a chair by the door, and on it a mud-splashed pair of trousers and a dirty shirt, with a pair of old slippers, trodden down at the heels, underneath; a black, shiny armchair, its horsehair stuffing protruding in places; a deal chest of drawers – this was all the furniture. No kind of ornament, bare walls, not a spot of colour to relieve the cheerlessness.

Yet presently, as one looked, two or three details betrayed something of the individuality of the occupant.

The papers on the writing-table were arranged in neat stacks; the shirt on the chair had been carefully folded; the slippers lay side by side; but it was the mechanical precision of habit, and not a love of tidiness; for the room was far from clean, and looked almost squalid.

But when he came in, he noticed none of these things.

A lean young man, with a hesitating gait and tired stoop; lank hair streaked with grey; a yellow, parchment-like skin that puckered in wrinkles round the eyes, and gave a shrivelled look to the whole face; and in the eyes a startling dulness.

He lit the little lamp with the green cardboard shade, hung up his hat and his overcoat behind the door, took off his boots and laid them together, just as he had done every evening for the last five years. He lifted up the dirty shirt, and, after looking closely at the cuffs, folded it again, and replaced it on the chair. Then he fetched a brush from off the chest of drawers, and began carefully to clean the mud-splashed trousers.

When he had nearly finished, the servant-girl brought in his dinner.

'Good evening,' he said, without looking up.

'Good evening, Mr. Gorridge,' she answered.

And he began to eat the cold mutton and the boiled potatoes methodically.

As a rule, when his dinner was finished, he seated himself at the writing-table, to copy manuscripts at a half-penny a folio or to address envelopes at fourpence a hundred. It was not so much for the sake of the money, for he had but few wants, and his salary was more than enough to supply them. He had taken to it long ago, when the mechanical work had kept him from brooding over his trouble; and gradually the habit had grown upon him, till it was an inseparable part of his existence. Narrower and narrower had become the groove in which his life ran, and now each day was a counterpart of the preceding one.

But to-night, when the servant girl had taken away the half-finished leg of mutton, he turned round his chair and stared into the empty grate.

February 18th, said the almanack on the wall opposite. February 18th, the day on which she had gone. With a yearning, dull and immense, like the yearning for home of the solitary traveller, he was thinking of his married life – quite hazily; for five years of unconscious crystallization had vaguely beautified them for him.

And then he lived over again the moment when he had come back from the City* to find her gone, gone with not a word of explanation.

Most of that night and all the next day he had spent in wild search for her. The next three days he was in bed, unable to get up. On the morning of the fourth day, fearing to lose his place, he had dragged himself down to the City as usual. And afterwards, for weeks, every evening as he mounted the stairs, his heart thumped excitedly with the hope that he would find her back again. But she never came.

He changed his lodgings, for the hundred and one little things that brought her back to him made the rooms unbearable.

* * * * *

Outside, a drizzling rain. The gas lamps shone a dim, filthy yellow, streaking the slimy pavement with their reflections. There was no sky, only a murky atmosphere overhead. And save for a woman creeping along, the street was deserted. Her slatternly clothes hung loosely about her; her skirt trailed in the mud. She was quite wet, for she had no umbrella.

Underneath his window she stopped, and for a moment she stood in the doorway out of the rain.

During that moment, the thoughts of the man in the little bedroom above, sitting staring into the empty grate, and the thoughts of the bedraggled figure in the doorway below, went out towards each other.

She could only think in a foggy sort of way, for she had already had a drink or two. There were many things which were blurred; many things about which she was not sure. Her recollection of their separation was dim; she scarcely understood how it had come about. She wondered feebly where he was, what he was doing. Yet her cunning instinct told her he would take her back, in spite of it all, and that once more, she could do with him what she would. It seemed that they were

* The financial district of London.

together. He was so simple, so confiding,* that during the day when he was down at the City, she did what she liked. She would be careful, of course, so that he never found out anything.

Then she moved out again into the wet, and stumbled along towards the lights of the publichouse at the corner.

* * * * *

It was inevitable that it would come, sooner or later, for she slept over the public-house at the end of the street, and he passed it every day on his way to the City. Yet it was several days before she saw him. When he went by in the morning, she was seldom out of bed, and when he came back in the evening, she was generally drunk.

But once she woke early, and looked out through the grimy window-pane.

There he was! She could see his back, as he hurried away down the street. But there was no mistaking the narrow, sloping shoulders, the jerky, nervous gait, with the head thrust forward. She even remembered the black overcoat; he had bought it just after their marriage. It used to be a shiny one, several sizes too large for him, and to hang in baggy wrinkles about the armpits. And she fell to dreaming, recalling vague, half-blurred little incidents.

He was found now. A quarter to nine. He was on his way to the City; well she knew that, when evening came, he would return by the same way. All she had to do was to wait for him, and to keep her head clear. So back she went to her dirty bed and fell into a fitful sleep.

About three o'clock, with a low, sickly feeling, she awoke. But as she slipped into her tawdry garments, her spirits rose. This was the last day; to-morrow she would be a respectable married woman in comfortable lodgings, with a man to earn money for her. She went down to the bar, and ordered a large pewter of beer. She always lunched off a large pewter, never having any appetite till evening.

Presently two women, one of whom she knew, came in. She felt in her pocket. Half a crown. Her last. But what odds?† To-morrow he would give her plenty more. So she recklessly stood drinks to the new-comers.

And thus through the afternoon, and with the idea that she must catch him on his return increasing in force as she grew more and more drunk.

She talked loudly and volubly, explaining to the two others all about

* 'Confiding' means 'trusting' here.

† What did it matter?

him, and dilating on all the things she would do when he had taken her back. They listened stupidly, nodding gravely at intervals.

About six o'clock they found themselves with no more money and with nothing more to drink, so, holding each other by the arm, they sallied forth into the street to wait for him.

* * * * *

He was hastening home, thinking of the bundle of manuscript which bulged his pocket, whether he would be able to copy it all before eleven, the hour when he always went to bed.

Of a sudden something clutching at his arm – a woman! – looking up into his face, with the glare of the gas-lamp lighting up her senseless leer. She did not speak, only leered the more, and hung heavier and heavier on his arm.

He made a half frightened, half indignant movement to shake her off. Next he recognised her. She did not know that he had done so, for he did not start, nor make any sound. Only first his features, then his whole body stiffened, till he stood as if petrified.

'Don't you know me Frank?' she stuttered. There was no reply, and it dawned upon her that he did.

'What are you looking so scared at? One would think you'd never seen me before,' she continued with a sickly smile. 'I'm not as I was, I know that. I've had a hard time of it, a cruel hard time of it,' she whined; 'but I've come back to be your dutiful wife once more,' and she leered the same, senseless leer. 'Where are your digs? Somewhere along this way, eh?' And pulling him by the arm, she dragged him down the street. His feeble resistance only lasted an instant.

When they reached the door, his hand shook so violently, that it was nearly a minute before he could fit the key into the keyhole. Automatically he lit the little lamp with the green cardboard shade, hung up his hat and overcoat behind the door, and was about to take off his boots, when his eye fell on her. With a start he stopped short.

She was lying in an armchair, looking round the room.

' No great shakes, this drawing-room of yours. Just you wait till I've been here a day or two, and see how I'll smarten it up. It's beastly cold and no fire.'

At this moment the servant-girl came in to lay the cloth. On seeing the stranger, she stepped back, looking in astonishment from one to the other.

'Well, stupid, what are you staring at? Look sharp. I'm hungry. Let's see. Soup – soup to begin with. Fish, no, no fish – beastly smelly stuff; I can't stomach it. Tripe and baked potatoes to follow, and here, fetch a bottle of beer, look alive; don't stand there like a blasted lamp-post.'

The servant-girl fled, slamming the door behind her. And the two relapsed into silence, he, standing staring at her, in terror-stricken rigidity.

Exasperated, she turned to him.

'What the devil's the matter with you? A nice way to receive back your loving wife, after all these years. Good God! man, you look like a blooming mummy!'

The door opened violently. In burst a heavy, stout woman, her face flushed with passion.

'Now, Mr. Gorridge,' she cried. 'What's the meaning of this? I'm not going to stand it, d'ye hear? What are you looking so dazed at? Why, God bless my soul, I believe the man's off his head!' And raising her voice still louder: 'Now then, hussy, clear out quick. What do you take me for, I should like to know? I've always kept a respectable house, and I ain't goin' to begin to have the likes of you about now!'

'Dry up your damned impudence,' stuttered the other, staggering to her feet. 'Why, I'm his lawful wife. We were married in church. I've been away on business, these last three years. And it's a hard time of it that I've had,' and she wound up with a whine.

'Get out, you drunken beast,' shouted the elder woman, 'or if you don't I'll soon make you.'

And, seizing her by the shoulders, she began to push her towards the door. The other kicked and struggled, but it was of no use. There was a scuffle on the staircase, an oath from the drunken woman, a crash as of something falling, and the front door banged.

'If you ever dare to set foot inside my house again,' called the landlady through the door, 'I'll send the police after you.'

And, as she re-entered the room: 'Mr. Gorridge, just you understand this, I'll have none of these goings on in my house. You ought to be ashamed of yourself, at your age.'

But he lay in a heap in the armchair, staring fixedly into the empty grate.

Seeing that he paid no heed, she bounced out of the room with a snort of contempt.

Quite still he lay, his limbs huddled together while the servant-girl, openly casting indignant glances at him, prepared his dinner.

Half an hour passed. The food was untouched. He had not moved.

'Ain't you going to have no dinner, Mr. Gorridge?' asked the girl, with a touch of compassion in her voice.

He made no sound, so she took away the things.

How long he had been there he did not know. He was cold; the cramped position had stiffened his legs; the lamp had gone out; it was quite dark.

He struck a match, and clumsily lit it again. Then, undressing, crept into bed.

* * * * *

When he awoke his mind was blank. Mechanically he looked at the chair on which his clothes always lay folded. It was empty. In a heap, there they were on the floor.

A quick spasm, contracting his features, and he remembered, and, with a gesture of indescribable weariness, began to dress.

That day he did his work at the office as usual, only he looked more yellow and more wizened than ever. But no one noticed it.

In the evening, he no longer hurried along the street towards home, absently with his head thrust forward. Slowly he crept, with cautious, cat-like movements.

From a doorway, out burst a boy with a basket. He started aside like a frightened animal.

It was only when he had passed the spot where she had met him yesterday, that he seemed reassured. Quickening his pace, he fell again into his accustomed, jerky gait.

But presently, he caught sight of something coming in the distance. By instinct he knew that it was she. On he hastened, his eyes on the pavement, till they came face to face.

'Frank,' she began in a voice broken by maudlin sobs, 'don't you think that I'm going to bother you any more. I'm a miserable, lost creature. I know I am. I'll never trouble you again, Frank; only give me something to keep body and soul together. I haven't a blessed sixpence,' here she stopped, watching him intently.

He had pulled out his purse, and was emptying its contents into his hand. Three half-crowns, a shilling and four coppers – he handed them all to her, and, without a word, turned to go in.

'Good-night, Frank my darling,' she called after him. 'You're a trump, you are.'

* * * * *

The next three days passed, and she never appeared.

Back his life dropped into the old groove, till it all seemed like a bad dream, and sometimes he wondered whether it had really happened.

Then she met him again, with the same maudlin tears. He gave her a sovereign, for that morning he had received his salary.

After this she took to waylaying him almost every evening. Sometimes, he could only give her a copper or two, sometimes half a crown, sometimes – on Saturdays – gold. He scarcely ever spoke to her, and seemed relieved when she left him on the doorstep. Once she spoke of coming up.

'To-morrow is Saturday,' he said in a hurried voice. She understood, and went away.

At the end of a fortnight, he was unable to pay his weekly bill. This was the first time since he had lodged there, and the thought gnawed him night and day.

His landlady said nothing, but when at the end of the second week no money was forthcoming, she grumbled sullenly.

And he began to age strangely, thinner and thinner his hair became, till he was almost quite bald.

* * * * *

. . . About three weeks later – night-time – the little street was black and still – on the doorstep, two figures.

'I am going on Saturday,' said he.

'Going? Why? Where?' she answered.

'I can't pay the rent,' he said simply.

Face to face, they stood. In his eyes the vacant stare of complete weariness; in hers a look of silent suffering. Quicker and quicker her face quivered. Big tears rolled down her cheeks.

And as he watched her, his vacant stare passed away; in its place came the soft light of compassion.

'Don't cry, Mag,' he said gently.

At the sound of this little pet name, coming again for the first time at the end of all these years, she broke down.

It was the hysterical sobbing of a ruined nervous system; it was very painful to hear.

'Don't cry, Mag,' he repeated.

But she sobbed on, her frame rocking with convulsive throbs.

Bewildered he looked about him. Then timidly, he put his arm round her saying once more:

'Don't cry, little Mag.'

By degrees the fit spent itself. She stood quite still at last, her head resting on his shoulder. After a moment, she stepped back and looked again into his eyes.

The features were quite composed, but the lips were bloodless.

'Frank,' she said with an intenseness that revealed the tumult within. 'Frank, will you forgive me?'

The old spasm of pain, contracting the features, came back.

She saw it.

'I don't mean that,' she said hurriedly. 'I'm too bad for that. Only say that you forgive me.'

He pondered a moment perplexed, his eyes blinking rapidly.

Then looking at her, and seeing that she was waiting for his answer:

'I forgive you,' he murmured.

Holding out her hand – 'Good-bye,' she said.

'Good-bye,' he answered mechanically.

And she stepped on to the pavement, and moved slowly away down the street.

1891–1892

Appendices

A note on the appendices

The texts in the following seven appendices have been chosen to illustrate aspects of Crackanthorpe's thinking about fiction and to provide a context for the writing in *Wreckage*. The first two texts – 'Realism in France and England: An Interview with M. Emile Zola' and 'Reticence in Literature' – indicate how Crackanthorpe saw the literary scene in the early 1890s. The former is a lively, slightly irreverent, affectionate and admiring picture of one of the greatest of European novelists, a figure of intense controversy and high regard in the 1890s. The latter shows how Crackanthorpe himself, in a nuanced fashion, saw literary trends of his day. The text deserves to be better known, as it is a complex endorsement of the innovation that many younger and older writers were aware of and aspired to in the *fin-de-siècle*.

Appendices 3–5 contain work by Crackanthorpe from the time after the publication of *Wreckage*. 'The Haseltons' was published independently in *The Yellow Book* in April 1895, but appeared as the second half of 'A Commonplace Chapter' in *Sentimental Studies*, published later that year. Both 'The White Maize' and the extracts from *Vignettes* show the young author attempting different types of writing from those in *Wreckage*: an austere study of French rural life and subjective evocations of French landscape, English *mœurs* of the mid-1890s and London cityscape.

As Crackanthorpe is often seen as an English disciple of Guy de Maupassant's work, I thought it would be of interest to the Anglophone reader to consider a short story by the French author in translation, and to assess where Crackanthorpe is in some measure working over similar themes and deploying similar techniques to those of Maupassant. The translation is mine, and I have usually chosen to reflect French vocabulary and syntax more than I would under other circumstances. Crackanthorpe, I believe, is thematically and technically close to some of Maupassant's work, but he does not actually employ the same syntax as the French author. It is worth stressing, too, that Maupassant's range is much greater than Crackanthorpe's had a chance to become.

The final appendix contains a short story by Crackanthorpe's wife,

Leila Macdonald, published in *The Yellow Book* in October 1894. The similarities in the couple's work – French provincial life, the cruelty of circumstance and persons – are immediately apparent. However, the religious motifs of Macdonald's writing are rarely reflected in her husband's texts, and certainly not to the degree that they are in 'Jeanne-Marie'.

Appendix 1

Realism in France and England: An Interview with M. Emile Zola*
The Albemarle 1.2 (February 1892): 39–43

'*Les parvenus se meublent toujours le salon qu'ils ont ambitionné autrefois dans leurs souhaits de jeunes gens pauvres.*'† I had never completely realized the truth of this remark of Balzac's until I stood the other day in M. Zola's gorgeously furnished study in the Rue de Bruxelles, Paris.

I called to mind the struggles of his early years; how, having failed in the one examination which in France leads to everything,‡ he had started in a wretched situation in the docks, not worth three pounds a month. I thought of the three whole years of hand-to-hand battling with starvation, that had followed. . . . Adrift on the pavement, doing nothing, with no future before him. . . . Hunger, misery, debts, and constant visits to the pawn-shop. How strange life is!

Yes, Balzac was right, '*l'ameublement trahit l'homme.*'§ M.¶ Zola began his literary career under the influence of Victor Hugo and the poets of 1830,** and it is singular how every object in the workroom of the great realist of today answers to the romanticist of thirty years ago . . . the heavy, Oriental carpet, medieval tapestries on the walls, stained glass in the windows, old Italian and Dutch furniture scattered here and there, the splendidly carved black oak writing-table, with an enormous high-backed chair – almost a throne – behind.

But, as I gaze curiously around, the entry of the great man himself suddenly interrupts my reflections.

'*Bonjour,*' he says, buttoning up his smoking-jacket. 'Ugh! how cold

* Émile Zola (1840–92) was one of the greatest and most controversial French novelists of the nineteenth century. He was known for his championship of realist writing, aspirations to make fiction a scientific depiction of society, and a predilection for the seamier aspects of life.

† 'Those who have made it always furnish the salon that they once aspired to in their wishes when they were young and poor' (French).

‡ In 1859, Zola failed the *baccalauréat*, a school-leaving examination, success in which would have made it possible to attend university or pursue a profession.

§ 'furnishing betrays the man' (French). This seems not to be a direct quotation from Balzac's work.

¶ A standard abbreviation for Monsieur: that is, Mr.

** Victor Hugo (1802–85) is one of the most prominent French nineteenth-century writers. He enjoyed great (and sometimes controversial) success in poetry, fiction and theatre, and was and is seen as the chief French Romantic author.

it is!' and drawing in a chair, vigorously stirs the wood fire on the hearth.

I at once notice several changes in him since we last met. He is considerably thinner, the pointed beard is more grey, the hair – in the old days always cut short – is now long and brushed back; there is, too, a tired, worn look about the cheeks. Yet, after all, it is the same short, thick-set figure, the heavy gait, which is characteristic of another famous '*littérateur*' – Mr. Walter Pater* – the complexion a strange, dull yellow, the eyes small and keen. The most striking feature in his physiognomy is the neck. Its short and bull-like column gives to the whole face a look of power and solid strength.

'Well,' continued M. Zola, '*causons.*† What are they saying about me in England? My friends over there tell me that one or two of your leading reviews have been devoting articles to the supposed death of realism in France.'

'Yes, and is it not so? Are there not on all sides signs of a reaction?'

'Realism dead!' interrupted M. Zola, fidgeting nervously with a paper-cutter. 'But you don't know what you are saying. No more realism! You might as well say that there will be no more sun, no more stars, no more trees. Realism, naturalism, whatever name you give it, is but the result of man's continued search after truth. And that search after truth will exist as long as the human race continues to progress. Now, with regard to the literary situation in France. Our conception of realistic fiction is probably destined to be developed, transformed. It would be absurd, were it not so. In nature, everything is by degrees developed, transformed. It is the same in art. It may be that we – Flaubert, Daudet, Goncourt and myself‡ – have been a little sectarian, a little dogmatic. After all, it was but natural, for as leaders of a movement we were obliged to make our formula as definite and as precise as possible. Yes,' he added meditatively, 'there will be an expansion of our formula.'

'And what shape do you think this expansion will take?'

'Ah!' he answered, shaking his head. '*je ne sais pas . . . je ne sais pas . . . que voulez-vous que je vous dise?*§ We have perhaps been too

* Walter Pater (1839–94), author of essays in *The Renaissance* (1873) and of the novel *Marius the Epicurean* (1885), was a considerable influence on *avant-garde* writers of the 1880s and 1890s. A *littérateur* is a man of letters.

† 'Let us chat' (French).

‡ Gustave Flaubert (1821–80) and Alphonse Daudet (1840–97) were eminent French novelists. Zola is probably referring in the singular to Edmond Goncourt (1822–96), who, with his shorter-lived brother Jules (1830–70), was an influential realist novelist. Crackanthorpe takes the epigraph to *Wreckage* from one of their novels.

§ 'I don't know . . . I don't know . . . what do you want me to tell you?' (French).

absolute, too positive. We have studied the human being a little too much from the point of view of the senses; and there will be, I think, a new movement towards the great Unknown – towards – *mais je ne sais pas . . . que voulez-vous que je vous dise?*'

'Do you think then that this reaction is near at hand?'

'First of all,' rapidly answered M. Zola, restlessly shifting his position, 'You must remember that I am not yet dead, and the present naturalistic formula will find it hard to die without me. But besides, I see no signs of its dying at present. Every great movement in literature is the outcome of a corresponding great social movement. Literature is an expression of the life of the nation, and the best literature of each epoch is that which best expresses the national life of that epoch. Now our age is an age which is thirsting after truth. We see this in many ways; in the progress of Positivism,* in the development of democracy, and above all in the enormous strides made by science. Our realistic movement represents all these things; thus we are the outcome of the temper of our age. This temper is so far from decaying that it is being developed further and further. And moreover among our young men there is no one strong enough to become the leader of a new school. I therefore see no reason for expecting an immediate reaction in literature, at least as far as the novel is concerned.'

'But what about poetry?'

'Ah! Poetry! Yes, that is a little different. In 1789 we killed our gods, and set up in their place Science.† From her, during these last hundred years, we have been expecting everything, and though I believe that she has done much to brighten our lives, our progress is but gradual and slow, while man's aspirations advance by leaps and bounds. That the weaker and more impatient spirits should at last revolt against her was inevitable. Hence all this so-called symbolist movement in poetry, these attempts to return to the first beginnings of art, only resulting in vague scribbling, in obscure, stuttering verses.‡ These symbolist poets seem to think that by their senseless reaction they can overthrow the literary formula of their epoch. And when we point out to them the

* Positivism was an important and influential nineteenth-century philosophy of history, society and action. Promulgated in the work of the French philosopher Auguste Comte (1798–1857), it promoted an objective observation of social circumstances that many mid- and late nineteenth-century novelists (the English George Eliot among them) found inspiring.

† The year 1789 is a traditional date used to mark the beginning of the French Revolution.

‡ In French literary history, the term symbolist poetry is usually taken to refer to the work of Charles Baudelaire (1821–67), Arthur Rimbaud (1854–91), Paul Verlaine (1844–96) and Isidore Ducasse (Lautréamont) (1846–70).

folly of it all, they throw the romanticist movement at our heads. The romanticist movement indeed!' continued M. Zola, getting up and walking excitedly up and down the room, 'that was the logical outcome of the Revolution and the wars of the first Empire.* The language, worn out by three centuries of classicism, was in need of fresh blood, of enrichment, in fact of a complete renovation. But what need has it to-day of enrichment, of renovation? And what social movement does this symbolism represent? *C'est de la littérature de brasserie.*'†

'Now, tell me about the novel in England,' he said, evidently desirous of changing the subject. '*Qu'est-ce qu'on y fait?*‡ Unfortunately your literature is a sealed book to me, except through translations, and so few of your new writers have been translated. The fact is that we French are very ignorant, and what is worse, we are very indifferent to what goes on beyond our frontiers. Who are your realists?'

'Well, there is Mr. George Moore.'§

'Ah! Yes, of course, my friend Moore. *Il a beaucoup de talent.*¶ I think very highly of his 'Mummer's Wife'**: it is full of power. But he is almost alone, is he not? Ah! I thought so. You English are so essentially Protestant. We over here cannot understand your Protestantism, just as you can never understand our Catholicity. All this puritanism†† of yours is very curious. It would seem as if it were almost an element in your national genius, yet I know no literature more healthily brutal and vigorous than that of Shakespeare, Jonson, and their contemporaries.‡‡ However, you have got under the yoke of the puritans, and as long as you remain so, you will never have a really fine literary outburst. But, from what I hear, there are signs of an approaching reaction. Our work is attracting more attention, is it not? It is more freely discussed than it was. And your stage, too, is getting emancipated. This Independent

* The First Empire is the name later given to the French state after Napoleon Bonaparte's declaration of himself as Emperor in 1804 until the defeat of French Imperial forces in the years 1814–15. The Second French Empire designates the regime of Napoleon III (Louis-Napoléon Bonaparte, the nephew of the first Napoleon), who, after a coup d'état in 1851, was proclaimed Emperor in 1852. The Second Empire lasted until France's defeat by Prussia and her allies in the Franco-Prussian War of 1870.

† 'It's the literature of the bar-room' (French).

‡ 'What are they up to there?' (French).

§ George Moore (1852–1933), Irish novelist.

¶ 'He has lots of talent' (French).

** *A Mummer's Wife* was published in 1885.

†† In what follows, it becomes clear that by puritanism Zola means prudery and a reluctance to deal with the sordid aspects of human life.

‡‡ William Shakespeare (1564–1616) and Ben Jonson (1573–1637), Elizabethan and Jacobean playwrights and poets. The late sixteenth- and early seventeenth-century English stage was always seen as a provocation to the neo-classical and rule-bound French theatre.

Theatre* is an excellent sign. My little "Thérese [sic] Raquin" excited quite a little battle, they tell me.† All that is good.'

'And Ibsen too,' I put in. 'We have had several of Ibsen's plays produced in London this year, and one of them at least was a great success.'‡

M. Zola was turning over the uncut pages of M. Ferdinand Fabre's last novel§: he did not seem to hear what I was saying.

'What do you think about Ibsen's work,' I continued.

'Ibsen!' he answered without raising his eyes, '*c'est bien obscur*.'¶

'But wouldn't you say – ?'

'*C'est bien obscur. Tout cela est bien obscur*,' he repeated, shrugging his shoulders – '*parlons d'autre chose*.'**

It was hopeless, I saw. The great man declined to be drawn.

'Which of our English novelists are most appreciated in France?'

'There is no difficulty in answering that question,' he replied, smiling at my sudden change of front; 'Dickens and Scott,†† without a doubt, and for this very obvious reason: the novel in France has always been more or less emancipated, while the works of Dickens and Scott can be put into the hands of anyone, which is more than can be said even for the works of George Sand.‡‡ Besides, Dickens is a poet, a great poet in many ways. He is less English than most of your writers, and that is why we understand him better. But he ignores all the greater side of man – love, and all the big emotions of life – and above all, woman. He knows nothing at all about women.'

'And Scott?'

* The Independent Theatre Society was established in London in 1891 in order to stage plays (such as those by Henrik Ibsen or by Zola) that would never have received a licence to be performed publicly from the British government office responsible for stage censorship. The Society performed plays to members only. Crackanthorpe and his parents belonged to it.

† *Thérèse Raquin* (1868), a novel of adultery and murder, was turned into a play by Zola himself in 1873.

‡ The plays of Henrik Ibsen (1828–1906) were performed successfully, if controversially, in London in the late 1880s and early 1890s. Crackanthorpe is probably referring to an 1891 production of Ibsen's *Ghosts*.

§ Ferdinand Fabre (1827–98), French novelist. In the nineteenth century, new novels often came with the edges of every set of two pages attached to each other.

¶ 'That's pretty obscure' (French).

** 'That's pretty obscure. All that is pretty obscure . . . let's speak about something else.'

†† Charles Dickens (1812–1870) and Walter Scott (1771–1832), British novelists. Scott, who was Scottish, was the most influential English-language novelist in continental Europe in the nineteenth century. Zola is not very up to date here.

‡‡ George Sand (1804–76), French novelist. Sand was the pseudonym of Aurore Dupin, who wrote novels of intense emotional states, often of women, and politically committed novels.

'Scott!' he answered with a wave of his hand, '*littérature de pensionnat*.* There is another reason for Dickens's success over here,' he continued, following up his train of thought. 'Our opponents have taken him up to use him as an argument against our conception of realism, and at one time our reviews were flooded with articles on Dickens. Tolstoi† has been taken up in the same way, but his success was never real, like that of Dickens.'

'And Thackeray?'‡

'Thackeray! Ah! *Je ne sais pas*,'§ with a shrug of the shoulders . . . 'deeper than Dickens, yes, certainly deeper than Dickens. But it is so difficult to understand it all. It is so English. For instance, there is George Eliot,¶ who has been lauded up to the skies by Brunetière and the Academic party.** *Eh bien! Ça n'a pas pris du tout*.†† She was *très savante, très instruite*,‡‡ but she had no real knowledge of humanity. She gives me the impression of never having been outside her library door. She seems only to know her humanity through books. "The Mill on the Floss" – *voyons, ça ne vaut pas grand'chose en somme, hein*?§§ Do you think much of it in England?'

I nodded.

'It is all,' he repeated, 'so utterly opposed to the genius of the French people.'

Then after a pause –

'*Voyons, tous les trois ensemble ne valent pas les grandes machines de Balzac?*'¶¶

At this moment our conversation was interrupted by the furious entry of a little black spaniel, who flew barking and snapping round my chair.

I rose to go.

* 'Boarding-school literature' (French).

† Lev Nikolayevich Tolstoi (or Tolstoy) (1828–1910), celebrated Russian novelist.

‡ William Makepeace Thackeray (1811–63), English novelist.

§ 'I don't know' (French).

¶ George Eliot (Mary Anne/Marion Evans) (1819–1880), English novelist.

** Ferdinand Brunetière (1849–1906), French critic and scholar, no friend to realist fiction, especially Zola's.

†† 'Well! That didn't ever catch on' (French).

‡‡ 'She was very knowledgeable, very well educated' (French).

§§ 'Let's see, it's not worth much altogether, eh?' (French). *The Mill on the Floss* is – *pace* Zola – George Eliot's magnificent novel of 1860.

¶¶ 'See, all the three together are no match for Balzac's great machines?' (French). Honoré de Balzac (1799–1850), French novelist, author of many ambitious and powerful depictions of French society, in an interlinked sequence of novels entitled *La Comédie humaine* (The Human Comedy).

'*Il ne faut pas que Bibi vous chasse*,'* said M. Zola, holding out his hand. 'You have been lucky,' he said, 'to get a drawing from Whistler for your first number,† . . . a great artist, . . . a great artist. Well, good-bye. I am very glad to have seen you. I wish you all success. Send me your review when you get another Whistler. Down, Bibi! Down! . . . don't be afraid, he won't bite,' and as I went down the staircase – '*Il faut de la patience en Angleterre . . . de la patience. Tout vient à qui sait attendre*.'‡

* 'Bibi doesn't have to chase you away' (French).

† James Abbott McNeill Whistler (1834–1903), American-born artist, trained in Paris and settled in England. He contributed a drawing to the first number of *The Albemarle* in January 1892.

‡ 'You need patience in England . . . patience. All things come to him who waits' (French).

Appendix 2

Reticence in Literature: Some Roundabout Remarks
The Yellow Book 2 (July 1894): 259–69

During the past fifty years, as every one knows, the art of fiction has been expanding in a manner exceedingly remarkable, till it has grown to be the predominant branch of imaginative literature. But§ the other day we were assured that poetry only thrives in limited and exquisite editions; that the drama, here in England at least, has practically ceased to be literature at all. Each epoch instinctively chooses that literary vehicle which is best adapted for the expression of its particular temper: just as the drama flourished in the robust age of Shakespeare and Ben Jonson; just as that outburst of lyrical poetry, at the beginning of the century in France, coincided with a period of extreme emotional exaltation; so the novel, facile and flexible in its conventions, with its endless opportunities for accurate delineation of reality, becomes supreme in a time of democracy and of science – to note but these two salient characteristics.

And, if we pursue this light [sic] of thought, we find that, on all sides, the novel is being approached in one especial spirit, that it would seem to be striving, for the moment at any rate, to perfect itself within certain definite limitations. To employ a hackneyed, and often quite unintelligent, catchword – the novel is becoming realistic.

Throughout the history of literature, the jealous worship of beauty – which we term idealism – and the jealous worship of truth – which we term realism – have alternately prevailed. Indeed, it is within the compass of these alternations that lies the whole fundamental diversity of literary temper.

Still, the classification is a clumsy one, for no hard and fast line can be drawn between the one spirit and the other. The so-called idealist must take as his point of departure the facts of Nature; the so-called realist must be sensitive to some one or other of the forms of beauty, if each would achieve the fineness of great art. And the pendulum of production is continually swinging, from degenerate idealism to degenerate realism, from effete vapidity to slavish sordidity.†

Either term, then, can only be employed in a purely limited and

§ Only.
† Sordidness, coarseness, the squalid, baseness.

relative sense. Completely idealistic art – art that has no point of contact with the facts of the universe, as we know them – is, of course, an impossible absurdity; similarly, a complete reproduction of Nature by means of words is an absurd impossibility. Neither emphasization* nor abstraction can be dispensed with: the one, eliminating the details of no import; the other, exaggerating those which the artist has selected. And, even were such a thing possible, it would not be Art. The invention of a highly perfected system of coloured photography, for instance, or a skilful recording by means of the phonograph† of scenes in real life, would not subtract one whit from the value of the painter's or the playwright's interpretation. Art is not invested with the futile function of perpetually striving after imitation or reproduction of Nature; she endeavours to produce, through the adaptation of a restricted number of natural facts, an harmonious and satisfactory whole. Indeed, in this very process of adaptation and blending together, lies the main and greater task of the artist. And the novel, the short story, even the impression of a mere incident, convey each of them, the imprint of the temper in which their creator has achieved this process of adaptation and blending together of his material. They are inevitably stamped with the hall-mark of his personality. A work of art can never be more than a corner of Nature, seen through the temperament of a single man.‡ Thus, all literature is, must be, essentially subjective; for style is but the power of individual expression. The disparity which separates literature from the reporter's transcript is ineradicable. There is a quality of ultimate suggestiveness to be achieved; for the business of art is, not to explain or to describe, but to suggest. That attitude of objectivity, or of impersonality towards his subject, consciously or unconsciously, assumed by the artist, and which nowadays provokes so considerable an admiration, can be attained only in a limited degree. Every piece of imaginative work must be a kind of autobiography of its creator – significant, if not of the actual facts of his existence, at least of the inner working of his soul. We are each of us conscious, not of the whole world, but of our own world; not of naked reality, but of that aspect of reality which our peculiar temperament enables us to appropriate. Thus, every narrative of an external circumstance is never anything else than the transcript of the impression produced upon ourselves by that circumstance, and, invariably, a degree of individual

* This word is not recorded in *The New Shorter Oxford English Dictionary*.

† An early version of the gramophone, using a cylinder, not a disc. It was possible to record as well as play sounds on it.

‡ Crackanthorpe is echoing Zola's observations in *Le Roman expérimental* (The Experimental Novel) (1880).

interpretation is insinuated into every picture, real or imaginary, however objective it may be. So then, the disparity between the so-called idealist and the so-called realist is a matter, not of æsthetic philosophy, but of individual temperament. Each is at work, according to the especial bent of his genius, within precisely the same limits. Realism, as a creed, is as ridiculous as any other literary creed.

Now, it would have been exceedingly curious if this recent specialisation of the art of fiction, this passion for draining from the life, as it were, born, in due season, of the general spirit of the latter half of the nineteenth century, had not provoked a considerable amount of opposition – opposition of just that kind which every new evolution in art inevitably encounters. Between the vanguard and the main body there is perpetual friction.

But time flits quickly in this hurried age of ours, and the opposition to the renascence of fiction as a conscientious interpretation of life is not what it was; its opponents are not the men they were. It is not so long since a publisher was sent to prison for issuing English translations of celebrated specimens of French realism*; yet, only the other day, we vied with each other in doing honour to the chief figure-head of that tendency across the Channel,† and there was heard but the belated protest of a few worthy individuals, inadequately equipped with the jaunty courage of ignorance, or the insufferable confidence of second-hand knowledge.

And during the past year things have been moving very rapidly. The position of the literary artist towards Nature, his great inspirer, has become more definite, more secure. A sound, organised opinion of men of letters is being acquired; and in the little bouts with the *bourgeois* – if I may be pardoned the use of that wearisome word – no one has to fight single-handed. Heroism is at a discount; Mrs. Grundy‡ is becoming mythological; a crowd of unsuspected supporters collect from all sides, and the deadly conflict of which we had been warned becomes but an interesting skirmish. Books are published, stories are printed, in old-established reviews, which would never have been tolerated a few years ago.§ On all sides, deference to the tendency of the time is spreading. The truth must be admitted: the roar of unthinking prejudice is dying away.

* In 1888 and 1889, Henry Vizetelly (1820–94) was prosecuted, fined and eventually imprisoned for publishing translations of Zola's fiction.

† Zola. See Appendix 1, note on page 103.

‡ Mrs Grundy is a personification of convention and prudishness.

§ Crackanthorpe presumably has in mind novels such as Thomas Hardy's *Tess of the d'Urbervilles* (1891) or George Moore's *Esther Waters* (1894).

All this is exceedingly comforting: and yet, perhaps, it is not a matter for absolute congratulation. For, if the enemy are not dying as gamely as we had expected, if they are, as I am afraid, losing heart, and in danger of sinking into a condition of passive indifference, it should be to us a matter of not inconsiderable apprehension. If this new evolution in the art of fiction – this general return of the literary artist towards Nature, on the brink of which we are to-day hesitating – is to achieve any definite, ultimate fineness of expression, it will benefit enormously by the continued presence of a healthy, vigorous, if not wholly intelligent, body of opponents. Directly or indirectly, they will knock a lot of nonsense out of us, will these opponents; – why should we be ashamed to admit it? They will enable us to find our level, they will spur us on to bring out the best – and only the best – that is within us.

Take, for instance, the gentleman who objects to realistic fiction on moral grounds. If he does not stand the most conspicuous to-day, at least he was pre-eminent the day before yesterday. He is a hard case, and it is on his especial behalf that I would appeal. For he has been dislodged from the hill top, he has become a target for all manner of unkind chaff, from the ribald youth of Fleet Street and Chelsea.* He has been labelled a Philistine†: he has been twitted with his middle-age; he has been reported to have compromised himself with that indecent old person, Mrs. Grundy. It is confidently asserted that he comes from Putney, or from Sheffield, and that, when he is not busy abolishing the art of English literature, he is employed in safeguarding the interests of the grocery or tallow-chandler's trade.‡ Strange and cruel tales of him have been printed in the monthly reviews; how, but for him, certain well-known popular writers would have written masterpieces; how, like the ogre in the fairy tale, he consumes every morning at fast a hundred pot-boiled young geniuses. For the most part they have been excellently well told, these tales of this moral ogre of ours; but why start to shatter brutally their dainty charm by a soulless process of investigation? No, let us be shamed rather into a more charitable spirit, into making generous amends, into rehabilitating the greatness of our moral ogre.

He is the backbone of our nation; the guardian of our mediocrity;

* Louche journalists and bohemians.

† In *Culture and Anarchy* (1867–8/1869), Matthew Arnold used the term 'Philistine' to refer to the middle classes. 'Barbarians' are the aristocracy, and the 'Populace' are the working classes.

‡ Putney, Sheffield, grocery and tallow-chandler all suggest a vulgar suburban or provincial materialism and a lack of interest in higher things. A tallow-chandler makes and sells candles made of animal fats.

the very foil* of our intelligence. Once, you fancied that you could argue with him, that you could dispute his dictum.† Ah! how we cherished that day-dream of our extreme youth. But it was not to be. He is still immense; for he is unassailable; he is flawless, for he is complete within himself; his lucidity is yet unimpaired; his impartiality is yet supreme. Who amongst us could judge with a like impartiality the productions of Scandinavia and Charpentier, Walt Whitman, and the Independent Theatre?‡ Let us remember that he has never professed to understand Art, and the deep debt of gratitude that every artist in the land should consequently owe to him; let us remember that he is above us, for he belongs to the great middle classes; let us remember that he commands votes, that he is candidate for the County Council§; let us remember that he is delightful, because he is intelligible.

Yes, he is intelligible; and of how many of us can that be said? His is no complex programme, no subtly exacting demand. A plain moral lesson is all that he asks, and his voice is as of one crying in the ever fertile wilderness of Smith and of Mudie.¶

And he is right, after all – if he only knew it. The business of art is to create for us fine interests, to make of our human nature a more complete thing: and thus, all great art is moral in the wider and the truer sense of the word. It is precisely on this point of the meaning of the word 'moral' that we and our ogre part company. To him, morality is concerned only with the established relations between the sexes and with fair dealing between man and man: to him the subtle, indirect morality of Art is incomprehensible.

Theoretically, Art is non-moral. She is not interested in any ethical code of any age or any nation, except in so far as the breach or observance of that code may furnish her with material on which to work. But, unfortunately, in this complex world of ours, we cannot satisfactorily pursue one interest – no, not even the interest of Art, at the expense of all others – let us look that fact in the face, doggedly, whatever pangs it may cost us – pleading magnanimously for the survival of our moral ogre, for there will be danger to our cause when his voice is no more heard.

* A thin leaf of metal used to enhance the brilliance of a precious stone.

† Utterance, expression of opinion.

‡ See Appendix 1, notes on Independent Theatre Society and Ibsen on page 108. Marc-Antoine Charpentier (1643–1704) was a French Baroque composer. Walt Whitman (1819–92) was a controversial US poet. Crackanthorpe means that the reader to whom he is referring thinks he knows a lot about many matters.

§ Local government.

¶ W. H. Smith's is a chain of booksellers. Mudie's was a subscription library. Both exercise(d) vigilant control of their stock of books.

If imitation be the sincerest form of flattery, then our moral ogre must indeed have experienced a proud moment, when a follower came to him from the camp of the lovers of Art, and the artistic objector to realistic fiction started on his timid career. I use the word timid in no disparaging sense, but because our artistic objector, had he ventured a little farther from the vicinity of the coat-tails of his powerful protector, might have secured a more adequate recognition of his performances. For he is by no means devoid of adroitness. He can patter to us glibly of the 'gospel of ugliness'; of the 'cheerlessness of modern literature'; he can even juggle with that honourable property-piece, the maxim of Art for Art's sake.* But there have been moments when even this feat has proved ineffective, and some one has started scoffing at his pretended 'delight in pure rhythm or music of the phrase,' and flippantly assured him that he is talking nonsense, and that style is a mere matter of psychological suggestion. You fancy our performer nonplussed, or at least boldly bracing himself to brazen the matter out. No, he passes dexterously to his curtain effect – a fervid denunciation of express trains, evening news papers, Parisian novels, or the first number of THE YELLOW BOOK.† Verily, he is a versatile person.

Sometimes, to listen to him you would imagine that pessimism and regular meals were incompatible; that the world is only ameliorated by those whom it completely satisfies, that good predominates over evil, that the problem of our destiny had been solved long ago. You begin to doubt whether any good thing can come out of this miserable, inadequate age of ours, unless it be a doctored survival of the vocabulary of a past century. The language of the coster and cadger‡ resound in our midst, and, though Velasquez [sic] tried to paint like Whistler, Rudyard Kipling cannot write like Pope.§ And a weird word has been invented to explain the whole business. Decadence, decadence: you are all decadent nowadays. Ibsen, Degas, and the New English Art Club; Zola, Oscar Wilde, and the Second Mrs. Tanqueray.¶ Mr. Richard Le Gallienne is hoist with his own petard;

* The Aesthetic School, aiming at beauty in art above all, and the antithesis of the realists, who favoured the ugly and the sordid.

† Crackanthorpe means here everything that is modern and *avant-garde*.

‡ A coster is a low-class street vendor, and a cadger continually begs and scrounges from one.

§ Diego Velázquez (1599–1660), eminent Spanish painter. For Whistler, see Appendix 1, note on page 110. Rudyard Kipling (1865–1936), British short-story writer and poet. Alexander Pope (1688–1744), great English neo-classical poet. The joke is that the modern innovative artist belongs to a great tradition, but the modern traditional poet cannot successfully imitate a great writer of the past.

¶ For Ibsen, see Appendix 1, note on page 108. For Zola, see Appendix 1, note on even the British playwright has not escaped the taint.* Ah, what a hideous spectacle. All whirling along towards one common end. And the elegant voice of the artistic objector floating behind: '*Après vous le déluge*.'† A wholesale abusing of the tendencies of the age has ever proved, for the superior mind, an inexhaustible source of relief. Few things breed such inward comfort as the contemplation of one's own pessimism – few things produce such discomfort as the remembrance of our neighbour's optimism.

And yet, pessimists though we may be dubbed, some of us, on this point at least, how can we compete with the hopelessness enjoyed by our artistic objector, when the spectacle of his despondency makes us insufferably replete with hope and confidence, so that while he is loftily bewailing or prettily denouncing the completeness of our degradation, we continue to delight in the evil of our ways?‡ Oh, if we could only be sure that he would persevere in reprimanding this persistent study of the pitiable aspects of life, how our hearts would go out towards him! For the man who said that joy is essentially, regrettably inartistic, admitted in the same breath that misery lends itself to artistic treatment twice as easily as joy, and resumed the whole question in a single phrase.§ Let our artistic objector but weary the world sufficiently with his despair concerning the permanence of the cheerlessness of modern realism, and some day a man will arise who will give us a study of human happiness, as fine, as vital as anything we owe to Guy de Maupassant or to Ibsen.¶ That man will have accomplished the infinitely difficult, and in admiration and in awe shall we bow down our heads before him.

In one radical respect the art of fiction is not in the same position as the other arts. They – music, poetry, painting, sculpture, and the

page 103. Edgar Degas (1834–1917), major French artist, linked with the still *avant-garde* Impressionist movement. *The Second Mrs Tanqueray*, Arthur Wing Pinero's play of sexual hypocrisy and misconduct, was very successful in London in 1893. When Crackanthorpe was writing, Wilde was an extremely famous author and public figure; his disgrace was a year away.

* Richard Le Gallienne (1866–1947), *avant-garde* author and friend of Crackanthorpe's. To be 'hoist with your own petard' means to be blown up by your own bomb, or destroyed by your own cleverness or cunning. The phrase comes from Shakespeare's *Hamlet* III, iv.

† 'After you [comes] the flood' (French) – attributed to various historical personages and used in various contexts with various contextual meanings.

‡ The phrase echoes several passages in the Authorised Version of the Bible – for example, Ezekiel 33 and 36.

§ 'Resumed' means summed up here.

¶ Guy de Maupassant (1850–93), French novelist and short-fiction writer. Crackanthorpe was often associated by critics with his work.

drama – possess a magnificent fabric of accumulated tradition. The great traditions of the art of fiction have yet to be made. Ours is a young art, struggling desperately to reach expression, with no great past to guide it. Thus, it should be a matter for wonder, not that we stumble into certain pitfalls, but that we do not fall headlong into a hundred more.

But, if we have no great past, we have the present and the future – the one abundant in facilities, the other abundant in possibilities. Young men of to-day have enormous chances: we are working under exceedingly favourable conditions. Possibly we stand on the threshold of a very great period. I know, of course, that the literary artist is shamefully ill-paid, and that the man who merely caters for the public taste, amasses a rapid and respectable fortune. But how is it that such an arrangement seems other than entirely equitable? The essential conditions of the two cases are entirely distinct. The one man is free to give untrammelled expression to his own soul, free to fan to the full the flame that burns in his heart: the other is a seller of wares, a unit in national commerce. To the one is allotted liberty and a living wage; to the other, captivity and a consolation in Consols.* Let us whine, then, no more concerning the prejudice and the persecution of the Philistine, when even that misanthrope, Mr. Robert Buchanan,† admits that there is no power in England to prevent a man writing exactly as he pleases. Before long the battle for literary freedom will be won. A new public has been created – appreciative, eager and determined; a public which, as Mr. Gosse‡ puts it, in one of those admirable essays of his, 'has eaten of the apple of knowledge, and will not be satisfied with mere marionnettes [sic]. Whatever comes next,' Mr. Gosse continues, 'we cannot return, in serious novels, to the inanities and impossibilities of the old well-made plot, to the children changed at nurse, to the madonna-heroine and the god-like hero, to the impossible virtues and melodramatic vices. In future, even those who sneer at realism and misrepresent it most wilfully, will be obliged to put their productions more in accordance with veritable experience. There will still be novel-writers who address the gallery, and who will keep up the gaudy old convention,

* Consols are government bonds that have existed in Britain since the mid-eighteenth century. They have historically offered secure investment and a safe source of income for the British middle classes.

† Robert Buchanan (1841–1901), a Scottish poet, novelist and dramatist. In an essay entitled 'The Fleshly School of Poetry' (1871), he wrote a controversial attack on contemporary verse and painting.

‡ Edmund Gosse (1849–1928), English author, translator and critic. The quotation is taken from *Questions at Issue* (1893).

and the clumsy *Family Herald** evolution, but they will no longer be distinguished men of genius. They will no longer sign themselves George Sand or Charles Dickens.'

Fiction has taken her place amongst the arts. The theory that writing resembles the blacking of boots, the more boots you black, the better you do it, is busy evaporating. The excessive admiration for the mere idea of a book or a story is dwindling; so is the comparative indifference to slovenly treatment. True is it that the society lady, dazzled by the brilliancy of her own conversation, and the serious-minded spinster, bitten by some sociological theory, still decide in the old jaunty spirit, that fiction is the obvious medium through which to astonish or improve the world. Let us beware of the despotism of the intelligent amateur, and cease our toying with that quaint and winsome bogey of ours, the British Philistine, whilst the intelligent amateur, the deadliest of Art's enemies, is creeping up in our midst.

For the familiarity of the man in the street with the material employed by the artist in fiction, will ever militate against the acquisition of a sound, fine, and genuine standard of workmanship. Unlike the musician, the painter, the sculptor, the architect, the artist in fiction enjoys no monopoly in his medium. The word and the phrase are, of necessity, the common property of everybody; the ordinary use of them demands no special training. Hence the popular mind, while willingly acknowledging that there are technical difficulties to be surmounted in the creation of the sonata, the landscape, the statue, the building, in the case of the short story, or of the longer novel, declines to believe even in their existence, persuaded that in order to produce good fiction, an ingenious idea, or 'plot,' as it is termed, is the one thing needed. The rest is a mere matter of handwriting.

The truth is, and, despite Mr. Waugh,† we are near recognition of it, that nowadays there is but scanty merit in the mere selection of any particular subject, however ingenious or daring it may appear at first sight; that a man is not an artist, simply because he writes about heredity or the *demi-monde*,‡ that to call a spade a spade requires no extraordinary

* *The Family Herald: A Domestic Magazine of Useful Information & Amusement*, an inexpensive weekly containing fiction, published between 1842 and 1940.

† Arthur Waugh's essay, 'Reticence in Literature', was published in *The Yellow Book* 1 (January 1894): 201–19. Crackanthorpe's essay is a response to this text. Arthur Waugh (1866–1943) was a critic, biographer and man of letters. He was father of the celebrated twentieth-century authors Alec Waugh and Evelyn Waugh. See: David Crackanthorpe (1977), p. 84 ff.

‡ Literally, French for 'half-world': that is, the world of prostitutes, demi-reps, semi-prostitutes, mistresses and kept women. In *Ghosts* (1881), Ibsen wrote of the transmission of venereal disease over generations.

literary gift, and that the essential is contained in the frank, fearless acceptance by every man of his entire artistic temperament, with its qualities and its flaws.

Appendix 3

'The Haseltons'
The Yellow Book 5 (April 1895): 132–163
This story was published as Part II of 'A Commonplace Chapter' in *Sentimental Studies* in 1895

I

She sat in a corner of a large London drawing-room, and the two men stood before her – Hillier Haselton, her husband, and George Swann, her husband's cousin; and, beyond them, the mellow light of shaded candles, vague groupings of black coats, white shirt-fronts, and gay-tinted dresses, and the noisy hum of conversation.

The subject that the two men were discussing – and more especially Swann's blunt earnestness – stirred her, though throughout it she had been unpleasantly conscious of a smallness, almost a pettiness, in Hillier's aspect.

'Well, but why not, my dear Swann? Why not be unjust: man's been unjust to woman for so many years.'

Hillier let his voice fall listlessly, as if to rebuke the other's vehemence; and to hint that he was tired of the topic, looked round at his wife, noting at the same time that Swann was observing how he held her gaze in his meaningly. And the unexpectedness of his own attitude charmed him – his hot defence of an absurd theory, obviously evoked by a lover-like desire to please her. Others, whose admiration he could trust, would, he surmised, have reckoned it a pretty pose. And she, perceiving that Swann seemed to take her husband's sincerity for granted, felt a sting of quick regret that she had ever come to understand him, and that she could not still view him as they all viewed him.

Hillier moved away across the room, and Swann drew a stool beside her chair, and asking her for news of Claude, her little boy, talked to her of other things – quite simply, for they were grown like old friends. He looked at her steadily, stroking his rough fair beard, as if he were anxious to convey to her something which he could not put into words. She divined; and, a little startled, tried to thank him with her eyes; but, embarrassed by the clumsiness of his own attempt at sympathetic perception, he evidently noticed nothing. And this obtuseness of his disappointed her, since it somehow seemed to confirm her isolation.

She glanced round the room. Hillier stood on the hearth-rug, his elbow on the mantel-piece, busily talking, with slight deferential gestures, to the great English actress in whose honour the dinner had been given. The light fell on his smooth glistening hair, on his quick sensitive face; for the moment forcing herself to realise him as he appeared to the rest, she felt a thrill of jaded pride in him, in his cleverness, in his reputation, in his social success.

Swann, observing the direction of her gaze, said, almost apologetically, 'You must be very proud of him.'

She nodded, smiled a faint, assumed smile; then added, adopting his tone, 'His success has made him so happy.'

'And you too?' he queried.

'Of course,' she answered quickly.

He stayed silent, while she continued to watch her husband absently.

II

Success, an atmosphere of flattery, suited Hillier Haselton, and stimulating his weaknesses, continually encouraged him to display the handsomer portion of his nature. For though he was yet young – and looked still younger – there was always apparent, beneath his frank boyish relish of praise, a semblance of serious modesty, a strain of genuine reserve. And society – the smart literary society that had taken him up – found this combination charming. So success had made life pleasant for him in many ways, and he rated its value accordingly; he was too able a man to find pleasure in the facile forms of conceit, or to accept, with more than a certain cynical complacency, the world's generous judgment on his work. Indeed, the whole chorus of admiration did but strengthen his contempt for contemporary literary judgments, a contempt which – lending the dignity of deliberate purpose to his indulgence of his own weakness for adulation – procured him a refined, a private, and an altogether agreeable self-satisfaction. When people set him down as vastly clever, he was pleased; he was unreasonably annoyed when they spoke of him as a great genius.

Life, he would repeat, was of larger moment than literature; and, despite all the freshness of his success, his interest in himself, in the play of his own personality, remained keener, and, in its essence, of more lasting a nature, than his ambition for genuine achievement. The world – people with whom he was brought into relation – stimulated him so far as he could assimilate them to his conception of his own attitude; most forms of art too, in great measure – and music altogether – attracted him in the proportion that they played upon his intimate emotions. Similarly, his friendships; and for this reason he preferred the companionship of women. But since his egoism was uncommonly dexterous, he seemed endowed with a rare gift of artistic perception, of psychological insight, of personal charm.

It had always been his nature to live almost exclusively in the present; his recollection of past impressions was grown scanty from habitual disuse. His sordid actions in the past he forgot with an ever-increasing facility; his moments of generosity or self-sacrifice he remembered carelessly, and enjoyed a secret pride in their concealment; and the conscious embellishment of subjective experience for the purpose of 'copy,' he had instinctively disdained.

Since his boyhood, religion had been distasteful to him, though, at rare moments, it had stirred his sensibilities strangely. Now, occasionally, the thought of the nullity of life, of its great unsatisfying quality, of the horrid squalor of death, would descend upon him with its crushing, paralysing weight; and he would lament, with bitter, futile regret, his lack of a secure stand-point, and the continual limitations of his self-absorption; but even that, perhaps, was a mere literary melancholy, assimilated from certain passages of Pierre Loti.*

But now he had published a stout volume of critical essays, and an important volume of poetry, and society had clamorously ratified his own conception of himself. Certainly, now, in the eyes of the world, it was agreed beyond dispute that she, his wife, was of quite the lesser importance. 'She was nice and quiet,' which meant that she seemed mildly insignificant; 'she had a sense of humour,' which meant that an odd note of half-stifled cynicism sometimes escaped her. He was evidently very devoted to her, and on that account women trusted him – all the more because her personality possessed no obvious glamour. Perhaps, now and then, his attentions to her in public seemed a little ostentatious; but then, in these modern uncourtly days, that in itself was distinctive. In private too, especially at the moments when he found life stimulating, he was still tactful and expansive with sympathetic impulse; from habit; from pride in his comprehension of women; from dislike to cheap hypocrisy. How could he have divined that bitter suppressed seriousness, with which she had taken her disillusionment; when not once in three months did he consider her apart from the play of his own personality; otherwise than in the light of her initial attitude towards him?

And her disillusionment, how had it come? Certainly not with a rush of sudden overwhelming revelation; certainly it was in no wise inspired

* Pierre Loti (Louis Marie-Julien Viaud) (1850–1923), French novelist and travel writer.

by the tragedy of Nora Helmer.* It had been a gradual growth, to whose obscure and trivial beginnings she had not had the learning to ascribe their true significance. To sound the current of life was not her way. She was naive by nature; and the ignorance of her girlhood had been due rather to a natural inobservance than to carefully managed surroundings. And yet, she had come to disbelieve in Hillier; to discredit his clever attractiveness: she had become acutely sensitive to his instability, and, with a secret, instinctive obstinacy, to mistrust the world's praise of his work. Perhaps, had he made less effort in the beginning to achieve a brilliancy of attitude in her eyes, had he schooled her to expect from him a lesser loftiness of aspiration, things might have been very different; or, at least, there might have resulted from the process of her disillusionment a lesser bitterness of conviction. But she had taken her marriage with so keen an earnestness of ideal, had noted every turn in his personality with so intense an expectation. Perhaps, too, had he detected the first totterings of her ideal conception of him, had he aided her, as it were, to descend his figure from that pedestal where he himself had originally planted it, together they might have set it uninjured on a lower and less exposed plane. But he had never heeded her subtle indications of its insecurity; alone, she had watched its peril, awaiting with a frightened fascination the day when it should roll headlong in the dust. And, at intervals, she would vaguely marvel, when she observed others whose superior perspicacity she assumed, display no perception of his insincerity. Then the oppressive sense that she – she, his wife, the mother of his child – was the only one who saw him clearly, and the unsurmountable shrinking from the relief of sharing this sense with any one, made her sourly sensitive to the pettiness, the meanness, the hidden tragic element in life.

A gulf had grown between – that was how she described it to herself. Outwardly their relations remained the same; but, frequently, in his continuance of his former attitude, she detected traces of deliberate effort; frequently when off his guard, he would abandon all pretension to it, and openly betray how little she had come to mean to him. There were, of course, moments also, when, at the echo of his tenderness, she would feverishly compel herself to believe in its genuineness; but a minute later he would have forgotten his exaltation, and, almost with irritation, would deliberately ignore the tense yearning that was glowing within her.

* Nora Helmer is the principal female character in Henrik Ibsen's *A Doll's House* (1879). The controversial play was given its first public performances in Britain in 1889.

And so, the coming of his success – a brilliant blossoming into celebrity – had stirred her but fitfully. Critics wrote of the fine sincerity of his poetry; while she clung obstinately to her superstition that fine poetry must be the outcome of a great nobility of character. And, sometimes, she hated all this success of his, because it seemed to emphasise the gulf between them, and in some inexplicable way to lessen her value in his eyes: then again, from an impulse of sheer unselfishness, she would succeed in almost welcoming it, because, after all, he was her husband.

But of all this he noted nothing: only now and then he would remind himself vaguely that she had no literary leanings.

The little Claude was three years old. Before his birth, Hillier had dilated much on the mysterious beauty of childhood, had vied with her own awed expectation of the wonderful coming joy. During her confinement, which had been a severe one, for three nights in succession he had sat, haggard with sleepless anxiety, on a stiff-backed dining-room chair, till all danger was passed. But afterwards the baby had disappointed him sorely; and later she thought he came near actively disliking it. Still, reminding herself of the winsomeness of other children at the first awakening of intelligence, she waited with patient hopefulness, fondly fancying a beautiful boy-child; wide baby eyes; a delicious prattle. Claude, however, attained no prettiness, as he grew: from an unattractive baby he became an unattractive child, with lanky, carroty hair; a squat nose, an ugly, formless mouth. And in addition, he was fretful, mischievous, self-willed. Hillier at this time paid him but a perfunctory attention; avoided discussing him; and, when that was not possible, adopted a subtle, aggrieved tone that cut her to the quick. For she adored the child; adored him because he was hers; adored him for his very defects; adored him because of her own suppressed sadness; adored him for the prospect of the future – his education, his development, his gradual growth into manhood.

From the house in Cromwell Road the Haseltons had moved to a flat near Victoria Station*: their means were moderate; but now, through the death of a relative, Hillier was no longer dependent upon literature for a living.

III

George Swann was her husband's cousin; and besides, he had stood godfather to the little Claude. He was the elder by eight years; but Hillier always treated him as if their ages were reversed, and, before

* This is a move up in the world. A 'flat' is an apartment.

Ella, used to nickname him the 'Anglo-Saxon,' because of his loose physical largeness, his flaxen hair and beard, his strong simplicity of nature. And Swann, with a reticent good-humour, acquiesced in Hillier's tone towards him; out of vague regard for his cousin's ability; out of respect for him as Ella's husband.

Swann and Ella were near friends. Since their first meeting, the combination of his blunt self-possession and his uncouth timidity with women, had attracted her. Divining his simplicity, she had felt at once at her ease with him, and, treating him with open cousinly friendliness, had encouraged him to come often to the house.

A while later, a trivial incident confirmed her regard for him. They had been one evening to the theatre together – she and Hillier and Swann – and afterwards, since it was raining, she and Hillier waited under the door-way while he sallied out into the Strand to find them a cab. Pushing his way along the crowded street, his eyes scanning the traffic for an empty hansom, he accidentally collided with a woman of the pavement, jostling her off the kerb into the mud of the gutter. Ella watched him stop, gaze ruefully at the woman's splashed skirt, take off his hat, and apologise with profuse, impulsive regret. The woman continued her walk, and presently passed the theatre door. She looked middle-aged: her face was hard and animal-like.

One Sunday afternoon – it was summer-time – as she was crossing the park* to pay a call in Gloucester Square, she came across him sauntering alone in Kensington Gardens. She stopped and spoke to him: he seemed much startled to meet her. Three-quarters of an hour later, when she returned, he was sitting on a public bench beside her path; and immediately, from his manner, she half-guessed that he had been waiting for her. It was a fortnight after Claude's christening: he started to speak to her of the child, and so, talking together gravely, they turned on to the turf, mounted the slope, and sat down on two chairs beneath the trees.

Touched by his waiting for her, she was anxious to make friends with him; because he was the baby's godfather; because he seemed alone in the world; because she trusted in his goodness. So she led him, directly and indirectly, to talk of himself. At first, in moody embarrassment, he prodded the turf with his stick; and presently responded, unwillingly breaking down his troubled reserve, and alluding to his loneliness confidingly, as if sure of her sympathy.

Unconsciously he made her feel privileged thus to obtain an insight

* Hyde Park in west central London.

into the inner workings of his heart, and gave her a womanly, sentimental interest in him.

Comely cloud-billows were overhead, and there was not a breath of breeze.

They paused in their talk, and he spoke to her of Kensington Gardens, lovingly, as of a spot which had signified much to him in the past – Kensington Gardens, massively decorous; ceremoniously quiet; pompous, courtly as a king's leisure park; the slow, opulent contours of portly foliage, sober-green, immobile and indolent; spacious groupings of tree-trunks; a low ceiling of leaves; broad shadows mottling the grass. The Long Water, smooth and dark as a mirror; lining its banks, the rhododendrons swelling with colour, cream, purple, and carmine. The peacock's insolent scream; a silently skimming pigeon; the joyous twitterings of birds; the patient bleating of sheep*. . . .

At last she rose to go. He accompanied her as far as the Albert Memorial,† and when he had left her, she realised, with a thrill of contentment, that he and she had become friends.

IV

That had been the beginning of George Swann's great love for her. His was a slowly-moving nature: it was gradually therefore that he came to value, as a matter of almost sacred concern, the sense of her friendship; reverencing her with the single-hearted, unquestioning reverence of a man unfamiliar with women; regarding altogether gravely her relations with him – their talks on serious subjects, the little letters she wrote to him, the books that he had given to her – Swinburne's *Century of Roundels*; a tiny edition of Shelley, bound in white parchment; Mrs. Meynell's *Rhythm of Life*.‡ He took to studying her intellectual tastes, the topics that were congenial to her, her opinions on men and women, with a quiet, plodding earnestness; almost as if it were his duty. Thus he learned her love of simple country things; gained a conception of her girlhood's home; of her father and mother,

* Despite Kensington Gardens' location in the middle of a great city, sheep were employed at various times in the nineteenth century to crop the grass there. One can see a similar use of sheep and goats in modern Paris on, for example, the avenue de Breteuil near Les Invalides.

† The Albert Memorial is a neo-Gothic monument to the dead husband of Queen Victoria. It has stood in Kensington Gardens since 1872.

‡ Algernon Charles Swinburne (1837–1909), controversial English poet. Percy Bysshe Shelley (1792–1822), major English Romantic poet. Alice Meynell (1847–1922), English poet, author of religious verse, and in the early 1900s campaigner for women's rights. *The Rhythm of Life* (1893) is a volume of essays.

staid country folk. He did not know how to him alone she could talk of these things; or of the warm, deep-seated gratitude she bore him in consequence; but he reverted constantly to the topic, because, under its influence, she always brightened, and it seemed to ratify the bond of sympathy between them.

How much, as the months went by, she came to mean to him, he had not in the least realised: he had never thought of her as playing a part in his own life; only as a beautiful-natured woman, to whom he owed everything, because, by some strange chance, she had made him her friend.

Not even in his moments of idle vagrant reverie, did he think to ask more of her than this. To intrude himself further into her life, to offer her more than exactly that which she was expecting of him, naturally never occurred to him. Yet, in a queer uncomfortable way, he was jealous of other men's familiarity with her – vaguely jealous lest they should supplant him, mistrustful of his own modesty. And there was no service which, if she had asked it of him, he would not have accomplished for her sake; for he had no ties.

But towards Hillier, since he belonged to her, Swann's heart warmed affectionately: she had loved and married him; had made him master of her life. So he instinctively extended to his cousin a portion of the unspoken devotion inspired by Ella. Such was the extent of his reverence for her, and his diffidence regarding himself, that he took for granted that Hillier was an ideal husband, tender, impelled by her to no ordinary daily devotion: for, that it should be otherwise, would have seemed to him a monstrous improbability. Yet latterly, since the coming of Hillier's success, certain incidents had disconcerted him, riled him with ill-defined uneasiness.

From the first, he had been one of Hillier's warmest admirers; praising, whenever an opportunity offered, out of sheer loyalty to Ella, and pride in his cousin, the fineness of form that his poetry revealed. To her, when they were alone, he had talked in the same enthusiastic strain: the first time she had seemed listless and tired, and afterwards he had blamed himself for his want of tact; on another occasion, he had brought her a laudatory article, and she had turned the conversation brusquely into another channel. And, since his love for her of which as yet he was himself unconscious caused him to brood over means of pleasing her (he lived alone in the Temple*), this indication that he had jarred her sensibilities was not lost upon him.

* The Temple is an area of central London near the River Thames, associated with lawyers' offices.

Hillier's attitude towards the little Claude, and the pain that it was causing her, would in all probability have escaped him, had she not alluded to it once openly, frankly assuming that he had perceived it. It was not indeed that she was in any way tempted to indulge in the transitional treachery of discussing Hillier with him; but that, distressed, yearning for counsel, she was prompted almost irresistibly to turn to Swann, who had stood godfather to the child, who was ready to join her in forming anxious speculations concerning the future.

For of course he had extended his devotion to the child also, who, at Hillier's suggestion, was taught to call him Uncle George. Naturally his heart went out to children: the little Claude, since the first awakening of his intelligence, had exhibited a freakish, childish liking for him; and, in his presence, always assumed something of the winsomeness of other children.

The child's preference for Swann, his shy mistrust of his father, were sometimes awkwardly apparent; but Hillier, so it seemed to Ella, so far from resenting, readily accepted his cousin's predominance. 'Children always instinctively know a good man,' he would say; and Ella would wince inwardly, discerning, beneath his air of complacent humility, how far apart from her he had come to stand.

Thus, insensibly, Swann had become necessary to her, almost the pivot, as it were, of her life: to muse concerning the nature of his feelings towards her, to probe its sentimental aspects, to accept his friendship otherwise than with unconscious ease, that was not her way.

But Hillier noted critically how things were drifting, and even lent encouragement to their progress in a way that was entirely unostentatious; since so cynical an attitude seemed in some measure to justify his own conduct.

V

For he was unfaithful to his wife, it was inevitable that the temptation, in the guise of a craving for change, should come not from the outside, but from within himself. And he had no habit of stable purpose with which to withstand it. Not altogether was it a vagrant, generalised lusting after women other than his wife; not a mere harking back to the cruder experiences of his bachelorhood; though, at first it had seemed so to manifest itself. Rather was it the result of a moody restlessness, of a dissatisfaction (with her, consciously, no; for the more that he sinned against her, the more lovable, precious her figure appeared to him) kindled by continual contact with her natural goodness. It was as if, in his effort to match his personality with hers, he had put too severe a strain upon the better part of him.

He himself had never analysed the matter more exhaustively than this. The treacherous longing had gripped him at certain moments, holding him helpless as in a vice. He had conceived no reckless passion for another woman: such an eventuality, he dimly surmised, was well-nigh impossible. In his case brain domineered over heart; to meet the first outbursting of his adoration for his wife, he had drained every resource of his sentimentality.

Was it then an idle craving for adventure, a school-boy curiosity clamouring for fresh insight into the heart of women? Mere experience was unnecessary for the attainment of comprehension: 'to have lived' did not imply 'to have understood': the most pregnant adventures, as he knew, were those which entailed no actual unfaithfulness.

And for these subtle, psychological intimacies ample occasion offered. Yet the twist in his nature led him to profess to treat them heedlessly; and, in reality, to prosecute them with no genuine strenuousness. They would have been obvious lapses; Ella would have been pained, pitied perhaps: from that his vanity and his sham chivalry alike shrank.

His unfaithfulness to her, then, had been prompted by no evident motive. Superficially considered, it seemed altogether gratuitous, meaningless. The world – that is, people who knew him and her – would probably have discredited the story, had it come to be bruited. And this fact he had not omitted to consider.

She, the other woman, was of little importance. She belonged to the higher walks of the demi-monde*: she was young; beautiful, too, in a manner; light-hearted; altogether complaisant. She was not the first: there had been others before her; but these were of no account whatsoever: they had but represented the bald fact of his unfaithfulness. But she attracted him: he returned to her again and again; though afterwards, at any rate in the beginning, he was wont to spare himself little in the matter of self-reproach, and even to make some show of resisting the temptation. The discretion of her cynical camaraderie, however, was to be trusted; and that was sufficient to undermine all virtuous resolution. She had the knack, too, of cheering him when depressed, and, curiously enough, of momentarily reinstating him in his own conceit, though later, on his return to Ella, he would suffer most of the pangs of remorse.

* Literally, French for 'half-world': that is, the world of prostitutes, demi-reps, semi-prostitutes, mistresses and kept women.

There was something mannish about her – not about her physiognomy, but about her mind – derived, no doubt, from the scantiness of her intercourse with women. Her cynicism was both human and humorous: she was a person of little education, and betrayed none of the conventionality of her class: hence her point of view often struck him as oddly direct and unexpected. He used to talk to her about himself, candidly discussing all manner of random and intimate matters before her, without shyness on his part, without surprise on hers – almost at times as if she were not present – and with an assumption of facile banter, to listen to which tickled his vanity. Only to Ella did he never allude; and in this, of course, she tacitly acquiesced. She possessed a certain quality of sympathetic tact; always attentive to his talk, never critical of it; mindful of all that he had previously recounted. He could always resume his attitude at the very point where he had abandoned it. Between them there was never any aping of sentimentality.

That she comprehended him – with so fatuous a delusion he never coquetted: nor that she interested him as a curious type. She saw no subtle significance in his talk: she understood nothing of its complex promptings: she was ordinary, uneducated, and yet stimulating – and that was the contrast which attracted him towards her. Concerning the course of her own existence he did not trouble himself: he accepted her as he found her; deriving a sense of security from the fact that towards him her manner varied but little from visit to visit. But, as these accumulated, becoming more and more regular, and his faith in her discretion blunted the edge of his remorse, he came to notice how she braced him, reconciled him to his treachery (which, he argued, in any case was inevitable); lent to it a spice almost of pleasantness. Neither had he misgivings of the future, of how it would end. One day she would pass out of his life as easily as she had come into it. His relations with her were odd, though not in the obvious way. About the whole thing he was insensibly coming to feel composed.

And its smoothness, its lack of a disquieting aspect, impelled him to persevere towards Ella in cheerfulness, courteous kindness, and a show of continuous affection; and to repent altogether of those lapses into roughness which had marred the first months of their marriage.

VI

The hansoms whirled their yellow, gleaming eyes down West: hot, flapping gusts went and returned aimlessly; and the mirthless twitterings of the women fell abruptly on the sluggishly shuffling crowd. All the sin of the city seemed crushed to listlessness; vacantly wistful, the figures waited by the street corners.*

Then the storm burst. Slow, ponderous drops: a clap of the thunder's wrath; a crinkled rim of light, unveiling a slab of sky, throbbing, sullen and violet; small, giggling screams of alarm, and a stampede of bunchy silhouettes. The thunder clapped again, impatient and imperious; and the rain responded, zealously hissing. Bright stains of liquid gold straggled across the road way; a sound of splashing accompanied the thud of hoofs, the rumble of wheels, the clanking of chains, and the ceaseless rattle of the drops on the hurried procession of umbrellas.

Swann, from the corner of a crowded omnibus, peered absently through the doorway, while the conductor, leaning into the street, touted mechanically for passengers.

The vehicle stopped. A woman, bare-headed and cloaked, escorted by the umbrella of a restaurant official, hurried to the shelter of a cab, across the wet pavement. A man broke the stream of the hastening crowd; halted beside the wheel to stare. The woman laughed in recognition, noisily. The man stepped rapidly on to the foot-board, and an instant stood there, directing the driver across the roof. The light from a lamp-post caught his face: it was Hillier. The next moment he was seated beside the woman, who was still laughing (Swann could see the gleaming whiteness of her teeth): the driver had loosened the window strap, the glass had slid down, shutting them in. The omnibus jolted forward, and the cab followed in its wake, impatiently, for the street was blocked with traffic.

Immediately, with a fierce vividness, Ella's image sprang up before Swann's eyes – her face with all its pure, natural, simple sweetness. And there not ten yards distant, behind the obscurity of that blurred glass, Hillier was sitting with another woman – a woman concerning whose status he could not doubt.

He clenched his gloved fists. The wild impulse spurted forth, the impulse to drag the cur from the cab, to bespatter him, to throw him into the mud, to handle him brutally, as he deserved. It was as if Hillier had struck him a cowardly blow in the face.

Then the hansom started to creep past the omnibus. Swann sprang into the roadway. A moment later he was inside another cab, whirling in pursuit down Piccadilly hill.†

The horse's hoofs splashed with a rhythmical, accelerated precision:

* Prostitutes and other denizens of the *demi-monde*.

† Piccadilly is a fashionable street in central London. It is apparent later that the cabs are travelling west toward Hyde Park Corner.

he noticed dully how the crupper-strap* flapped from side to side, across the animal's back. Ahead, up the incline, pairs of tiny specks, red and green, were flitting.

'It's the cab with the lady what come out of the restaurant, ain't it, sir?'

'Yes,' Swann called back through the trap.

The reins tightened: the horse quickened his trot.

Hyde Park Corner stood empty and resplendent with a glitter of glamorous gold. The cab turned the corner of Hamilton Place, and the driver lashed the horse into a canter up Park Lane.

'That's 'im – jest in front.'

'All right. Follow.' Swann heard himself answering. And, amid his pain, he was conscious that the man's jaunty tone seemed to indicate that this sort of job was not unfamiliar.

He struggled to tame the savageness of his indignation; to think out the situation; to realise things coolly, that he might do what was best for her. But the leaping recollection of all her trustfulness, her goodness, filled him with a burning, maddening compassion. . . . He could see nothing but the great wrong done to her. . . .

Where were they going – the green lights of that cab in front – that woman and Hillier? . . . Where would it end, this horrible pursuit – this whirling current which was sweeping him forward. . . . It was like a nightmare. . . .

He must stop them – prevent this thing . . . but, evidently, this was not the first time. . . . Hillier and this woman knew one another. He had stopped, on catching sight of her, and she had recognised him. . . . The thing might have been going on for weeks – for months. . . .

. . . Yet he must stop them – not here, in the crowded street (they were in the Edgware Road), but later, when they had reached their destination – where there were no passers – where it could be done without scandal. . . .

. . . Yes, he must send Hillier back to her. . . . And she believed in him – trusted him. . . . She must know nothing at all costs, he must spare her the hideous knowledge the pain of it. . . . And yet and yet? . . . Hillier – the blackguard – she would have to go on living with him, trusting him, confiding in him, loving him. . . .

And for relief he returned wearily to his indignation.

How was it possible for any man married to her to be so vile, so false? . . . The consummate hypocrisy of it all. . . .

Swann remembered moments when Hillier's manner towards her

* A strap running along the back of a horse and looped under its tail.

had appeared redolent of deference, of suppressed affection. And he – a man of refinement – not a mere coarse-fibred, sensual brute – he who wrote poetry – Swann recalled a couplet full of fine aspiration – that he should have done this loathsome thing – done it callously, openly – any one might have seen it – deceived her for some common vulgar, public creature. . . .

Suddenly the cab halted abruptly.

'They're pulled up, across the street there,' the driver whispered hoarsely, confidentially; and for his tone Swann could have struck him.

It was an ill-lit street, silent and empty. The houses were low, semi-detached,* and separated from the pavement by railings and small gardens.

The woman had got out of the cab and was pushing open the swing-gate. Hillier stood on the foot-board, paying the cab man. Swann, on the opposite side of the street, hesitated. Hillier stepped on to the pavement, and ran lightly up the door step after the woman. She unlocked the door: it closed behind them. And the hansom which had brought them turned, and trotted away down the street.

Swann stood a moment before the house, irresolute. Then re-crossed the street slowly. And a hansom, bearing a second couple, drew up at the house next door.

VII

'You can go to bed, Hodgson. I will turn off the light.'

The man retired silently. It was a stage-phrase that rose unconsciously to her lips, a stage-situation with which she was momentarily toying.

Alone, she perceived its absurd unreality. Nothing, of course, would happen to-night: though so many days and nights she had been waiting. The details of life were clumsy, cumbersome: the simplification of the stage, of novels, of dozing dreams, seemed, by contrast, bitterly impossible.

She took up the book again, and read on, losing herself for a while in the passion of its pages – a passion that was all glamorous, sentimental felicity, at once vague and penetrating. But, as she paused to reach a paper-knife, she remembered the irrevocable, prosaic groove of existence, and that slow drifting to a dreary commonplace – a com-

* A semi-detached house is one in which one building is divided into two separate homes. The action has moved downmarket to Edgware Road from earlier locales in Kensington Gardens, Piccadilly and the Temple.

monplace that was *hers* -brought back all her aching listlessness. She let the book slip to the carpet.

Love, she repeated to herself, a silken web, opal-tinted, veiling all life; love, bringing fragrance and radiance; love with the moonlight streaming across the meadows; love, amid summer-leafed woods, a-sparkle in the morning sun; a simple clasping of hands; a happiness, child-like and thoughtless, secure and intimate. . . .

And she – she had nothing – only the helpless child; her soul was brave and dismantled and dismal; and once again started the gnawing of humiliation – inferior even to the common people, who could be loved and forget, in the midst of promiscuous squalor. Without love, there seemed no reason for life.

Away her thoughts sailed to the tale of the fairy-prince, stepping to shore in his silver armour, come to deliver and to love. She would have been his in all humility, waited on him in fearful submission; she would have asked for nought but his love.

Years ago, once or twice, men had appeared to her like that. And Hillier, before they were married, when they were first engaged. A strange girl she must have been in those days! And now – now they were like any husband and any wife.

'It happened by chance,' the old tale began. Chance! Yes, it was chance that governed all life; mocking, ironical chance, daintily sportive chance, hobbled to the clumsy mechanism of daily existence.

Twelve o'clock struck. Ten minutes more perhaps, and Hillier would be home. She could hear his tread; she could see him enter, take off his coat and gloves gracefully, then lift her face lightly in his two hands, and kiss her on the forehead. He would ask for an account of her day's doings; but he would never heed her manner of answering, for he would have begun to talk of himself. And altogether complacently would he take up the well-worn threads of their common life.

And she would go on waiting, and trifling with hopelessness, for in real life such things were impossible. Men were dull and incomplete, and could not understand a woman's heart. . . .

And so she would wait till he came in, and when he had played his part, just as she had imagined he would play it, she would follow him, in dumb docility, up-stairs to bed.

* * * * *

It was past one o'clock when he appeared. She had fallen asleep in the big arm-chair: her book lay in a heap on the carpet beside her. He crossed the room, but she did not awake.

One hand hung over the arm of the chair, limp and white and fragile;

her head, bent over her breast, was coyly resting in the curve of her elbow; her hair was a little dishevelled; her breathing was soft and regular, like a child's.

He sat down noiselessly, awed by this vision of her. The cat, which had lain stretched on the hearth-rug, sprang into his lap, purring and caressing. He thought it strange that animals had no sense of human sinfulness, and recalled the devotion of the dog of a prostitute, whom he had known years and years ago. . . .

He watched her, and her unconsciousness loosed within him the sickening pangs of remorse. . . . He mused vaguely on suicide as the only fitting termination. . . . And he descended to cheap anathemas upon life. . . .

* * * * *

By-and-by she awoke, opening her eyes slowly, wonderingly. He was kneeling before her, kissing her hand with reverential precaution.

She saw tears in his eyes: she was still scarcely awake: she made no effort to comprehend; only was impulsively grateful, and slipping her arms behind his head, drew him towards her and kissed him on the eyes. He submitted, and a tear moistened her lips.

Then they went up-stairs.

And she, passionately clutching at every memory of their love, feverishly cheated herself into bitter self-upbraiding, into attributing to him a nobility of nature that set him above all other men. And he, at each renewed outburst of her wild straining towards her ideal, suffered, as if she had cut his bare flesh with a whip.

It was his insistent attitude of resentful humility that finally wearied her of the fit of false exaltation. When she sank to sleep, the old ache was at her heart.

VIII

Swann strode into the room. Hillier looked up at him from his writing-table in unfeigned surprise; greeted him cordially, with a couple of trite, cheery remarks concerning the weather, then waited abruptly for an explanation of this morning visit; for Swann's trouble was written on his face.

'You look worried. Is there anything wrong?' Hillier asked presently.

'Yes.'

'Well, can I do anything? If I can be of any service to you, old fellow, you know I – '

'I discovered last night what a damned blackguard you are.' He spoke savagely, as if his bluntness exulted him: his tone quivered with suppressed passion.

Hillier, with a quick movement of his head, flinched as if he had been struck in the face. And the lines about his mouth were set rigidly.

There was a long, tense silence. Hillier was drawing circles on a corner of the blotting-pad; Swann was standing over him, glaring at him with a fierce, hateful curiosity. Hillier became conscious of the other's expression, and his fist clenched obviously.

'I saw you get into a cab with that woman,' Swann went on. 'I was in an omnibus going home. I followed you – drove after you. I wanted to stop you – to stop it – I was too late.'

'Ah!' An exasperated, sneering note underlined the exclamation. Hillier drove the pen-point into the table. The nib curled and snapped.

The blood rushed to Swann's forehead. In a flash he caught a glimpse of the thought that had crossed Hillier's mind. It was like a personal indignity; he struggled desperately to control himself.

Hillier looked straight into his cousin's distorted face. At the sight the tightness about his own mouth slackened. His composure returned.

'I'm sorry. Forgive me,' he said simply.

'How can you be such a brute?' Swann burst out unheeding. 'Don't you care? Is it nothing to you to wreck your wife's whole happiness – to spoil her life, to break her heart, to deceive her in the foulest way, to lie to her. Haven't you any conscience, any chivalry?'

The manly anguish in his voice was not lost upon Hillier. He thought he realised clearly how it was for Ella, and not for him, that Swann was so concerned. Once more he took stock of his cousin's agitation, and a quick glitter came into his eyes. He felt as if a mysterious force had been suddenly given to him. Still he said nothing.

'How could you, Hillier? How came you to do it?'

'Sit down.' He spoke coldly, clearly, as if he were playing a part which he knew well.

Swann obeyed mechanically.

'It's perfectly natural that you should speak to me like that. You take the view of the world. The view of the world I accept absolutely. Certainly I am utterly unworthy of Ella' (he mentioned her name with a curious intonation of assertive pride). 'How I have sunk to this thing – the whole story of how I have come to risk my whole happiness for the sake of another woman, who is nothing – absolutely nothing – to me, to whom I am nothing, I won't attempt to explain. Did I attempt to do so, I see little probability of your understanding it, and little to be gained even if you did so. I choose to let it remain for you a piece of incomprehensible infamy: I have no wish to alter your view of me.'

'You don't care ... you've no remorse ... you're callous and cynical. ... Good God! it's awful.'

'Yes, Swann, I care,' Hillier resumed, lowering his voice, and speaking with a slow distinctness, as if he were putting an excessive restraint upon his emotions. 'I care more than you or any one will ever know.'

'It's horrible. ... I don't know what to think. ... Don't you see the awfulness of your wife's position? ... Don't you realise the hideousness of what you've done?'

'My dear Swann, nobody is more alive to the consequences of what I've done than I am. I have behaved infamously – I don't need to be told that by you. And whatever comes to me out of this thing' (he spoke with a grave, resigned sadness) 'I shall bear it.'

'Good God! Can you think of nothing but yourself? Can't you see that you've been a miserable, selfish beast – that what happens to you matters nothing? Can't you see that the only thing that matters is your wife? You're a miserable, skulking cur – ... She trusted you – she believed in you, and you've done her an almost irreparable wrong.'

Hillier stood suddenly erect.

'What I have done, Swann, is more than a wrong. It is a crime. Within an hour of your leaving this room, I shall have told Ella everything. That is the only thing left for me to do, and I shall not shirk it. I shall take the full responsibility. You did right to come to me as you did. You are right to consider me a miserable, skulking cur' (he brought the words out with an emphasised bravery). 'Now you can do no more. The remainder of the matter rests between me and my wife – '

He paused.

'And to think that you – ' Swann began passionately.

'There is no object to be gained by our discussing the matter further,' Hillier interrupted a little loudly, but with a concentrated calm. 'There is no need for you to remain here longer.' He put his thumb to the electric bell.

'The maid will be here in a moment to show you out,' he added.

Swann waited, blinking with hesitation. His personality seemed to be slipping from him.

'You are going to tell her?' he repeated slowly.

The door opened: he hurried out of the room.

The outer door slammed: Hillier's face turned a sickly white; his eyes dilated, and he laughed excitedly – a low, short, hysterical laugh. He looked at the clock: the whole scene had lasted but ten minutes. He pulled a chair to the fire, and sat staring at the flames moodily. ... The tension of the dramatic situation snapped. Before his new prospect, once again he thought weakly of suicide. ...

IX

He had told her – not, of course, the whole story – from that his sensitivity had shrunk. Still he had besmirched himself bravely; he had gone through with the interview not without dignity. Beforehand he had nerved himself for a terrible ordeal; yet, somehow, as he reviewed it, now that it was all over, the scene seemed to have fallen flat. The tragedy of her grief, of his own passionate repentance, which he had been expecting, had proved unaccountably tame. She had cried, and at the sight of those tears of hers he had suffered intensely; but she had displayed no suppressed, womanish jealousy; had not, in her despair, appeared to regard his confession as an overwhelming shattering of her faith in him, and so provoked him to reveal the depth of his anguish. He had implored her forgiveness; he had vowed he would efface the memory of his treachery; she had acquiesced dreamily, with apparent heroism. There had been no mention of a separation.

And now the whole thing was ended: to-night he and she were dining out.

He was vaguely uncomfortable; yet his heart was full of a sincere repentance, because of the loosening of the strain of his anxiety; because of the smarting sense of humiliation, when he recollected Swann's words; because he had caused her to suffer in a queer, inarticulate way, which he did not altogether understand, of which he was vaguely afraid. . . .

X

When at last he had left her alone, it was with a curious calmness that she started to reflect upon it all. She supposed it was very strange that his confession had not wholly prostrated her; and glancing furtively backwards, catching a glimpse of her old girlish self, wondered listlessly how it was that, insensibly, all these months, she had grown so hardened. . . .

* * * * *

By-and-by, the recent revelation of his unfaithfulness seemed to recede slowly into the misty past, and, fading, losing its sharpness of outline, its distinctness of detail, to resemble an irreparable fact to which familiarity had inured her.

And all the uneasiness of her mistrustfulness, and pain of her fluctuating doublings ceased; her comprehension of him was all at once clarified, rendered vivid and indisputable; and she was conscious of a certain sense of relief. She was eased of those feverish, spasmodic gaspings of her half-starved love; at first the dulness of sentimental atrophy seemed the more endurable. She jibed at her own natural artlessness; and insisted to herself that she wanted no fool's paradise, that she was even glad to see him as he really was, to terminate, once for all, this futile folly of love; that, after all, his unfaithfulness was no unusual and terrible tragedy, but merely a commonplace chapter in the lives of smiling, chattering women, whom she met at dinners, evening parties, and balls. . . .

* * * * *

There were some who simpered to her over Hillier as a model of modern husbands; and she must go on listening and smiling. . . .

. . . And the long years ahead would unroll themselves a slow tale of decorous lovelessness. . . .

He would be always the same – that was the hardest to face. His nature could never alter, grow into something different . . . never, never change . . . always, always the same. . . .

Oh! it made her dread it all – the restless round of social enjoyments; the greedy exposure of the petty weaknesses of common acquaintance; the ill-natured atmosphere that she felt emanating from people herded together. . . . All the details of her London life looked unreal, mean, pitiful. . . .

And she longed after the old days of her girlhood, of the smooth, staid country life; she longed after the simple, restful companionship of her old father and mother; after the accumulation of little incidents that she had loved long ago. . . . She longed too – and the straining at heart-strings grew tenser – she longed after her own lost maidenhood; she longed to be ignorant and careless; to see life once again as a simple, easy matter; to know nothing of evil; to understand nothing of men; to trust – to trust unquestioningly.

... All that was gone; she herself was all changed; those days could never come again. . . .

And she cried to herself a little, from weakness of spirit, softly. . . .

* * * * *

Then, gradually, out of the weary turmoil of her bitterness, there came to her a warm impulse of vague sympathy for the countless, unknown tragedies at work around her; she thought of the sufferings – of outcast women of loveless lives, full of mirthless laughter; she thought of the long loneliness of childless women. . . .

She clutched for consolation at the unhappiness of others; but she only discovered the greater ugliness of the world. And she returned to a tired contemplation of her own prospect. . . .

* * * * *

He had broken his vows to her – not only the solemn vow he had taken in the church (she recalled how his voice had trembled with emotion as he had repeated the words) – but all that passionate series of vows he had made to her during the spring-time of their love. . . .

. . . Yes, that seemed the worst part of it – that, and not the making love to another woman. . . . What was she like? . . . What was it in her that had attracted him? . . . Oh! but what did that matter? . . . – only why were men's natures so different from women's? . . .

. . . Now, she must go on – go on alone. Since her marriage she had lost the habit of daily converse with Christ: here in London, somehow, He had seemed so distant, so difficult of approach. . . .

. . . She must just go on. . . . She had the little Claude. . . . It was to help her that God had given her Claude. . . . Oh! she would pray to God to make him good – to give him a straight, strong, upright, honest nature. And herself, every day, she would watch over his growth, guide him, teach him. . . . Yes, he must grow up good . . . into boyhood . . . different from other boys. . . . into manhood, simple, honourable manhood. . . . She would be everything to him: he and she would come to comprehend each other, to read into each other's hearts. . . . Perhaps, between them, would spring up perfect love and trust. . . .

XI

Swann had written to her:

'You are in trouble: let me come.'

Gradually, between the lines of the note, she understood it all – she read how his love for her had leapt up, now that he knew that she was unhappy; how he wanted to be near her, to comfort her, and perhaps . . . perhaps . . .

She was filled with great sorrow for him and warm gratitude, too, for his simple, single-hearted love – but sorrow, that she could give him nothing in return, and because it seemed that, somehow, he and she were about to bid one another good-bye; she thought she dimly foresaw how their friendship was doomed to dwindle. . . .

So she let him come.

* * * * *

. . . And all this she fancied she read again in the long, grave glance of his greeting, and the firm clasp of his big hand.

When he spoke, his deep, steady voice dominated her: she knew at once that he would do what was right.

'Ella, my poor Ella, how brave you are!' She looked up at him, smiling tremulously, through her quick-starting tears. . . . The next moment it was as if the words had escaped him almost as if he regretted them.

He sat down opposite her, and, lightening his voice, asked just as he always did for news of the little Claude.

And so their talk ran on.

After awhile, she came to realise that he meant to say no more: the strength of his great reserve became apparent, and a sense of peace stole over her. He talked on, and to the restful sound of his clear, strong voice, she abandoned herself dreamily. . . . This he had judged the better course. . . . that he should have adopted any other now seemed inconceivable. Beside him she felt weak and helpless: she remembered the loneliness of his life: he seemed to her altogether noble; and she was vaguely remorseful that she had not perceived from the first that it was from him that her help would come. . . .

She divined, too, the fineness of his sacrifice – that manly, human struggle with himself, through which he had passed to attain it – how he had longed for the right to make her his . . . and how he had renounced. The sureness of his victory, and the hidden depths of his nature which it revealed awed her . . . now he would never swerve from what he knew to be right. . . . And on, through those years to come, she could trust him, always, always. . . .

. . . At last he bade her good-bye: even at the last his tone remained unchanged.

It was close upon seven o'clock. She went upstairs to dress for dinner, and kneeling beside the bed, prayed to God with an outburst of passionate, pulsing joy. . . .

Ten minutes later Hillier came in from his dressing-room. He clasped his hands round her bare neck, kissing her hair again and again.

'I have been punished, Nellie,' he began in a broken whisper. 'Good God! it is hard to bear. . . . Help me, Nellie, . . . help me to bear it.'

She unclasped his fingers, and started to stroke them a little mechanically, as if it were her duty to ease him of his pain. . . .

Appendix 4

'The White Maize'
Published in *A Set of Village Tales* in 1895

Old Cauhapé said it was the end of the world.

For eight days and eight nights the ceaseless hiss of the rain. During the day-time, neither sky nor sun, nor breath of wind – only the grey veil of mist, enshrouding all things. The nights were dark as pitch, and full of the hiss of the rain; and from sunset to sunrise the frogs chanted their long, dismal mass.

On the eighth day of the rain, about six o'clock in the afternoon, I went out. A sickly glimmer of muddy light flickered from the west; a breeze was shaking the drops from the trees; the road was powdered with acacia-bloom, lying thick like sodden snow; great pools of yellow water were in possession of the lanes; and new-born streams, bubbling of their own importance, trickled, sleek and swollen, across the fields and under the hedges.

Eudore stood in his doorway: inside the house I could hear the clattering of Anna's sabots.* He looked up at me, as I trudged towards him, across the spongy ox-bedding; but he gave me no greeting, nor moved his hand to his beret, military wise, as was his habit. In an instant, it flashed upon me that some great trouble had come to Eudore, and I hesitated whether to go forward or to go back.

Eudore was young and brawny and obstinate: but, as I had reason to know, he had been hard put to it these last months. And the third baby was on its way.

I came close up to him; but still he said nothing, just held his open palm towards me. In it lay a young maize-sprout, fresh-plucked.

I understood. My gaze met his, and there was the solidness of despair in his dull face.

The maize had come up white.

We went inside without speaking, and Anna bustled about to make me welcome, and knelt on the hearth to blow up the fire. Marcellin, the little boy, lay on the floor, playing with a cockchafer.† He had tied a thread to its hind legs, and was trying to persuade the creature to fly. But the cockchafer was lazy with the damp, and refused to do more

* A simple wooden shoe.
† A large flying beetle (*Melolontha melolontha*).

than crawl. Whereupon Marcellin dumped his podgy fist on the floor, and threw the cockchafer, thread and all, into the yard.

Eudore took him by the hand, and the two went out to bring in the geese. And when they were gone there was an end of Anna's cheeriness. She began to grumble, pursing her dark-red lips, dilating her round, black eyes, scattering her words, as it were, all over the room.

It was while Eudore was with the regiment* at Mont-de-Monsan that he had courted her. She was a *bonne-à-tout-faire*† in those days. And now that the luck was dead against Eudore, that every year things went worse and worse with them, and that most of the place was mortgaged to Etienne Mattou,‡ the money-lender, she grumbled whenever she could find a listener, and when there was no one she emptied her heart to little Marcellin, concerning the dreariness of life in the country, the cursed greed of the land which devoured everything, and grudged even a tainted fruit, concerning the spitefulness of God in Heaven.

Then Eudore returned, and little Marcellin drove the young geese towards the fire, and Anna's grumbling ceased.

Eudore pulled the maize-sprout from his pocket, and turned it over once more in his hand, looking stolidly across at Anna. Then he threw it among the fizzling logs.

The maize had come up white. The fields were all dotted with thousands and thousands of rotten sprouts, and Eudore was altogether ruined.

At the Toussaint§ he was sold up, and the great tragedy of his life started to drag its course.

* Performing compulsory military service.

† A general maid of all work.

‡ Mattou is the principal character in a later story in the collection.

§ The Feast of All Saints or All Saints' Day is celebrated by the Roman Catholic Church (and other Western Christian churches) on 1 November.

Appendix 5

From *Vignettes: A Miniature Journal of Whim and Sentiment*

'At Villeneuve-lès-Avignon'* (23 April)

On the roof of the ruined church we lay, basking amid the hot, powdery heather; the cinder-coloured roofs of the town flattened out beneath us – a ragged patch of dead, decayed colour, burnt, as it seemed, out of the luscious green of the Rhône valley. Overhead, a thick, blue sky hung heavy, and away and away, into the steamy haze of mid-day heat, filtered the Tarascon road, a streak of dazzling white. To the east, the sun was beating on the sandy slopes; to the west, the old papal palace, like a great, grey, sleeping beast, lifted its long, bare back above the roofs of Avignon.

The lizards scurried from cranny to cranny across the crumbling wall. Below, in the cloister, a cat was curled by the black stack of brushwood. The little *place*† stood empty, and stillness seemed to have fallen over all things.

The warmth lulled one to a delicious torpor. I was thinking of the bustling Regent Street pavement, of the rumble of Piccadilly, of newsboys yelling special editions in the Strand, drowsily conjuring up these and other commonplace contrasts.‡

Then Jeanne-Marie Latou began to speak. She sat between us, with her legs hunched under her coarse, colourless skirt, and some stray wisps of hair looking dingily yellow against the clean white of her *coiffe*.§ As she talked, her brown skin puckered oddly about her tiny, shrunken eyes, and her hands – browned also and squat – clasped themselves around her knees. It was not often that Jeanne-Marie Latou spoke French; her vocabulary was quite simple and limited, and every now and then, with an impatient shake of her head, she would break out into *patois*.¶

* All the French place names in this vignette – Villeneuve-lès-Avignon, Tarascon, Ardèche – are towns in southern France near the River Rhône. Marseilles is a large city on the Mediterranean in the same region.

† A square (French).

‡ These are all busy streets in central London.

§ A peasant woman's cap. The word has become 'coif' in English.

¶ A local language or dialect of French.

She was telling us of her nephew in Tunis – '*Un pays où on ne voit que des sauvages*'* – and of the sweetheart he had left behind at Barbentane; repeating by heart, one after another, his queer, bald, little letters – how he had been kicked by his horse (he was a *spahi*; '*zouave à cheval*,' she called it†), and had been sick ten days in the hospital; and how, without telling anyone, she had scraped together a hundred sous‡ to send out to him. Somehow, irresistibly, while she chattered, I seemed to see that soldier nephew of hers – broad and straight and bronzed, his fez§ stuck nonchalantly on the back of his head, noisily *noçant avec des camarades*¶ with those hundred sous, which old Tante Latou** had sent out to him.

By-and-bye, she related her journey to Valence, in the time when she had worked hard as a cherry-packer for Madame Charbonnier in the Rue Joseph-Vernet, insisting with comical, energetic wrinklings of her forehead on her contempt for the *jargon de L'Ardèche.*†† . . . She had been to Marseilles, too, last year – that was a great journey – eighteen of them had gone from Villeneuve, '*femmes et filles et trois garçons, dans un train 'ambulant' – quatre francs et douze sous, aller et retour. . . . Marseilles, vous savez,*' Jeanne-Marie Latou reiterated, '*c'est quelque chose . . . c'est quelque chose . . . c'est quelque chose . . . enfin, c'est la plus jolie ville que j'ai trouvée.*'‡‡

Afterwards, starting to recall bygone times, she described the breaking up of the *Chartreuse* in *quatre-vingt-douze*,§§ and the selling of the whole building by auction in the little *place*, there below us (not for money – no one in the *pays*¶¶ had any money in those days – but for

* A country where you see only savages (French).

† A *spahi* was a soldier in a mounted French cavalry unit, serving in North Africa. *Spahis* were mainly North Africans, but a significant number of soldiers and most officers were French. A *zouave à cheval* would be a 'Zouave on horseback'. The Zouaves were light infantry in the French Army, marked by their distinctive oriental uniforms. They would be unlikely to be on horseback.

‡ A sou was an ancient French coin, no longer in existence at the time Crackanthorpe is writing. The word continued to be used to mean the twentieth part of a franc. Hence, a hundred sous is Jeanne-Marie Latou's way of saying five francs. The word 'sou' is still used in modern French, meaning 'money'.

§ A North African hat, part of the *spahis*' oriental-style uniform.

¶ On a spree with his pals (French).

** Aunt Latou (French)

†† The Ardèche dialect (French).

‡‡ . . . women and girls and three boys, in a [slow, local] train – four francs twelve sous, there and back. . . . Marseilles, you know . . . it's something . . . it's something . . . it's something . . . well, it's the prettiest city I've found (French).

§§ The reference is to the dissolution of a Carthusian nunnery during the French Revolution in 1792.

¶¶ Country (French).

*assignats**), and Jeanne-Marie Latou explained, '*Ceux qui avaient peur, n'en prenaient pas, et ceux qui n'avaient pas peur en prenaient.*'† And her father, who had been a stone-worker, over there at Les Angles, had bid *douze cent francs d'assignats*‡ for the house where the *supérieure*§ had lived – *douze cents francs d'assignats* which no one had ever asked him to pay. There Jeanne-Marie Latou had always lived – seventy-seven years, it was now, as near as she could remember – she, and her husband who had been dead these twenty-three years. She could remember the time when the frescoes on the cloister walls were bright and beautiful, and no grass grew between the flags.¶ Yes, she had seen all the other houses pass from family to family; there were six of them now who had the right to use the old church as a barn, '*ma foi, elle est bien grande, l'église,*' Jeanne-Marie Latou concluded, smiling knowingly at us, '*Mais, quand même, ils se chicanent toujours.*' . . .**

And with that, she rose slowly and bid us good-bye, and wished us good health, toddling grotesquely away down the steps.

After she had gone, we stayed a long while up on the hot roof, watching the dark shadows creep from under the broken bridge across the rippling Rhône, as it swept past towards the sea. And I wondered more drowsily than ever concerning old Jeanne-Marie Latou, and her soldier nephew, with the *spahis*, away over there in Tunis, and the great journey of hers to Marseilles – eighteen of them from the dead little town below, '*femmes et filles et trois garçons, dans un train 'ambulant' – quatre francs et douze sous, aller et retour.*'

'Rêverie' (25 December)

I dreamed of an age grown strangely picturesque – of the rich enfeebled by monotonous ease; of the shivering poor clamouring nightly for justice; of a helpless democracy, vast revolt of the ill-informed; of priests striving to be rational; of sentimental moralists protecting iniquity; of middle-class princes; of sybaritic†† saints; of complacent and pompous politicians; of doctors hurrying the degeneration of the race; of artists discarding possibilities for limitations; of pressmen befooling

* *Assignats* were promissory notes issued by the French Revolutionary Government in the late eighteenth century.

† Those who were afraid didn't take any, and those who weren't afraid did (French).

‡ Twelve hundred francs in *assignats* (French).

§ Superior (female). The head of a religious house.

¶ Large paving stones.

** By my faith, it's really big, the church. . . . But, all the same, they argue all the time (French).

†† Self-indulgent, given over to luxury.

a pretentious public; of critics refining upon the 'busman's methods; of inhabitants of Camberwell* chattering of culture.

And I dreamed of this great, dreamy London of ours; of her myriad fleeting moods; of the charm of her portentous† provinciality; and I awoke all a-glad and hungering for life. . . .

'In the Strand'‡ (27 January)

The city disgorges.

All along the Strand, down the great, ebbing tide, the omnibuses, a congested press of gaudy craft, drift westwards, jostling and jamming their tall, loaded decks, with a clanking of chains, a rumble of lumbering wheels, a thudding of quick-loosed brakes, a humming of hammering hoofs.§ . . .

The empty hansoms slink silently past; the street hawkers¶ – a long row of dingy figures – line the pavement edge; troops of frenzied newsboys dart yelling through the traffic; and here and there a sullen-faced woman struggles to stem the tide of men.

Somewhere, behind Pall Mall,** unheeded the sun has set: the sky is powdered with crimson dust; one by one the shops gleam out, blazing their windows of burnished glass; the twilight throbs with a ceaseless shuffle of hurrying feet; and over all things hovers the spirit of London's grim unrest.

* A district in south London.

† Here the word means pompous, pretentious. This is an early use of the word with this meaning.

‡ A busy street in central London. It runs west into Trafalgar Square.

§ The vehicles are horse-drawn.

¶ Street-sellers of various goods. The word has negative and shabby connotations.

** Pall Mall runs westward from Trafalgar Square toward Green Park.

Appendix 6

'The Rendezvous' (*Le Rendez-vous*)
Guy de Maupassant
First published in *L'Écho de Paris*, 23 February 1889. Published in book form in *La Main gauche* in 1889

Hat on her head, coat on her back, a black veil down to her nose, another in her pocket that she would put over the first one when she had got into the guilty cab, she tapped the tip of her parasol on the tip of her ankle boot and stayed seated in her room, unable to decide whether to leave for this rendezvous.

How many times, however, for ten years, had she dressed thus, while her husband (a very fashionable broker) was working at the Stock Exchange, to join in his bachelor apartment the handsome Viscount de Martelet, her lover?

The clock behind her back ticked off the seconds in a brisk fashion; a half-read book lay open on the little bureau of rosewood, between the windows, and a strong perfume of violets, breathed out by two small bouquets bathing in two delicate Meissen vases over the fireplace, mingled with a vague scent of vervain breathed out slyly by the door of the toilette left ajar.

The hour struck – three o'clock – and brought her to her feet. She turned to look at the face, then smiled, fancying: He is waiting for me already. He will become upset. So, she left the room, advised the manservant that she would return in an hour at the latest – a lie – descended the stairs and ventured out into the street, on foot.

It was the last days of May, that delicious season when the spring from the countryside seems to have laid siege to Paris and to take it over the roofs, to invade the houses, through the walls, to make the city blossom, to spread a gaiety there over the stones of the façades of the buildings, the asphalt of the pavements and the stones of the streets, to bathe her, to make her tipsy with sap like a tree that is turning green.

Mme Haggan took several steps to the right intending to follow, as always, the Rue de Provence where she would hail a cab, but the gentleness of the air, that feeling of summer that enters our throat on certain days, penetrated her so brusquely that, changing her mind, she took the Rue de la Chaussée-d'Antin, without knowing why, obscurely drawn by a desire to see the trees in the Square of the Trinity. She thought: Bah! He'll wait ten minutes longer for me. This idea, once more, made her glad, and, taking little steps, in the crowd, she thought she saw him become impatient, look at the hour, open the window, listen at the door, sit down for a few instants, get up again, and, not daring to smoke, for she had forbidden him to do so on the days of their rendezvous, cast despairing glances at the cigarette box.

She walked gently, distracted by all she encountered, by the figures and the shops, slowing her step more and more and so little desiring to arrive that she sought, in the shop fronts, pretexts for stopping.

At the end of the street, before the church, the green of the little gardens drew her so strongly that she crossed the square, entered the garden, this cage for children, and twice took a turn round the narrow strip of grass, in the midst of the nannies beribboned, in full bloom, gaudy, flowery. Then she took a seat, sat down, and raising her eyes to the face round as a moon in the clock-tower, she watched the hand move.

Just at that moment, the half hour struck, and her heart thrilled with pleasure when she heard the bells of the carillon ring out. A half hour gained, a quarter of an hour more to reach the Rue de Miromesnil, and a few more minutes of strolling – an hour! An hour stolen from the rendezvous! She would stay there barely forty minutes, and it would be over once more.

God! How it bored her to go over there! Just like a patient going to the dentist's, she bore in her heart an intolerable memory of all the rendezvous in the past, one a week on average for two years, and the thought that another was going to take place, right now, made her wince with anguish from head to foot. Not that it was painful, painful like a visit to the dentist, but so boring, so boring, so complicated, so long, so arduous that anything, anything, even an operation, would have seemed preferable to her. However, she went on, very slowly, with tiny steps, stopping, sitting down, strolling everywhere, but on she went. Oh! she would have preferred to give him a miss, but she had stood up the poor viscount twice in succession last month, and she did not dare start again so soon. Why did she go back there? Ah! why? Because she had got into the habit, and she had no reason to give to poor Martelet when he wanted to know why! Why had she begun? Why? She no longer knew! Had she loved him? It was possible. Not a lot, but a little, so long ago! He was nice, in demand, elegant, gallant, and represented closely at first glance the perfect lover for a woman of the world. The courtship had lasted three months – the normal time, an honourable struggle, sufficient resistance – then she consented, with what emotion, what tingling, what horrid and charming fear, to the first rendezvous, followed by so many others, in the little bachelor's entresol,* on the Rue de Miromesnil. Her heart? What did it know then, her little heart of a woman seduced, defeated, conquered, passing for the first time the door of that house of nightmare? True, she no longer knew! She had forgotten! One remembered a fact, a date, a thing, but scarcely remembered, two years later, an emotion that had flown so fast because it was so light. Oh! for example, she had not forgotten the others, that strand of rendezvous, that way of the cross of love, its station so fatiguing, so monotonous, so similar, that nausea rose to her lips in looking ahead at what would be shortly.

God! these cabs you had to hail to go there; they didn't resemble the other cabs that you use for ordinary journeys! For sure, the cabmen guessed. She felt it just in the way they looked at her, and those eyes of the cabmen of Paris are terrible! When one thinks that at any moment, in court, they recognise after many years the criminals they carried one single time, deep in the night, from some street to a railway station, and that they deal with almost as many passengers as there are hours in the day, and that their memories are so sure that they can declare: That's the man I picked up on the Rue des Martyres and let down at the Gare de Lyon, at quarter past midnight, on the tenth of July last year! – wasn't there reason to tremble when you are risking what a young woman risks who is going to a rendezvous, trusting her reputation to the first cabman who comes by! For two years she'd used them for the trip from the Rue de Miromesnil, at least a hundred to a hundred and twenty, reckoning one a week. That's how many witnesses there were who could give evidence against her at a critical moment.

As soon as she was in the cab, she took from her pocket the other veil thick and black like a wolf, and hung it over her eyes. That hid the face, yes, but the rest, the dress, the hat, the parasol, could someone not notice them, have seen them already? Oh! in the Rue de Miromesnil, what a torment! She believed she recognised all the passers-by, all the servants, the whole world. With the cab hardly stopped, she jumped out and ran in in front of the concierge, always erect at the threshold to his lodge. Now there was someone who must know everything – her address – her name – her husband's profession – everything – for concierges are the most subtle of policemen! For two years she had wanted to buy him, to give him, to throw to him, one day or another, a hundred franc note while passing before him. Not once had she dared to make that little movement of throwing at his feet a little piece of rolled-up paper! She was afraid – of what? – She did not know! – To

* A low storey of a building lying between two floors, usually between ground and first floors.

be called back, if he didn't understand at all? Of a scandal? of a crowd gathered on the stair? of being arrested perhaps? To arrive at the viscount's door there was nothing but a half-floor to go up, and it seemed to her as high as the Tour Saint-Jacques! Scarcely in the vestibule, she felt herself caught in a trap, and the least noise, before or behind, made her suffocate. Impossible to go back, with the concierge and the street closing off her retreat; and if anyone came down the stairs just at that moment, she did not dare ring Martelet's bell and passed by the door as if she were going elsewhere! She would climb, climb, climb! She would go up four floors! Then, when all seemed to become peaceful again in the stairwell, she would go downstairs again running with anguish in her soul that she would not recognise the entresol!

He would be there, in a gallant suit of velvet lined with silk, very dainty, but a little ridiculous, and for two years he had changed nothing in his manner of greeting her, but nothing, not a gesture!

As soon as he had closed the door again, he would say to her: 'Let me kiss your hands, my dear, dear friend!' Then he would follow her into the bedroom, where with the shutters closed and the lamps lit, winter and summer, to be chic doubtless, he would kneel before her looking at her from below upwards with an air of adoration. The first day that had been very sweet, very successful, that movement! Now she thought she was seeing M. Delaunay* performing for the hundred-and-twentieth time the fifth act of a successful play. He needed to change his moves.

And then after, oh! my God! after! that was the hardest! No, he did not change his moves, the poor fellow! What a good fellow, but banal! . . .

God, it was difficult to undress without a lady's maid! Once, it was just acceptable, but every week it became odious! No, really, a man shouldn't demand of a woman forced labour like that! But if it was difficult to undress, getting dressed again became almost impossible and it became enervating to cry out, exasperating to bat off the gentleman who said, circling around her in a gauche manner: 'Would you like me to help you?' Help her! Ah yes! to do what? What could he do?? It was sufficient to see him with a tie-pin between his fingers to know that.

It was at that moment perhaps that she began to take a dislike to him. When he said 'Would you like me to help you?', she could have killed him. And then was it possible that a woman could not end up

* Delaunay is probably Louis-Arsène Delaunay (1826–1903), a well-known French actor noted for the length of his career. In 1889, the year of publication of 'Le Rendez-vous', he would be at the end of his career on stage.

detesting a man who for two years had forced her more than one hundred and twenty times to get dressed again without a lady's maid?

For sure, there were not many men as maladroit as he, as little loosened up, as monotonous. The little Baron de Grimbal would not have asked with that inane air: 'Would you like me to help you?' He would have helped, he would, so lively, so droll, so spirited. There you have it! He was a diplomat; he'd been around the world, had roved everywhere, had doubtless undressed and dressed again women attired in all the fashions of the earth, he had! . . .

The church clock struck the three-quarters of the hour. She rose up, looked at the clock face, began to laugh murmuring: 'Oh! he must be agitated!' Then she set off with a more lively step, and left the gardens.

She had not even made ten steps into the square when she found herself face to face with a gentleman who bowed deeply to her.

'Goodness, it's you, Baron?' she said surprised. She had just been thinking of him.

'Yes, Madame.'

And he enquired of her health, then after few vague remarks, he began again.

'You know that you are the only one – you will permit me to say of my friends, won't you? – who has still never come to see my Japanese collection.'

'But, my dear baron, a woman cannot go to a bachelor's just like that.'

'How so! How so! that is a mistake when it's a matter of visiting a rare collection!'

'In any case, she cannot go alone.'

'And why not? but I have received multitudes of ladies on their own, only there for the sake of my gallery! I receive them every day. Would you like me to name them? – no – then I won't do it. One must be discreet even when it is not open to censure. In principle it is not improper to visit a serious man, one known, in a certain situation, except when one goes there for a reason one cannot admit!'

'Well, that's right enough what you say.'

'So, you will come to see my collection.'

'When?'

'But right away.'

'Impossible, I'm in a hurry.'

'Come now. It's been a half-hour that you've been sitting in the gardens.'

'You are spying on me?'

'I was looking at you.'

'It's true, I'm in a hurry . . .'

'I am certain you're not. Admit you are not in a great hurry.'

Mme Haggan began to laugh and admitted,

'No . . . no . . . not . . . great. . . .'

A cab passed close by. The little Baron called out, 'Cab!', and the vehicle stopped. Then, opening the door,

'Please get in, Madame.'

'But, Baron, no, it is impossible, I cannot today'.

'Madame, what you are doing is imprudent, please get in! People are starting to look at us, you'll bring a mob down on us; people will think I'm carrying you off and they'll arrest both of us, get in, I beg you!'

She got in, startled, bewildered. Then he sat next to her, saying to the cab-driver,

'Rue de Provence.'

But suddenly she cried out,

'Oh! my goodness, I forgot an urgent telegram. Could you take me first to the nearest telegraph office?'

The cab stopped a little further on, on the Rue de Châteaudun, and she said to the Baron,

'Could you get me a fifty-centimes card? I promised my husband to invite Martelet to dinner for tomorrow, and I completely forgot.'

When the Baron returned, the blue card in his hand, she wrote in pencil:

'My dear friend, I am very unwell; I have atrocious neuralgia that keeps me in bed. Come to dine tomorrow evening so I may make amends. JEANNE.'

She moistened the sticky part, closed it carefully, with the address 'Viscount de Martelet, 240 Rue de Miromesnil', then, giving the card to the Baron:

'Now, would you be so kind as to place this in the telegram box?'

Translated by David Malcolm

Appendix 7

'Jeanne-Marie'
Leila Macdonald
Published in *The Yellow Book* 3 (October 1894): 215–40

I

Jeanne-Marie lived alone in the white cottage at the far end of the village street.

It was a long narrow street of tall houses, stretching each side of the white shining road, for two hundred yards or more. A street that was cool and shadeful even in the shadeless summer days, when the sun burned most hotly, when the broad roads dazzled between their avenues of plane-tree and poplar, and the mountains disappeared from the horizon in the blue haze of heat.

From her little garden Jeanne-Marie liked to look at the mountains each morning, and, when for two or three days following they were not to be seen, she would shake her head reproach fully, as at the failing of old friends.

'My boys, Jeanne-Marie is only thirty-seven,' Bourdet the innkeeper said to his companions, as they sat, one May afternoon, smoking under the chestnut-trees in front of the café. They all looked up as he spoke, and watched Jeanne-Marie, as she walked slowly past them to her cottage.

'Bourdet has been paying court,' said Leguillon, the fat, red-faced butcher, with a chuckle, as he puffed at his long pipe.

'You see, he is anxious we should think her of an age suitable, before he tells us the betrothals are arranged.'

'For my part I should give many congratulations,' said the village postman and tobacconist, gruffly. 'Jeanne-Marie is worth any of our girls of the village, with their bright dresses and silly giggles.'

Bourdet laughed. 'You shall come to the wedding, my friends,' he said, with a wink and a nod of the head to the retreating figure; 'and since our friend Minaud there finds the girls so distasteful, he shall wait till our babies are old enough, and be betrothed to one of them.'

The postmaster laughed with the rest. 'But seriously,' he said, 'Bourdet will pardon me if I tell him our Jeanne-Marie is a good deal past the thirties.'

Laurent, the good-looking young farmer, who stood leaning against the tree round which their chairs were gathered, answered him gravely. 'Wait, *beau-père*,* till you see her on Sunday coming from Mass on M. Bourdet's arm; the cap that hides the grey knot of hair at the back of the head is neat and bright oh! so bright pink or blue for choice, and if M. Bourdet chances to compliment the colour of the stockings he is gay, you know, always the yellow face turns rosy and all the wrinkles go.'

And laughing maliciously at Bourdet, the young fellow turned away homewards.

Bourdet looked grave. ''Tis your son-in-law that speaks like that, Minaud,' he said, 'otherwise I would say that in my day the young fellows found it better to amuse themselves with the young girls than to mock at the old ones.'

'You are right, my friend,' said Minaud. ''Tis the regiment† that taught Laurent this, and many other things. But it is a good boy, though with a sharp tongue. To these young ones it seems all foolishness to be an old girl.'

And the others nodded agreement.

So they sat, chatting, and drawing at their long pipes, while the afternoon sun gleamed on the little gardens and on the closed green shutters of the houses; and the slow, large oxen lumbered through the village street, their yoked heads pressed well down, and their tails flicking unceasingly at the swarm of flies.

Jeanne-Marie stood in her garden, blinking thoughtfully at the flowers, while she shaded her eyes with her hand. On her bare head the sparse brown hair was parted severely and neatly to each side, and the deep southern eyes looked steadily out of the tanned and wrinkled face. Her light cotton bodice fell away from the thin lines of her neck and shoulders, and her sabots clicked harshly as she moved about the garden.

'At least the good God has given me a fine crab-apple bloom this year,' Jeanne-Marie said, as she looked at the masses of rich blossom. On the wall the monthly roses were flowering thickly, and the Guelder roses‡ bent their heads under the weight of their heavy bunches. 'In six days I shall have the peonies, and the white rose-bush in the corner is coming soon,' said Jeanne-Marie contentedly.

* Father-in-law (French).

† Military service in the French Army.

‡ Guelder rose (*Viburnum opulus*), or dogberry, is a deciduous shrub native to Europe. It has splendid and complex white flowers in summer and bright red berries in autumn. It does not look like a rose at all.

II

It was four and a half years ago that Jeanne-Marie had come to the white cottage next to the mill, with the communal school opposite. Till that autumn day, when a pair of stout oxen had brought her goods to the door, she had lived with her brother, who was *métayer** to M. François, the owner of the big villa a quarter of a mile beyond the village. Her father had been *métayer*; and when he died, his son Firman – a fine-looking young man, not long home from his service† – had taken his place. So the change at the *métairie*‡ had very little affected Jeanne-Marie.

But she missed her father sorely every day at mid-day, when she remembered that there was one less to cook for; that the tall, straight old figure would not come in at the door, and that the black pudding§ might remain uncooked for all Firman's noticing; and Jeanne-Marie would put the bouillon by the fire, and sit down and cry softly to herself.

They were very kind to her at the villa, and at night, when Firman was at the café, she would take the stockings and the linen and darn them in the kitchen, while she listened to the servants talk, and suppressed her *patois*¶ as much as possible, for they were from the North, and would not understand.

Two years after her father's death, Jeanne-Marie began to notice that Firman went no more to the café in the evening, and had always his shirt clean, and his best black smocked** cape for the market in the town on Mondays, and for Mass on Sundays.

'It astonishes me,' she had said, when she was helping M. François cook that day the château-folk†† had come to *déjeuner*‡‡ unexpectedly – for Jeanne- Marie's cooking was very good indeed – 'because, you understand, that is not his way at all. Now, if it were Paul Puyoo or the young André, it would be quite ordinary; but with Firman, I doubt with him it is a different thing.'

And Anna had nodded her black head sagely over the *omelette*

* A farmer who pays rent in kind; a type of sharecropper.

† Compulsory military service.

‡ The kind of farm worked by a *métayer*.

§ Blood sausage; *boudin noir* – a mixture of blood and fat, a source of protein for European peasants for centuries.

¶ Dialect (French).

** Pleated and ornamented.

†† People from the local big house where the landowners and gentry live.

‡‡ Dinner – a midday meal.

*aux fines herbes** as she answered : 'Jeanne-Marie, Firman wishes to marry; Jeanne-Marie, for my own part, I say it's that little fat blue-eyed Suzanne from the *métairie* on the hill.'

III

Suzanne looked very pretty the day she came home to M. François' *métairie* leaning on her husband's arm; but Jeanne-Marie was not there to see; she was sitting in the large chair in the kitchen of the white cottage, and she was sobbing with her head in her hands. 'And indeed the blessed Virgin herself must have thought me crazy, to see me sitting sobbing there, with the house in confusion, and not a thing to cook with in the kitchen,' she said, shamefacedly, to Marthe Legrand from the mill, when she came in, later, to help her. 'You should have remained,' Marthe answered, nodding at her pityingly. 'You should have remained, Jeanne-Marie; the old house is the old house, and the good God never meant the wedding of the young ones to drive away the old ones from the door.'

Jeanne-Marie drew in her breath at the words 'old ones.' 'But the book says I am only thirty-four!' she told herself; and that night she looked in the old Mass-book, to be sure if it could be true; and there was the date set down very clearly, in the handwriting of Dubois, her father's oldest friend; for Jeanne-Marie's father himself could neither read nor write – he was, as he said with pride, of the old school, 'that kissed our sweethearts, and found that better than writing them long scribbles on white paper, as the young ones do now; and thought a chat with a friend on Sundays and holidays worth more than sitting cramped up, reading the murders and the adulteries in the newspapers.'

So it was Dubois who wrote down the children's births in the old Mass book. Yes, there they were. Catherine first of all; poor Catherine, who was so bright and pretty, and died that rainy winter when she was just twelve years old. Then '*Jeanne-Marie, née le 28 Novembre 1854, à minuit,*'† and added, in the same hand writing, '*On nous raconte qu'à cette heure-là nous étions en train de gagner une grande bataille en Russie! Que ça lui porte Bonheur!*'‡ Eight years later; '*Jacques Firman, né le 12 Février à midi.*'§ It all came back to Jeanne-Marie as she read;

* An omelette with herbs.

† Jeanne-Marie, born 28 November 1854, at midnight (French).

‡ They tell us that at that hour we were in the process of winning a great battle in Russia! May that bring her happiness! (French). The reference is to the Battle of Inkerman in the Crimean War (1853–6).

§ Jacques Firman, born 12 February at midday (French).

that scene of his birth, when she was just eight years old. She was sitting alone in the kitchen, crying, for they had told her her mother was very ill, and had been ill all the night, and just as the big clock was striking twelve she heard the voice of the neighbour who had spent the night there, calling to her; '*Jeanne-Marie, viens vite, ta mère veut te voir*'*; and she had gone, timid and hesitating, into the darkened room. The first thing she noticed was the large fire blazing on the open hearth – she had never known her father and mother have a fire before – and she wondered much whether it was being too cold that had made her mother ill, as it had little Catherine. She looked towards the bed and saw her mother lying there, her eyes closed, and very pale – so pale that Jeanne-Marie was frightened and ran towards her father; but he was smiling where he stood by the bed, and the child was reassured. She saw him stoop and kiss his wife on the forehead, and call her his '*bonne petite femme*,'† and taking Jeanne-Marie by the hand he showed her the *sage-femme*‡ – the *sage-femme* who had come the night before to make her mother well – sitting near the fire with a white bundle in her arms, and thanked the good God aloud that he had sent him a fine boy at last. Old Dubois had come in gently, his beret in his hand, as Jeanne-Marie's father was speaking, and turning to the bed had reiterated emphatically, '*Tu as bien fait, chère dame, tu as bien fait*.'§

Jeanne-Marie sat silently going over it all in her mind. '*Té*,'¶ she murmured, 'how quickly they all go; the father, the mother, old Dubois, even Jeanne the *voisine*** is gone. I alone am left, and the good God knows if there will be any to cry for me when my turn comes to go.' She shut the old Mass-book, and put it carefully back on the shelf, and she went to the old looking-glass and the tanned wrinkled face met its reflection very calmly and patiently. 'I think it was the hard work in the fields when I was young,' she said; 'certainly Marthe was right. It is the face of an old woman, a face more worn than hers, though she is beyond forty and has borne so many children.'

* Jeanne-Marie, come quickly, your mother wants to see you (French).

† Good little woman (French).

‡ Midwife (French). The word means literally 'wise woman'.

§ You have done well, dear lady, you have done well (French).

¶ An exclamation or greeting in the South of France.

** Neighbour (French).

IV

Firman had urged his sister to stay on at the *métairie* after his marriage. 'You should not go, it is not natural,' he said one evening a few weeks before his wedding, while they were piling the small wood in the shed. 'The old house will not be the old house without you. Suzanne wishes it also. *Parbleu*!* Is it the custom for the fathers to turn their sons out, when they marry? Then, why should I let the old sister go, now my time for marrying has come? Suzanne is a good girl and pretty; and has never even looked at any young fellow in the village for I, as you know, am particular, and I like not the manners in some villages, where a girl's modesty is counted nothing – but blood is worth the most, *ma foi*,† as the old father used to say; and badly must he think of me to see the old sister making room even for the little Suzanne.'

But Jeanne-Marie shook her head. 'I cannot well explain it, Firman,' she said. 'It's not that your Suzanne comes unwelcome to me – no, the good God knows it's not that but it would be so strange. I should see the old mother's shadow, at the table where you sat, and in the bed where you lay. I might get foolish, and angry, Firman. So let me go, and, when the little ones come, I shall be their grandmother, and Suzanne will forgive me.'

That was four and a half years ago, and it was a very lonely four and a half years at the white cottage. Even the cooking, when it was for herself alone, became uninteresting, and the zest went out of it. Jeanne-Marie, in her loneliness, hungered for the animal life that had unconsciously formed a great part of her existence at the *métairie*. Every springtime she would sit, sometimes for hours, in her garden, watching the flocks of callow‡ geese, as they wandered along the road in front of the mill, pecking at the ground as they went, and uttering all the time their little plaintive cries, that soothed her with its echo of the old home.

When the boys in their berets, with their long poles and their loud cries of 'guà, guà,' drove the cows and the oxen home from the fields at sunset, Jeanne-Marie would come out of her cottage, and watch the patient, sleek beasts, as they dawdled along. And she would think longingly of the evenings at the *métairie*, when she never missed going out to see the oxen, as they lay contentedly on their prickly bedding,

* An exclamation – my goodness, good God.
† By my faith (French).
‡ Young.

moving their heavy jaws slowly up and down, too lazy even to look up as she entered.

Firman loved his oxen, for they were well trained and strong, and did good work; but Jeanne-Marie would have laughed in those days, had she been told she loved the animals of the farm. 'I remember,' she said to Marthe of the mill one day, 'how I said to the old father years ago: When the children of M. François came to the *métairie*, it is "Oh, Jeanne-Marie, you will not kill that pretty little grey hen with the feathered legs," and "Oh! Jeanne-Marie, you must not drown so many kittens this time": but I say to them always : "My children, the rich have their toys and have the time and money to make toys of their animals; but to us poor folk they are the useful creatures God has given us for food and work, and they are not playthings." So I said then; but now, ah, now Marthe, it is different. Do you remember how old Dubois forever quarrelled with young Baptiste, but when they wrote from the regiment to tell him the boy was dead of fever, during the great manœuvres, do you remember how the old father mourned, and lay on his bed for a whole day, fasting? So it always is, Marthe. The cow butts the calf with her horns, but when the calf is gone, the mother moans for it all the day.'

Firman was too busy with his farm and his new family ties to come much to see his sister, or to notice how rarely she came up to the *métairie* now. For Suzanne had never forgiven, and that was why Jeanne-Marie walked up so seldom to M. François's *métairie*.

Did not all the village say that it was Suzanne's doing that Firman's sister left the farm on his marriage? That Suzanne's jealousy had driven Jeanne-Marie away? And when this came to the ears of Firman's wife, and the old folks shook their heads in her presence over the strange doings of young couples now-a-days, the relief that the dreaded division of supremacy with her husband's sister was spared her, was lost in anger against Jeanne-Marie, as the cause of this village scandal. The jealousy that she had always felt for the '*chère sœur*,'* whom Firman loved and respected, leapt up within her. 'People say he loves his sister, and that it is I who part them; they shall see yes, they shall see.'

And bit by bit, with all a woman's subtle diplomacy, she drew her husband away from his sister's affection, until in a year or two their close intimacy had weakened to a gradually slackening friendship.

At night-time, when Firman's passionate southern nature lay under the thrall of his wife's beauty, she would whisper to him in her soft *patois*, 'Love me well, my husband, for I have only you to love; others

* Dear sister (French).

are jealous of my happiness, and even Jeanne-Marie is envious of your wife, and of the babe that is to come.'

And the hot Spanish blood, that his mother had given him, would leap to Firman's face as he took her in his arms, and swore that all he loved, loved her; and those who angered her, he cared not for.

In the first year of their marriage, when Jeanne-Marie came almost every day, Suzanne would show her with pride all the changes and alterations in the old house. 'See here, my sister,' she said to her one day, only six months after the wedding, when she was taking her over the house, 'this room that was yours, we have dismantled for the time; did it not seem a pity to keep an unused room all furnished, for the sun to tarnish, and the damp to spoil?' And Jeanne-Marie, as she looked round on the bare walls and the empty corners of the little room, where she and Catherine had slept together in the old days, answered quietly,

'Quite true, Suzanne, quite true; it would be a great pity.'

That night when she and Marthe sat together in the kitchen she told her of the incident.

'But, Jeanne-Marie,' Marthe interrupted eagerly, 'how was it you had left your furniture there, since it was yours?'

'How was it? But because little Catherine had slept in the old bed, and sat in the old chairs, and how could I take them away from the room?'

'Better that than let Suzanne break them up for firewood,' Marthe replied shortly.

When little Henri was born, a year after the marriage, Suzanne would not let Jeanne-Marie be at the *métairie* and she sent Firman down beforehand to tell her that she feared the excitement of her presence. Jeanne-Marie knew she was disliked and distrusted; but this blow fell very heavily: though she raised her head proudly and looked her brother full in the face when he stammered out his wife's wishes.

'For the sake of our name, and what they will say in the village, I am sorry for this,' she said; and Firman went without a word.

But when he was gone Jeanne-Marie's pride broke down, and in the darkness of the evening she gathered her shawl round her, and crept up to the *métairie* door.

Hour after hour she sat there, not heeding the cold or the damp, her head buried in her hands, her body rocked backwards and forwards. 'I pray for Firman's child,' she muttered without ceasing. 'O dear Virgin! O blessed Virgin! I pray for my brother's child.' And when at length an infant's feeble cry pierced through the darkness, Jeanne-Marie rose and tottered home, saying to herself contentedly, 'The good God himself tells me that all is well.'

Perhaps the pangs of maternity quickened the capabilities for compassion in Suzanne's peasant mind. She sent for Jeanne-Marie two days later, and watched her with silent wonder, but without a sneer, as she knelt weeping and trembling before the small new bundle of humanity.

From that day little Henri was the idol of Jeanne-Marie's heart. All the sane instincts of wifehood and motherhood, shut up irrevocably within the prison of her maiden life, found vent in her devotion to her brother's child. The natural impulses, so long denied freedom, of whose existence and force she was not even aware, avenged their long suppression in this worship of Firman's boy.

To watch the growth of the childish being, the unveiling of his physical comeliness, and the gradual awakening of his perceptions, became the interest and fascination of her life. Every morning at eleven o clock, when the cottage showed within the open door all white and shining after her energetic scrubbings, she would put on a clean bodice, and a fresh pink handkerchief for the little coil of hair at the back of her head, and sit ready and impatient, knitting away the time, till one o'clock struck, and she could start for the farm.

She would always arrive at the same hour, when the *métairie* dinner was finished, and Suzanne's fretful complaints: 'Jeanne-Marie, you are so proud, you will not come for the dinner or stay for the supper,' met only a smile and a deprecating shake of the head.

On her arrival, if Suzanne were in a good temper, she would surrender Henri to her, and Jeanne-Marie's hour of heaven reached her. If it were cold, she would sit in the kitchen, crooning snatches of old tunes, or chattering soft nothings in *patois* to the sleeping child. If fine, she would wander round the garden with him in her arms, sometimes as far as the road, where a chance passer's exclamation of '*Oh, le beau bébé!*'* would flush her face with pleasure.

If Suzanne's temper chanced to be ruffled, if Firman had displeased her, or if the fitful jealousy that sprang up at times against her *belle-sœur*,† happened to be roused, she would insist that little Henri was tired, and must not be moved; and Jeanne-Marie would sit for hours sadly watching the cot, in which the child lay, not daring to touch him or comfort him, even when he moaned and moved his arms restlessly in his sleep.

So her life went on till Henri was about a year old, when Suzanne's gradually increasing exasperation reached an ungovernable pitch. To

* Oh, the beautiful baby! (French).

† Sister-in-law (French).

her jealous imagination it had seemed for some time that the boy clung more to her sister than to her, and one day things reached a climax.

Jeanne-Marie had arrived with a toy bought for three sous* from a travelling pedlar, and the child had screamed, and cried, because his mother, alleging that he was tired, refused to allow Jeanne-Marie to take him or show him the toy. The boy screamed louder and louder, and Jeanne-Marie sat, silent and troubled, in her corner. Even Firman, who was yoking his oxen in the yard, came in hurriedly, hearing the noise, and finding nothing wrong, pleaded with his wife. '*Mais, voyons*, Suzanne,' he began, persuasively, ' if *le petit* wants to see his toy, *la tante* may show it him, *n'est ce pas*?'† And Suzanne, unable to bear it any longer, almost threw her child into Jeanne-Marie's lap, bursting out, 'Take him, then, and draw my baby's love from me, as you please. I want no child who hates his mother.' And sobbing loudly, she rushed out. Firman followed her, his handsome face puckered with perplexity, and Jeanne-Marie and the baby were left alone. She bent low down over the deep Spanish eyes that were so like her own, and, while her tears dropped on his face, she held him to her feverishly. 'Adieu,' she whispered, 'adieu, petit Henri. *La tante* must not come to see him any more, and Henri must be a good boy and love his mother.' And with one long look at the child's eyes fixed on her so wonderingly, Jeanne-Marie rose softly and left the farm.

From that day started the great conflict between her love and her pride. Though, to her simple nature, the jealousy of a woman who seemed to her to have in abundance everything that made life worth living, was utterly incomprehensible, she said to herself over and over as she went home, that such a scene as that should never happen again. And as she lay in her narrow bed that night, and made her resolution for the future, she seemed to feel the very fibres of her heart break within her.

Firman came down next day to beg his sister to behave as if nothing had happened. 'You are pale and your face is all drawn, *chère sœur*,' he told her reproachfully; 'but you must not take the things like that. If poor Suzanne were herself and well, she would never have spoken as she did.' But Jeanne-Marie smiled at him.

'If I am pale, Firman, it is not for worrying over Suzanne. Tell her from me, I have been selfish all this time. I will not be so again. When she can spare the little Henri, she shall send him to play here with

* See note on *sou* on page 146.

† Macdonald interweaves French and English words here. 'But see here, Suzanne . . . if the little one wants to see his toy, his aunt may show it to him, can't she?'

me, by Anna.' Anna was Suzanne's sixteen-year-old sister, who lived almost entirely at the *métairie* since her sister's marriage. 'And every Sunday afternoon I will come up, and will sit with him in the garden as I used to do. Tell this to Suzanne, with my love.'

And Firman told her; and mingled with the relief that Suzanne felt, that the face and figure which had become like a nightmare to her strained nerves, would appear only once a week at the farm, was gratitude that her sister had taken things so well. 'Anna shall take him every other day,' she observed to Firman, 'she shall see I am not jealous; it was the pain that took me suddenly yesterday, while you were speaking. For that matter, in the afternoon there is always much for me to do, and little Henri can very well go with Anna to the cottage.'

And no doubt she meant to keep her promise, but she was occupied mind and body with other things. The second baby would be born in a month, and in the afternoons, when she sat, languid and tired, she liked to have her sister Anna by her, and Henri playing by her side.

And after little Catherine was born, there was much for Anna to do. 'I could not well spare her if I would,' Suzanne would say to herself; 'what with two babies and me so long in getting on my feet this time.'

And Jeanne-Marie put on the clean white bodice every day before her dinner, and sat in the little garden with her eyes fixed on the turning in the white road that led to M. François's *métairie*, but it was not more than one day a week that Anna would come in sight, with little Henri in her arms. The other days Jeanne-Marie would sit, shading her eyes and watching, till long after the hour when she could expect them to appear. There was great rejoicing in the cottage the day that Anna's white blouse and large green umbrella came in sight, and the three sat in the kitchen together: Anna eating smilingly the cakes and biscuits that grateful Jeanne-Marie made specially for her, and Henri crawling happily on the floor. 'He said "*Maman*"* to Suzanne yesterday,' Anna would announce, as Jeanne-Marie hurried to meet her at the gate; or, 'Firman says he heard him say "Menou,"† when the white cat ran across the yard this morning.' And many were the attempts to induce Henri to make these utterances again. '*Je t'aime, je t'aime*,'‡ Jeanne-Marie would murmur to him, as she kissed him again and again, and the little boy would look up at her with his dark eyes, and smile encouragingly.

All too quickly the time would go, and all too soon would come

* Mummy or Mommy (French).

† The name of the cat.

‡ I love you, I love you (French).

Anna's glance at the clock, and the dreaded words: 'Suzanne will make herself angry; we must go.'

And as Jeanne-Marie watched them disappear along the white road, the clouds of her loneliness would gather round her again.

The Sunday afternoons at the farm were looked forward to through all the week. There was little Catherine to admire, and in the summer days there was the orchard, where Henri loved to play, and where he and his aunt would sit together all the afternoon. If Suzanne were in a good temper, she would bring Catherine out in her arms, and the children would tumble about together in the long grass.

And so the time wore on, and as Henri grew in mind and body, and was able to prattle and run about the fields, Jeanne-Marie hungered for him with a love more absorbing than ever.

Two years had passed since Catherine s birth, and for the last year Anna would often bring her, when she came down to Jeanne-Marie's cottage. The one day a week had dropped gradually to every ten days; it was sometimes only every fortnight* that one or both children would appear, and the days that little Henri came were marked white days† on the simple calendar of Jeanne-Marie's heart.

V

Now, as Jeanne-Marie stood in her garden this hot May afternoon, and shaded her eyes, as she gazed at the broad white road, her face was troubled, and there was a drawn line of apprehension round the corners of her mouth. For lately Suzanne's jealous temper had flamed up again, and this alert jealousy boded evil days for Jeanne-Marie.

Several times within the last two months, little Henri – now going on for four years old – had come toddling down to the cottage by himself, to his aunt's unbounded amazement and delight. 'Maman is at market,' he explained with dignity the first time, in answer to the wondering queries. 'Papa yoked the oxen to the big cart after dinner, and they went; Anna is talking all the afternoon to Pierre Puyoo in the road; and Henri was alone. So Henri came; Henri loves his aunt, and would like some biscuits.' Great was the content of that hour in the cottage, when Jeanne-Marie sat in the big arm-chair, and the boy prattled and ate his biscuits on her knee. Anna's hard young smile, that scorned emotion, was always a *gêne* to this harmony of old and young; also, there was no need to glance anxiously at the clock; for the oxen

* Two weeks.

† Special days.

take two hours to get home from the market, and who leaves the town till late in the afternoon? 'Anna will miss *le petit*,' Jeanne-Marie suggested the first time; but he answered proudly: 'She will think *le petit* takes care of the geese in the meadow; do I not have charge of all the geese many afternoons? And when I am six years old, papa has promised I may guard the cows, and bring them home to milk at sundown, as André Puyoo and Georges Vidal do, each day. Also, why cannot Henri come to see *la tante* when he likes?'

But nevertheless, the second and third occasions of these happy visits, always on market-days, Jeanne-Marie became uneasy. Did Suzanne know of the boy's absences? Were those fitful jealousies she now displayed almost every Sunday, the result of her knowledge? And if she did not know, would there not be a burst of rage when she heard? Should Jeanne-Marie risk this joy by telling her of its existence, and asking her permission for its continuance? How well the hard tones of Suzanne's voice, framing each plausible objection, came to her mind, as she thought. No, she could not do it. Let the child come, and go on coming every market-day, for as long as he could. She would say no word to encourage his keeping it secret from his mother; he would tell her one day, if he had not told her already, and then, if anger there was, surely the simple words, 'May not your child visit his aunt alone?' must bring peace again.

So Jeanne-Marie reasoned away her fears. But now, as she stood in her garden, her lips were trembling with anxiety.

Last Sunday she had been too ill to go up to the farm. A sudden agonising breathlessness, together with great dizziness, had forced her to bed, and Marthe's boy had gone up with the message. But neither that day nor the next, which was market-day, nor any following day, had Suzanne, or Anna, or little Henri come to see her. And to-day was Saturday. And she realised wearily that to-morrow she could not get to the farm; she felt too ill and feeble. 'My heart aches,' she said to Marthe each day, 'my heart aches.'

The afternoon waned slowly, and the little group at the café increased in numbers, as the men sauntered through the village at sundown. The women stood at their doors, laughing and chatting with one another. M. le Curé* passed down the street, smiling at the children. From the meadows came the cows and oxen, driven slowly along, their bells beating low harmonies as they went. The festive air of evening after a hot day touched all the tiny town. And Jeanne-Marie stood in her garden, waiting.

* The parish priest.

Suddenly, while she watched, her heart bounded within her, and a spasm of sudden pain drove the colour from her face, for she recognised the figure that was passing from the white turning into the broad road. Suzanne – Suzanne, who had not been near her cottage for a year – Suzanne, alone. She pressed her two hands under her left breast, and moved forward to the gate. She felt now she had known it for long. All the suspense of many days had given way to a dull certainty: little Henri was ill, was dying perhaps, and Suzanne had come with the news.

Jeanne-Marie had her hand on the latch to let her through; but she stood outside the gate, and said hoarsely, 'I will not come in.' Her face was flushed, there was no cap over her coil of brown hair, and she had on the dark dress she never wore except at the farm. All this Jeanne-Marie noticed mechanically, while that suffocating hurry at her heart seemed to eat away her energy and her power of speech.

But Suzanne was going to speak. The colour flamed into her face, and her teeth ground together, as if to force down the violence of her feeling, and then she spoke: 'Jeanne-Marie, you have done your work well. We knew you loved our boy. You were careful always to show us how far greater was your love for him than ours. And as you could not well turn him against me before my eyes, you waited *ma foi*, how well you did it! you waited till I was well away, and then, you taught him to sneak down to see you, and sneak home again before my return. *Mon Dieu*!* it was a worthy son to us you wished to make of him. But it could not be, Jeanne-Marie. Your good God, you love so well, would not have it and so'; – there came a sob in her voice that she choked down, and Jeanne-Marie's face went a shade greyer as she listened – 'it happened that I was long at the market last week, and you, knowing this would be so, because it was a big market, brought him home late, when the fever was springing from the marshes – it was Marguerite Vallée saw him and came and told me – and now these four days he has lain with fever, and the *officier de santé*† tells us there grows something in his throat that may kill him in four days.'

The hard tones left her voice in the last phrase. A shadow of the love she persuaded herself she felt for Henri sprang up, and choked her anger. She forgot Jeanne-Marie for the moment, and saw only the little figure tossing with fever and delirium, and pity for her own sorrow filled her eyes with tears. She was surprised at the calm cruelty of her own words. Looking up curiously to see how her sister would take it,

* My God! (French).

† Health officer, a medical practitioner authorised to practise without a degree (French).

she started, for Jeanne-Marie's face seemed suddenly to have grown old and grey. She was struggling breathlessly to speak, and when her voice came, it sounded far off, and weak like the voice of a sick child:

'You know well that in your anger you have lied to me. Henri may be ill and dying; it is not I who have made him so. You shall listen to me now, though I will not keep you here long; for the hand that struck my mother suddenly through the heart, struck me while you were speaking. You have kept me all these days in suspense, and now you have given the blow. Be satisfied, Suzanne.'

She paused, and the sound of her heavy breathing struck Suzanne's frightened senses like the knell of a doom.

'Listen to me. Henri came to me of his own will, and never did I persuade him or suggest to him to come. Never did he go home later than four o'clock; there was nothing done in secret; neither I, nor any in the village, thought it a crime he came to visit me. Often I have seen him keeping the geese in the long grass of the meadows at six, at seven o'clock. Seek the fever there – not on the village road before the sunset. As the good God hears me, never have I stood between that boy and his mother. Gradually you took from me every privilege my affection knew; but I said nothing. Ah, I loved him dearly; I was content to wait. But all that is over. If God grants me life – but He is good, and I think He knows my suffering all these years – I swear before Him your house shall be to me a house of strangers, Henri the child of strangers, and my brother's face unknown to me. Never shall my father's daughter hear again what I have heard from you to-day. All these years you have played upon my heart. You have watched the suffering; you have known how each word seemed so innocent, but stabbed so deep. You have seen your child wind himself round my heart, and every day, every hour, you have struggled to pluck him from me. Now, I tell you I tear your children from my heart; you have killed not only my body, but my love. Go, and leave me for ever, or by my father, I will curse you where you stand.'

She tottered forward, and with one horrified look at the agony of her menacing face, Suzanne turned and ran.

And Jeanne-Marie fell all her length on the garden soil.

VI

The miller's boy saw her there, when he came past a few minutes later, and not daring to touch her, ran to the mill for help. Marthe and her husband came immediately and carried her into the cottage. At first, they thought she was dead, her face was so grey and sunken; but she came to herself, as they laid her on the bed, and shook her head faintly when Marthe suggested fetching the *officier de santé.*

As soon as she could speak she whispered: 'No, Marthe, it is the illness of the heart that killed my mother. The doctor told her she might have lived to be old, with much care, and if no great trouble or excitement had come to her; but, you see, I was much troubled just now, and so it has come earlier. Do not send for any doctor; he could but call it by the long name they called it when my mother died, and trouble one with vain touches and questions.'

So Marthe helped her to undress, and to get to bed quickly. The breathlessness and the pain had gone for a time, though she was very feeble, and could scarcely stand on her feet. But it was the grey look of her face that frightened Marthe, and her strained quietness. No questions could get out of her the story of the afternoon.

'Suzanne came to tell me little Henri was ill,' was all she would say; but Marthe only shook her head, and made her own deductions.

Jeanne-Marie would not hear of her staying with her for the night, and leaving her young children alone, and so it was settled the miller's boy should sleep below in the kitchen, and if Jeanne-Marie felt ill in the night, she would call to him, and he would fetch Marthe immediately.

Also, Marthe promised to call at the house of M. le Curé on her way home. He would be out late, since he had started only an hour ago to take the Host* to old Goupé, who lay dying four kilometres away; but she would leave a message, and certainly, when he returned, however late, he would come round. It was nine o'clock before Marthe would leave, and even then she stopped reluctantly at the door, with a last look at the thin figure propped up on her pillows. 'Let me stay, Jeanne-Marie,' she said; 'you are so pale, and yet your eyes burn. I do not like to think of the long night and you sitting here.'

'It is easier than when I lie down, which brings the breathlessness. Do not worry yourself, Marthe, I shall sleep perhaps, and if I need anything, I have but to call to Jean below. Good-night, and thank you, Marthe.'

The little house was very quiet. Jean had been asleep on his chair this hour past, and not a sound came from the slumbering village. There was no blind to the window of the bedroom, and Jeanne-Marie watched the moon, as it escaped slowly from the unwilling clouds, and threw its light on to the foot of the narrow bed.

For a long while she lay there, without moving, while through all her troubled, confused thoughts ran like an under-current the dull

* Consecrated bread or wafer.

pain that wrenched at her heart. It seemed to take the coherency from her thinking, and to be the one unquiet factor in the calm that had come over her. She was surprised, herself, at this strange fatigue that had swept away even her suffering. She thought of little Henri and his illness without a pang. He seemed like some far-off person she had read about, or heard of, long ago.

She thought to herself, vaguely, that she must be dying, since she seemed to have lost all feeling.

Bit by bit, various little scenes between her and Henri came to her mind, with an extraordinary vividness. He was sitting on her knee in the cottage, and his clear child's voice rang like a bell in the silent room so clearly, that Jeanne-Marie started, and wondered if she were light-headed or had been dreaming. Then the voice faded away, and she saw the cool, high grass of the orchard, and there was Henri laughing at her, and rolling among the flowers. How cool and fresh it looked; and Henri was asking her to come and play: '*Tante Jeanne-Marie, viens jouer avec ton petit. Tante Jeanne-Marie, tante Jeanne-Marie!*'* She must throw herself on the grass with him on the cool, waving grass. And she bent forward with outstretched arms; but the movement brought her to herself, and as she lay back on her pillows, suddenly the reality of suffering rushed back upon her, with the agonising sense of separation and of loss. Little Henri was dying; was dead perhaps; never to hear his voice, or feel his warm little arms round her neck. She could do nothing for him; he must die without her. '*Tante Jeanne-Marie! Tante Jeanne-Marie!*' Was he calling her, from his feverish little bed? If he called, she must go to him, she could not lie here, this suffering was choking her. She must have air, and space to breathe in; this room was suffocating her. She must go to Henri. With a desperate effort she struggled to her feet, and stood supporting herself by the bed-post. The moon, that had hidden itself in the clouds, struggled out, the long, old-fashioned glass hanging on the wall opposite the bed became one streak of light, and Jeanne-Marie, gazing at herself, met the reflection of her own face, and knew that no power on earth could make her reach the farm where little Henri lay.

She stood, as if spell-bound, marking the sunken look of the eyes, the grey–blue colour of the cheeks, the face that was the face of an old woman.

A sudden, fierce revolt against her starved life swept through her at the sight, and conquered even the physical pain raging at her heart.

* Aunt Jeanne-Marie, come and play with your little one. Aunt Jeanne-Marie, aunt Jeanne-Marie! (French).

Still struggling for breath, she threw up her arms and tore the cotton nightgown from her shoulders, and stood there beating her breast with her hands.

'Oh, good God! good God! see here what I am. How old and shrunken before my time! Cursed be these breasts, that no child has ever suckled; cursed be this withered body, that no man has ever embraced. I could have loved, and lived long, and been made beautiful by happiness. Ah, why am I accursed? I die, unloved and neglected by my own people. No children's tears, no husband to close my eyes; old, worn out, before my time. A woman only in name – not wife, not mother. Despised and hideous before God and men – God and men.'

Her voice died away in a moan, her head fell forward on her breast, and she stumbled against the bed. For a long time she lay crouched there, insensible from mere exhaustion, until, just as the clocks were striking midnight, the door opened gently, and Marthe and M. le Curé came in. Jean, awakened by the sounds overhead, had run quickly for Marthe, and coming back together, they had met M. le Curé on his way.

They raised her gently, and laid her on the bed, and finding she still breathed, Marthe ran to fetch brandy, and the Curé knelt by the bed in prayer.

Presently, the eyes opened quietly, and M. le Curé saw her lips move. He bent over her, and whispered: 'You are troubled, Jeanne-Marie; you wish for the absolution?'*

But her voice came back to her, and she said clearly:

'To die unloved, unmourned; a woman, but no wife; no mother.'

She closed her eyes again. There were noises singing in her head, louder and louder; but the pain at her heart had ceased. She was conscious only of a great loneliness, as if a curtain had risen, and shut her off from the room; and again the words came, whispered from her lips: 'A woman, accursed and wasted; no mother and no wife.'

But some one was speaking, speaking so loudly that the sounds in her head seemed to die away. She opened her eyes, and saw M. le Curé, where he knelt, with his eyes shining on her face, and heard his voice saying: 'And God said, Blessed be the virgins above all women; give unto them the holy places; let them be exalted and praised by My church, before all men, and before Me. Worthy are they to sit at My feet – worthy are they above all women.'†

* Forgiveness for sins.

† Rather than a Biblical quotation, this sentence appears an amalgam of passages relating to the Virgin Mary.

A smile of infinite happiness and of supreme relief lit up Jeanne-Marie's face.

'Above all women,' she whispered: 'above all women.'

And Jeanne-Marie bowed her head, and died

EU representative:
Easy Access System Europe
Mustamäe tee 50, 10621 Tallinn, Estonia
Gpsr.requests@easproject.com

www.ingramcontent.com/pod-product-compliance
Lightning Source LLC
Chambersburg PA
CBHW070646100726
47907CB00007B/2117

* 9 7 8 1 4 7 4 4 8 4 6 6 4 *